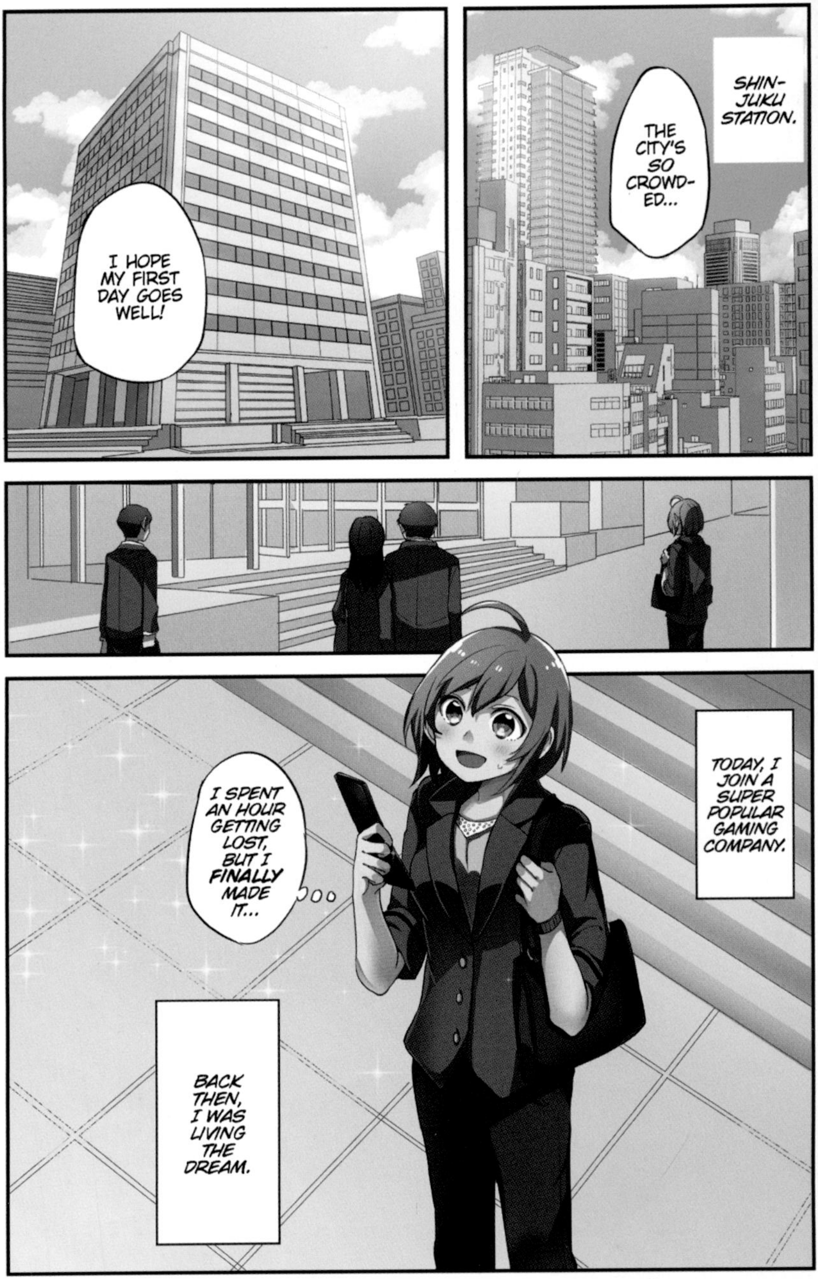
SHIN-JUKU STATION.
THE CITY'S SO CROWD-ED...
I HOPE MY FIRST DAY GOES WELL!
TODAY, I JOIN A SUPER POPULAR GAMING COMPANY.
I SPENT AN HOUR GETTING LOST, BUT I FINALLY MADE IT...
BACK THEN, I WAS LIVING THE DREAM.

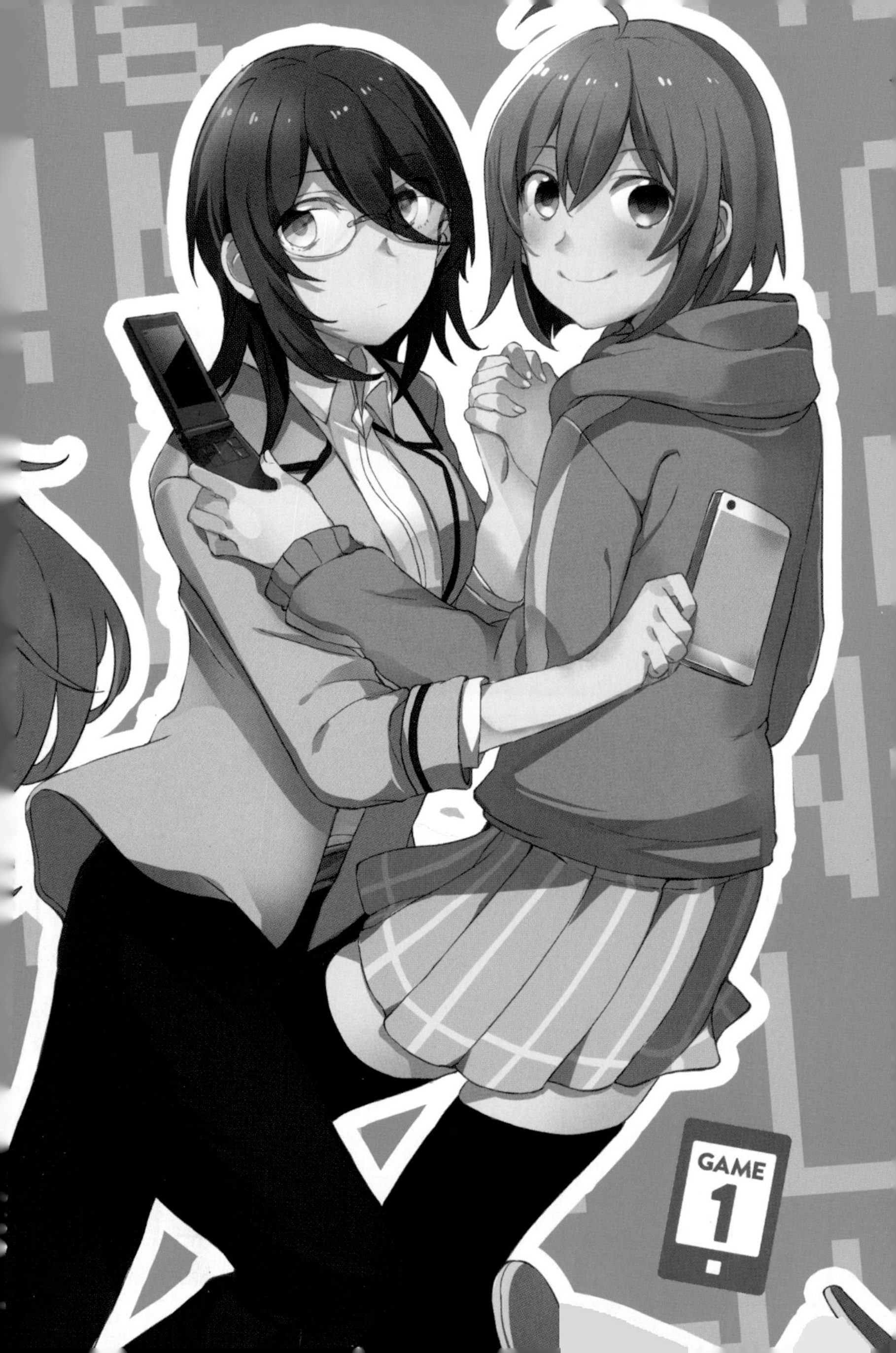
GAME
1

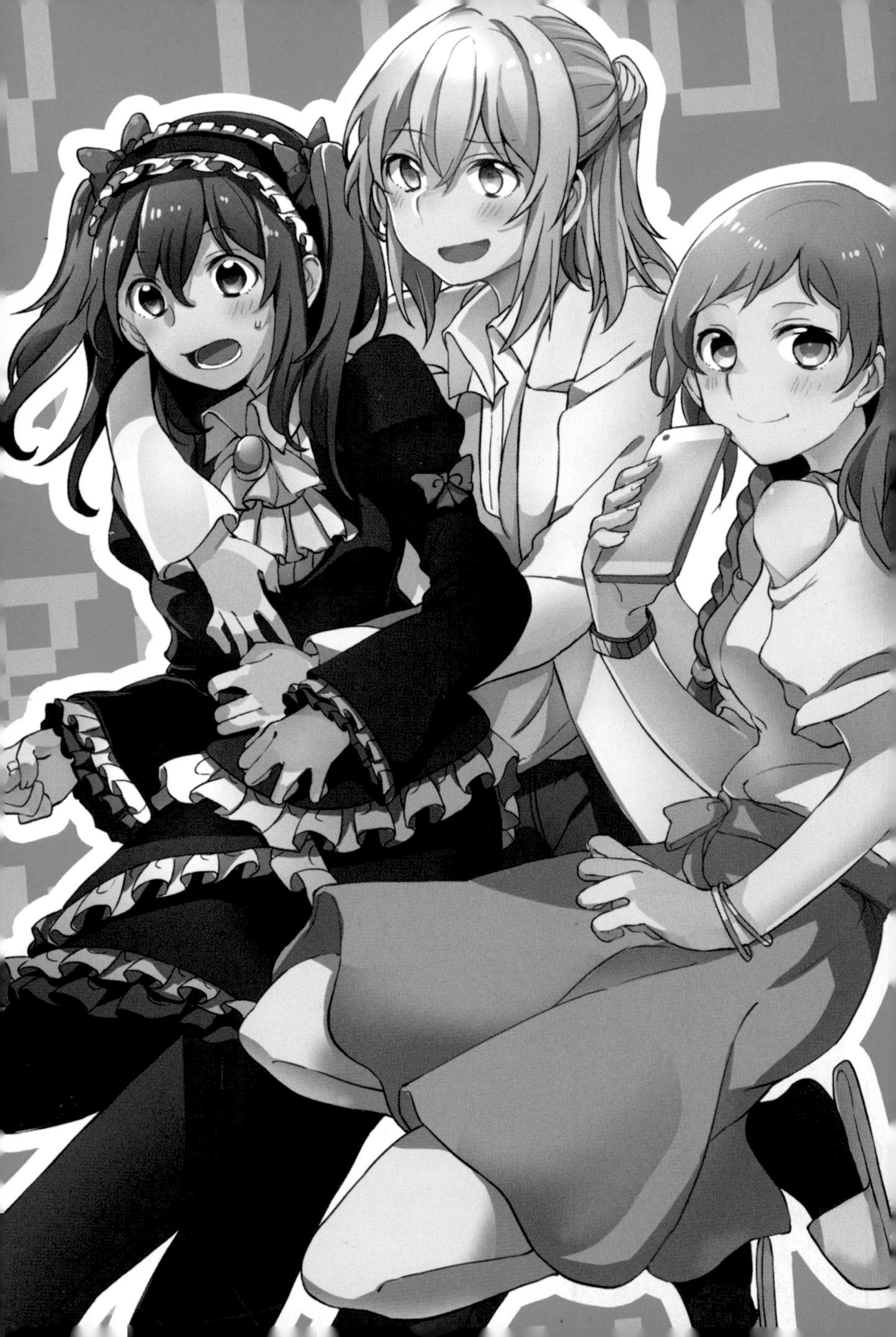

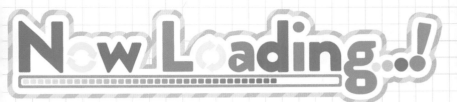
Now Loading...!

Contents

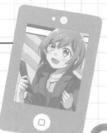
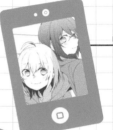
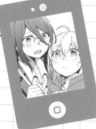
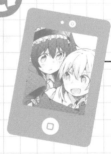
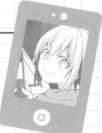
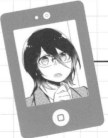

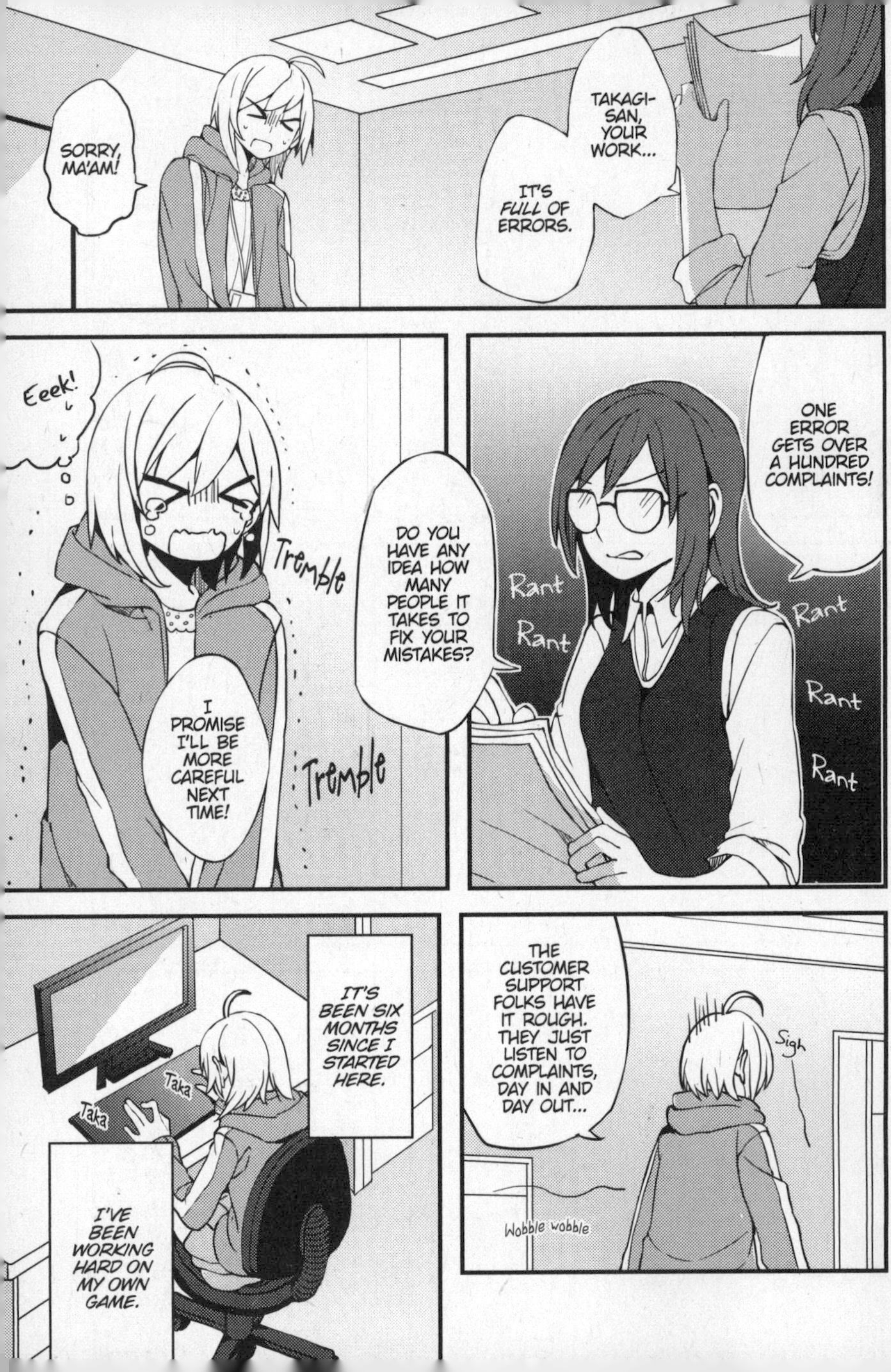
TAKAGI-SAN, YOUR WORK...
IT'S FULL OF ERRORS.
SORRY, MA'AM!
ONE ERROR GETS OVER A HUNDRED COMPLAINTS!
Rant
Rant
Rant
Rant
DO YOU HAVE ANY IDEA HOW MANY PEOPLE IT TAKES TO FIX YOUR MISTAKES?
Rant
Eeek!
Tremble
I PROMISE I'LL BE MORE CAREFUL NEXT TIME!
Tremble
THE CUSTOMER SUPPORT FOLKS HAVE IT ROUGH. THEY JUST LISTEN TO COMPLAINTS, DAY IN AND DAY OUT...
Sigh
Wobble wobble
IT'S BEEN SIX MONTHS SINCE I STARTED HERE.
Taka
Taka
I'VE BEEN WORKING HARD ON MY OWN GAME.

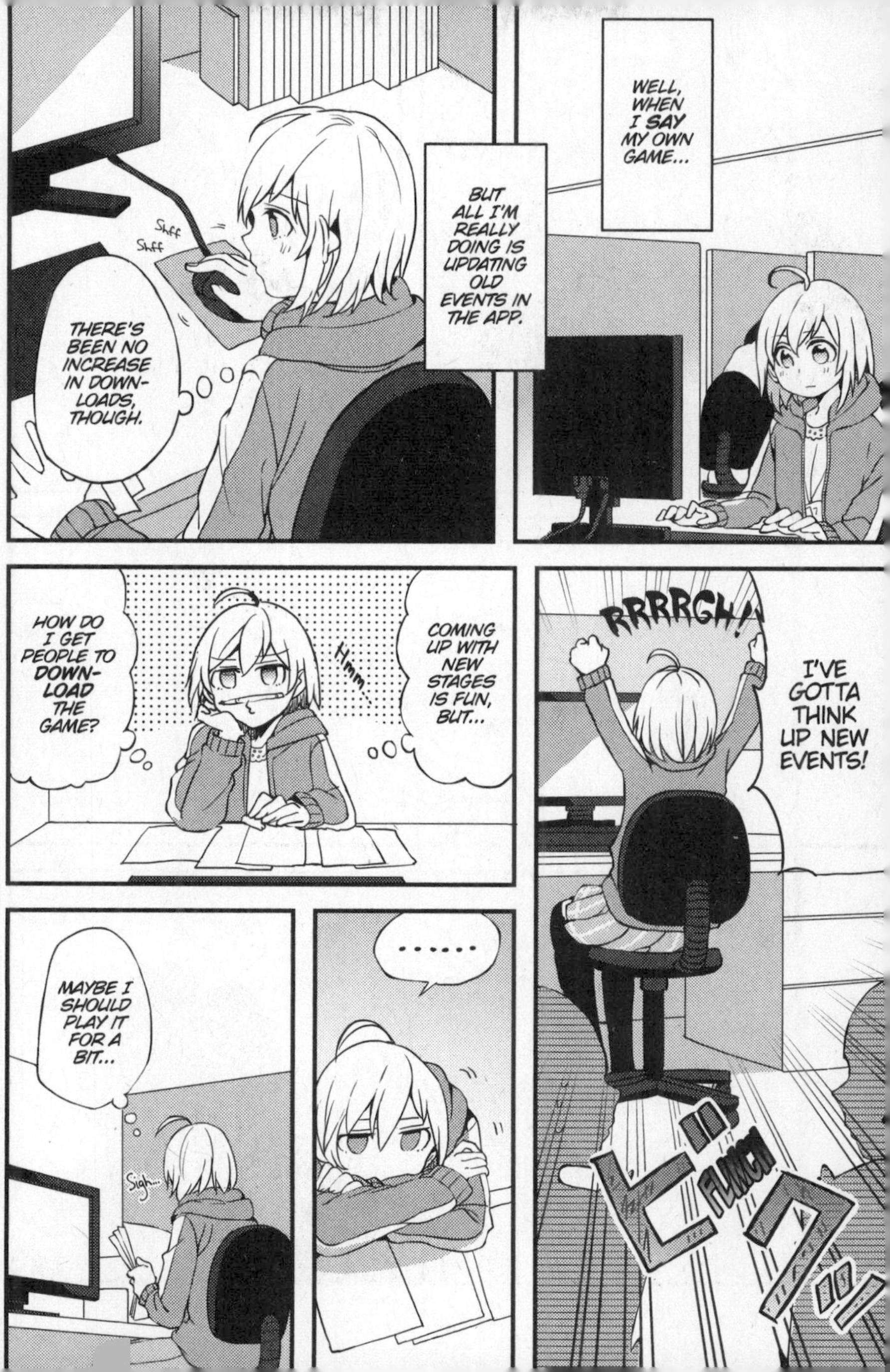
WELL, WHEN I SAY MY OWN GAME...
BUT ALL I'M REALLY DOING IS UPDATING OLD EVENTS IN THE APP.
Shff Shff
THERE'S BEEN NO INCREASE IN DOWN-LOADS, THOUGH.
RRRRGH!
I'VE GOTTA THINK UP NEW EVENTS!
FLINCH
COMING UP WITH NEW STAGES IS FUN, BUT...
Hmm...
HOW DO I GET PEOPLE TO DOWN-LOAD THE GAME?
......
MAYBE I SHOULD PLAY IT FOR A BIT...
Sigh...

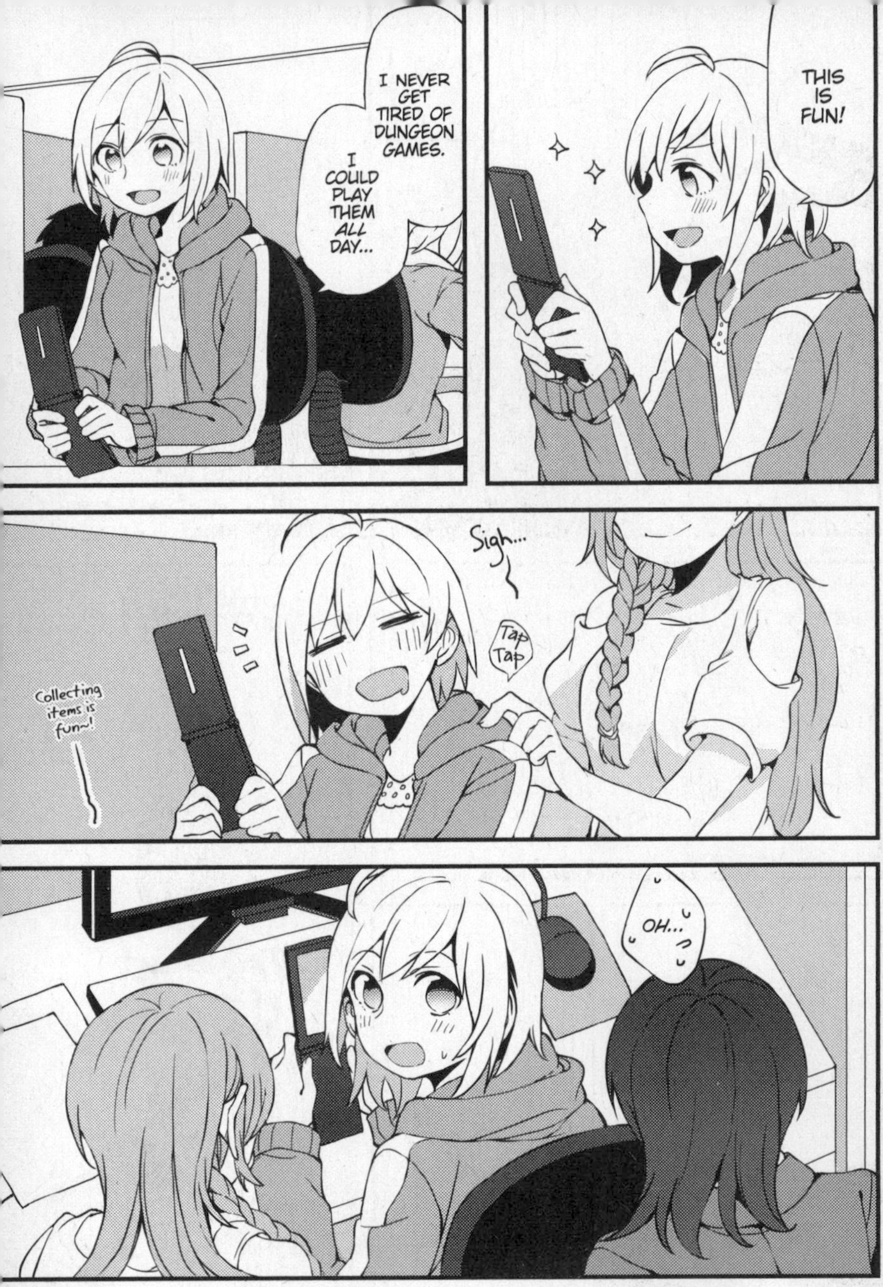
THIS IS FUN!
I NEVER GET TIRED OF DUNGEON GAMES.
I COULD PLAY THEM ALL DAY...
Sigh...
Tap Tap
Collecting items is fun~!
OH...

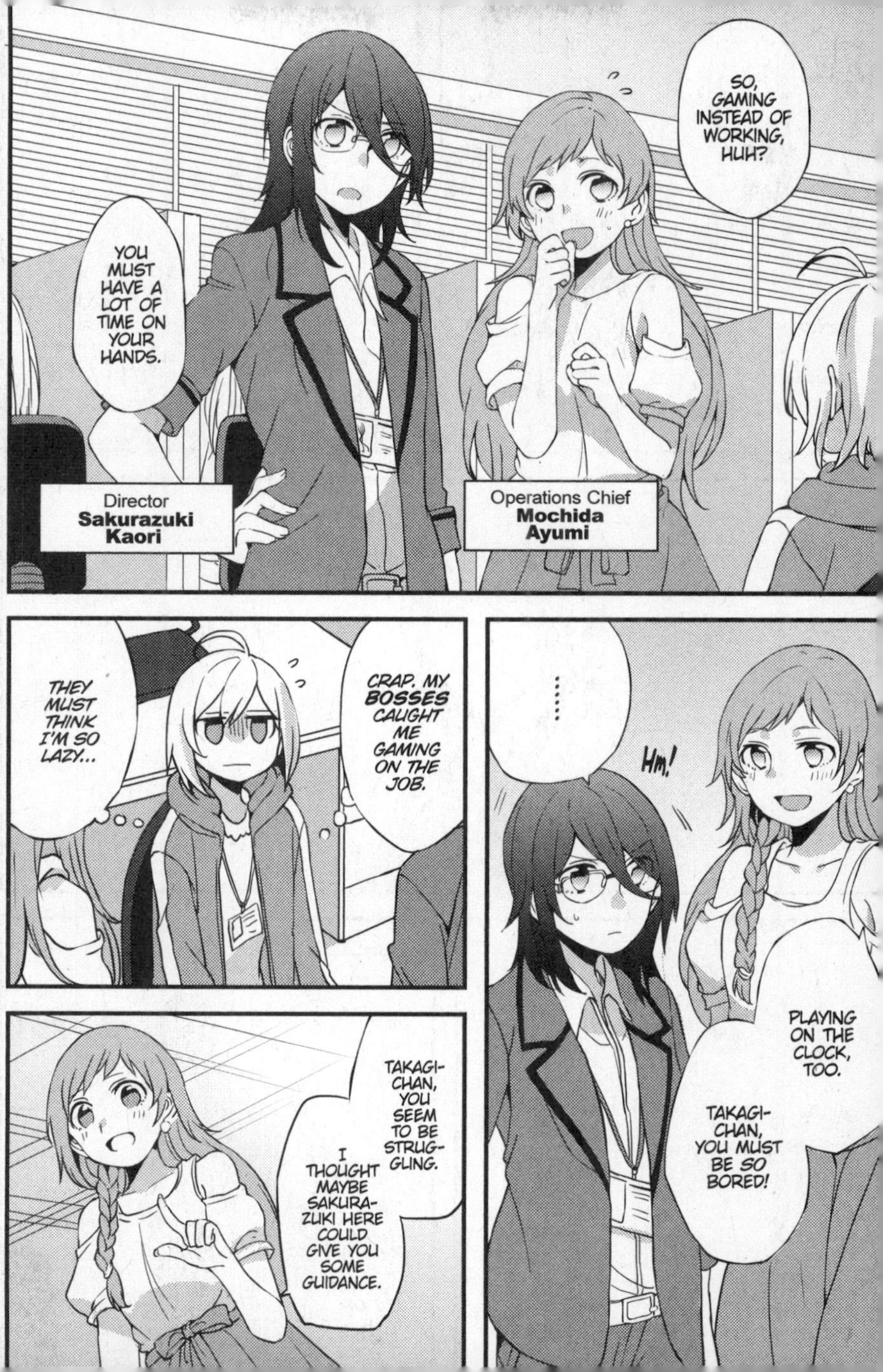
SO, GAMING INSTEAD OF WORKING, HUH?
YOU MUST HAVE A LOT OF TIME ON YOUR HANDS.
Operations Chief **Mochida Ayumi**
Director **Sakurazuki Kaori**
......
Hm!
PLAYING ON THE CLOCK, TOO.
TAKAGI-CHAN, YOU MUST BE SO BORED!
CRAP. MY BOSSES CAUGHT ME GAMING ON THE JOB.
THEY MUST THINK I'M SO LAZY...
TAKAGI-CHAN, YOU SEEM TO BE STRUG-GLING.
I THOUGHT MAYBE SAKURA-ZUKI HERE COULD GIVE YOU SOME GUIDANCE.

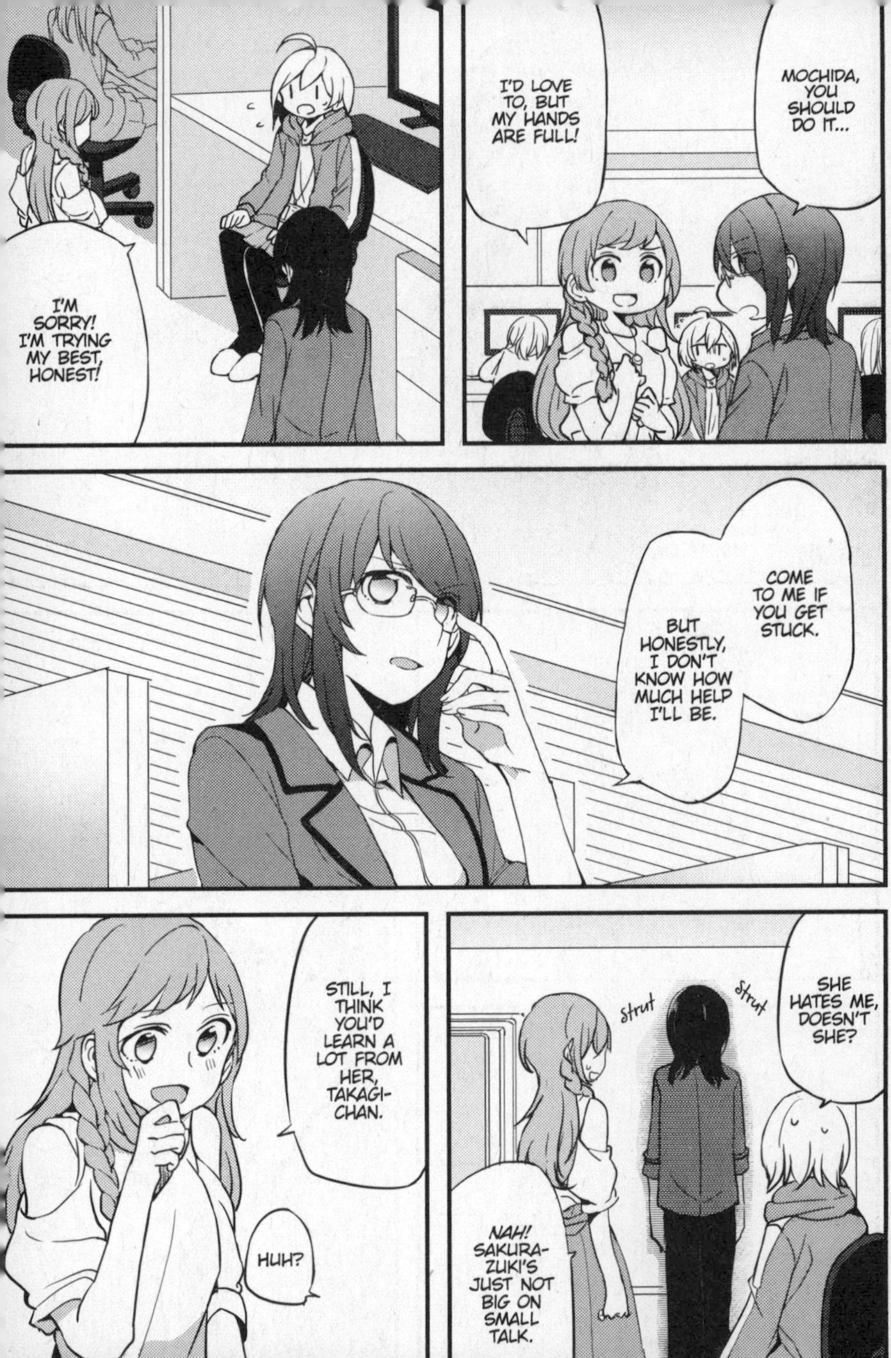
MOCHIDA, YOU SHOULD DO IT...
I'D LOVE TO, BUT MY HANDS ARE FULL!
I'M SORRY! I'M TRYING MY BEST, HONEST!
COME TO ME IF YOU GET STUCK.
BUT HONESTLY, I DON'T KNOW HOW MUCH HELP I'LL BE.
SHE HATES ME, DOESN'T SHE?
Strut
Strut
NAH! SAKURAZUKI'S JUST NOT BIG ON SMALL TALK.
STILL, I THINK YOU'D LEARN A LOT FROM HER, TAKAGI-CHAN.
HUH?

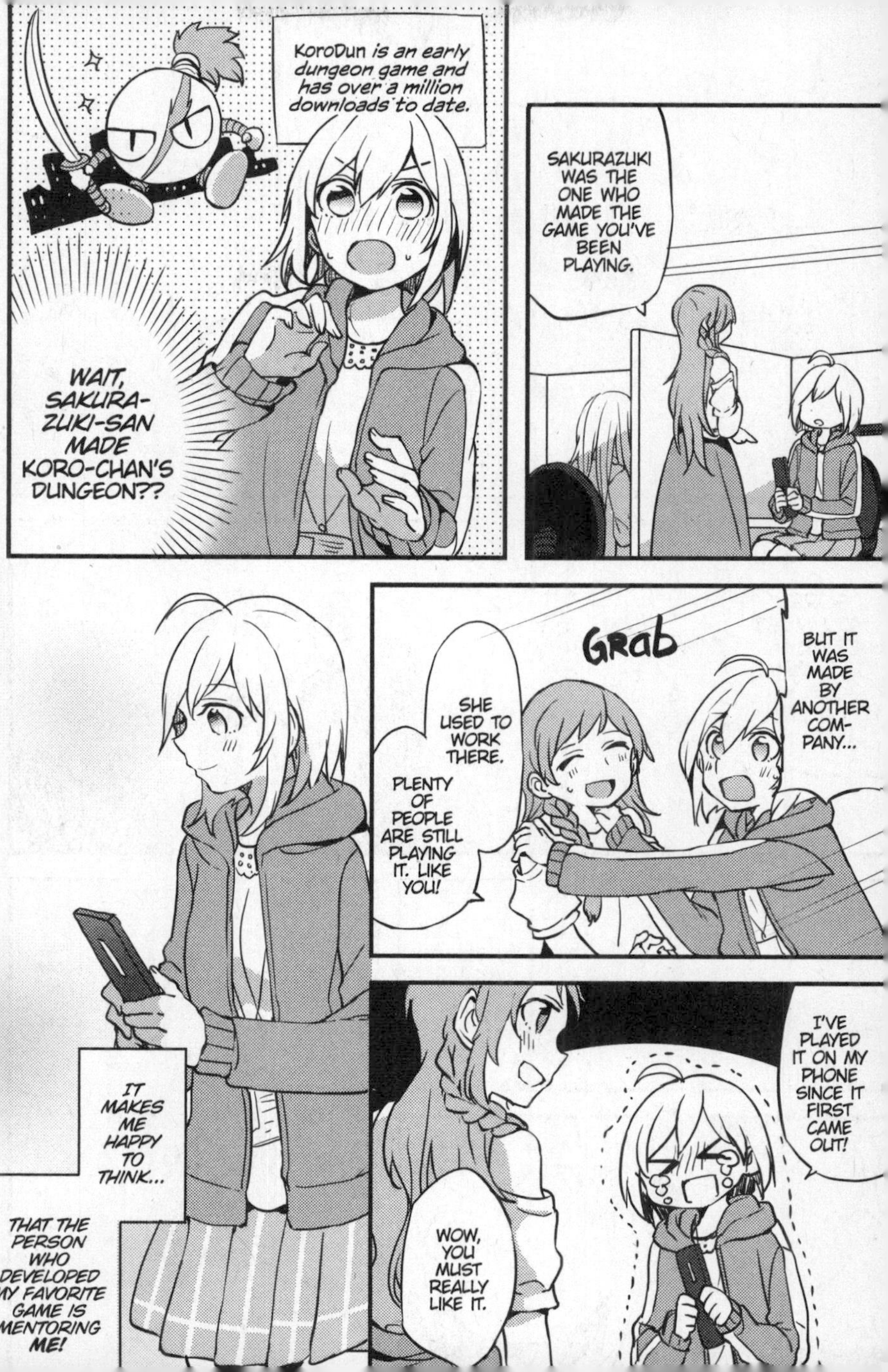
SAKURAZUKI WAS THE ONE WHO MADE THE GAME YOU'VE BEEN PLAYING.
KoroDun is an early dungeon game and has over a million downloads to date.
WAIT, SAKURA-ZUKI-SAN MADE KORO-CHAN'S DUNGEON??
BUT IT WAS MADE BY ANOTHER COM-PANY...
Grab
SHE USED TO WORK THERE.
PLENTY OF PEOPLE ARE STILL PLAYING IT. LIKE YOU!
I'VE PLAYED IT ON MY PHONE SINCE IT FIRST CAME OUT!
WOW, YOU MUST REALLY LIKE IT.
IT MAKES ME HAPPY TO THINK...
THAT THE PERSON WHO DEVELOPED MY FAVORITE GAME IS MENTORING ME!

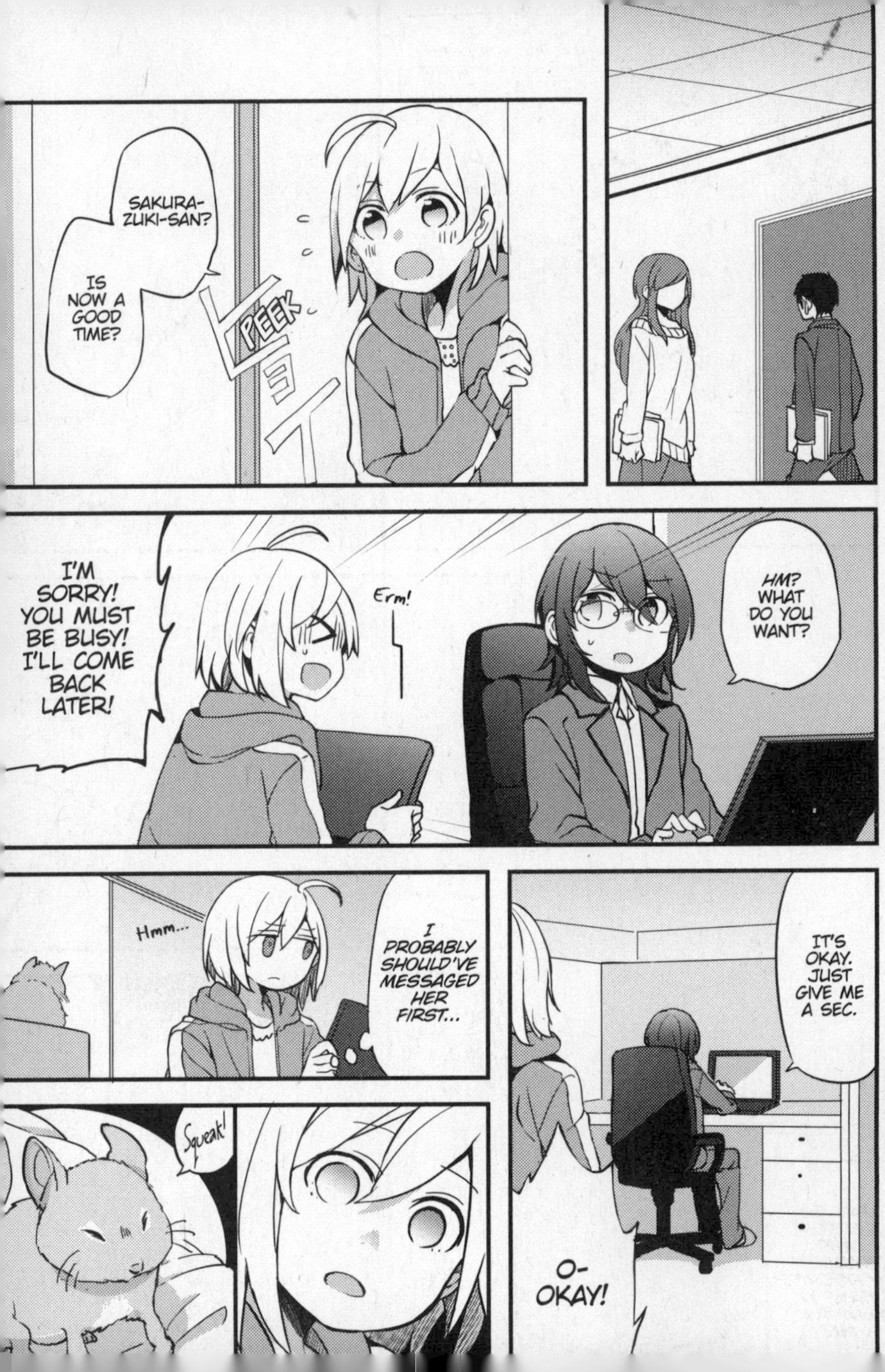
SAKURA-ZUKI-SAN?
IS NOW A GOOD TIME?
PEEK
ヒョイ
HM? WHAT DO YOU WANT?
Erm!
I'M SORRY! YOU MUST BE BUSY! I'LL COME BACK LATER!
IT'S OKAY. JUST GIVE ME A SEC.
O-OKAY!
I PROBABLY SHOULD'VE MESSAGED HER FIRST...
Hmm...
Squeak!

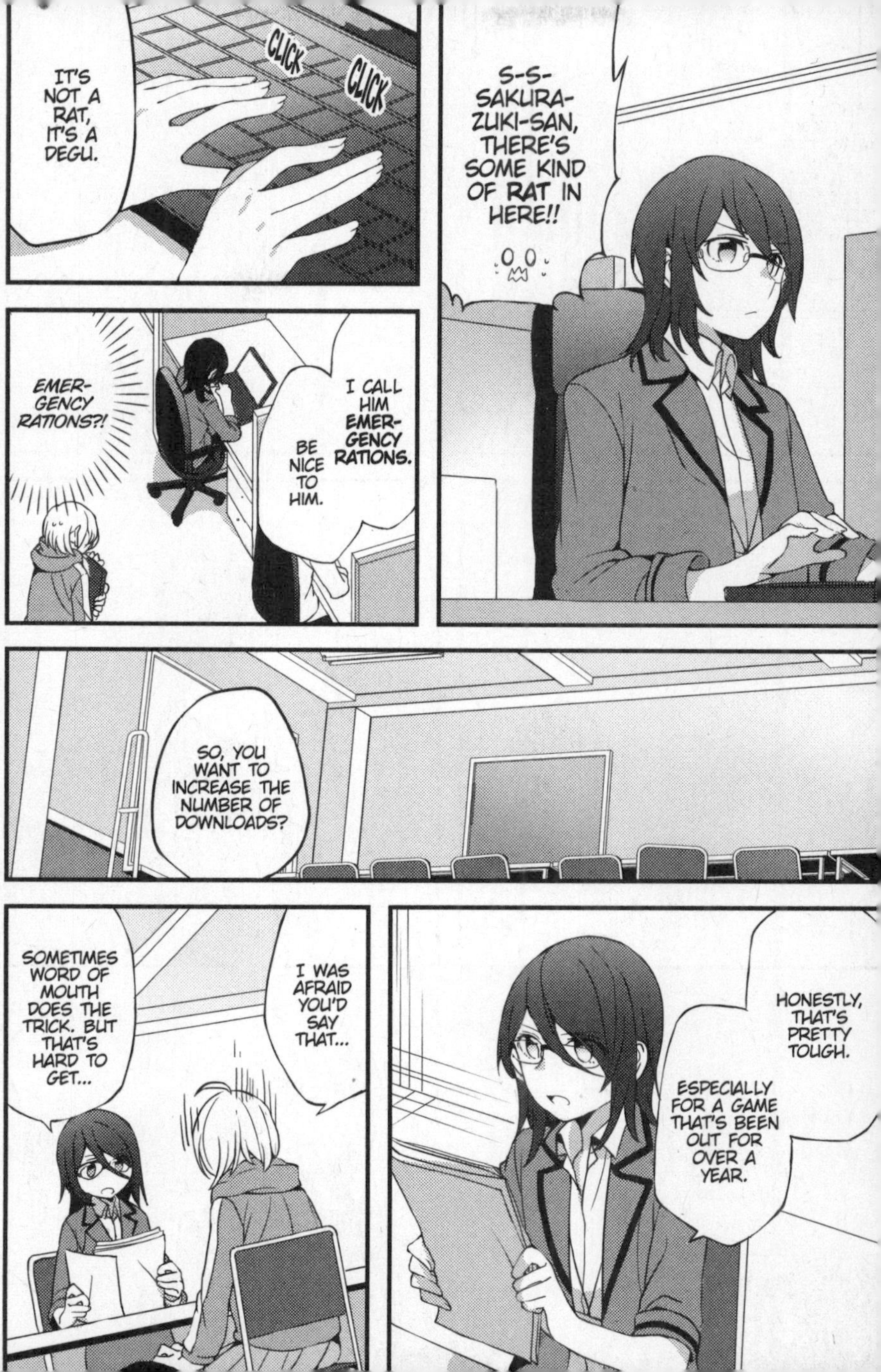
S-S-SAKURAZUKI-SAN, THERE'S SOME KIND OF RAT IN HERE!!
CLICK
CLICK
IT'S NOT A RAT, IT'S A DEGU.
I CALL HIM EMERGENCY RATIONS.
BE NICE TO HIM.
EMERGENCY RATIONS?!
SO, YOU WANT TO INCREASE THE NUMBER OF DOWNLOADS?
HONESTLY, THAT'S PRETTY TOUGH.
ESPECIALLY FOR A GAME THAT'S BEEN OUT FOR OVER A YEAR.
I WAS AFRAID YOU'D SAY THAT...
SOMETIMES WORD OF MOUTH DOES THE TRICK. BUT THAT'S HARD TO GET...

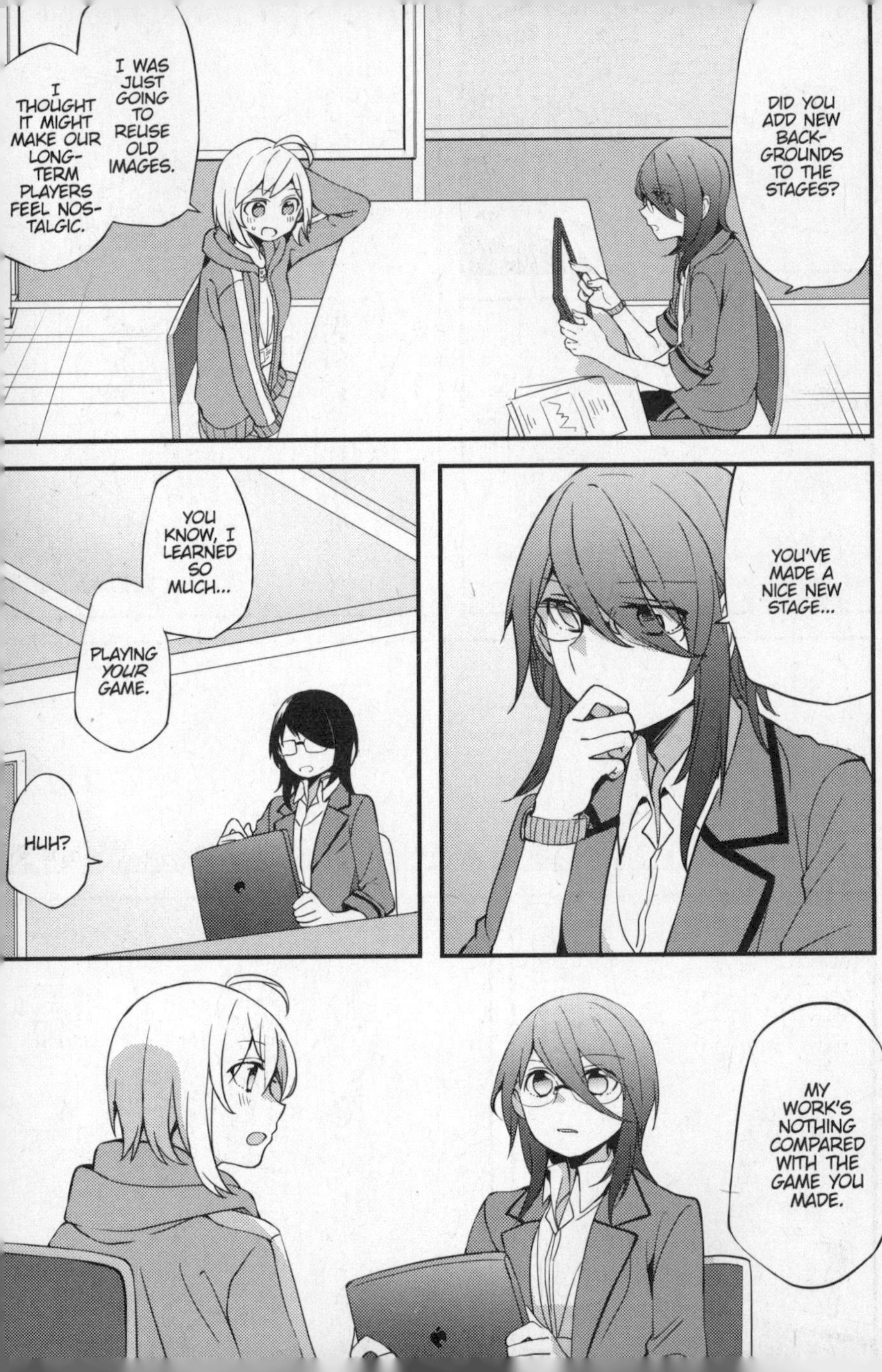
DID YOU ADD NEW BACKGROUNDS TO THE STAGES?
I WAS JUST GOING TO REUSE OLD IMAGES.
I THOUGHT IT MIGHT MAKE OUR LONG-TERM PLAYERS FEEL NOSTALGIC.
YOU'VE MADE A NICE NEW STAGE...
YOU KNOW, I LEARNED SO MUCH...
PLAYING *YOUR* GAME.
HUH?
MY WORK'S NOTHING COMPARED WITH THE GAME YOU MADE.

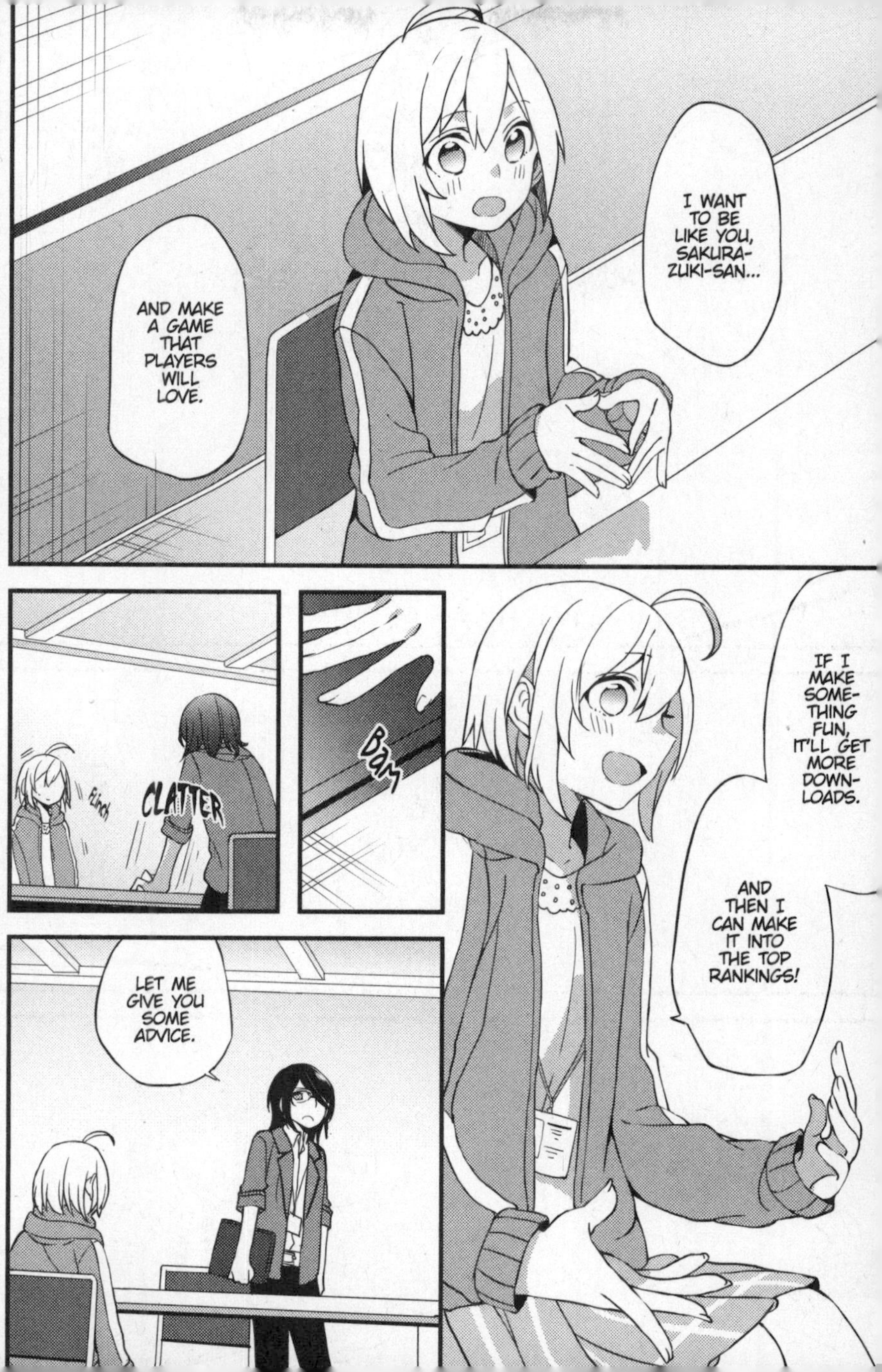
I WANT TO BE LIKE YOU, SAKURA-ZUKI-SAN...
AND MAKE A GAME THAT PLAYERS WILL LOVE.
IF I MAKE SOME-THING FUN, IT'LL GET MORE DOWN-LOADS.
AND THEN I CAN MAKE IT INTO THE TOP RANKINGS!
BAM
CLATTER
FLINCH
LET ME GIVE YOU SOME ADVICE.

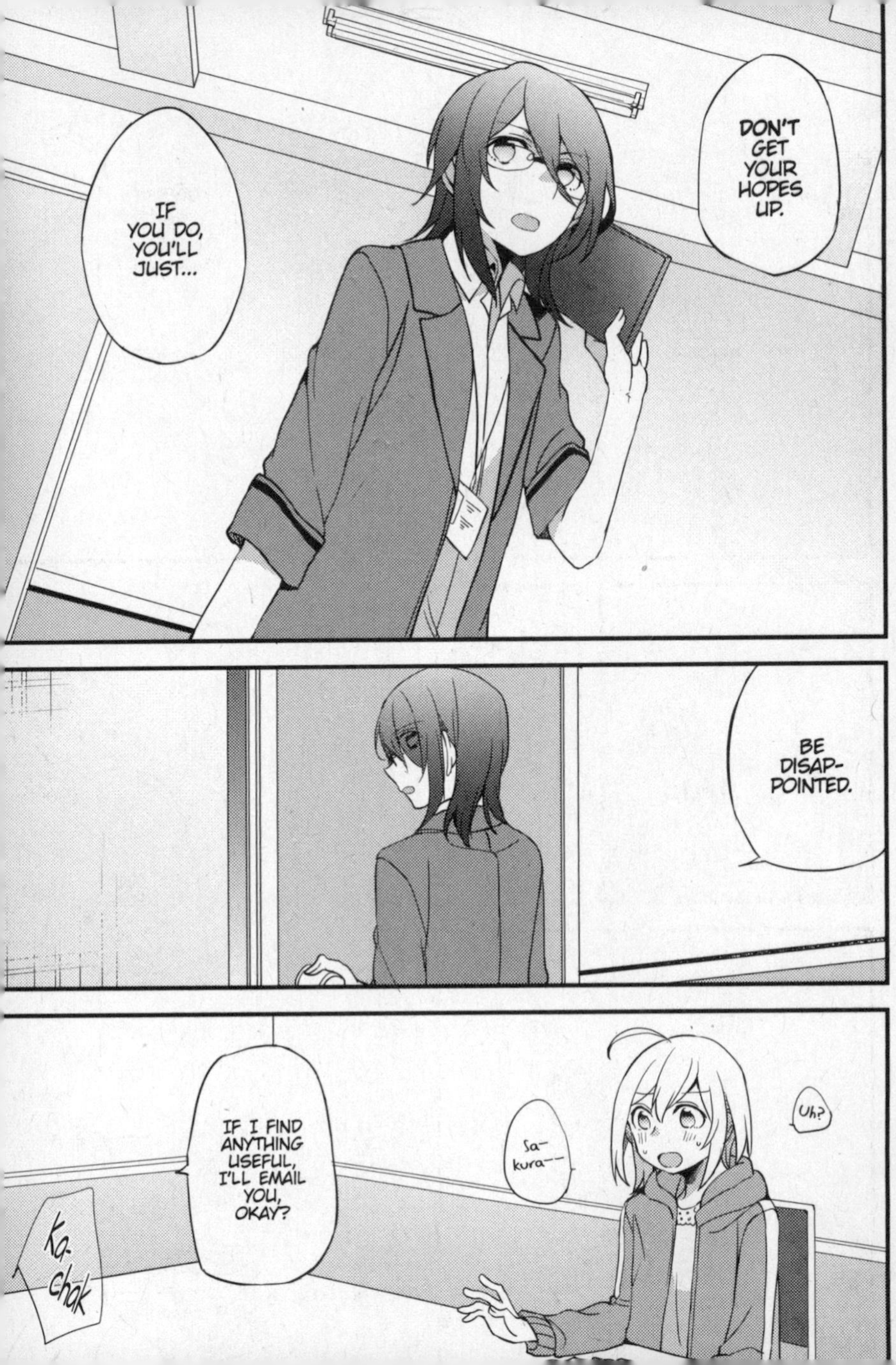
DON'T GET YOUR HOPES UP.
IF YOU DO, YOU'LL JUST...
BE DISAP-POINTED.
Uh?
Sa-kura--
IF I FIND ANYTHING USEFUL, I'LL EMAIL YOU, OKAY?
Ka-chak

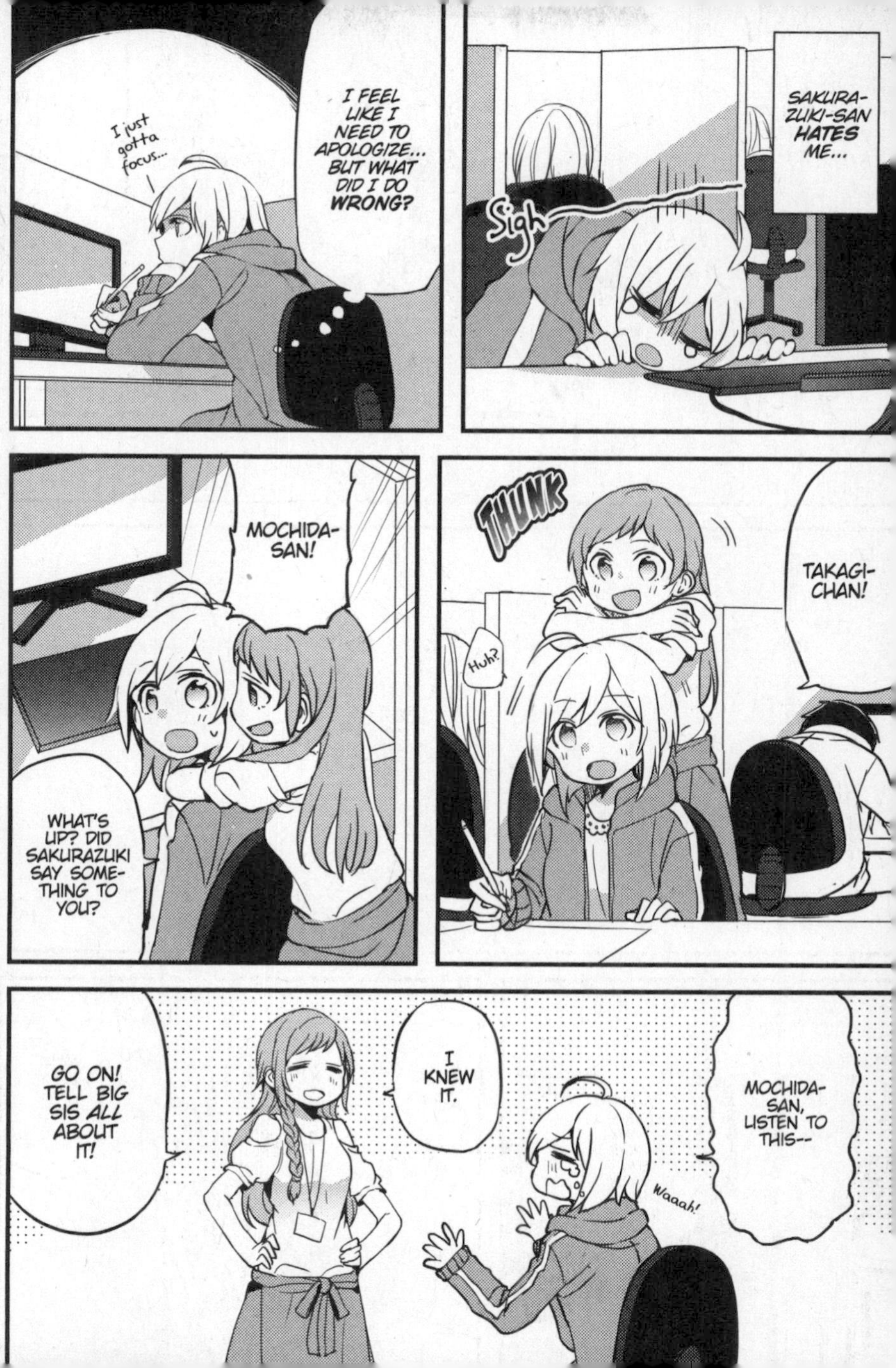
SAKURAZUKI-SAN HATES ME...
Sigh
I FEEL LIKE I NEED TO APOLOGIZE... BUT WHAT DID I DO WRONG?
I just gotta focus...
TAKAGI-CHAN!
THUNK
Huh?
MOCHIDA-SAN!
WHAT'S UP? DID SAKURAZUKI SAY SOME-THING TO YOU?
MOCHIDA-SAN, LISTEN TO THIS--
Waaah!
I KNEW IT.
GO ON! TELL BIG SIS ALL ABOUT IT!

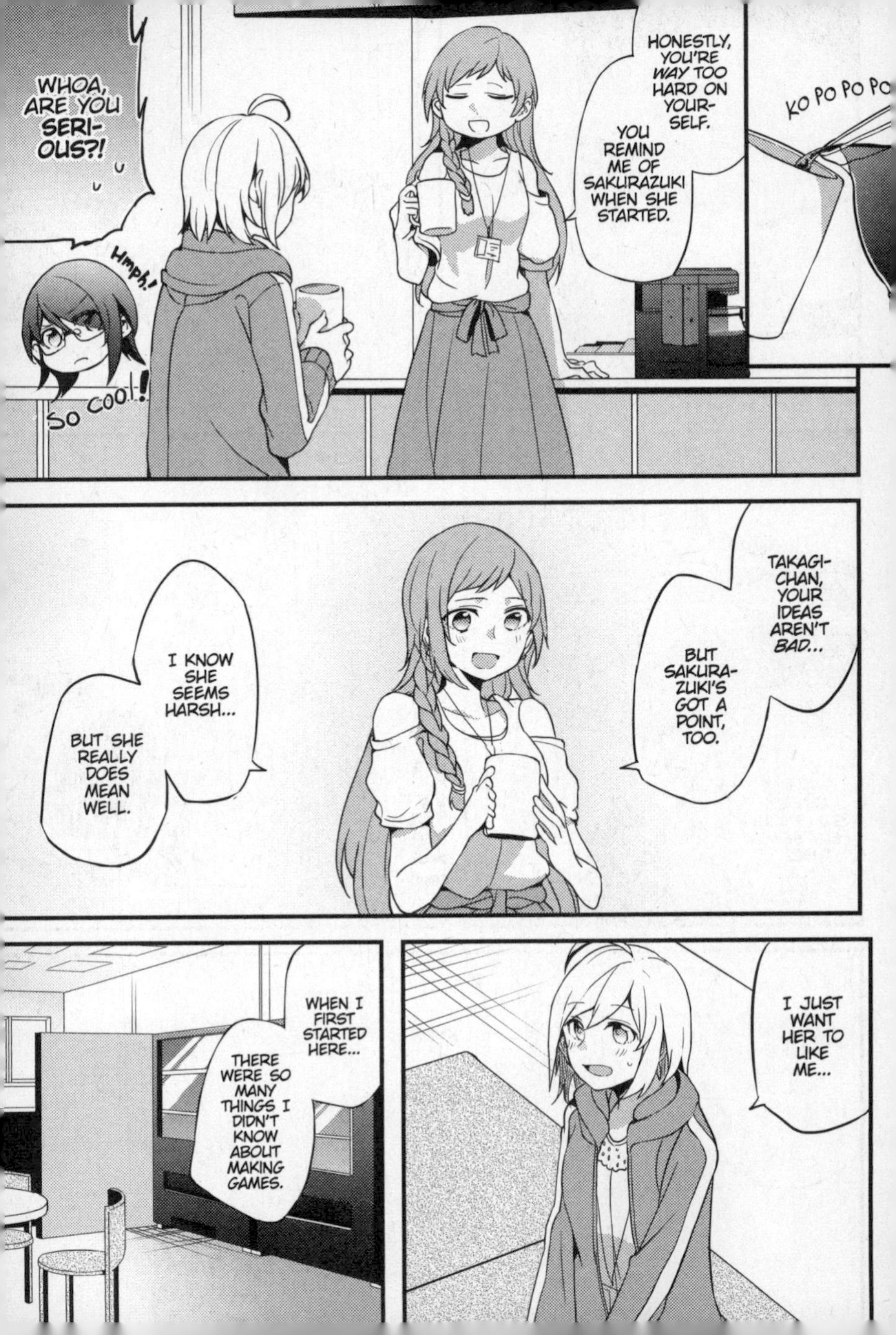
KO PO PO PO
HONESTLY, YOU'RE *WAY* TOO HARD ON YOURSELF.
YOU REMIND ME OF SAKURAZUKI WHEN SHE STARTED.
WHOA, ARE YOU SERIOUS?!
Hmph!
SO COOL!
TAKAGI-CHAN, YOUR IDEAS AREN'T *BAD*...
BUT SAKURAZUKI'S GOT A POINT, TOO.
I KNOW SHE SEEMS HARSH...
BUT SHE REALLY DOES MEAN WELL.
I JUST WANT HER TO LIKE ME...
WHEN I FIRST STARTED HERE...
THERE WERE SO MANY THINGS I DIDN'T KNOW ABOUT MAKING GAMES.

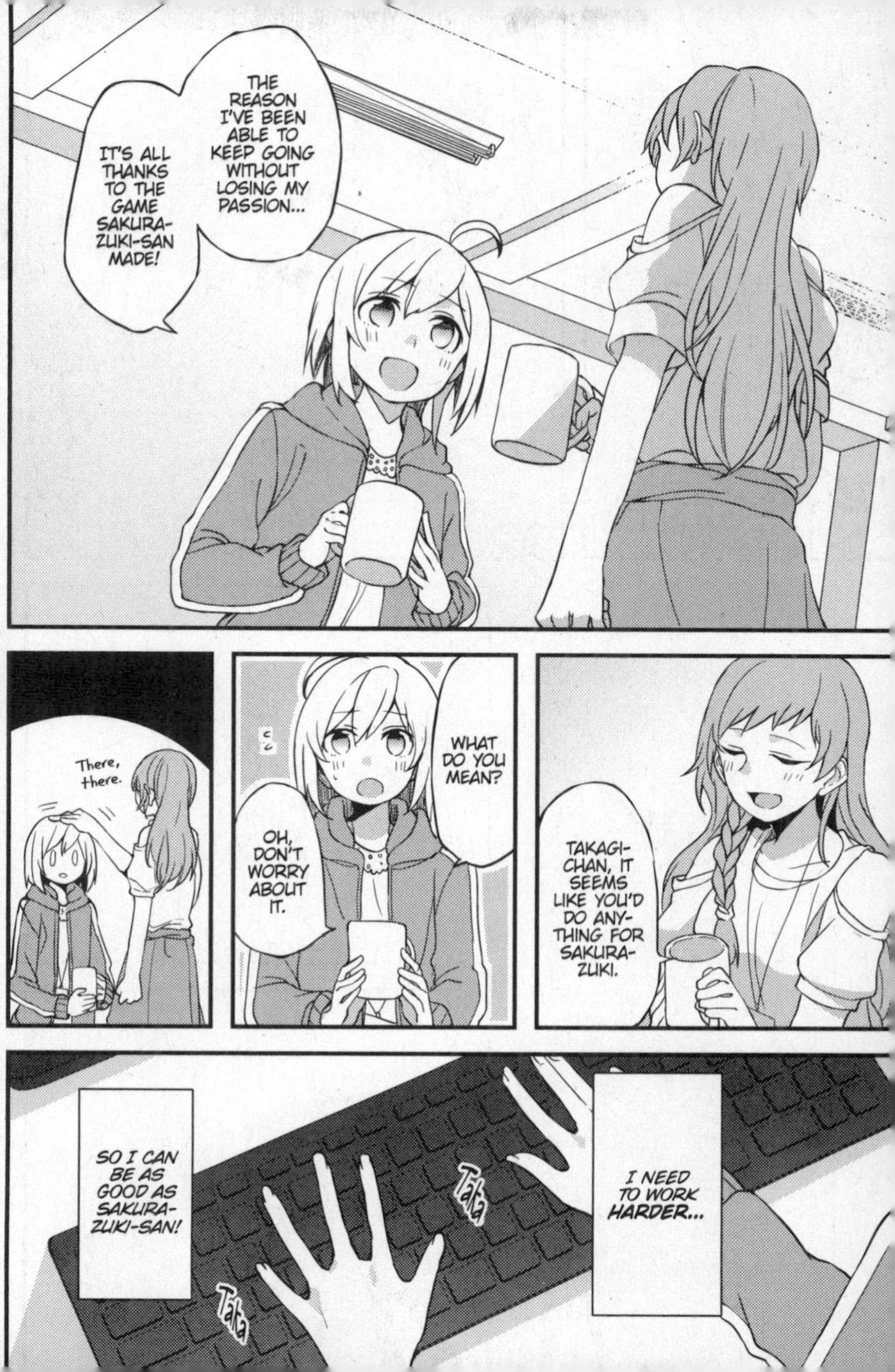
THE REASON I'VE BEEN ABLE TO KEEP GOING WITHOUT LOSING MY PASSION...
IT'S ALL THANKS TO THE GAME SAKURAZUKI-SAN MADE!
TAKAGI-CHAN, IT SEEMS LIKE YOU'D DO ANYTHING FOR SAKURAZUKI.
WHAT DO YOU MEAN?
OH, DON'T WORRY ABOUT IT.
There, there.
I NEED TO WORK HARDER...
Tata
SO I CAN BE AS GOOD AS SAKURAZUKI-SAN!
Tata

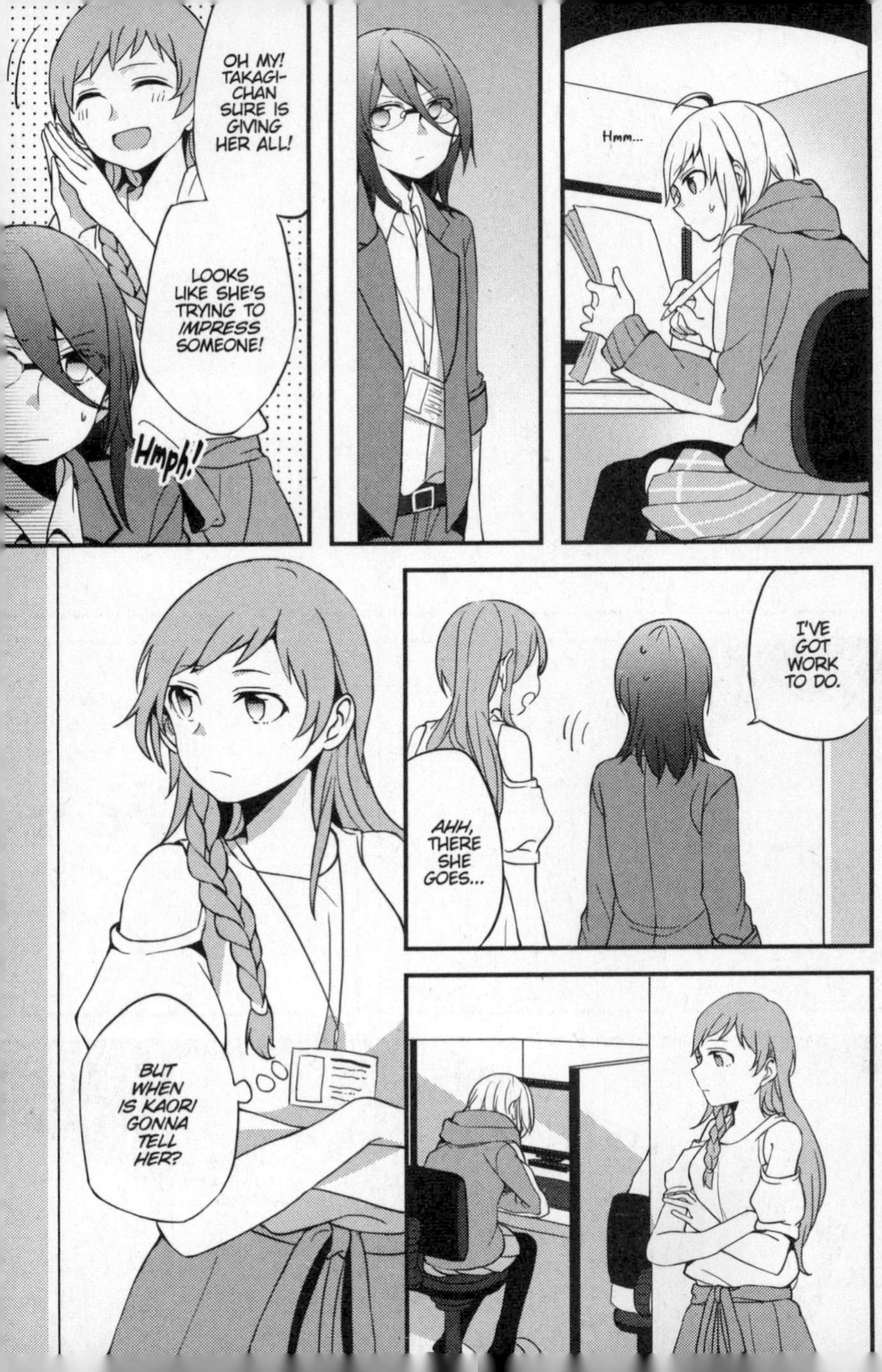
Hmm...
OH MY! TAKAGI-CHAN SURE IS GIVING HER ALL!
LOOKS LIKE SHE'S TRYING TO *IMPRESS* SOMEONE!
Hmph!
I'VE GOT WORK TO DO.
AHH, THERE SHE GOES...
BUT WHEN IS KAORI GONNA TELL HER?

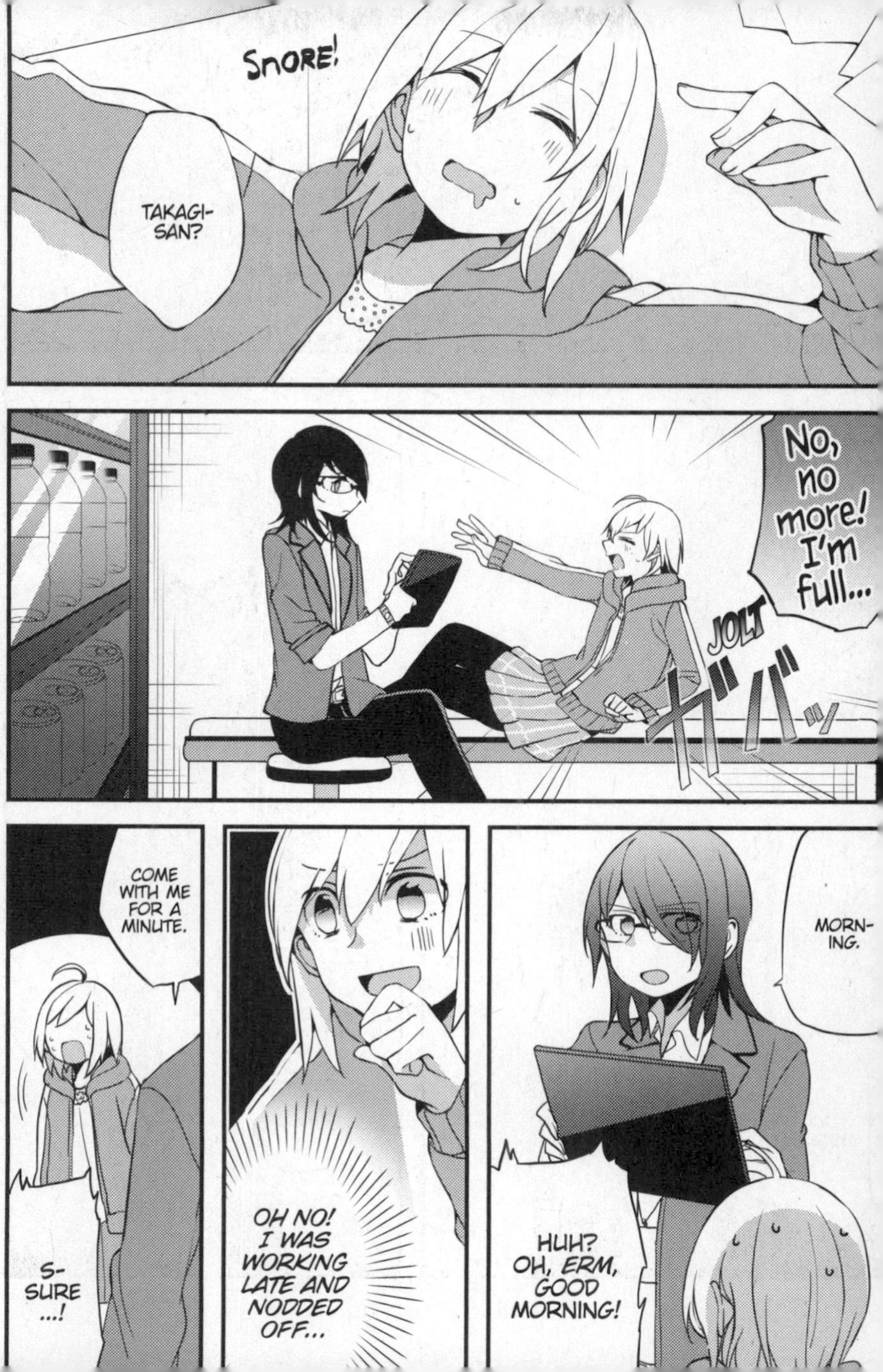
SNORE!
TAKAGI-SAN?
No, no more! I'm full...
JOLT
MORNING.
HUH? OH, ERM, GOOD MORNING!
OH NO! I WAS WORKING LATE AND NODDED OFF...
COME WITH ME FOR A MINUTE.
S-SURE ...!

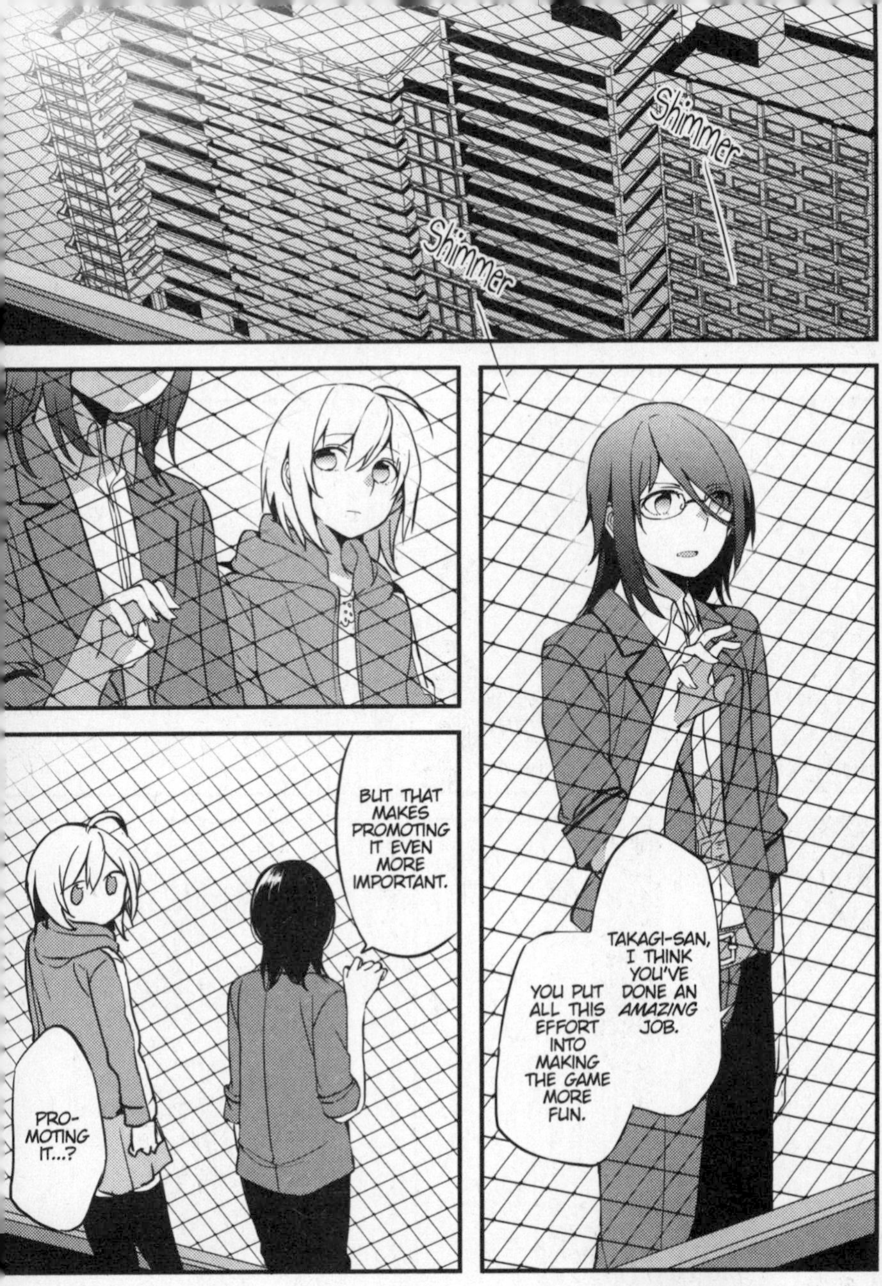
Shimmer
Shimmer
TAKAGI-SAN, I THINK YOU'VE DONE AN *AMAZING* JOB.
YOU PUT ALL THIS EFFORT INTO MAKING THE GAME MORE FUN.
BUT THAT MAKES PROMOTING IT EVEN MORE IMPORTANT.
PRO-MOTING IT...?

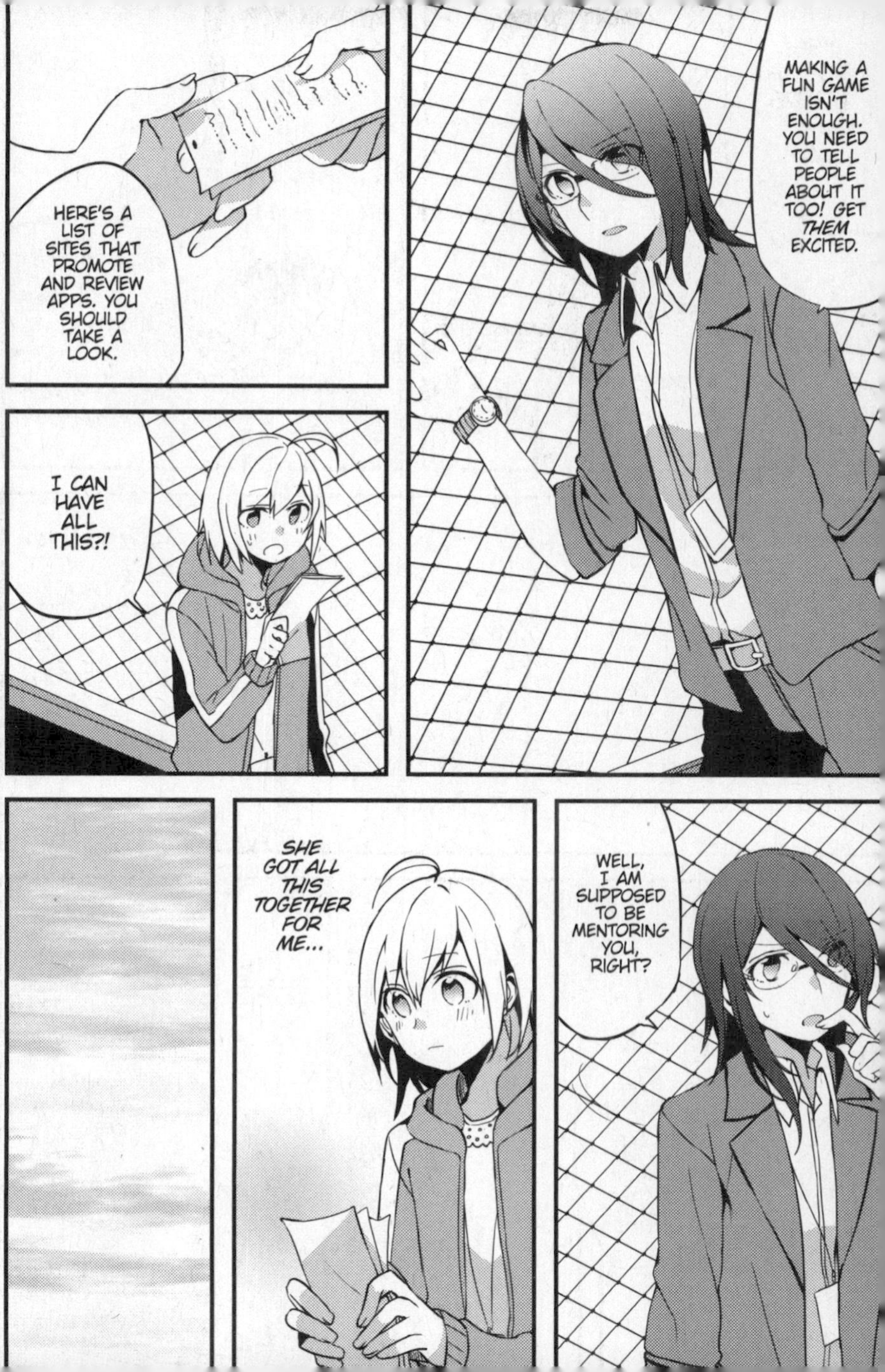
MAKING A FUN GAME ISN'T ENOUGH. YOU NEED TO TELL PEOPLE ABOUT IT TOO! GET *THEM* EXCITED.
HERE'S A LIST OF SITES THAT PROMOTE AND REVIEW APPS. YOU SHOULD TAKE A LOOK.
I CAN HAVE ALL THIS?!
WELL, I AM SUPPOSED TO BE MENTORING YOU, RIGHT?
SHE GOT ALL THIS TOGETHER FOR ME...

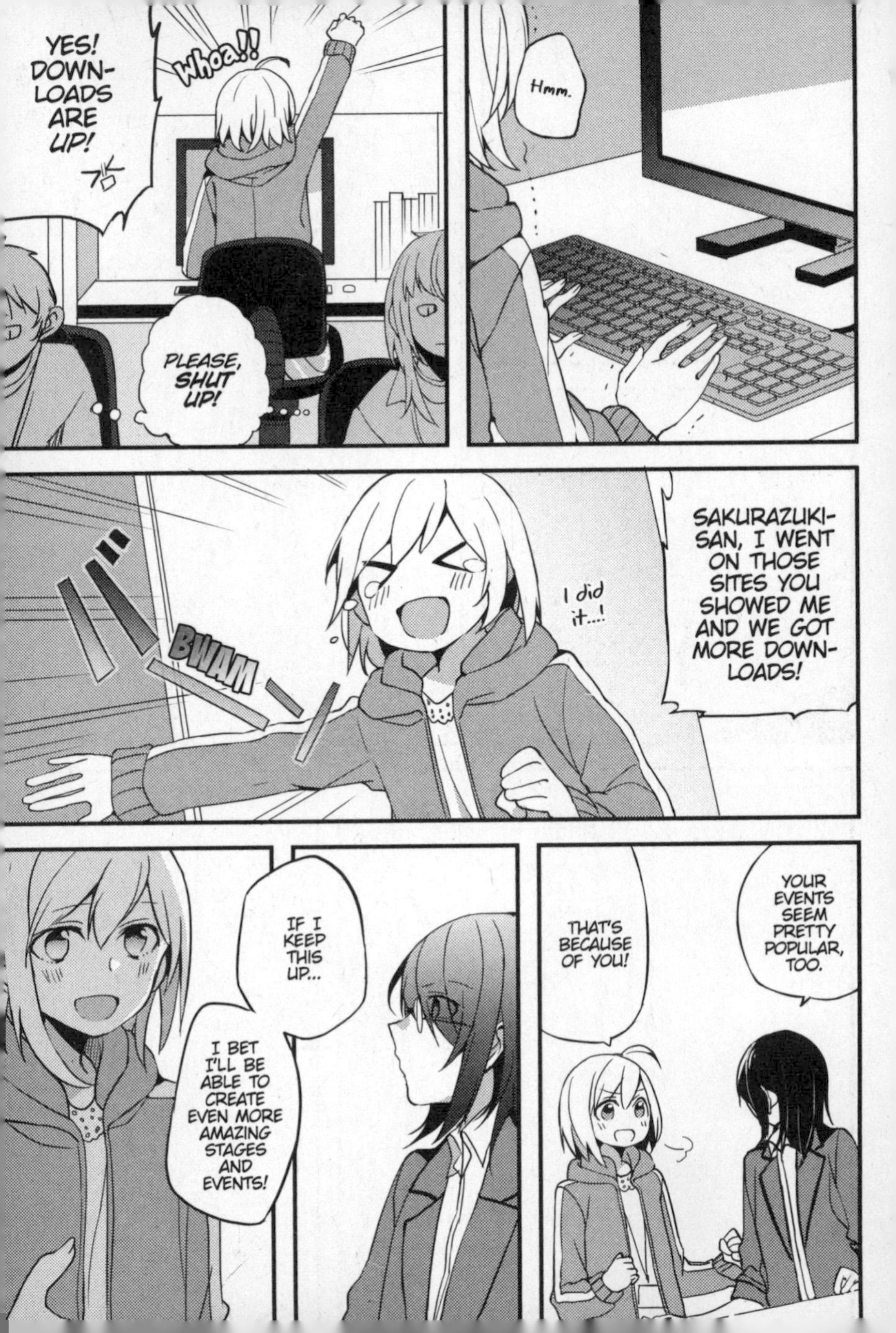
Hmm.
whoa!!
YES! DOWN-LOADS ARE UP!
PLEASE, SHUT UP!
SAKURAZUKI-SAN, I WENT ON THOSE SITES YOU SHOWED ME AND WE GOT MORE DOWN-LOADS!
I did it...!
BWAM
YOUR EVENTS SEEM PRETTY POPULAR, TOO.
THAT'S BECAUSE OF YOU!
IF I KEEP THIS UP...
I BET I'LL BE ABLE TO CREATE EVEN MORE AMAZING STAGES AND EVENTS!

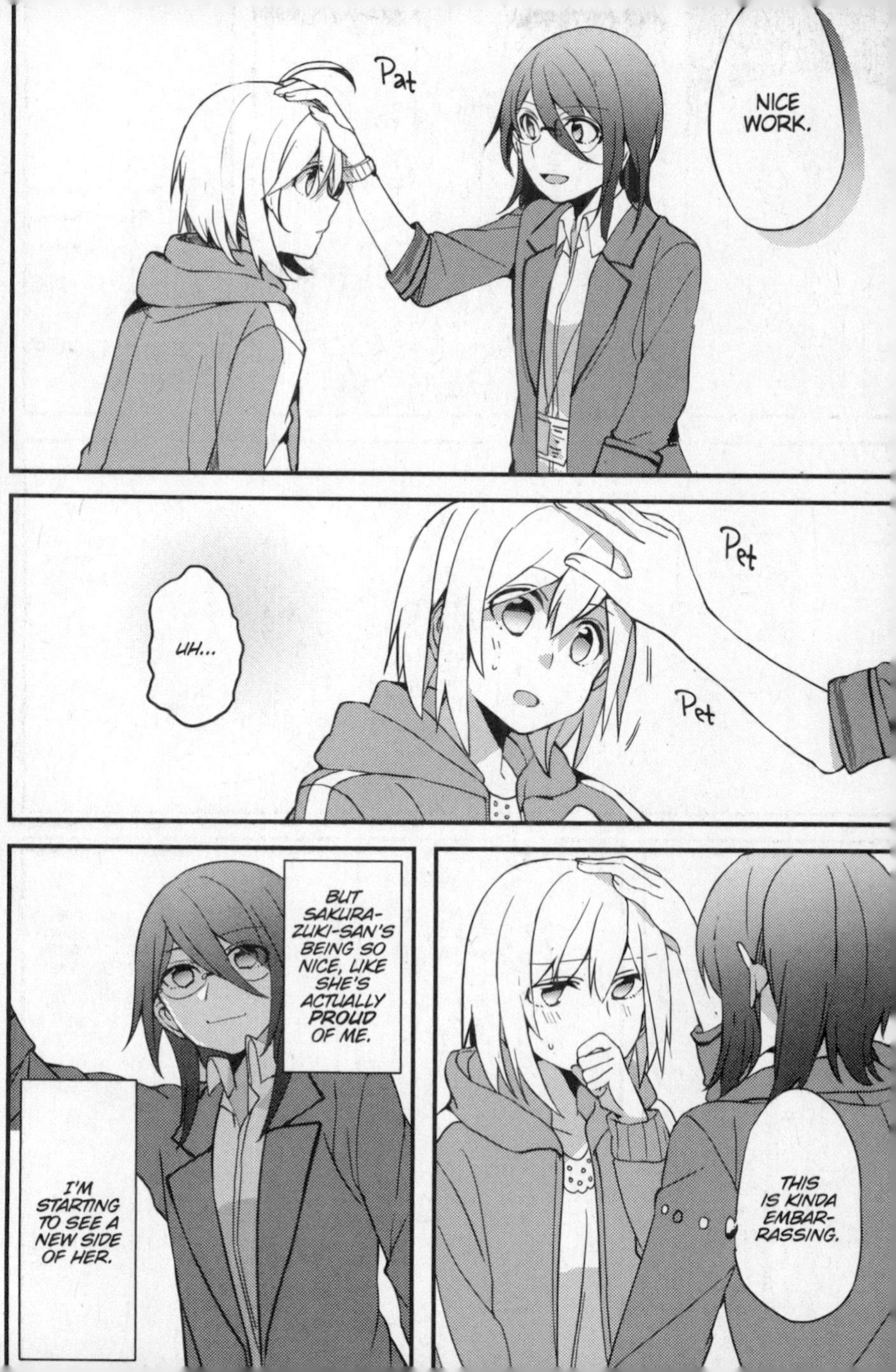
NICE WORK.
Pat
Pet
Pet
UH...
THIS IS KINDA EMBARRASSING.
BUT SAKURAZUKI-SAN'S BEING SO NICE, LIKE SHE'S ACTUALLY PROUD OF ME.
I'M STARTING TO SEE A NEW SIDE OF HER.

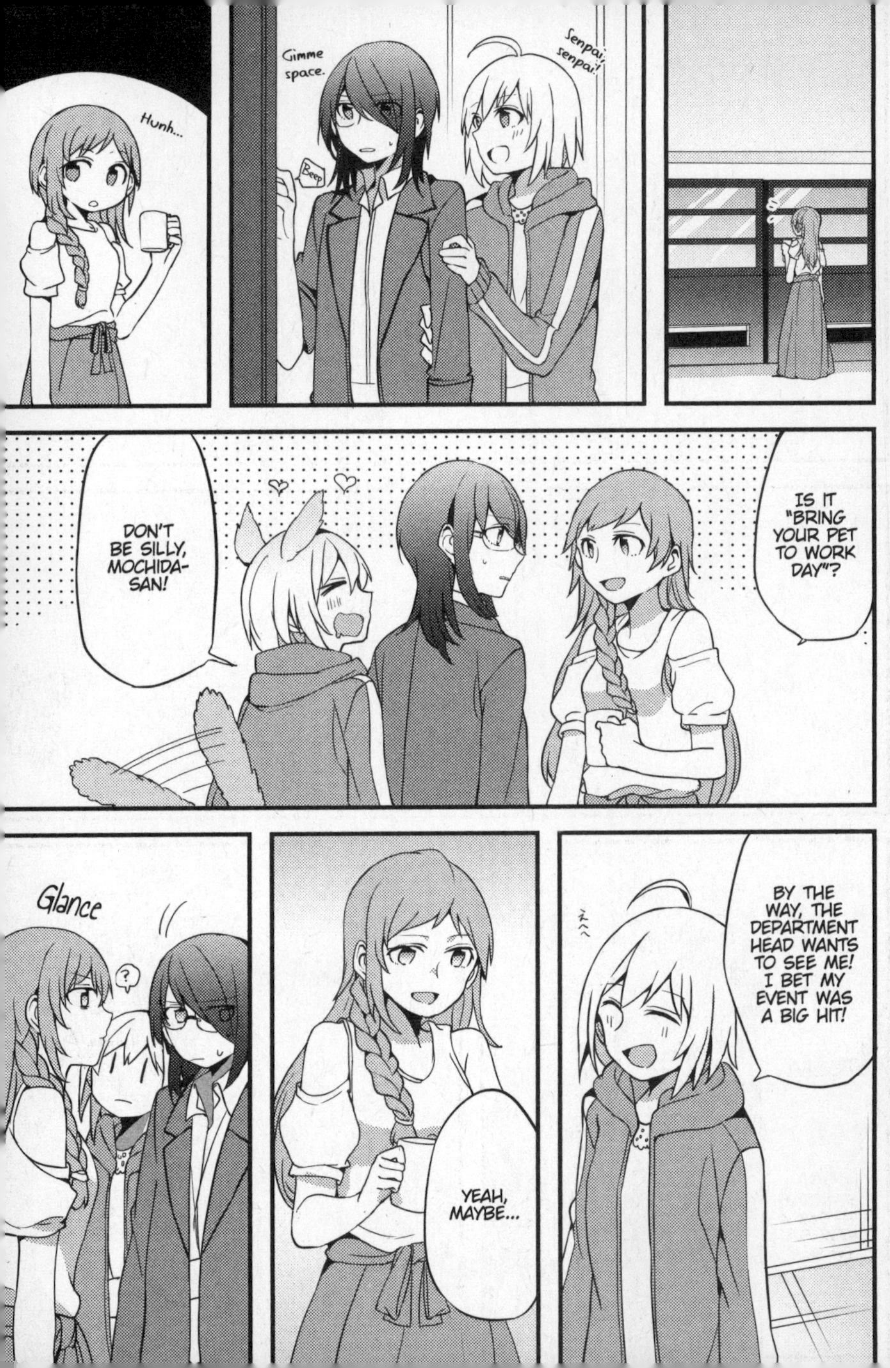
Senpai, senpai!
Gimme space.
Beep
Hunh...
IS IT "BRING YOUR PET TO WORK DAY"?
DON'T BE SILLY, MOCHIDA-SAN!
BY THE WAY, THE DEPARTMENT HEAD WANTS TO SEE ME! I BET MY EVENT WAS A BIG HIT!
YEAH, MAYBE...
Glance
?

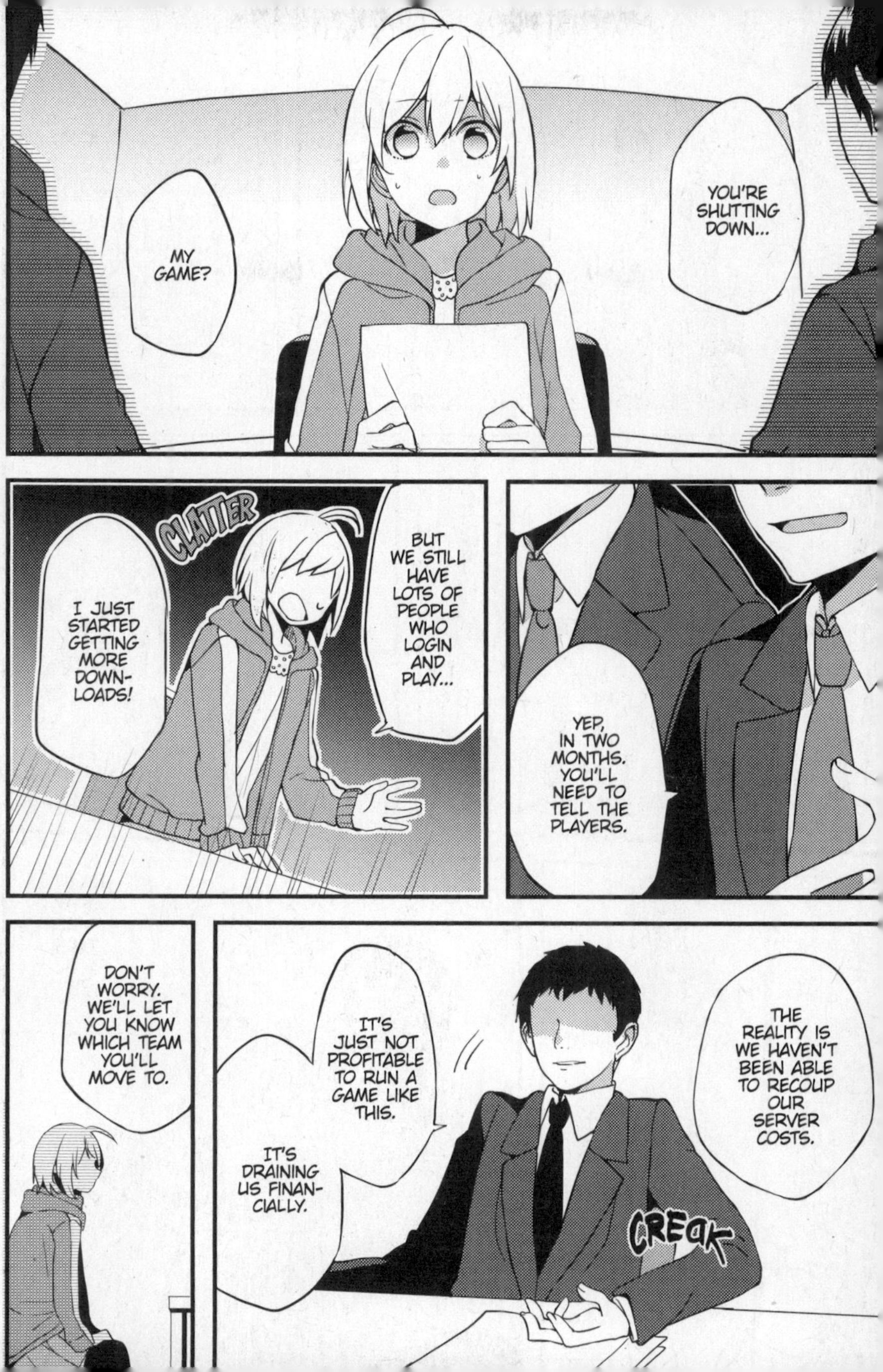
YOU'RE SHUTTING DOWN...
MY GAME?
YEP, IN TWO MONTHS. YOU'LL NEED TO TELL THE PLAYERS.
BUT WE STILL HAVE LOTS OF PEOPLE WHO LOGIN AND PLAY...
CLATTER
I JUST STARTED GETTING MORE DOWN-LOADS!
THE REALITY IS WE HAVEN'T BEEN ABLE TO RECOUP OUR SERVER COSTS.
IT'S JUST NOT PROFITABLE TO RUN A GAME LIKE THIS.
IT'S DRAINING US FINAN-CIALLY.
CREAK
DON'T WORRY. WE'LL LET YOU KNOW WHICH TEAM YOU'LL MOVE TO.

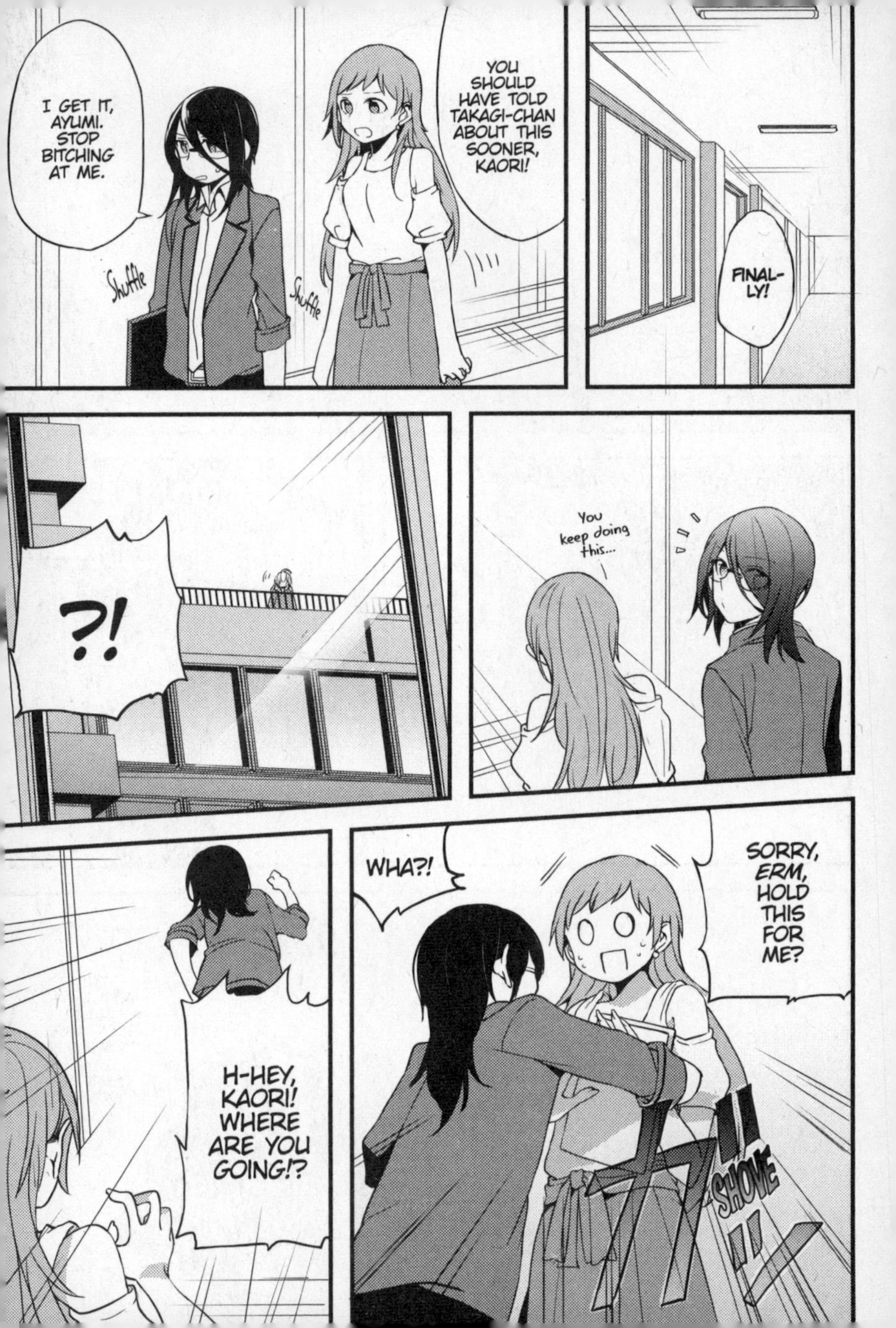
FINAL-LY!
YOU SHOULD HAVE TOLD TAKAGI-CHAN ABOUT THIS SOONER, KAORI!
Shuffle
Shuffle
I GET IT, AYUMI. STOP BITCHING AT ME.
You keep doing this...
?!
SORRY, ERM, HOLD THIS FOR ME?
WHA?!
SHOVE
H-HEY, KAORI! WHERE ARE YOU GOING!?

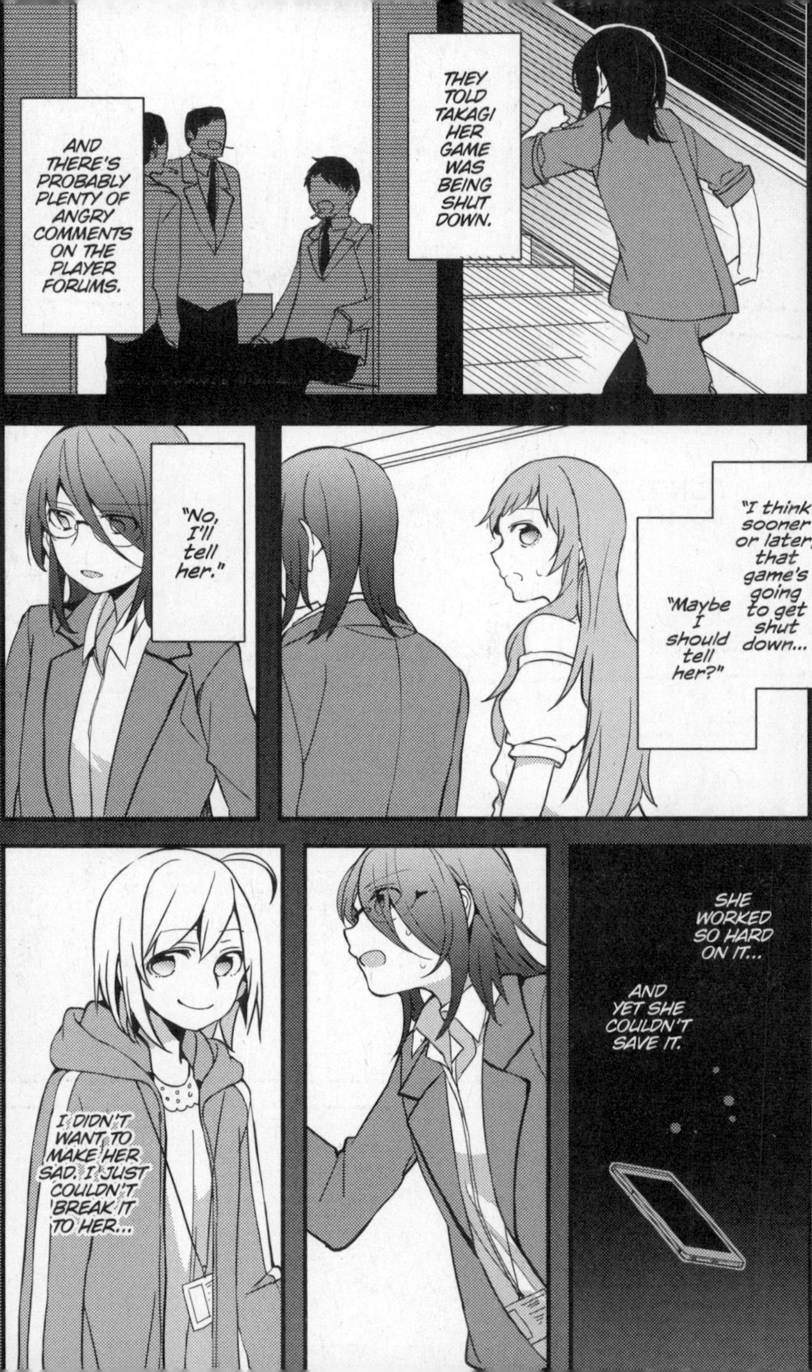
THEY TOLD TAKAGI HER GAME WAS BEING SHUT DOWN.
AND THERE'S PROBABLY PLENTY OF ANGRY COMMENTS ON THE PLAYER FORUMS.
"I think sooner or later, that game's going to get shut down...
"Maybe I should tell her?"
"No, I'll tell her."
SHE WORKED SO HARD ON IT...
AND YET SHE COULDN'T SAVE IT.
I DIDN'T WANT TO MAKE HER SAD. I JUST COULDN'T BREAK IT TO HER...

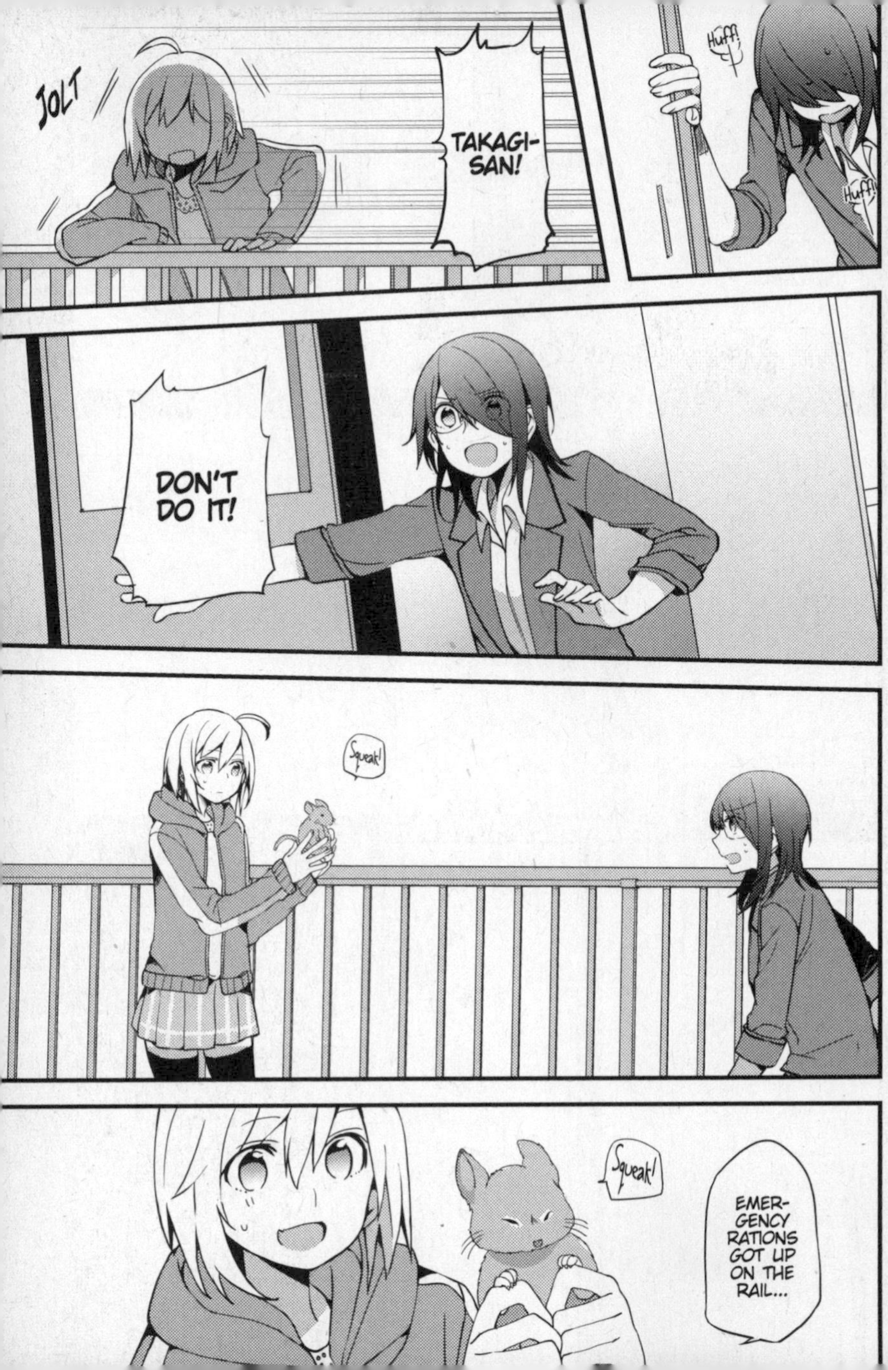
Huff!
Huff!
TAKAGI-SAN!
JOLT
DON'T DO IT!
Squeak!
EMERGENCY RATIONS GOT UP ON THE RAIL...
Squeak!

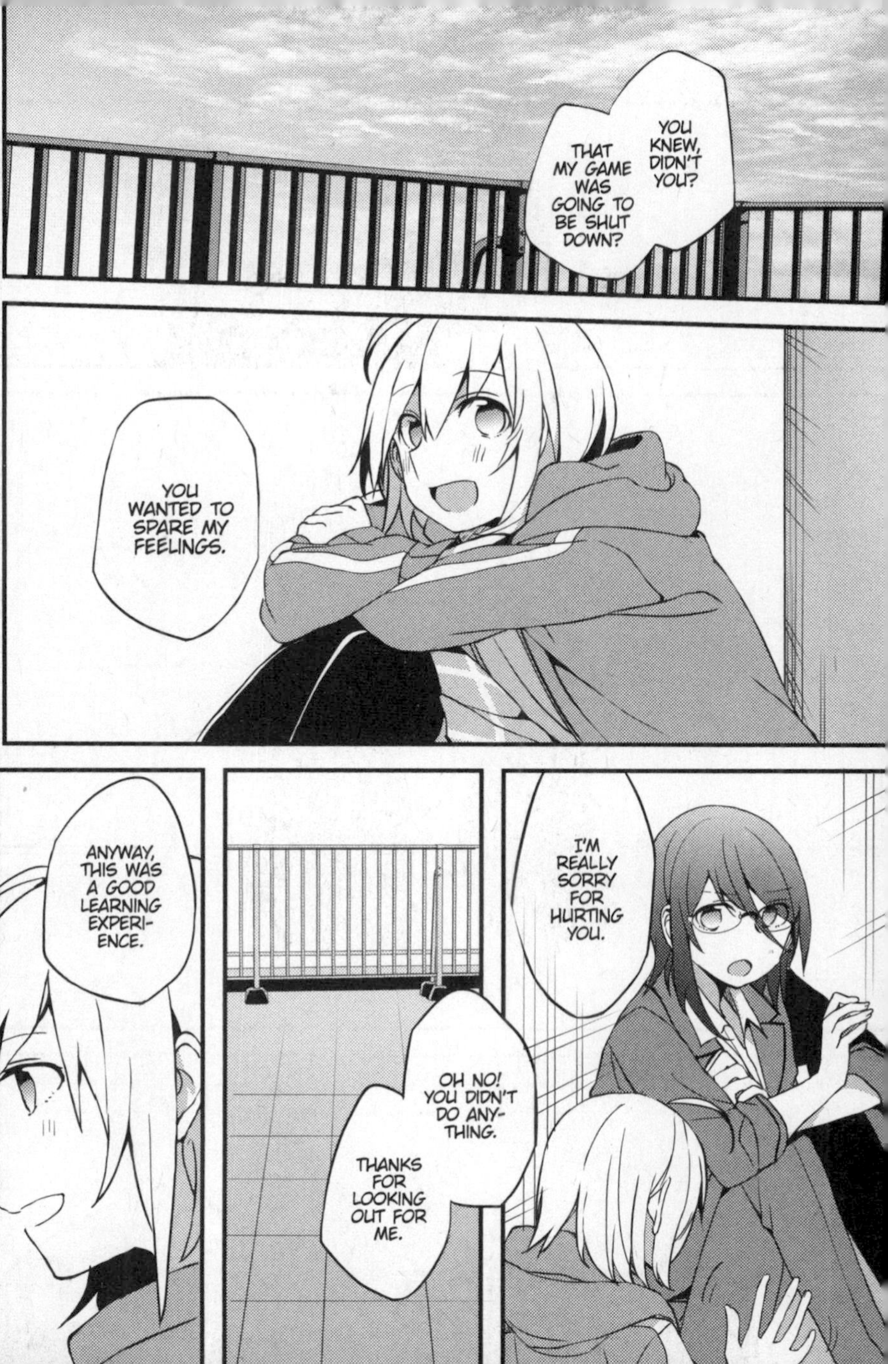
YOU KNEW, DIDN'T YOU?
THAT MY GAME WAS GOING TO BE SHUT DOWN?
YOU WANTED TO SPARE MY FEELINGS.
I'M REALLY SORRY FOR HURTING YOU.
OH NO! YOU DIDN'T DO ANY-THING.
THANKS FOR LOOKING OUT FOR ME.
ANYWAY, THIS WAS A GOOD LEARNING EXPERI-ENCE.

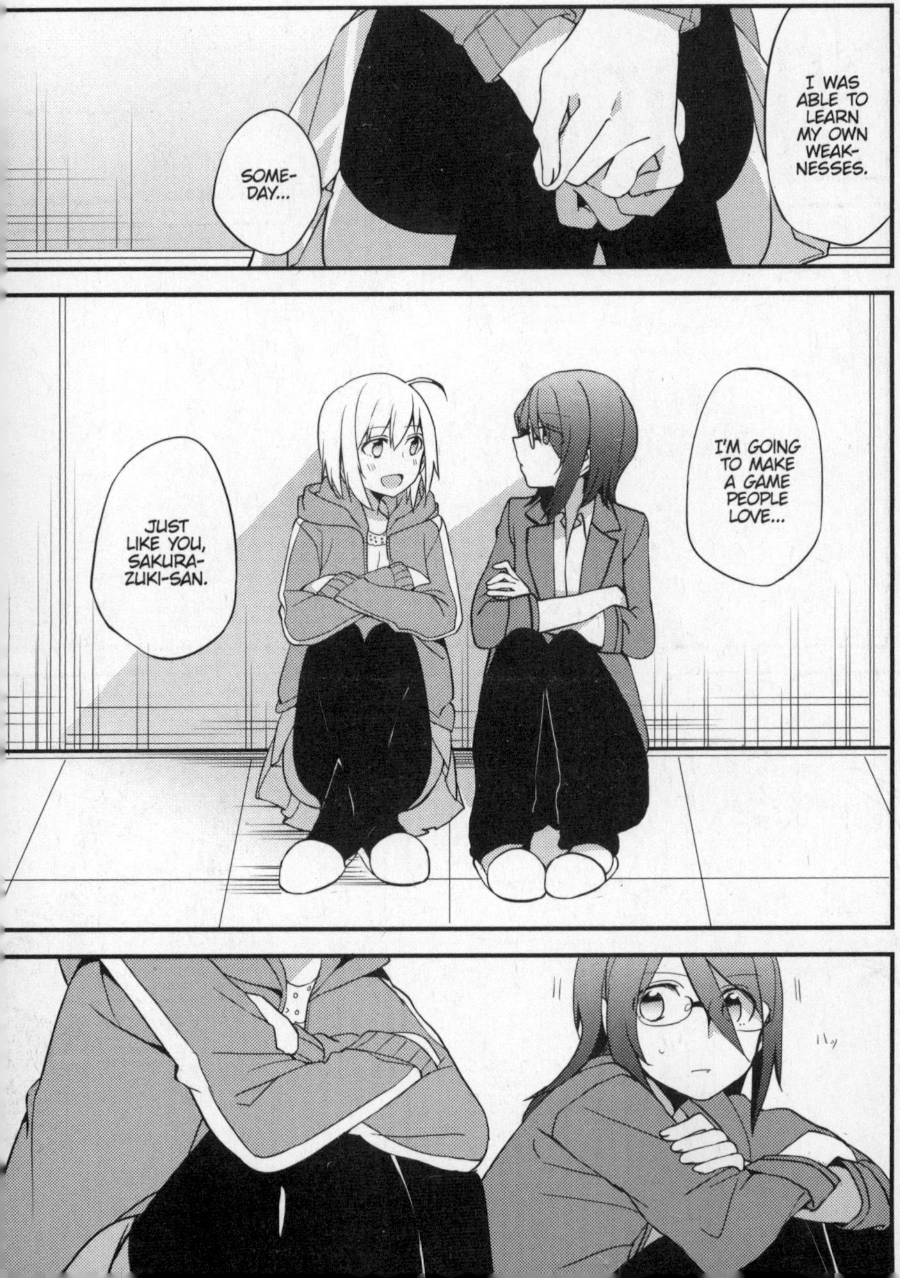
I WAS ABLE TO LEARN MY OWN WEAK-NESSES.
SOME-DAY...
I'M GOING TO MAKE A GAME PEOPLE LOVE...
JUST LIKE YOU, SAKURA-ZUKI-SAN.
ハッ

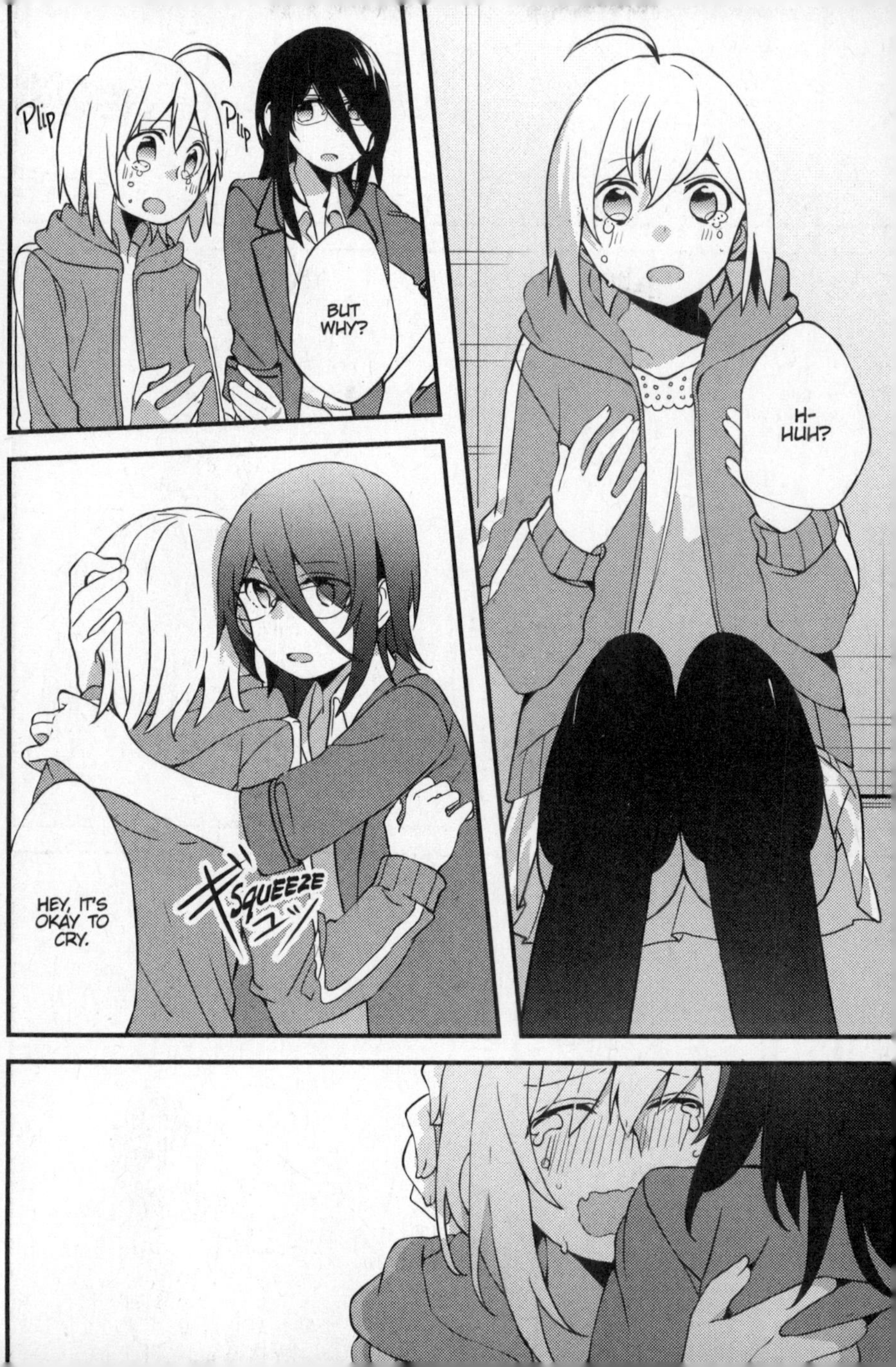
H-
HUH?
Plip
Plip
BUT
WHY?
SQUEEZE
HEY, IT'S
OKAY TO
CRY.

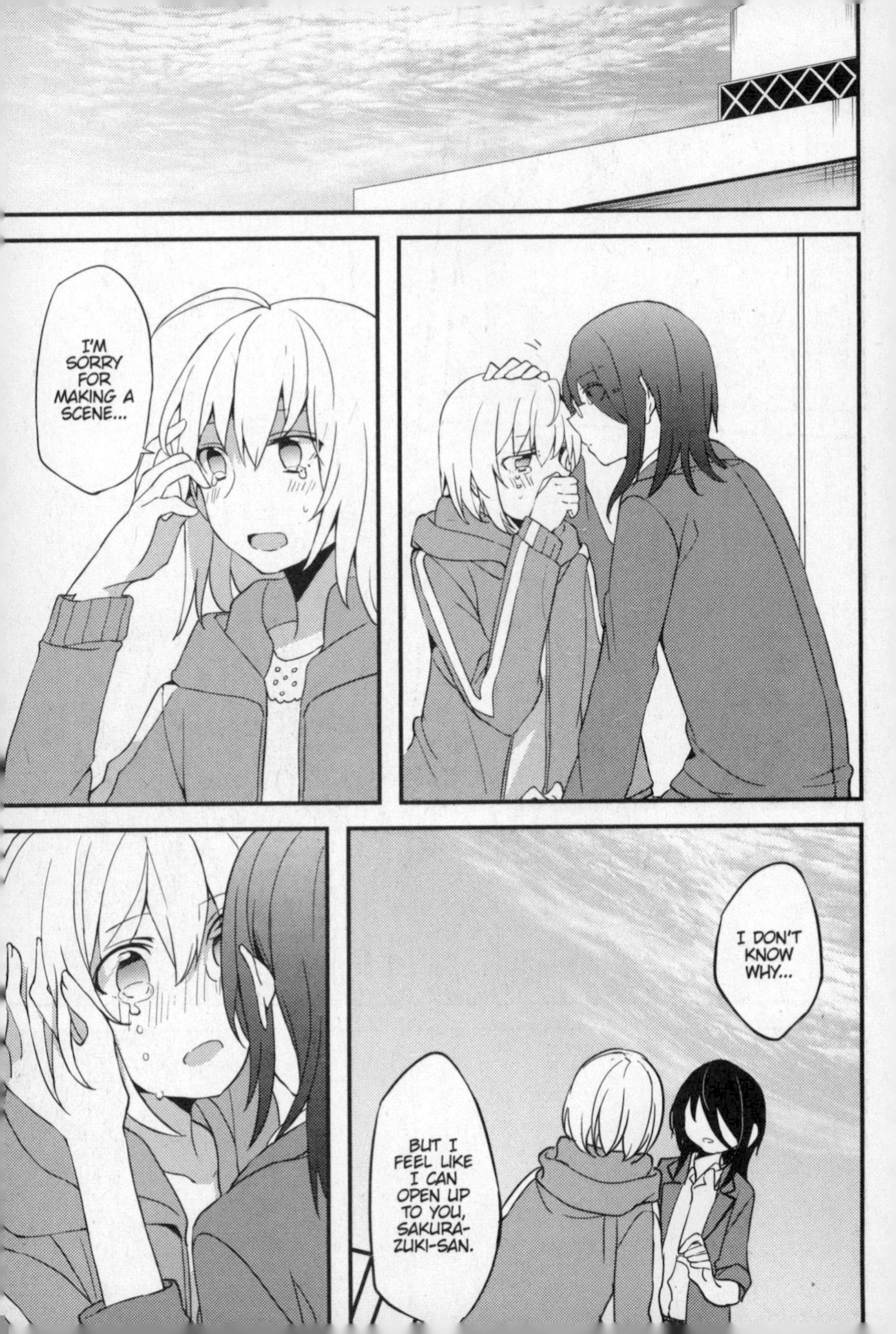
I'M SORRY FOR MAKING A SCENE...
I DON'T KNOW WHY...
BUT I FEEL LIKE I CAN OPEN UP TO YOU, SAKURAZUKI-SAN.

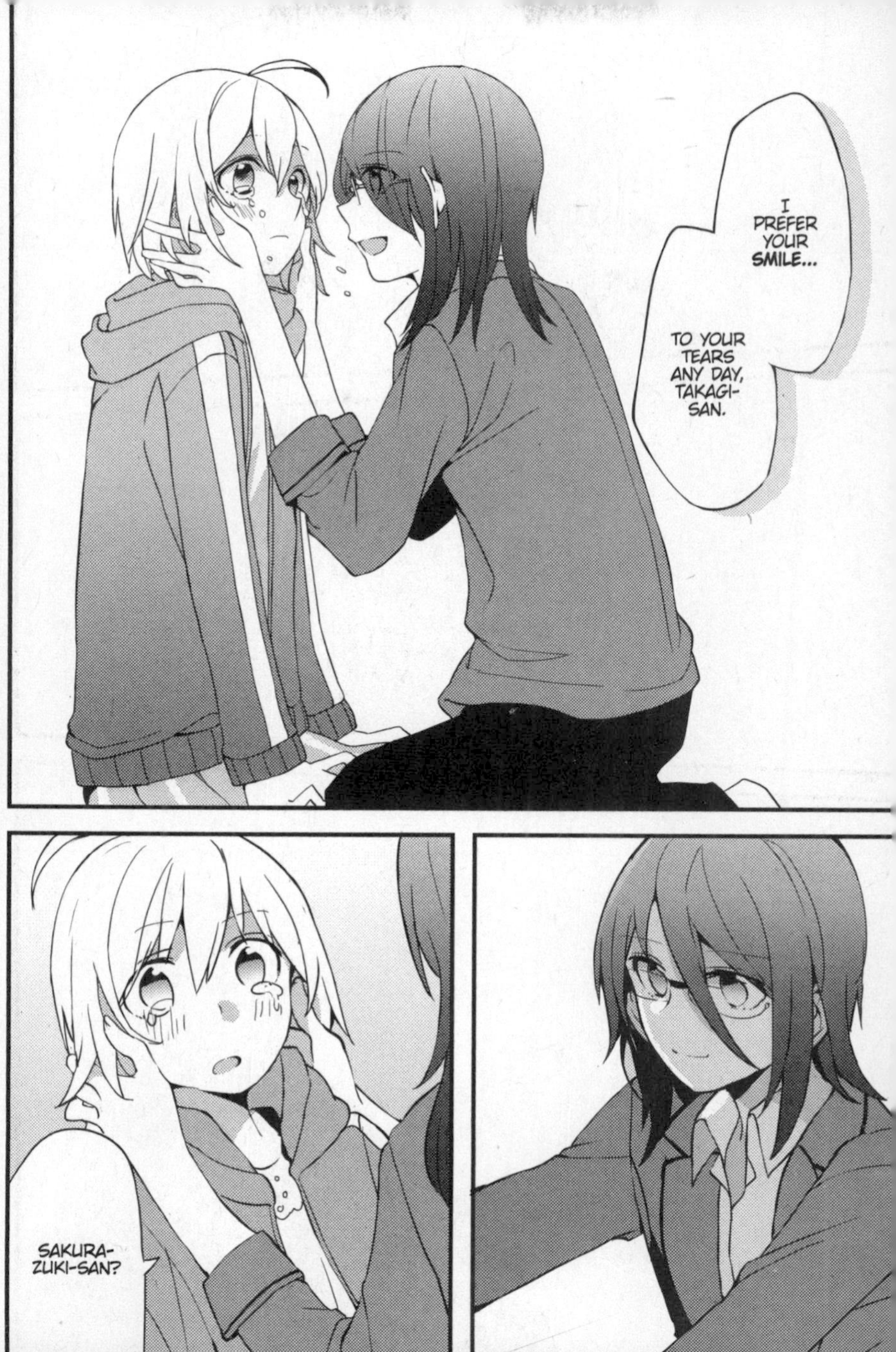
I PREFER YOUR SMILE...
TO YOUR TEARS ANY DAY, TAKAGI-SAN.
SAKURA-ZUKI-SAN?

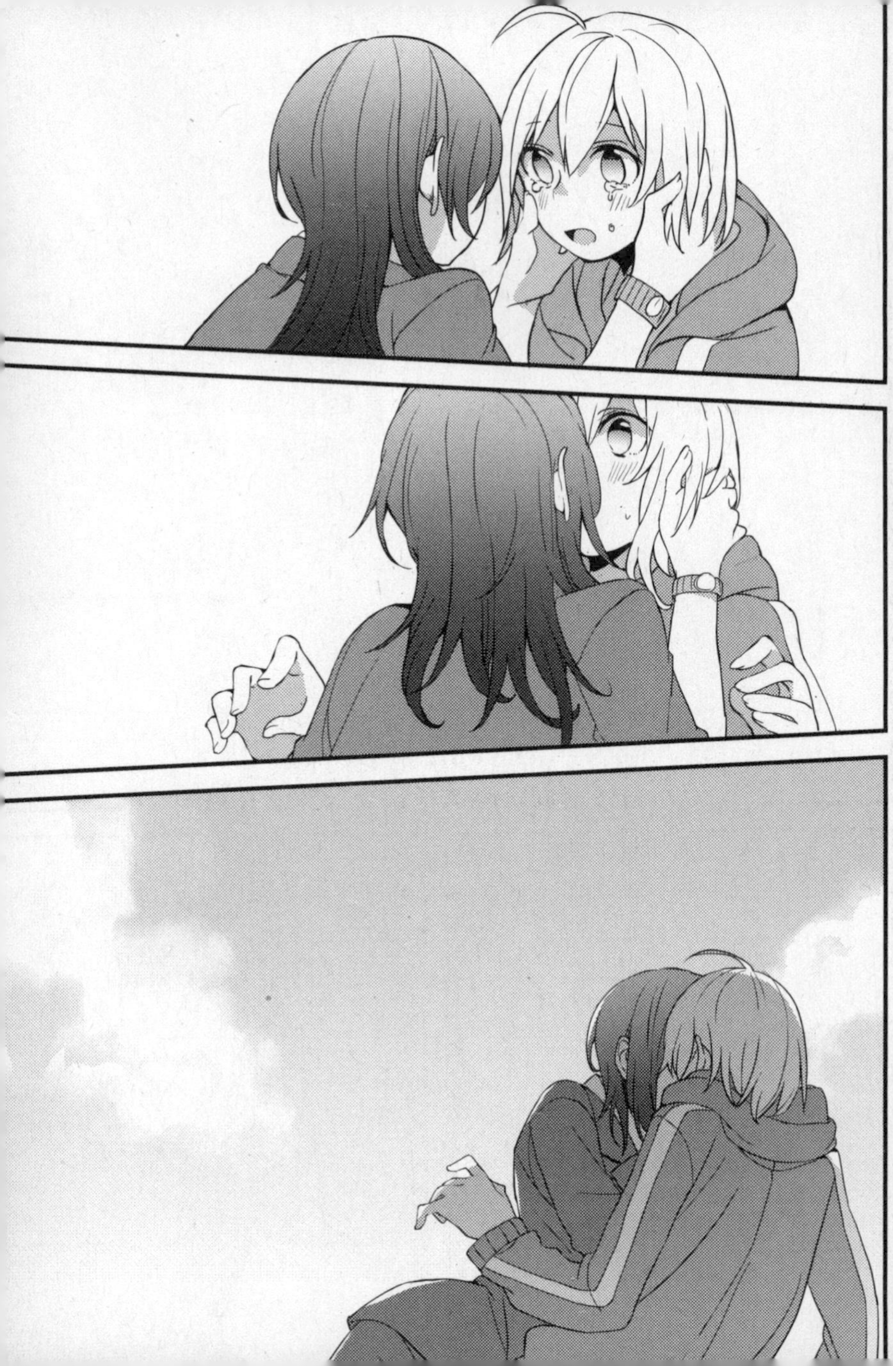

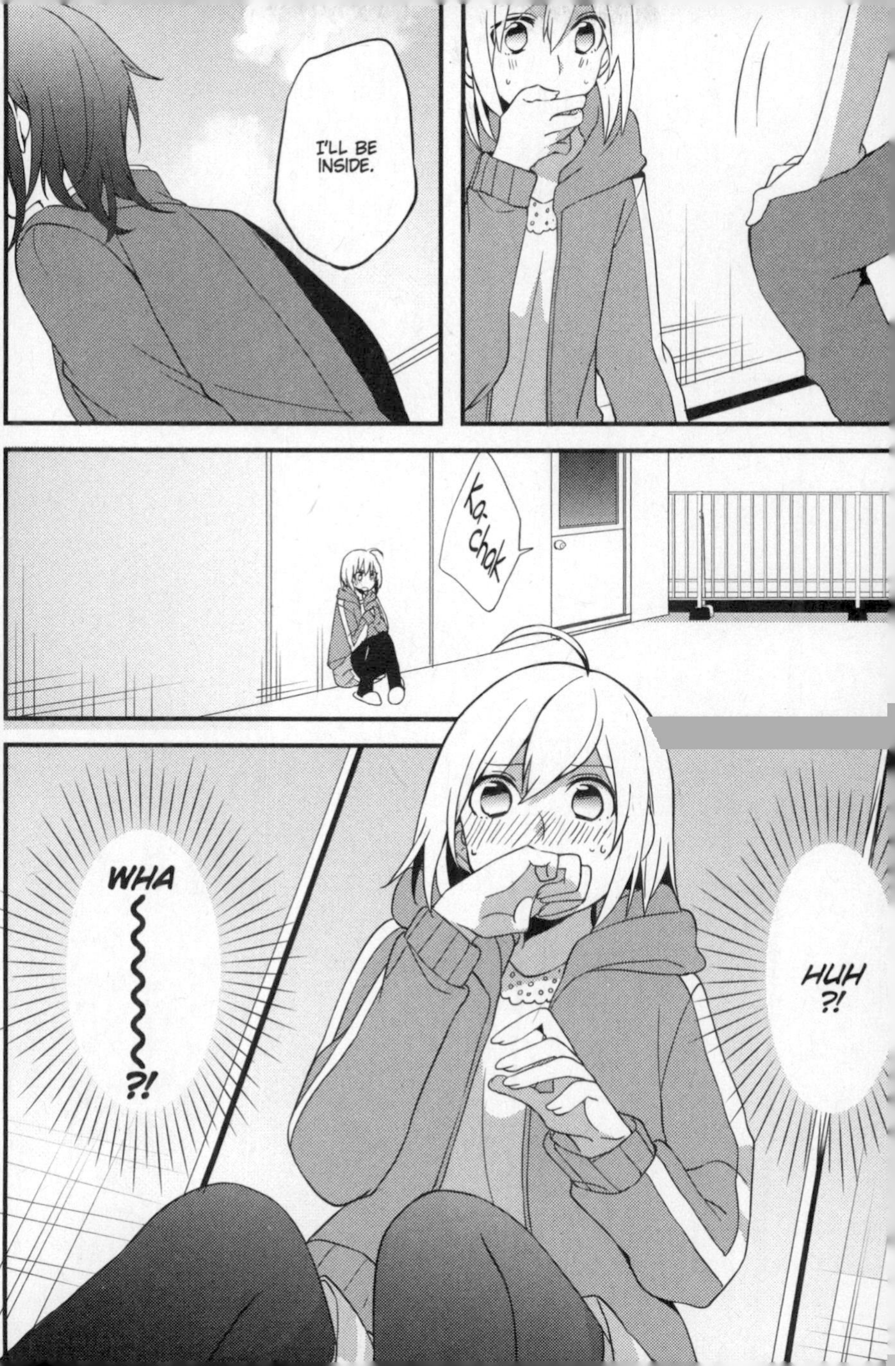
I'LL BE INSIDE.
Ka-chok
HUH ?!
WHA ~~~~ ?!

Now Loading...!

Now Loading...!

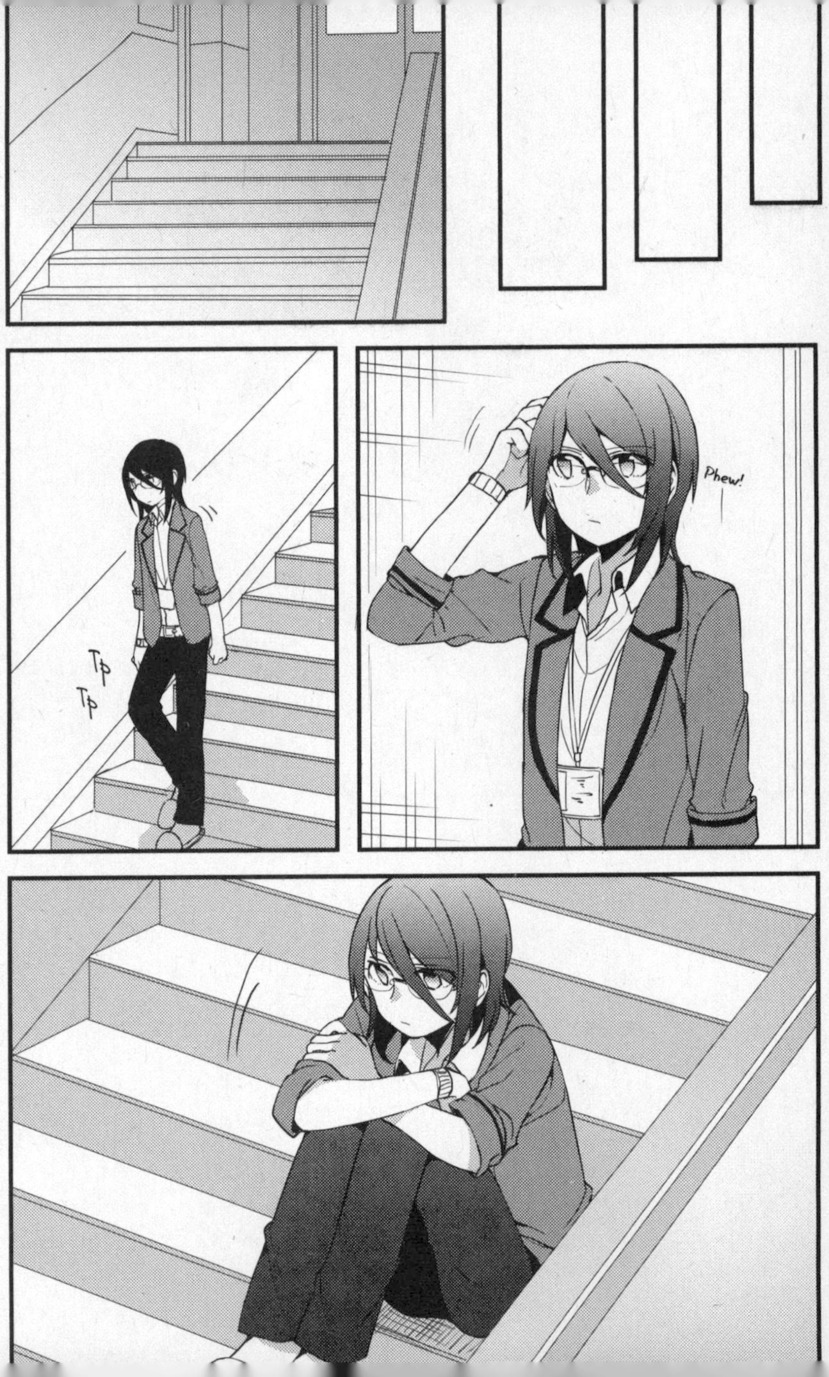
Phew!
Tp
Tp

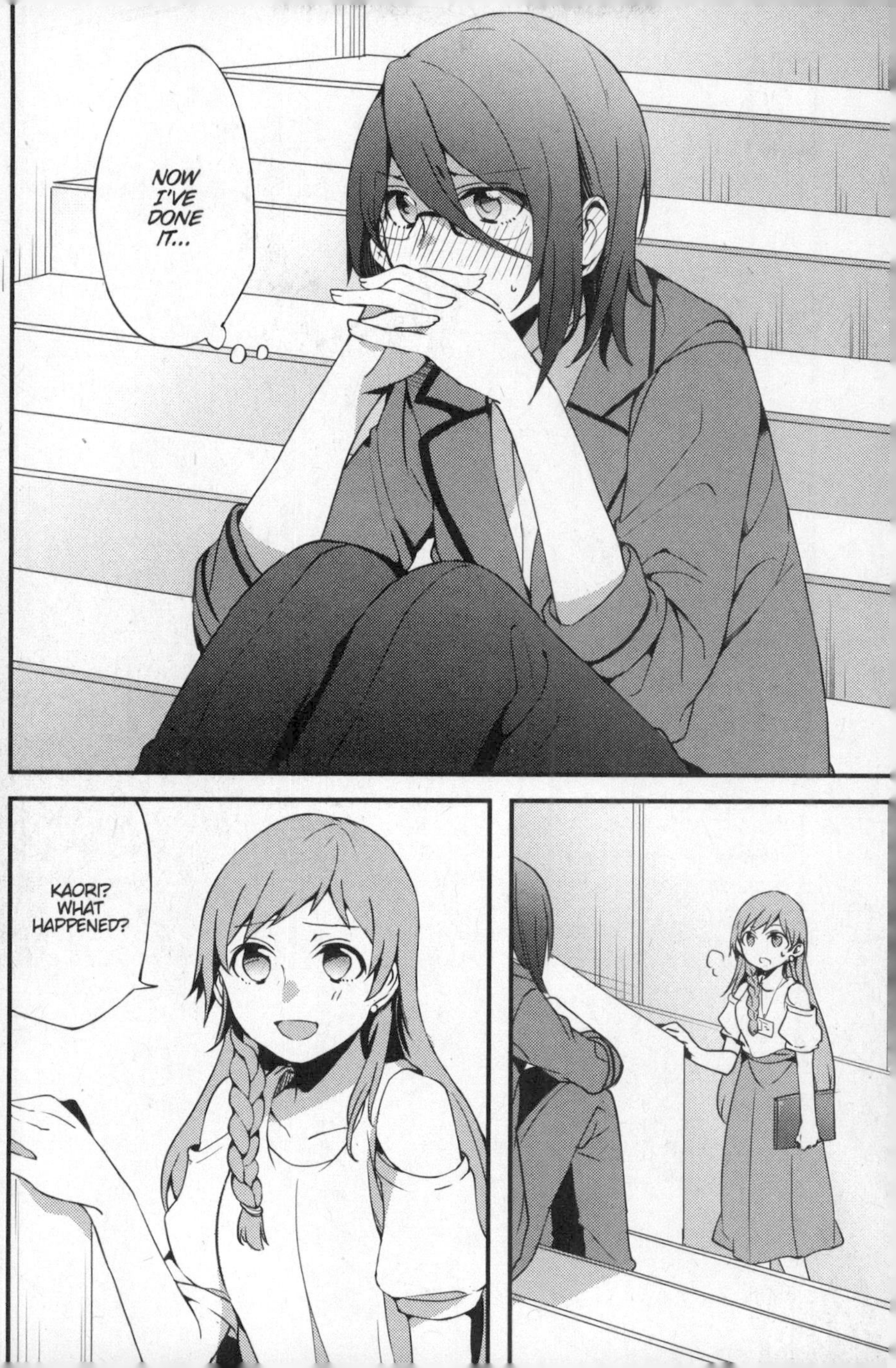
NOW I'VE DONE IT...
KAORI? WHAT HAPPENED?

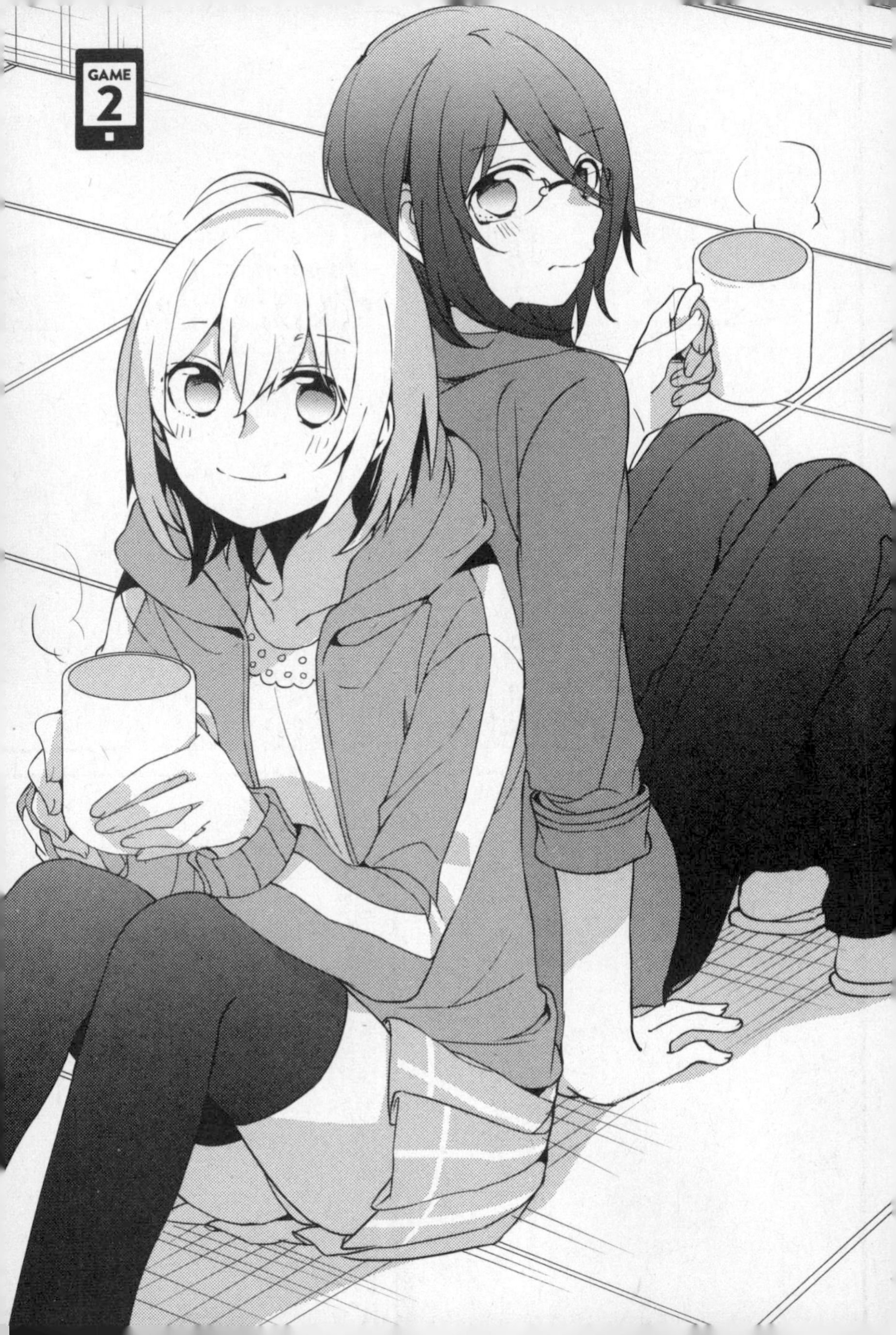
GAME
2

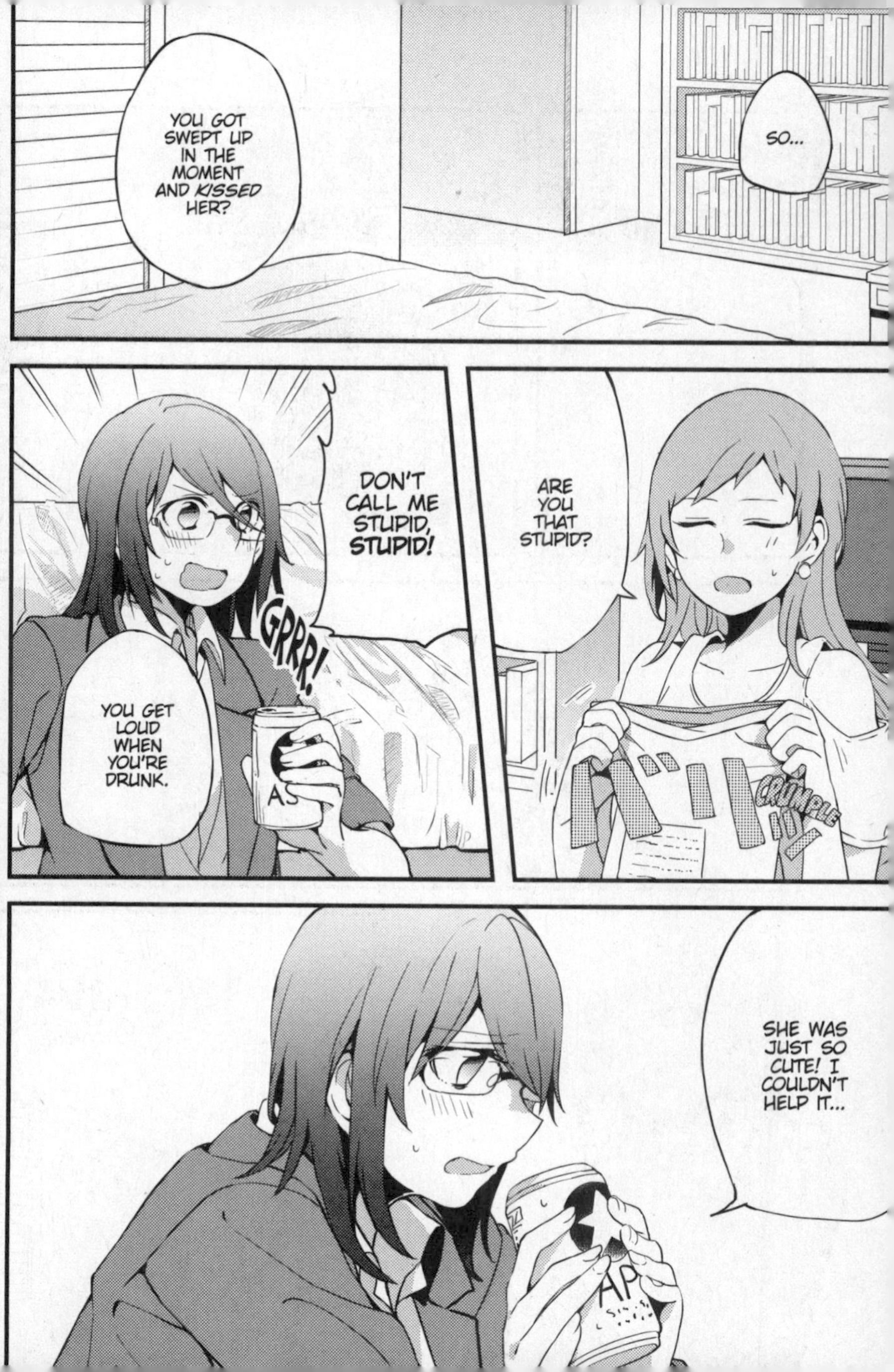
SO...
YOU GOT SWEPT UP IN THE MOMENT AND *KISSED* HER?
ARE YOU THAT STUPID?
CRUMPLE
DON'T CALL ME STUPID, STUPID!
GRRR!
YOU GET LOUD WHEN YOU'RE DRUNK.
SHE WAS JUST SO CUTE! I COULDN'T HELP IT...

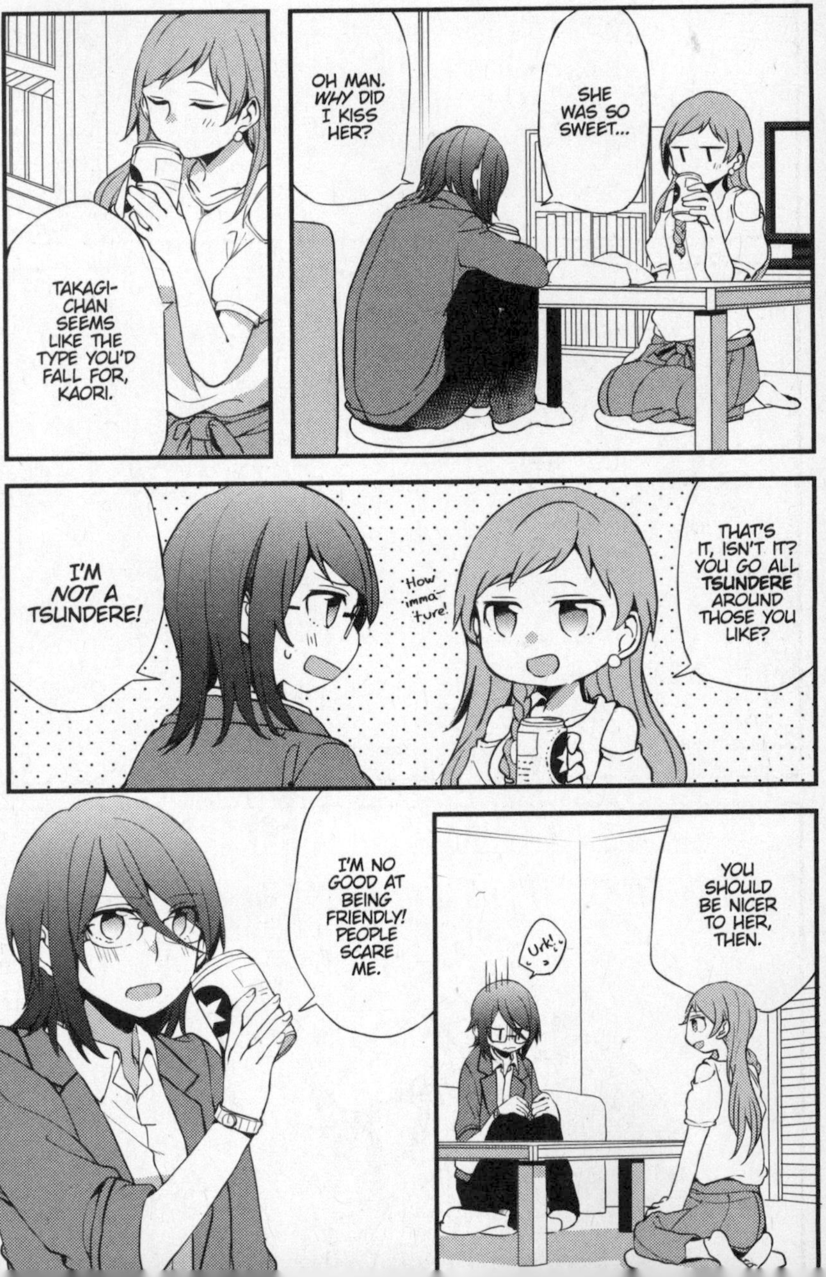
SHE WAS SO SWEET...
OH MAN. WHY DID I KISS HER?
TAKAGI-CHAN SEEMS LIKE THE TYPE YOU'D FALL FOR, KAORI.
THAT'S IT, ISN'T IT? YOU GO ALL TSUNDERE AROUND THOSE YOU LIKE?
How imma-ture!
I'M NOT A TSUNDERE!
YOU SHOULD BE NICER TO HER, THEN.
Urk!
I'M NO GOOD AT BEING FRIENDLY! PEOPLE SCARE ME.

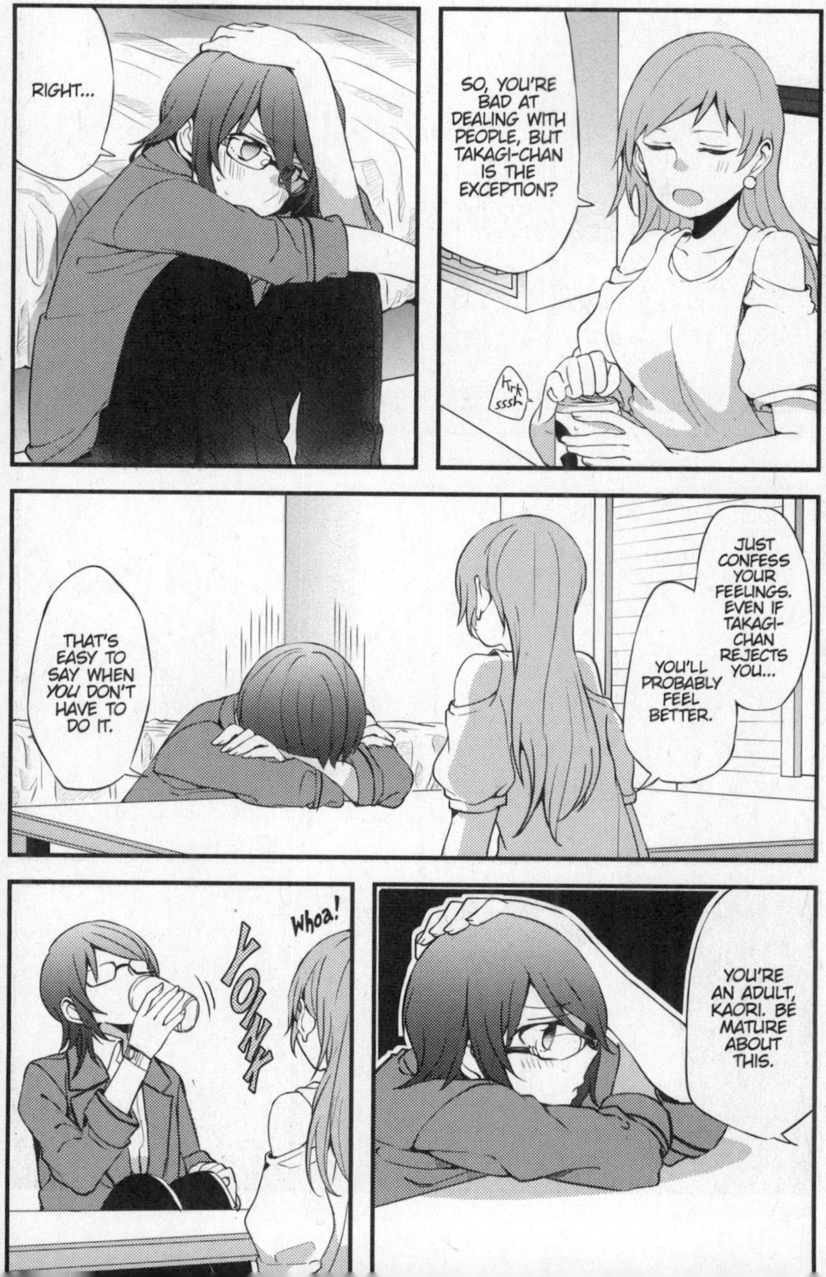
SO, YOU'RE BAD AT DEALING WITH PEOPLE, BUT TAKAGI-CHAN IS THE EXCEPTION?
Krk sssh
RIGHT...
JUST CONFESS YOUR FEELINGS. EVEN IF TAKAGI-CHAN REJECTS YOU...
YOU'LL PROBABLY FEEL BETTER.
THAT'S EASY TO SAY WHEN *YOU* DON'T HAVE TO DO IT.
YOU'RE AN ADULT, KAORI. BE MATURE ABOUT THIS.
Whoa!
YONK

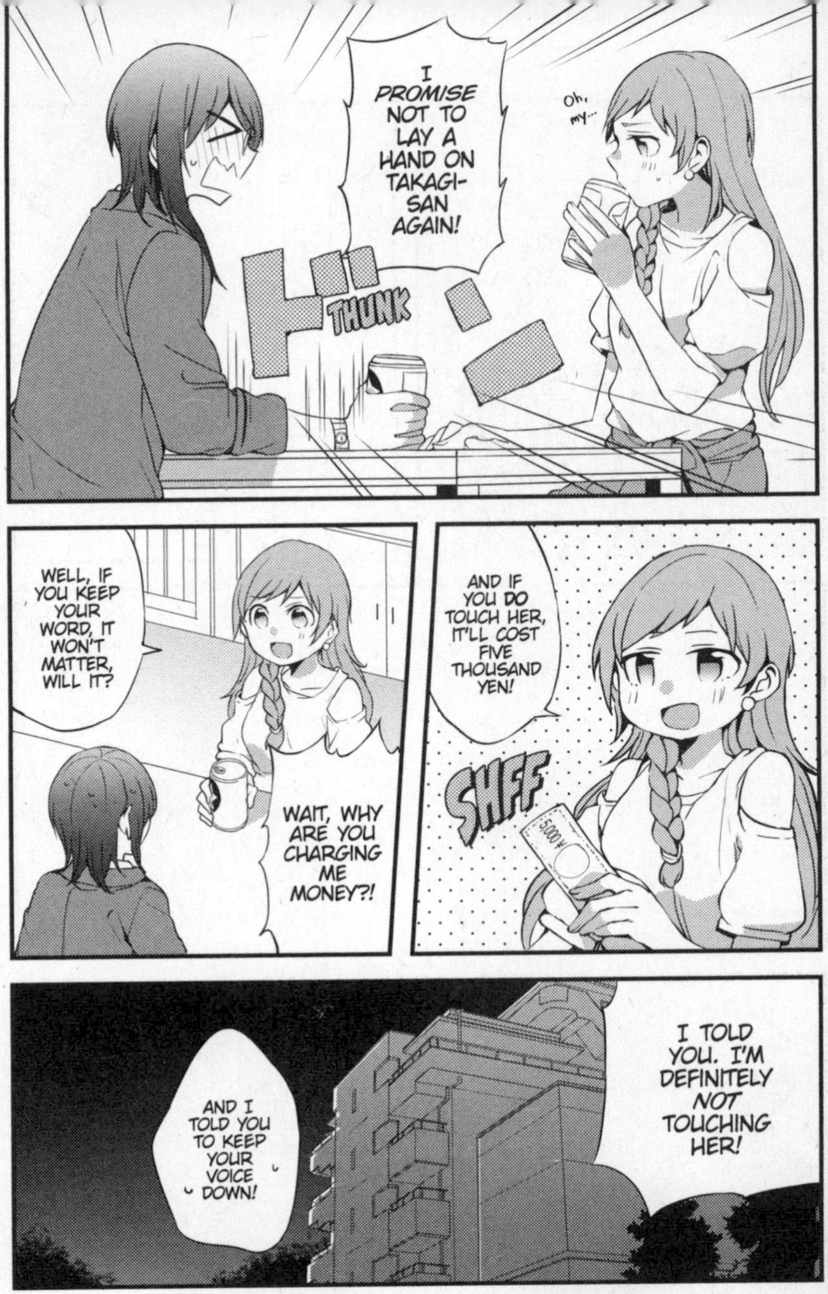
I *PROMISE* NOT TO LAY A HAND ON TAKAGI-SAN AGAIN!
THUNK
Oh, my...
AND IF YOU DO TOUCH HER, IT'LL COST FIVE THOUSAND YEN!
SHFF
5,000¥
WELL, IF YOU KEEP YOUR WORD, IT WON'T MATTER, WILL IT?
WAIT, WHY ARE YOU CHARGING ME MONEY?!
I TOLD YOU. I'M DEFINITELY *NOT* TOUCHING HER!
AND I TOLD YOU TO KEEP YOUR VOICE DOWN!

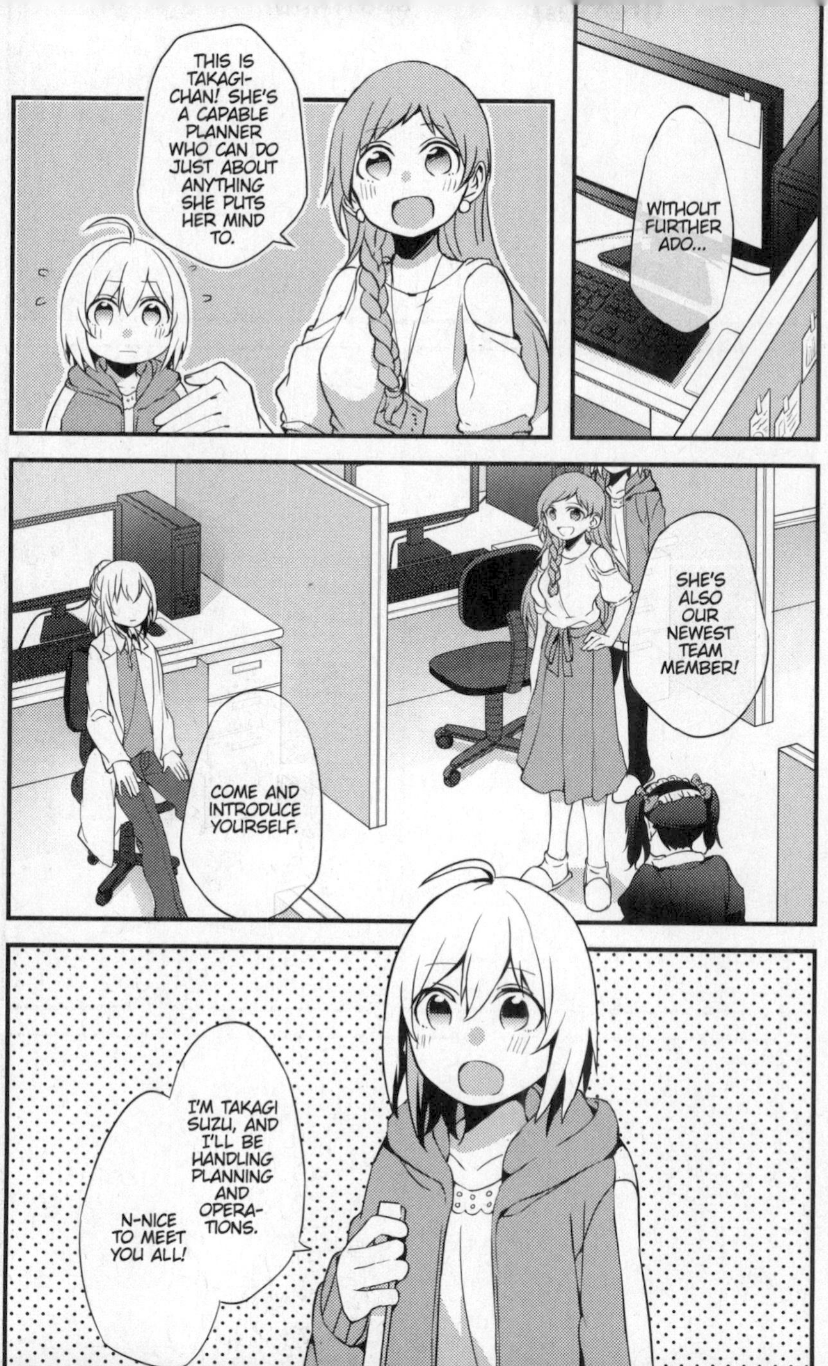
WITHOUT FURTHER ADO...
THIS IS TAKAGI-CHAN! SHE'S A CAPABLE PLANNER WHO CAN DO JUST ABOUT ANYTHING SHE PUTS HER MIND TO.
SHE'S ALSO OUR NEWEST TEAM MEMBER!
COME AND INTRODUCE YOURSELF.
I'M TAKAGI SUZU, AND I'LL BE HANDLING PLANNING AND OPERATIONS.
N-NICE TO MEET YOU ALL!

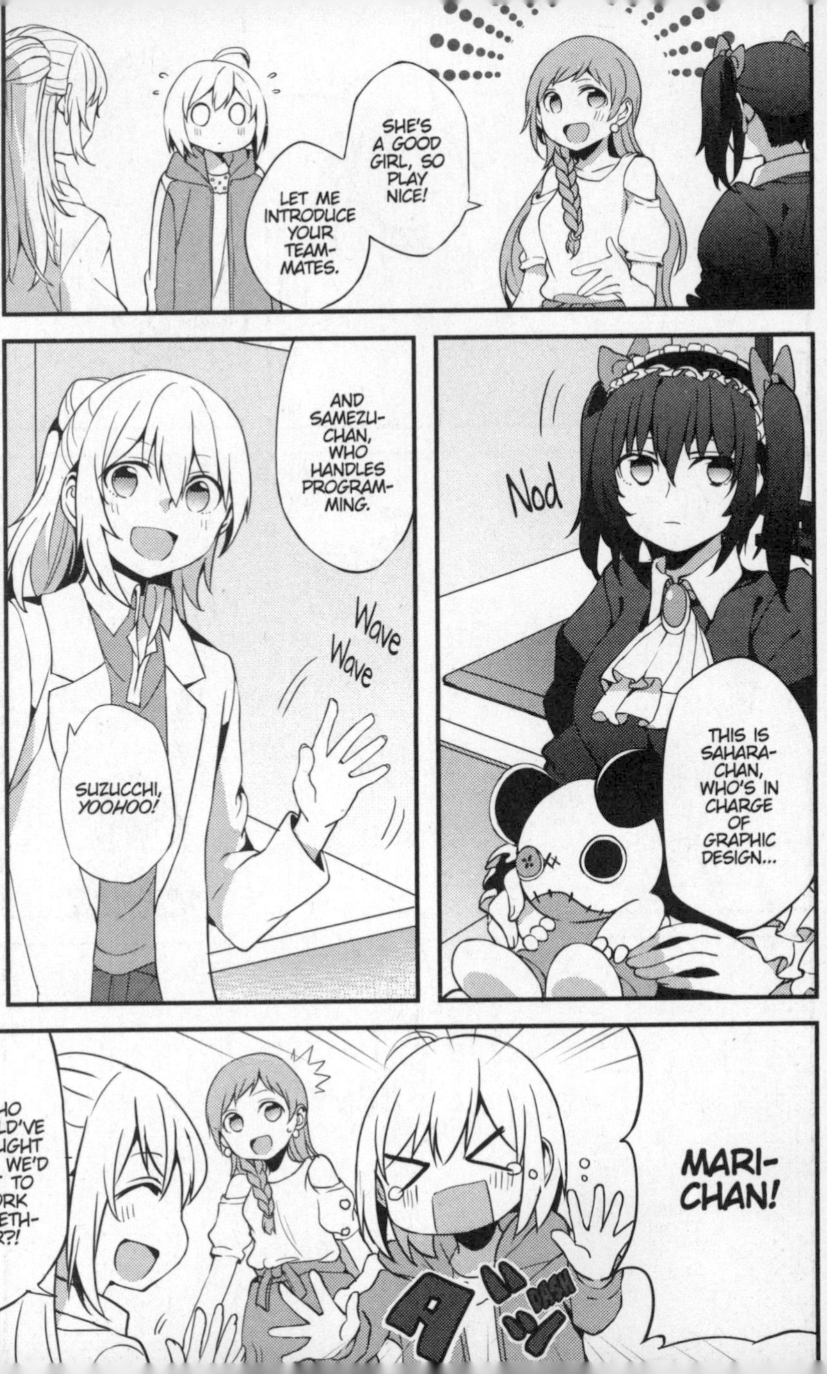
SHE'S A GOOD GIRL, SO PLAY NICE!
LET ME INTRODUCE YOUR TEAM-MATES.
THIS IS SAHARA-CHAN, WHO'S IN CHARGE OF GRAPHIC DESIGN...
Nod
AND SAMEZU-CHAN, WHO HANDLES PROGRAM-MING.
Wave Wave
SUZUCCHI, YOOHOO!
MARI-CHAN!
DASH
WHO WOULD'VE THOUGHT THAT WE'D GET TO WORK TOGETH-ER?!

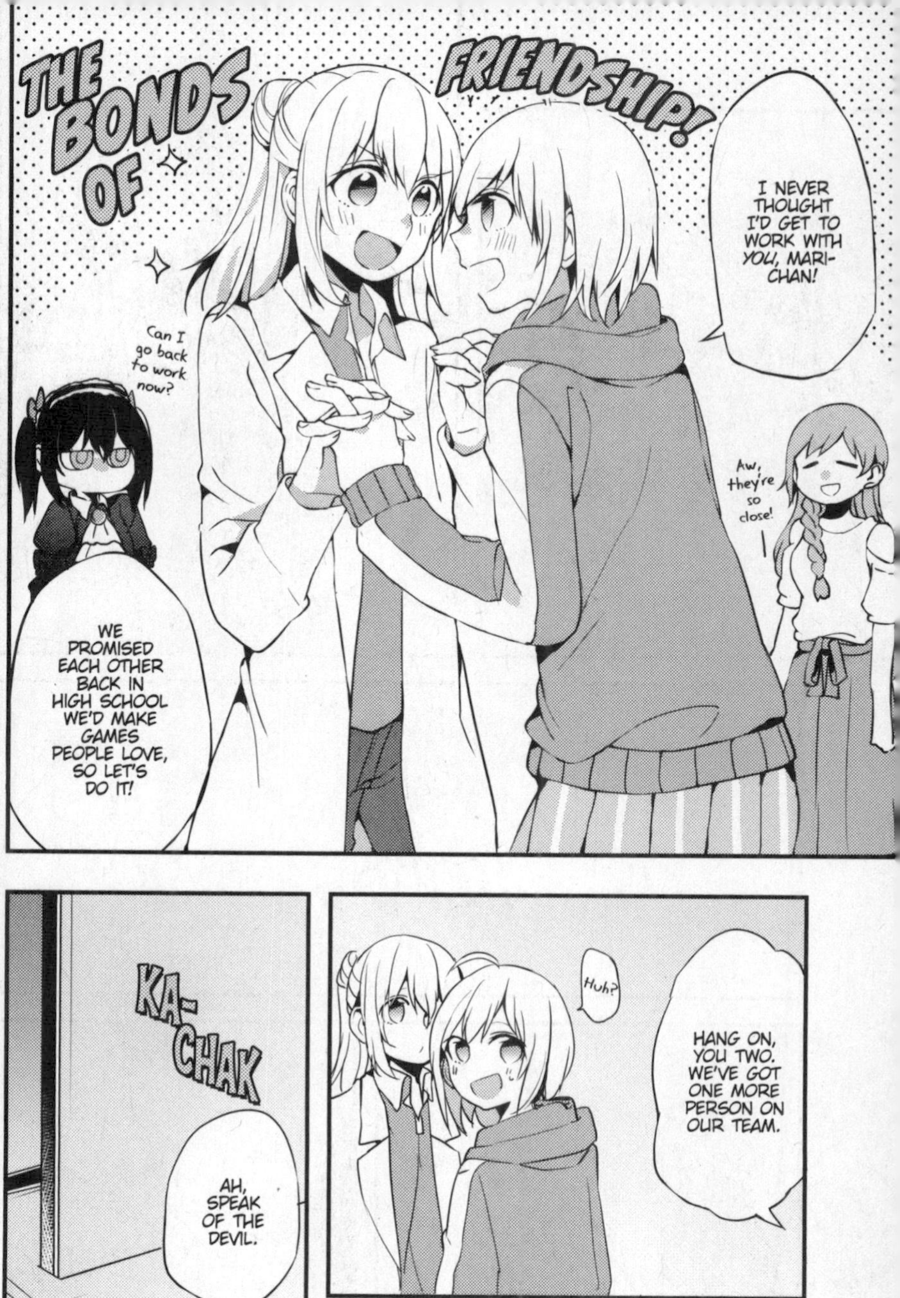
I NEVER THOUGHT I'D GET TO WORK WITH *YOU*, MARI-CHAN!
THE BONDS OF FRIENDSHIP!
Aw, they're so close!
Can I go back to work now?
WE PROMISED EACH OTHER BACK IN HIGH SCHOOL WE'D MAKE GAMES PEOPLE LOVE, SO LET'S DO IT!
HANG ON, YOU TWO. WE'VE GOT ONE MORE PERSON ON OUR TEAM.
Huh?
KA-CHAK
AH, SPEAK OF THE DEVIL.

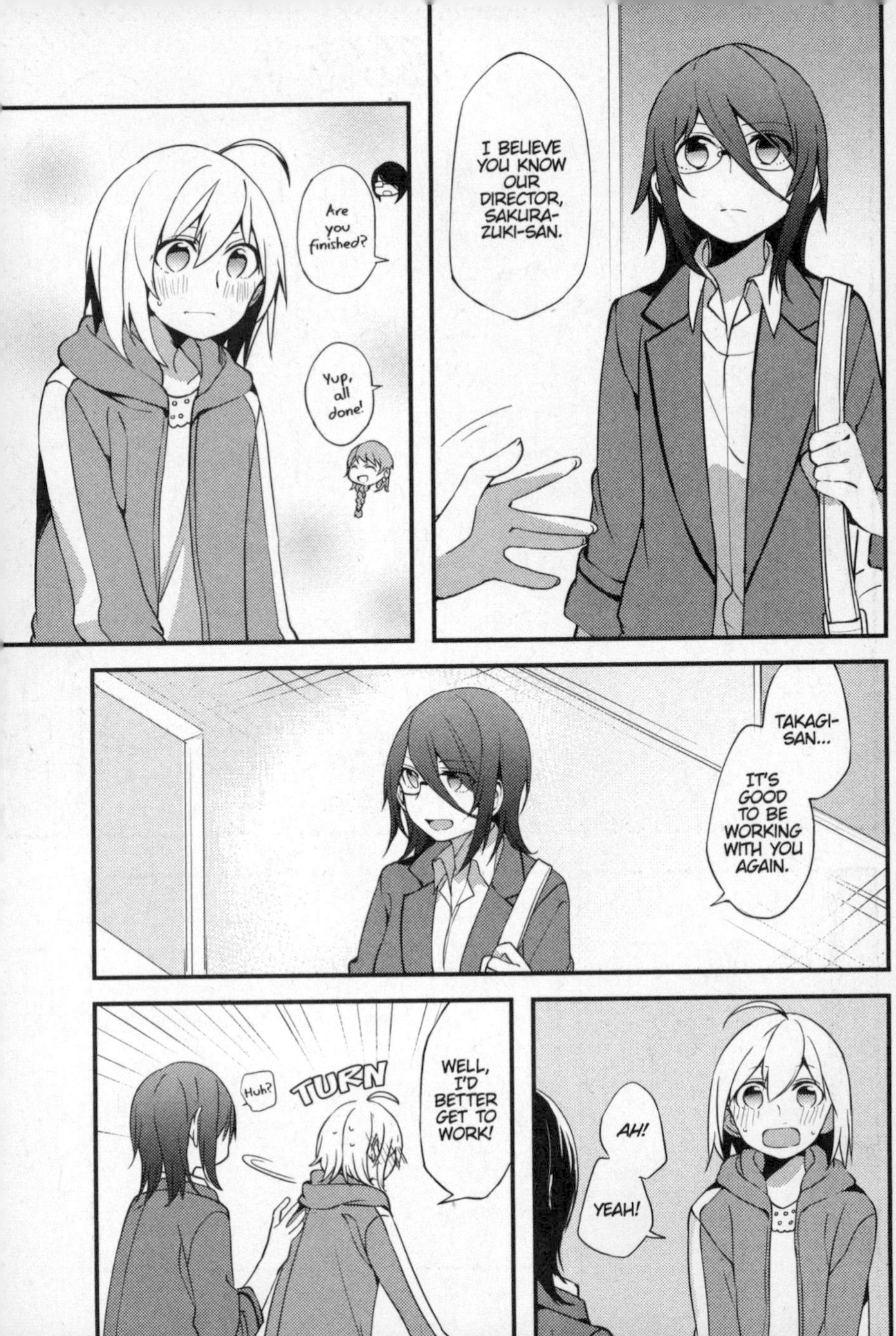
I BELIEVE YOU KNOW OUR DIRECTOR, SAKURA-ZUKI-SAN.
Are you finished?
Yup, all done!
TAKAGI-SAN...
IT'S GOOD TO BE WORKING WITH YOU AGAIN.
AH!
YEAH!
WELL, I'D BETTER GET TO WORK!
TURN
Huh?

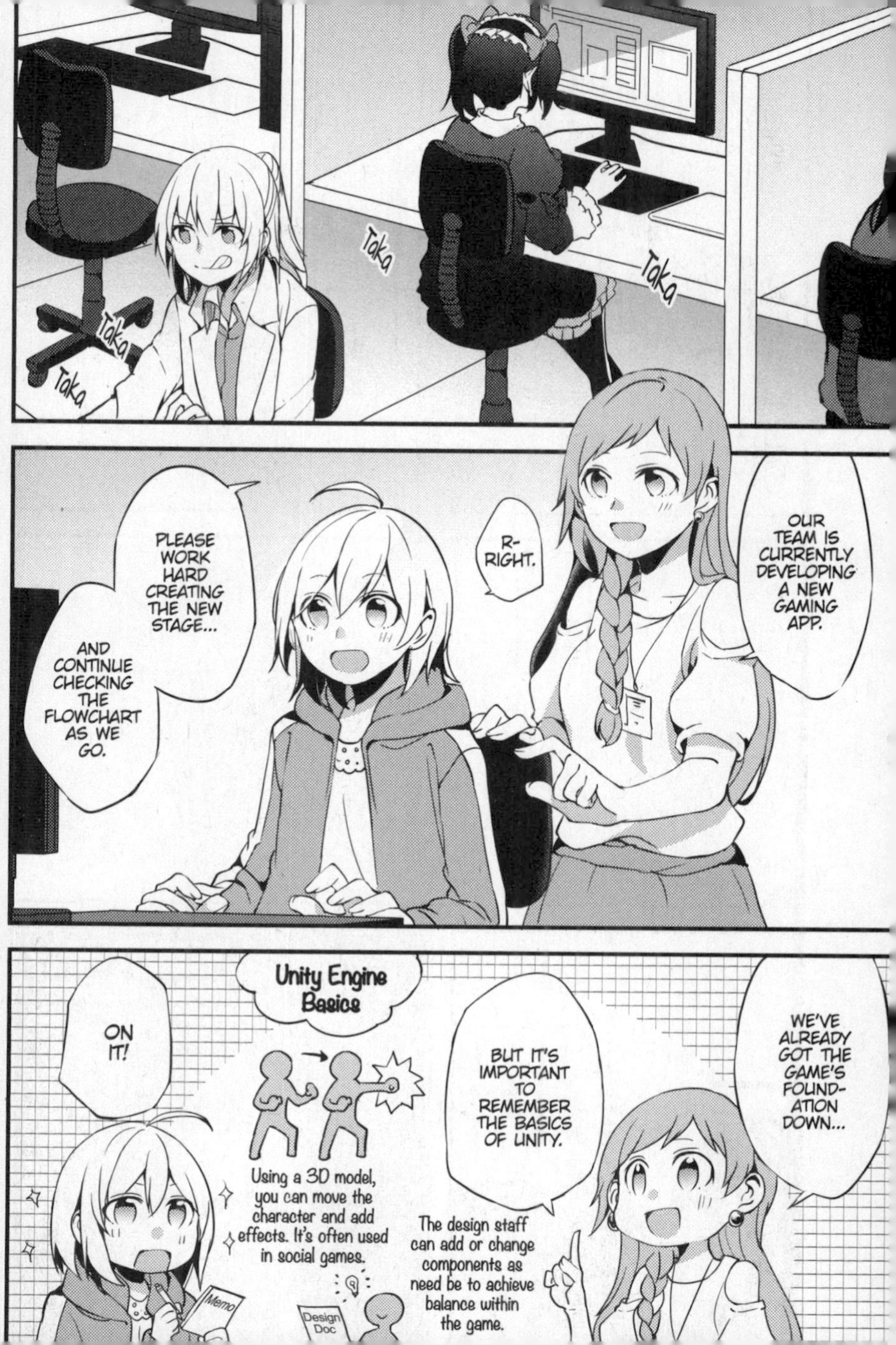
Taka
Taka
Taka
Taka
OUR TEAM IS CURRENTLY DEVELOPING A NEW GAMING APP.
R-RIGHT.
PLEASE WORK HARD CREATING THE NEW STAGE...
AND CONTINUE CHECKING THE FLOWCHART AS WE GO.
WE'VE ALREADY GOT THE GAME'S FOUND-ATION DOWN...
BUT IT'S IMPORTANT TO REMEMBER THE BASICS OF UNITY.
The design staff can add or change components as need be to achieve balance within the game.
Design Doc
Unity Engine Basics
Using a 3D model, you can move the character and add effects. It's often used in social games.
ON IT!
Memo

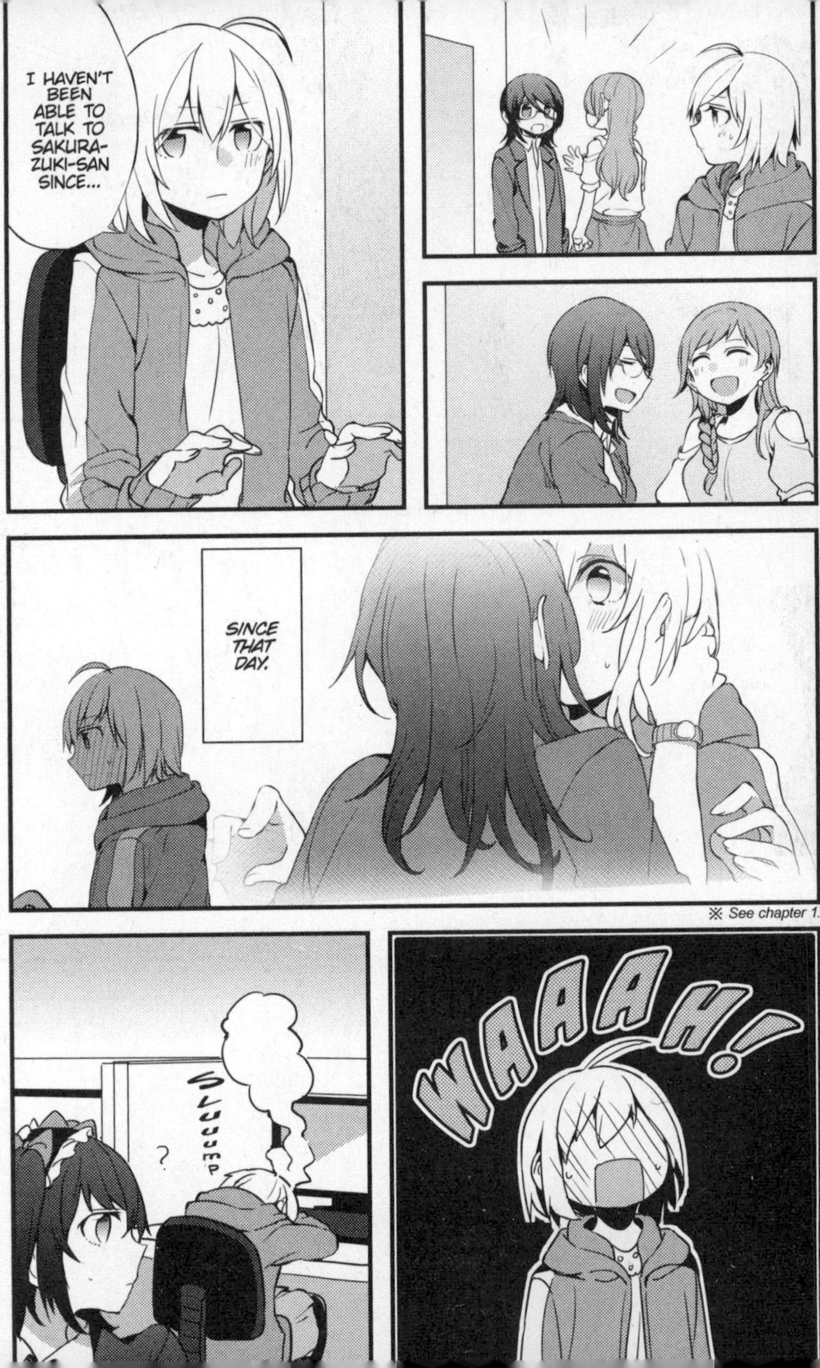
I HAVEN'T BEEN ABLE TO TALK TO SAKURAZUKI-SAN SINCE...
SINCE THAT DAY.
※ See chapter 1.
WAAAAH!!
SLUUUMP
?

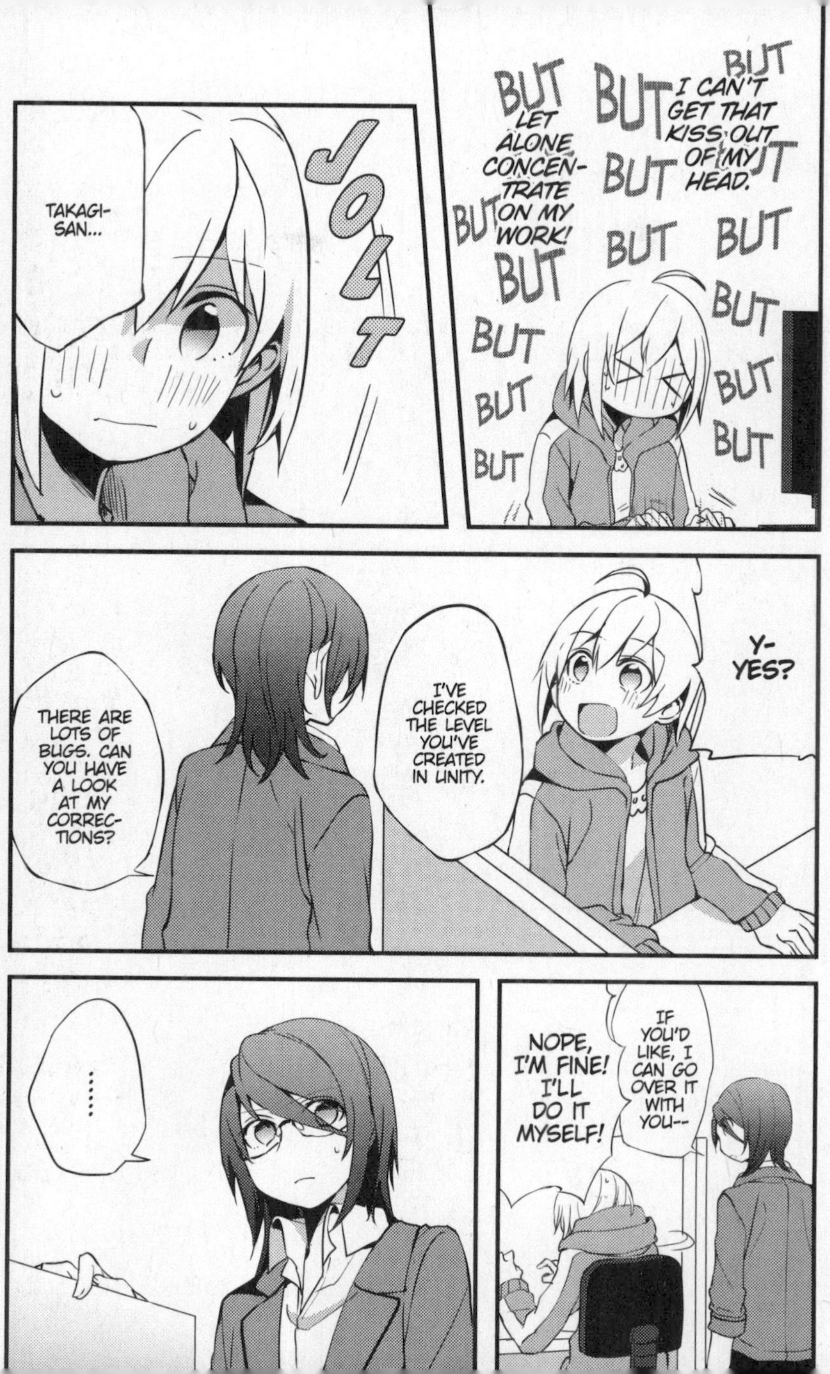

BUT
BUT
BUT
I CAN'T GET THAT KISS OUT OF MY HEAD.
LET ALONE CONCENTRATE ON MY WORK!
BUT
BUT
BUT
BUT
BUT
BUT
BUT
BUT
BUT
BUT
BUT
JOLT
TAKAGI-SAN...
Y-YES?
I'VE CHECKED THE LEVEL YOU'VE CREATED IN UNITY.
THERE ARE LOTS OF BUGS. CAN YOU HAVE A LOOK AT MY CORRECTIONS?
IF YOU'D LIKE, I CAN GO OVER IT WITH YOU--
NOPE, I'M FINE! I'LL DO IT MYSELF!
......

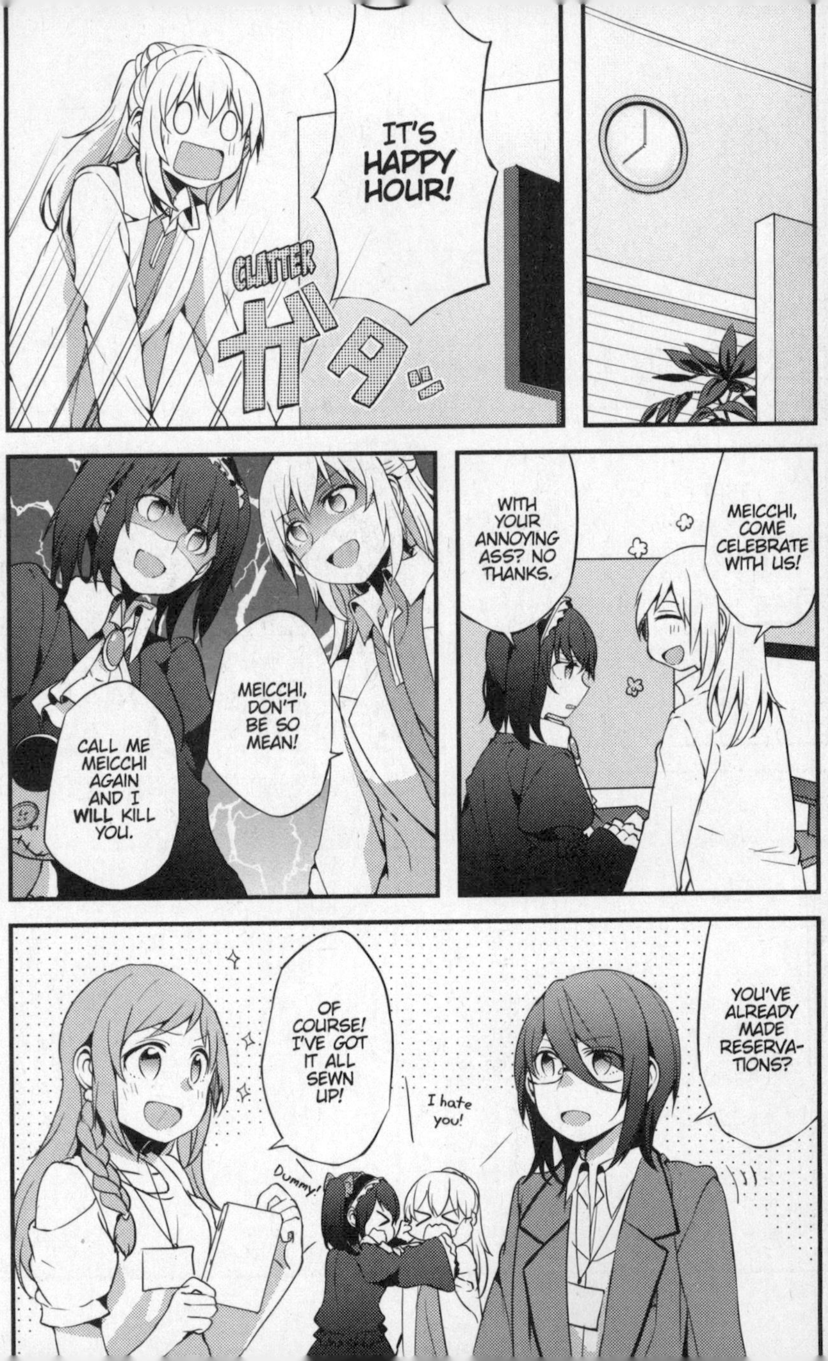
IT'S HAPPY HOUR!
CLATTER
ガタッ
MEICCHI, COME CELEBRATE WITH US!
WITH YOUR ANNOYING ASS? NO THANKS.
MEICCHI, DON'T BE SO MEAN!
CALL ME MEICCHI AGAIN AND I WILL KILL YOU.
YOU'VE ALREADY MADE RESERVA-TIONS?
OF COURSE! I'VE GOT IT ALL SEWN UP!
I hate you!
Dummy!

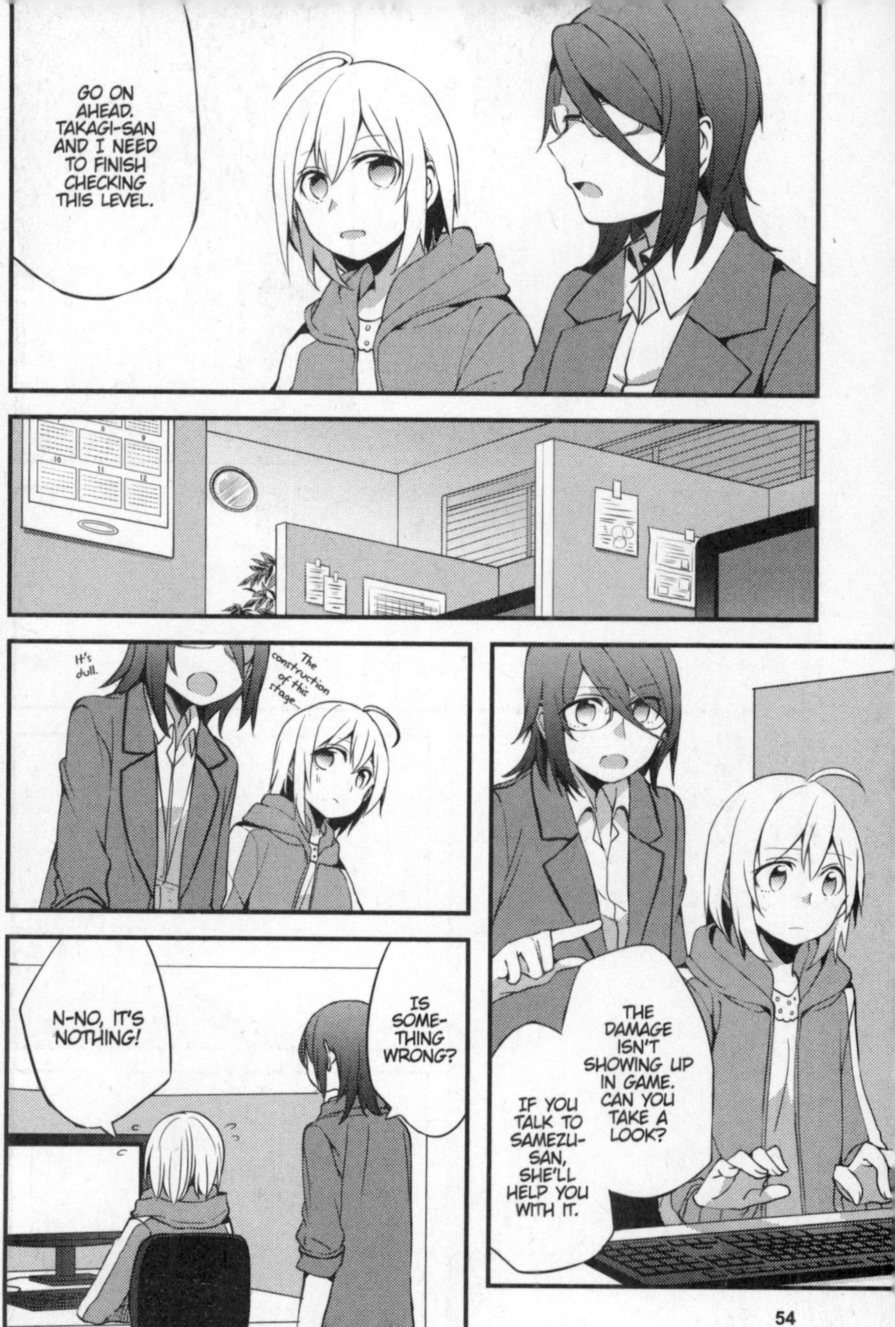
GO ON AHEAD. TAKAGI-SAN AND I NEED TO FINISH CHECKING THIS LEVEL.
THE DAMAGE ISN'T SHOWING UP IN GAME. CAN YOU TAKE A LOOK?
IF YOU TALK TO SAMEZU-SAN, SHE'LL HELP YOU WITH IT.
The construction of this stage...
It's dull.
IS SOME-THING WRONG?
N-NO, IT'S NOTHING!

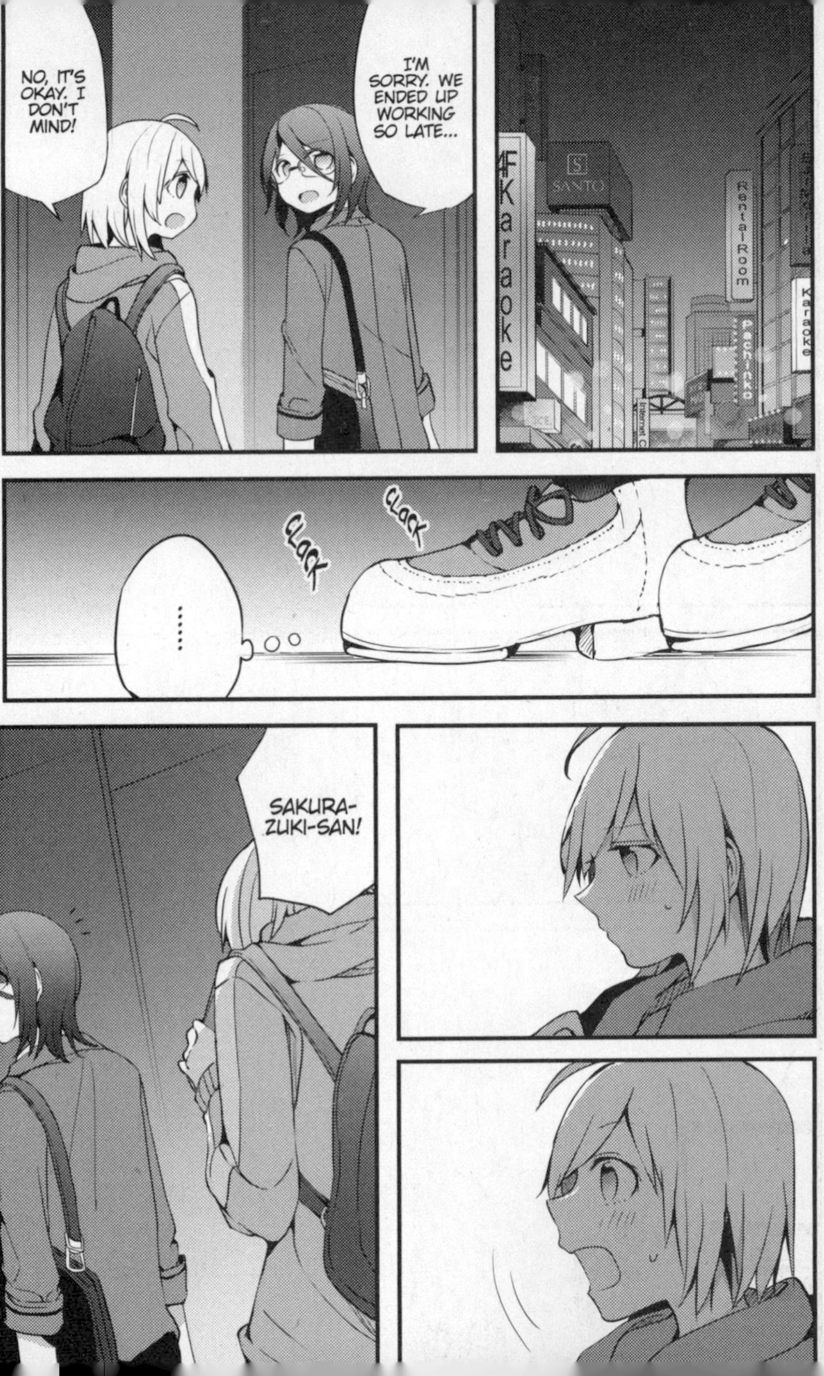
Rental Room
Karaoke
Pachinko
SANTO
4F Karaoke
I'M SORRY. WE ENDED UP WORKING SO LATE...
NO, IT'S OKAY. I DON'T MIND!
CLACK
CLACK
......
SAKURA-ZUKI-SAN!

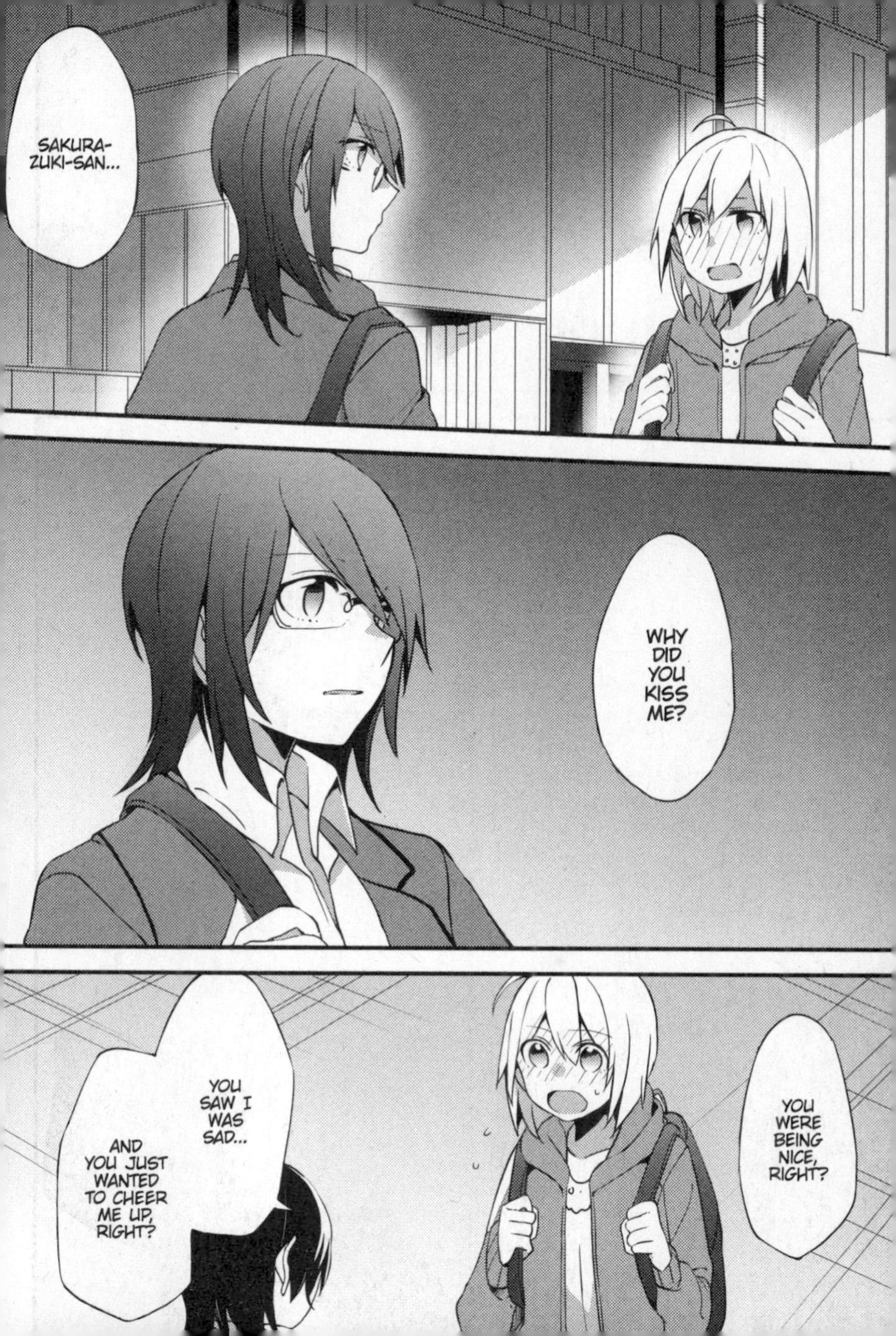
SAKURA-ZUKI-SAN...
WHY DID YOU KISS ME?
YOU WERE BEING NICE, RIGHT?
YOU SAW I WAS SAD...
AND YOU JUST WANTED TO CHEER ME UP, RIGHT?

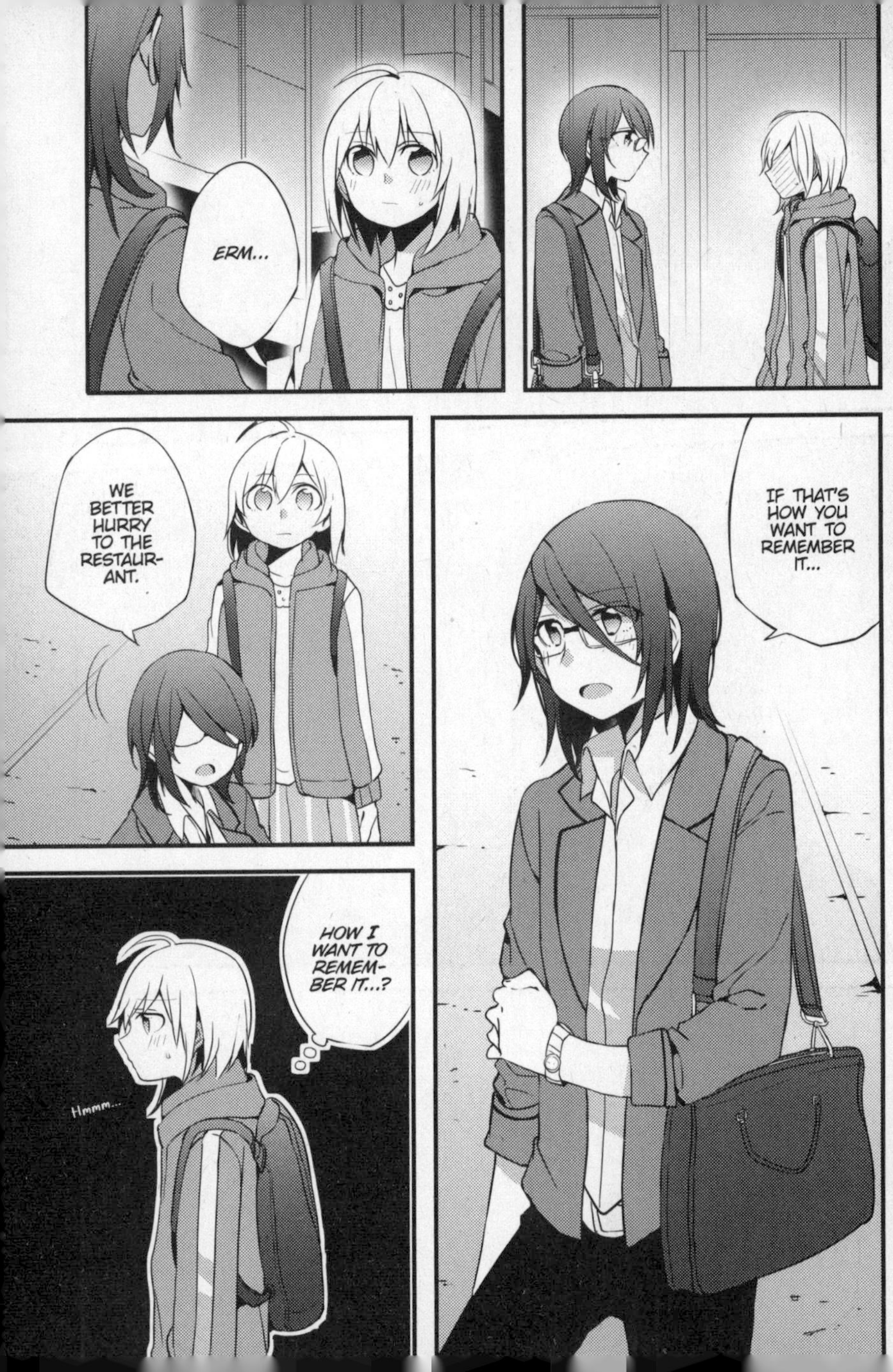
ERM...
IF THAT'S HOW YOU WANT TO REMEMBER IT...
WE BETTER HURRY TO THE RESTAURANT.
HOW I WANT TO REMEMBER IT...?
Hmmm...

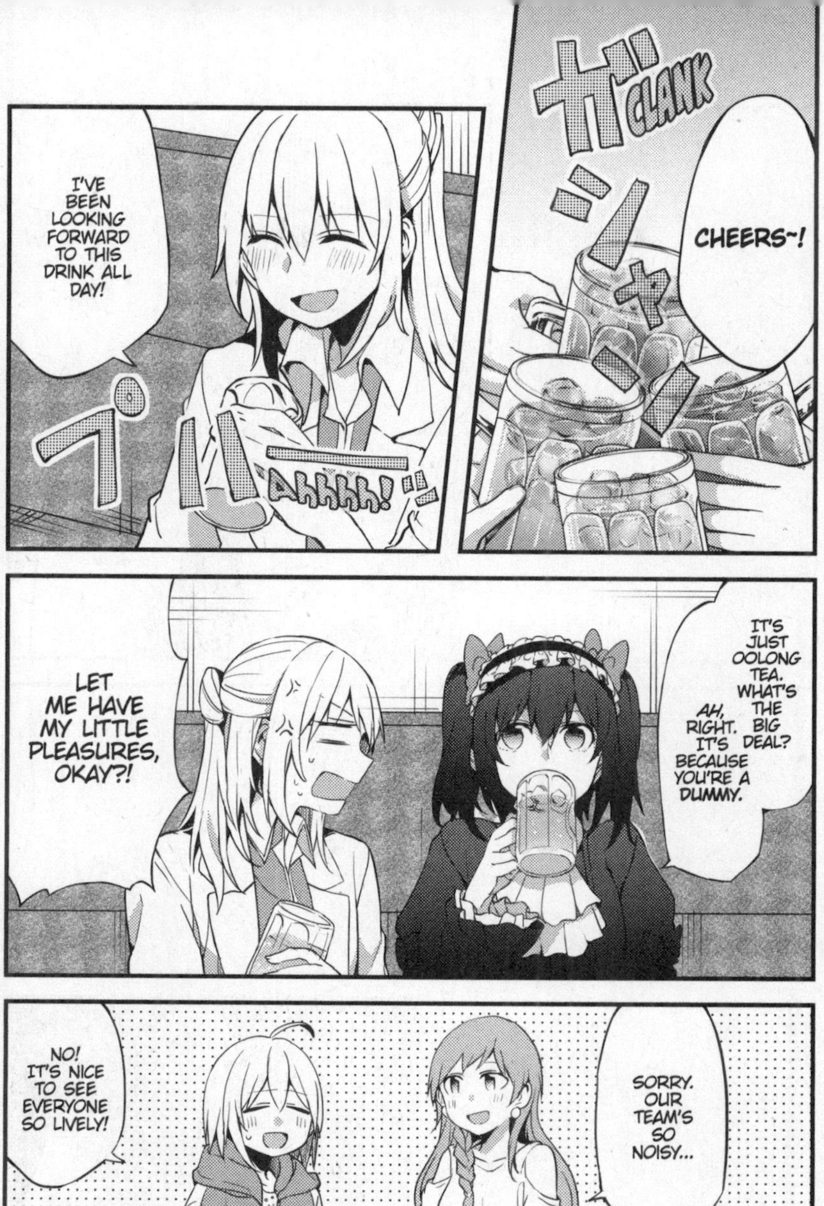
CLANK
CHEERS~!
I'VE BEEN LOOKING FORWARD TO THIS DRINK ALL DAY!
Ahhhh!
IT'S JUST OOLONG TEA. WHAT'S THE BIG DEAL?
AH, RIGHT. IT'S BECAUSE YOU'RE A DUMMY.
LET ME HAVE MY LITTLE PLEASURES, OKAY?!
SORRY. OUR TEAM'S SO NOISY...
NO! IT'S NICE TO SEE EVERYONE SO LIVELY!

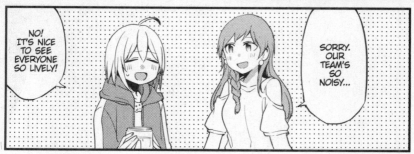

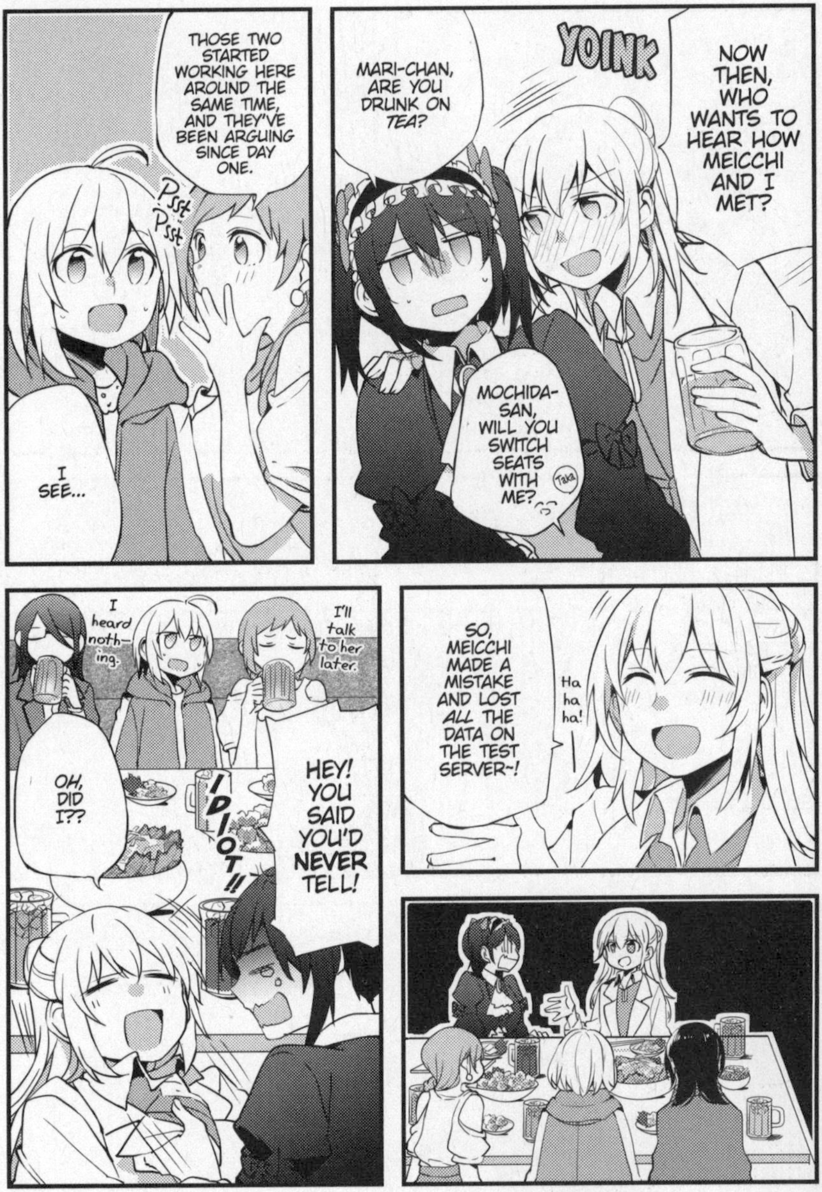
YOINK
NOW THEN, WHO WANTS TO HEAR HOW MEICCHI AND I MET?
MARI-CHAN, ARE YOU DRUNK ON *TEA*?
MOCHIDA-SAN, WILL YOU SWITCH SEATS WITH ME?
Taka
THOSE TWO STARTED WORKING HERE AROUND THE SAME TIME, AND THEY'VE BEEN ARGUING SINCE DAY ONE.
Psst Psst
I SEE...
SO, MEICCHI MADE A MISTAKE AND LOST *ALL* THE DATA ON THE TEST SERVER~!
Ha ha ha!
I'll talk to her later.
I heard nothing.
HEY! YOU SAID YOU'D NEVER TELL!
IDIOT!!
OH, DID I??

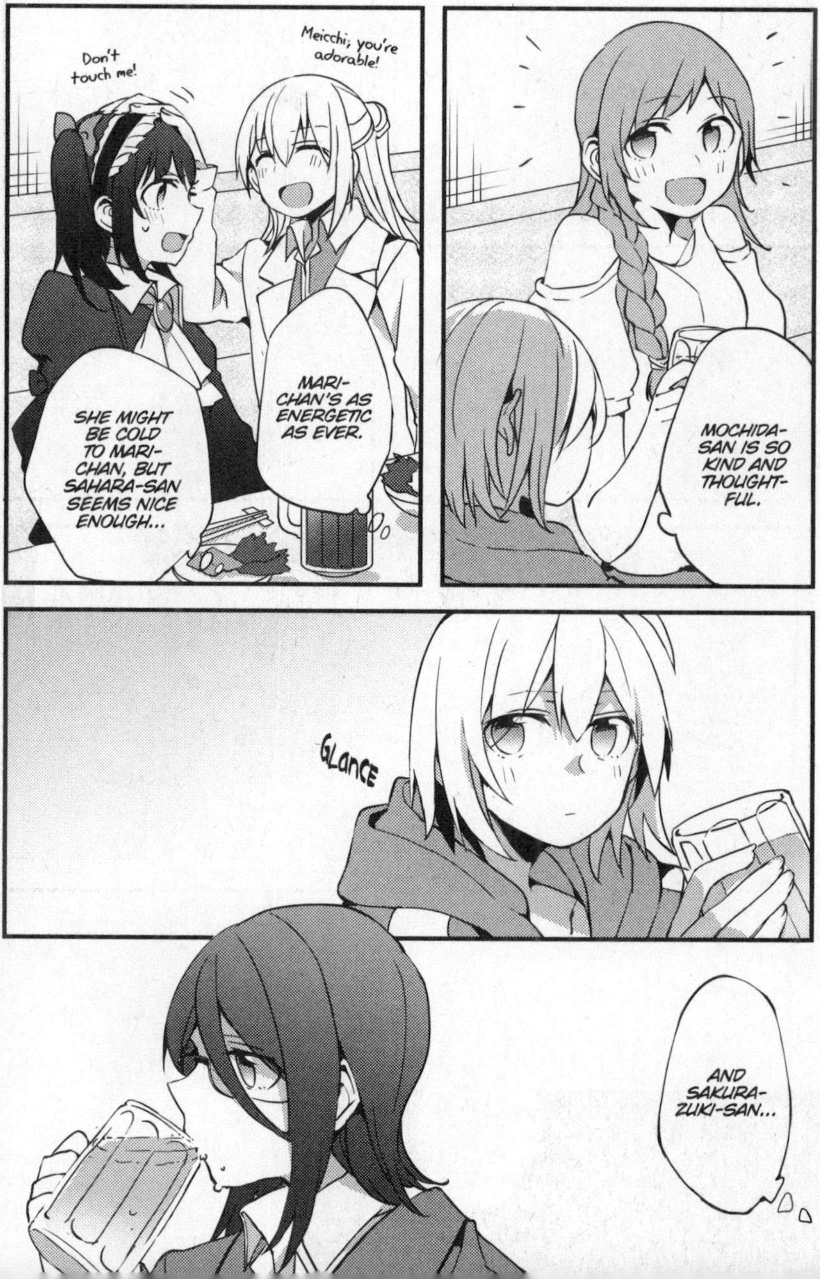
MOCHIDA-SAN IS SO KIND AND THOUGHTFUL.
Meicchi; you're adorable!
Don't touch me!
MARI-CHAN'S AS ENERGETIC AS EVER.
SHE MIGHT BE COLD TO MARI-CHAN, BUT SAHARA-SAN SEEMS NICE ENOUGH...
GLANCE
AND SAKURAZUKI-SAN...

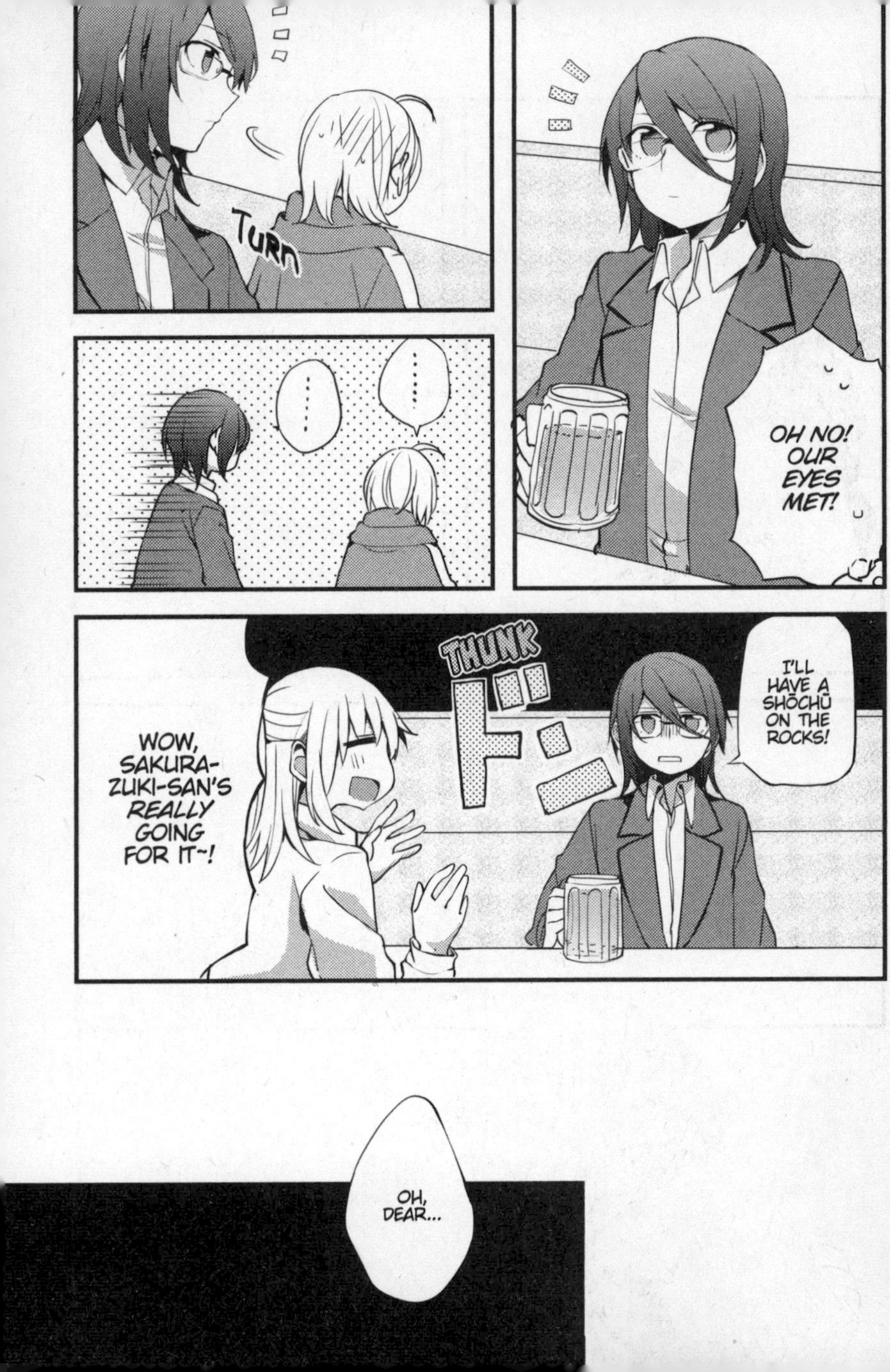
OH NO! OUR EYES MET!
Turn
...
...
I'LL HAVE A SHŌCHŪ ON THE ROCKS!
THUNK
ドン
WOW, SAKURA-ZUKI-SAN'S REALLY GOING FOR IT~!
OH, DEAR...

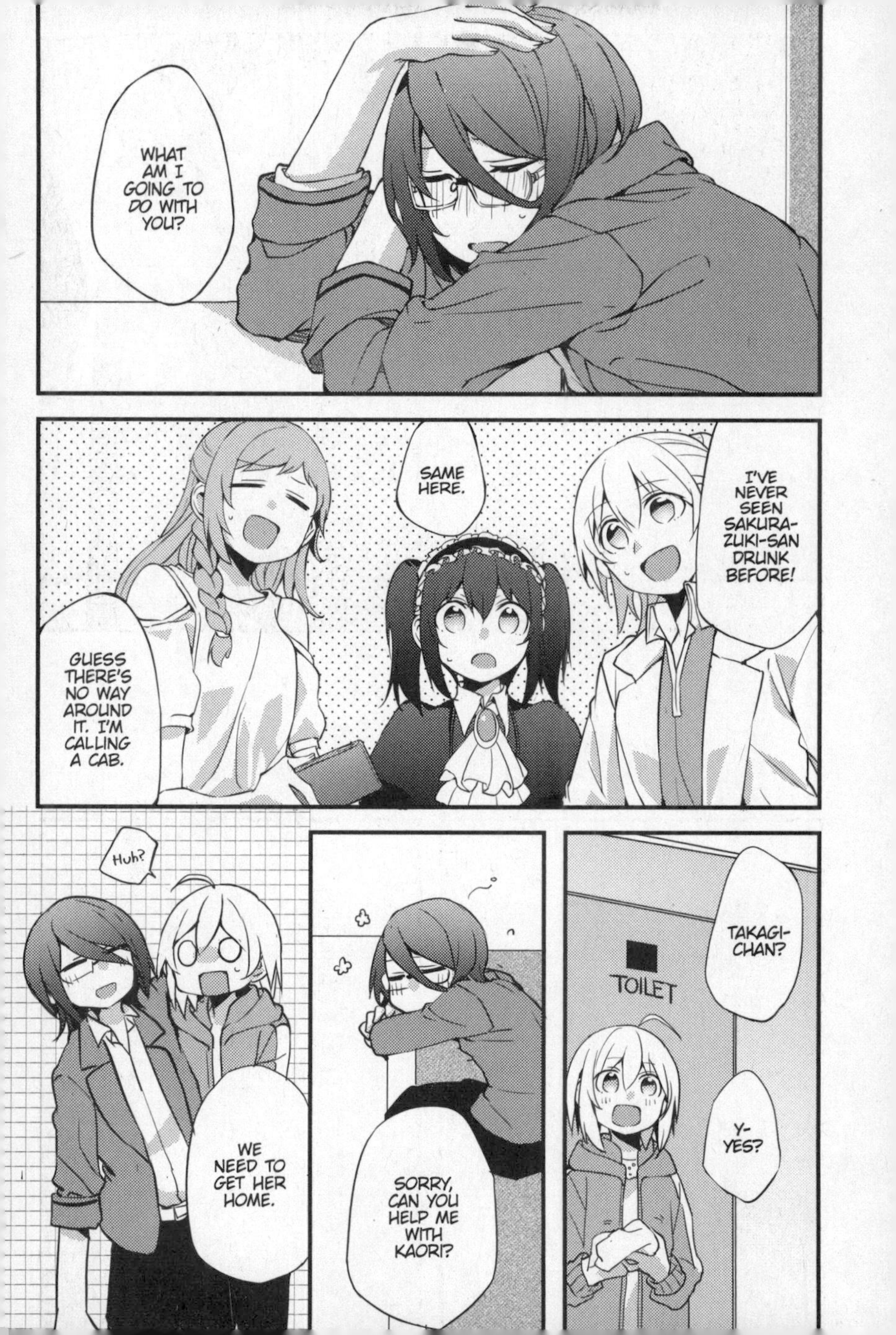
WHAT AM I GOING TO DO WITH YOU?
I'VE NEVER SEEN SAKURAZUKI-SAN DRUNK BEFORE!
SAME HERE.
GUESS THERE'S NO WAY AROUND IT. I'M CALLING A CAB.
TAKAGI-CHAN?
TOILET
Y-YES?
SORRY, CAN YOU HELP ME WITH KAORI?
Huh?
WE NEED TO GET HER HOME.

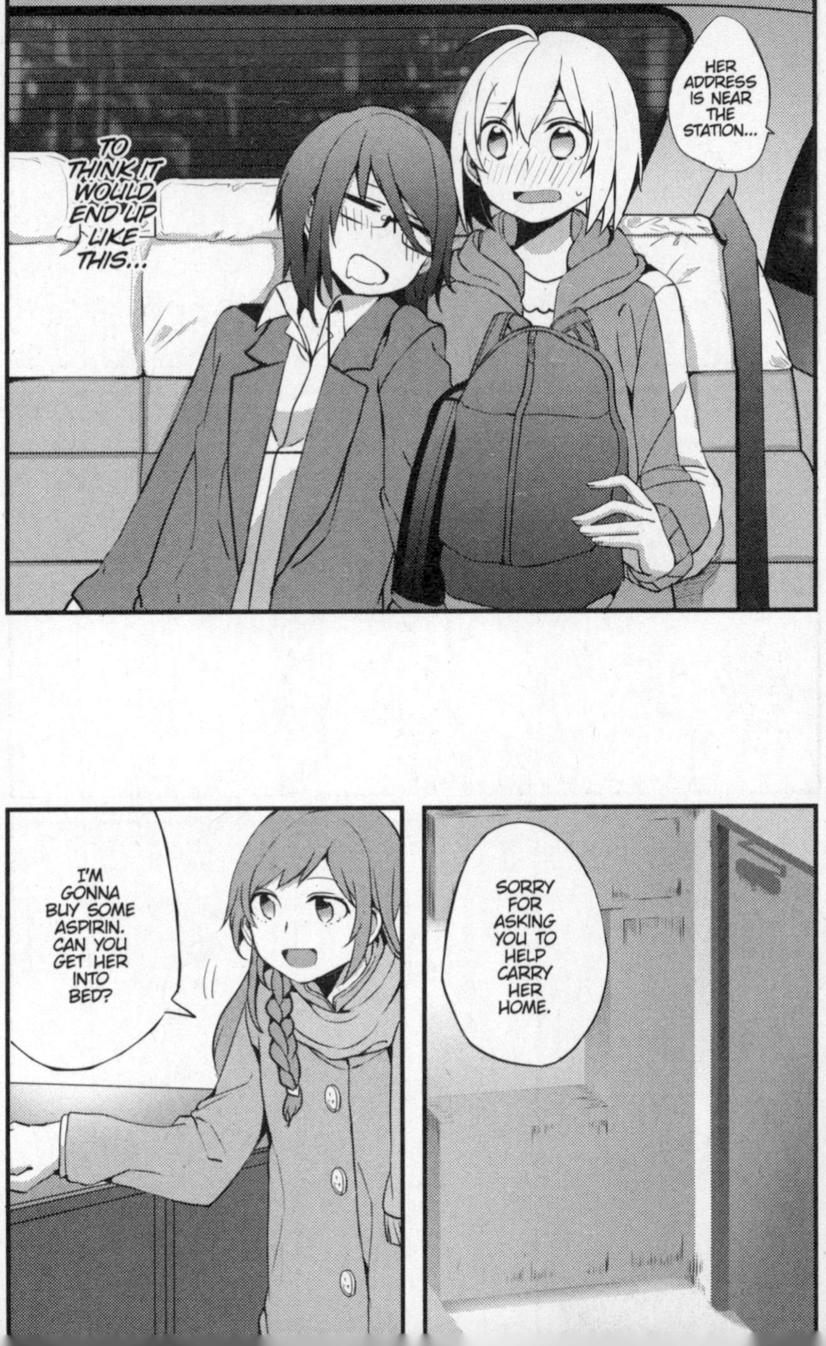
HER ADDRESS IS NEAR THE STATION...
TO THINK IT WOULD END UP LIKE THIS...
SORRY FOR ASKING YOU TO HELP CARRY HER HOME.
I'M GONNA BUY SOME ASPIRIN. CAN YOU GET HER INTO BED?

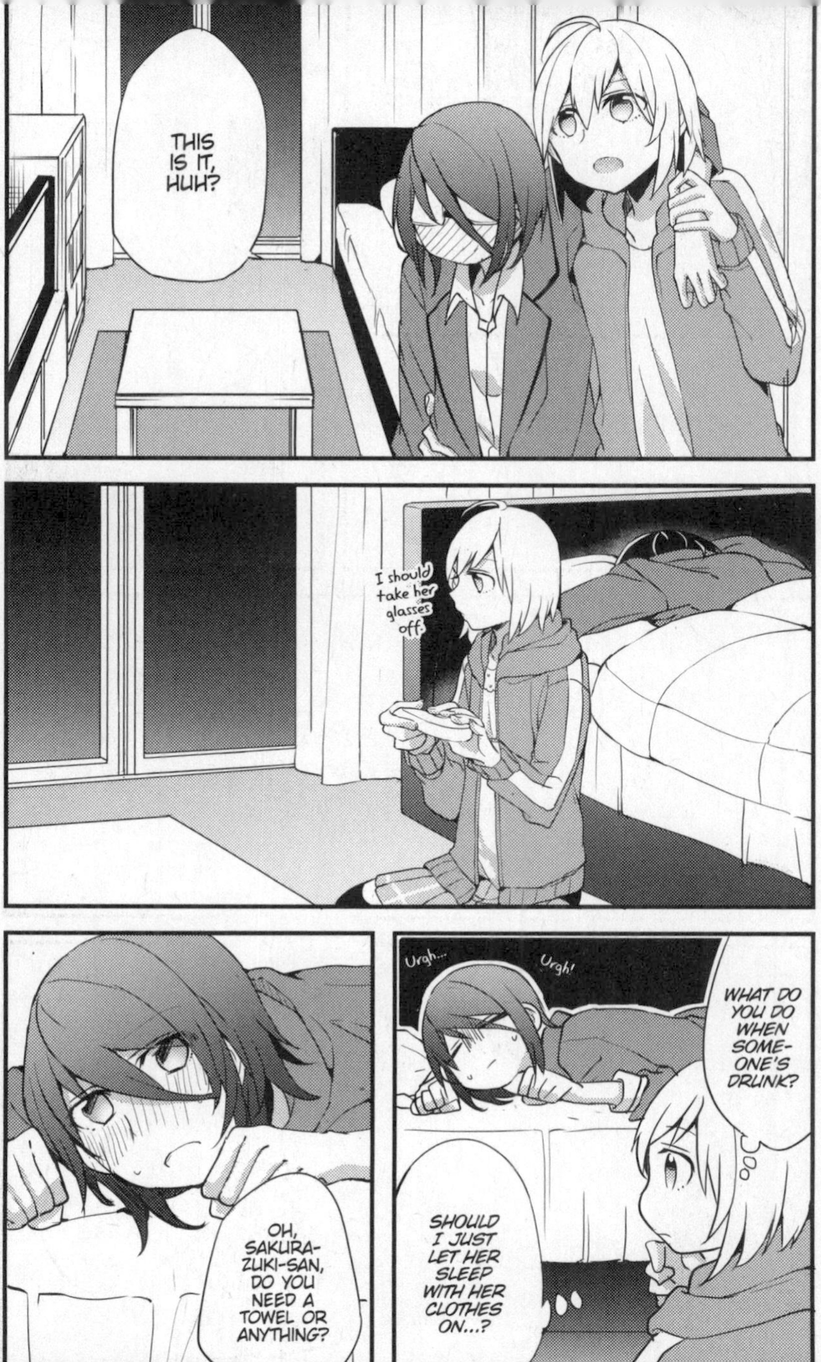
THIS IS IT, HUH?
I should take her glasses off.
WHAT DO YOU DO WHEN SOMEONE'S DRUNK?
Urgh!
Urgh...
SHOULD I JUST LET HER SLEEP WITH HER CLOTHES ON...?
OH, SAKURAZUKI-SAN, DO YOU NEED A TOWEL OR ANYTHING?

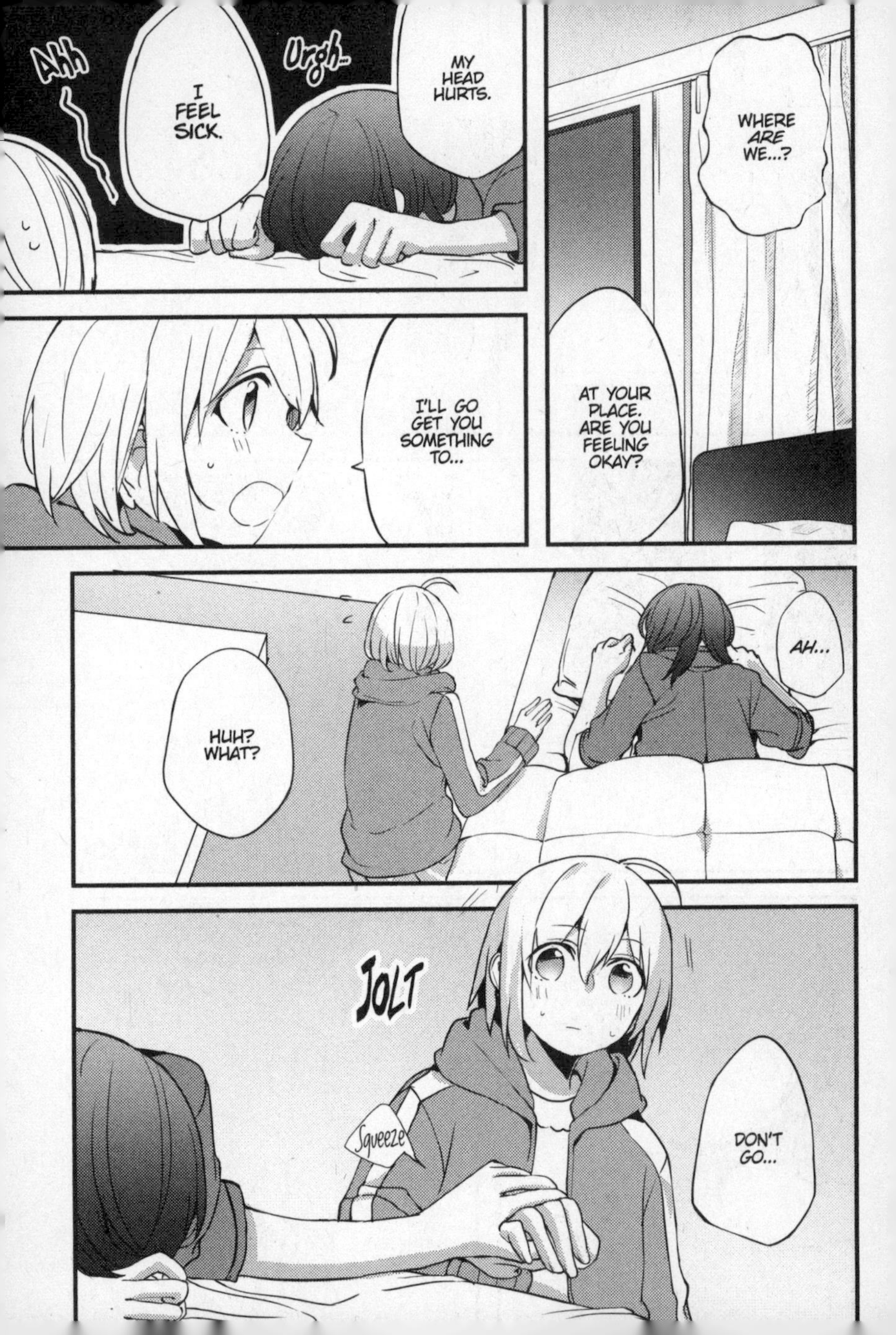
WHERE ARE WE...?
AT YOUR PLACE. ARE YOU FEELING OKAY?
MY HEAD HURTS.
Urgh..
I FEEL SICK.
Ahh~
I'LL GO GET YOU SOMETHING TO...
AH...
HUH? WHAT?
DON'T GO...
JOLT
Squeeze

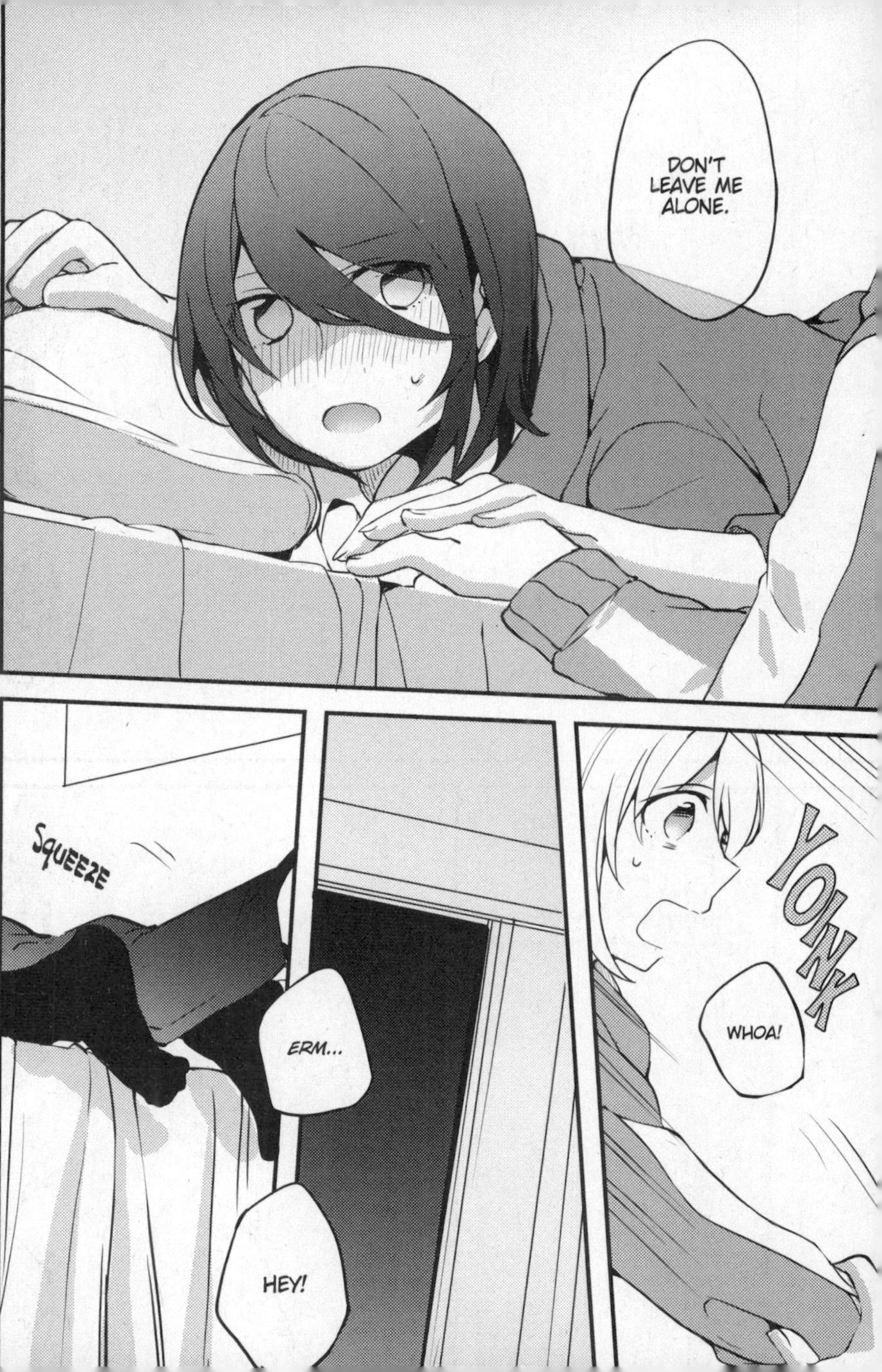
DON'T LEAVE ME ALONE.
YOINK
WHOA!
ERM...
Squeeze
HEY!

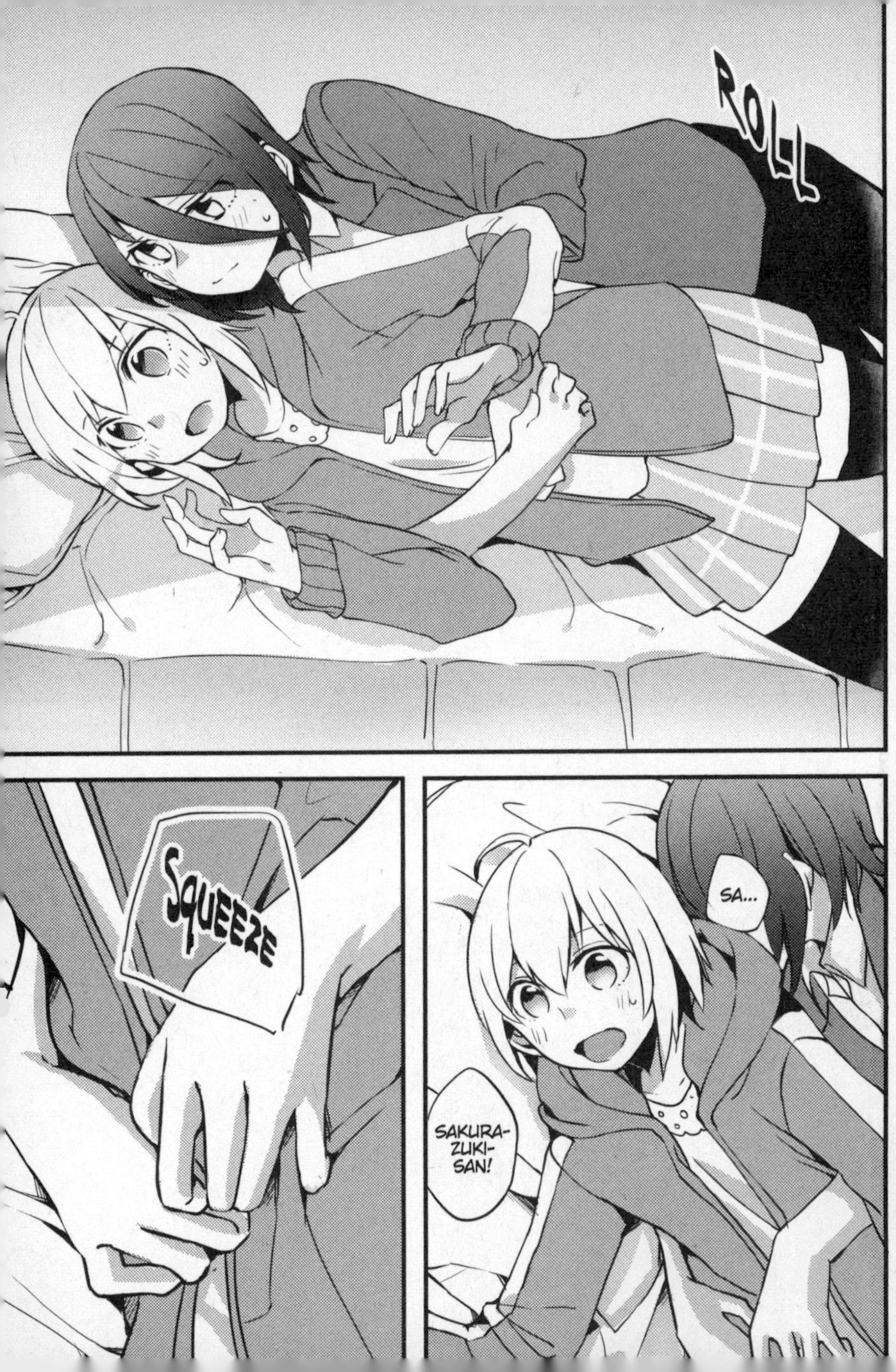
ROLL
SA...
SAKURA-ZUKI-SAN!
SQUEEZE

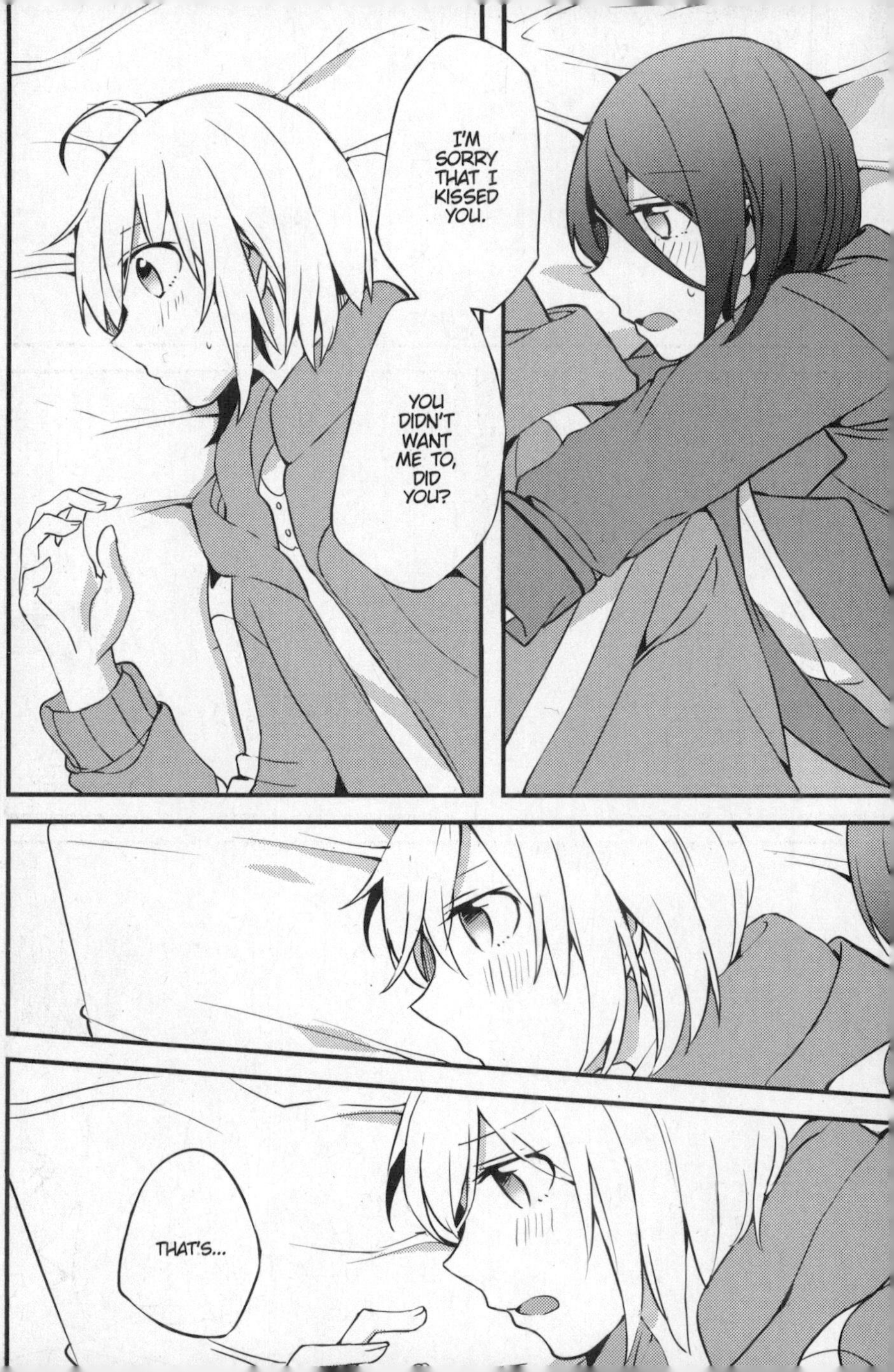
I'M SORRY THAT I KISSED YOU.
YOU DIDN'T WANT ME TO, DID YOU?
THAT'S...

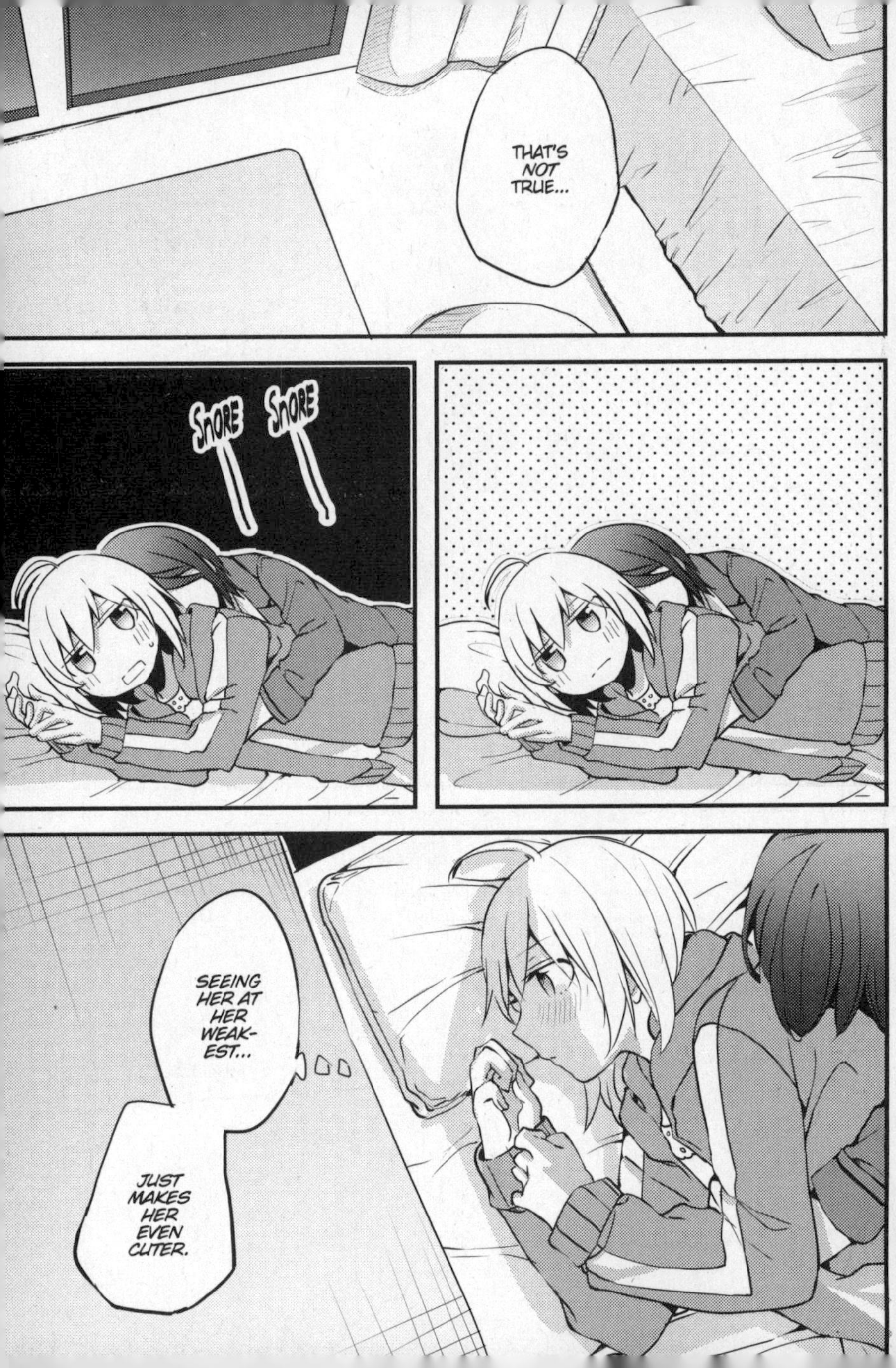
THAT'S NOT TRUE...
SNORE SNORE
SEEING HER AT HER WEAK- EST...
JUST MAKES HER EVEN CUTER.

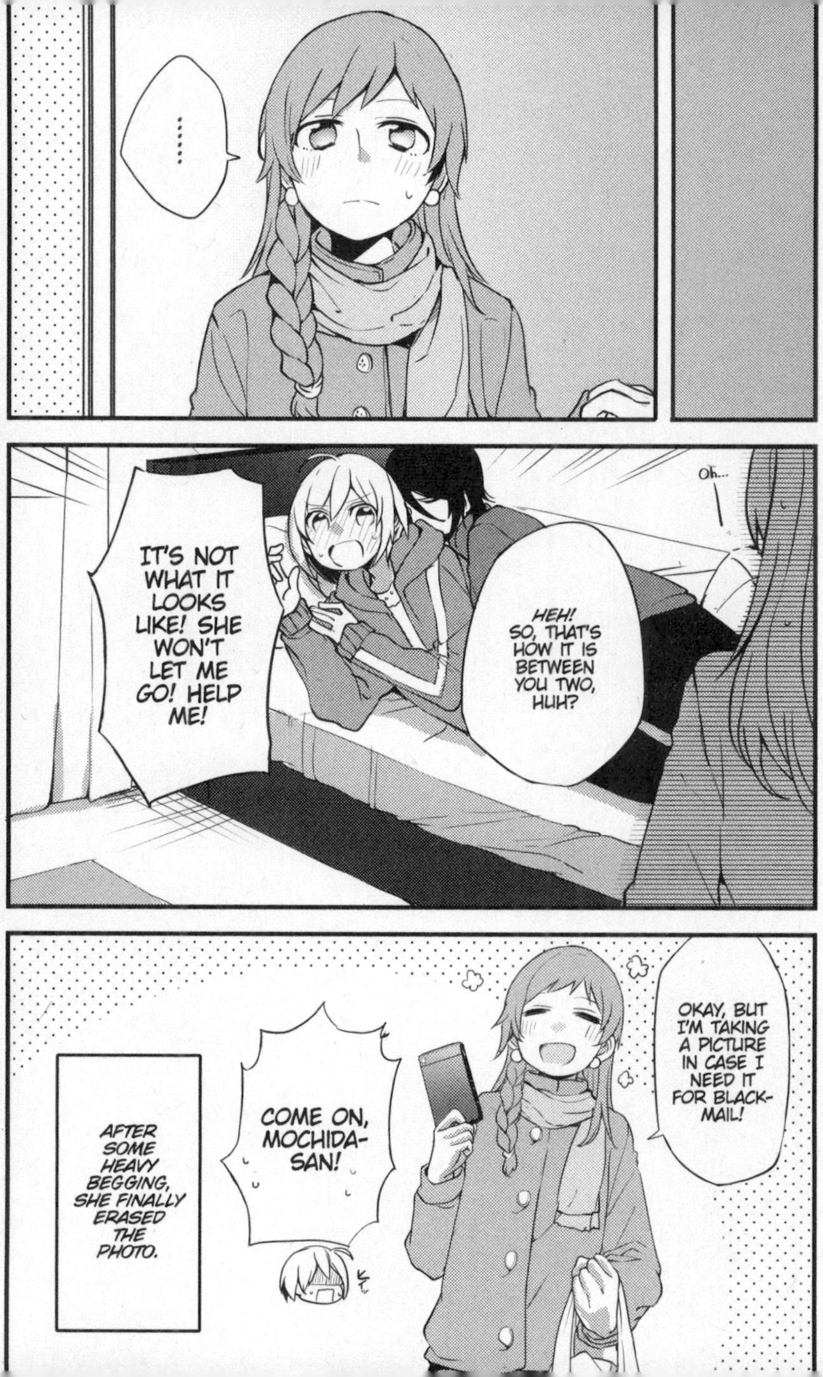
......
Oh...
HEH! SO, THAT'S HOW IT IS BETWEEN YOU TWO, HUH?
IT'S NOT WHAT IT LOOKS LIKE! SHE WON'T LET ME GO! HELP ME!
OKAY, BUT I'M TAKING A PICTURE IN CASE I NEED IT FOR BLACK-MAIL!
COME ON, MOCHIDA-SAN!
AFTER SOME HEAVY BEGGING, SHE FINALLY ERASED THE PHOTO.

Now Loading...!

Now Loading...!

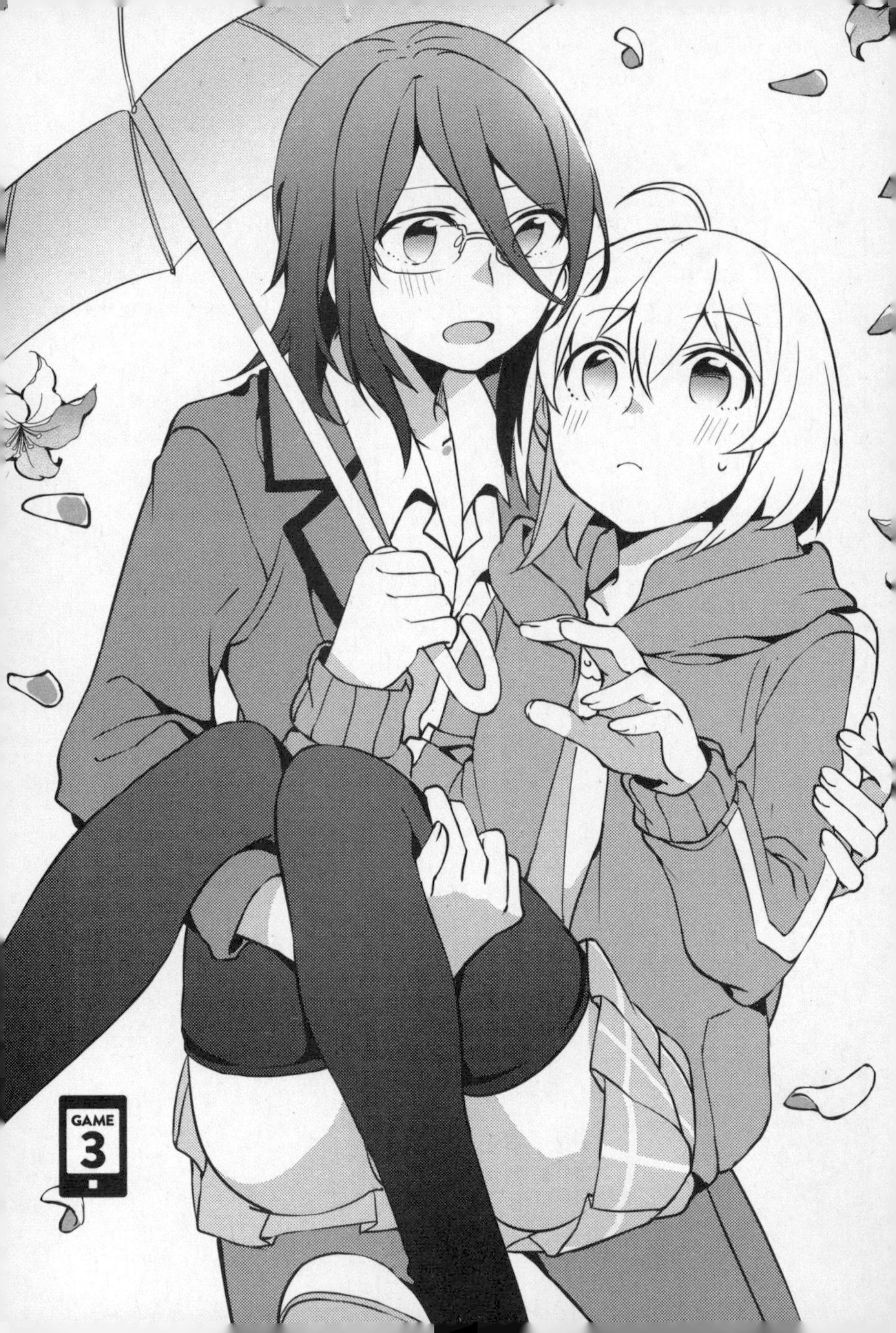
GAME
3

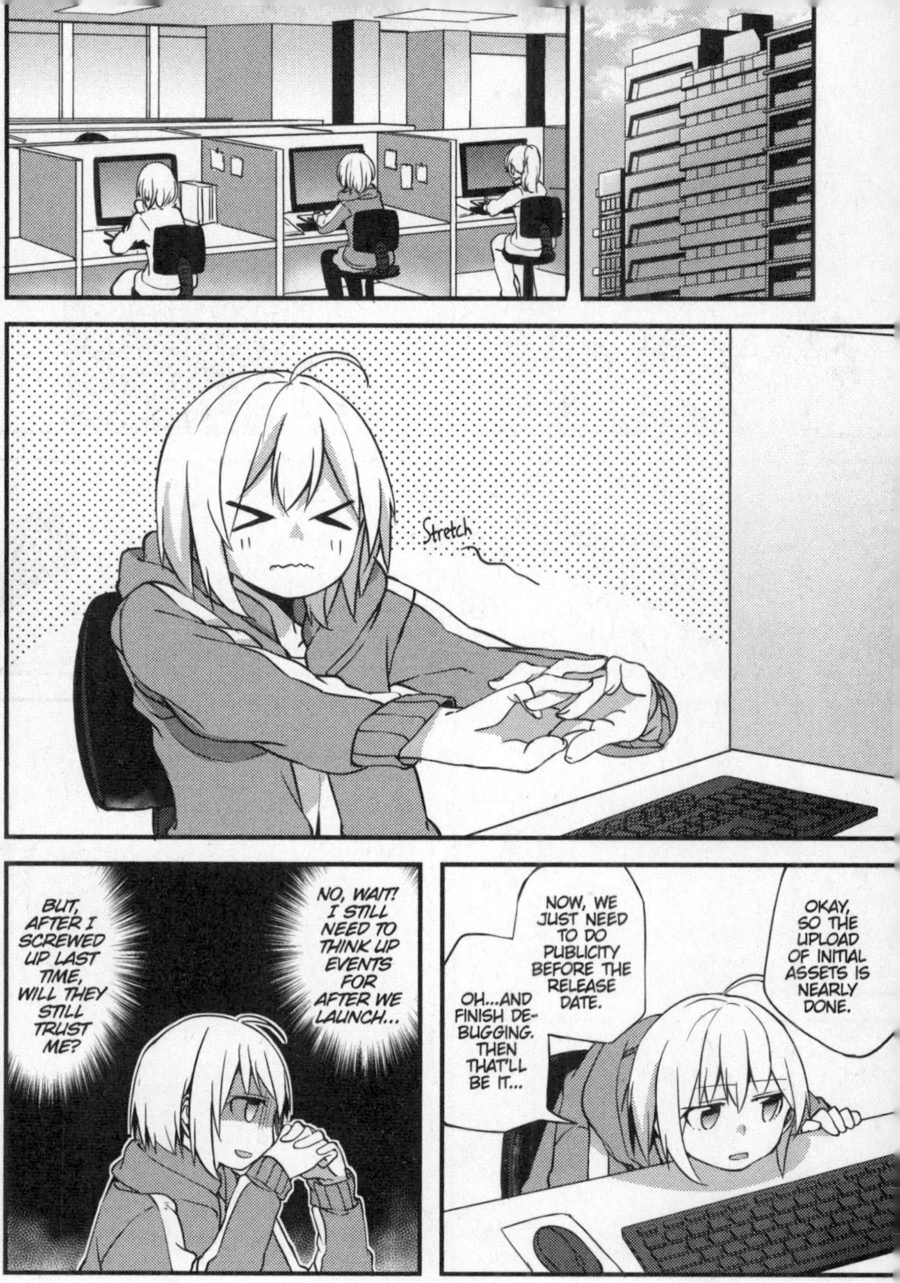
Stretch
OKAY, SO THE UPLOAD OF INITIAL ASSETS IS NEARLY DONE.
NOW, WE JUST NEED TO DO PUBLICITY BEFORE THE RELEASE DATE.
OH...AND FINISH DE-BUGGING. THEN THAT'LL BE IT...
NO, WAIT! I STILL NEED TO THINK UP EVENTS FOR AFTER WE LAUNCH...
BUT, AFTER I SCREWED UP LAST TIME, WILL THEY STILL TRUST ME?

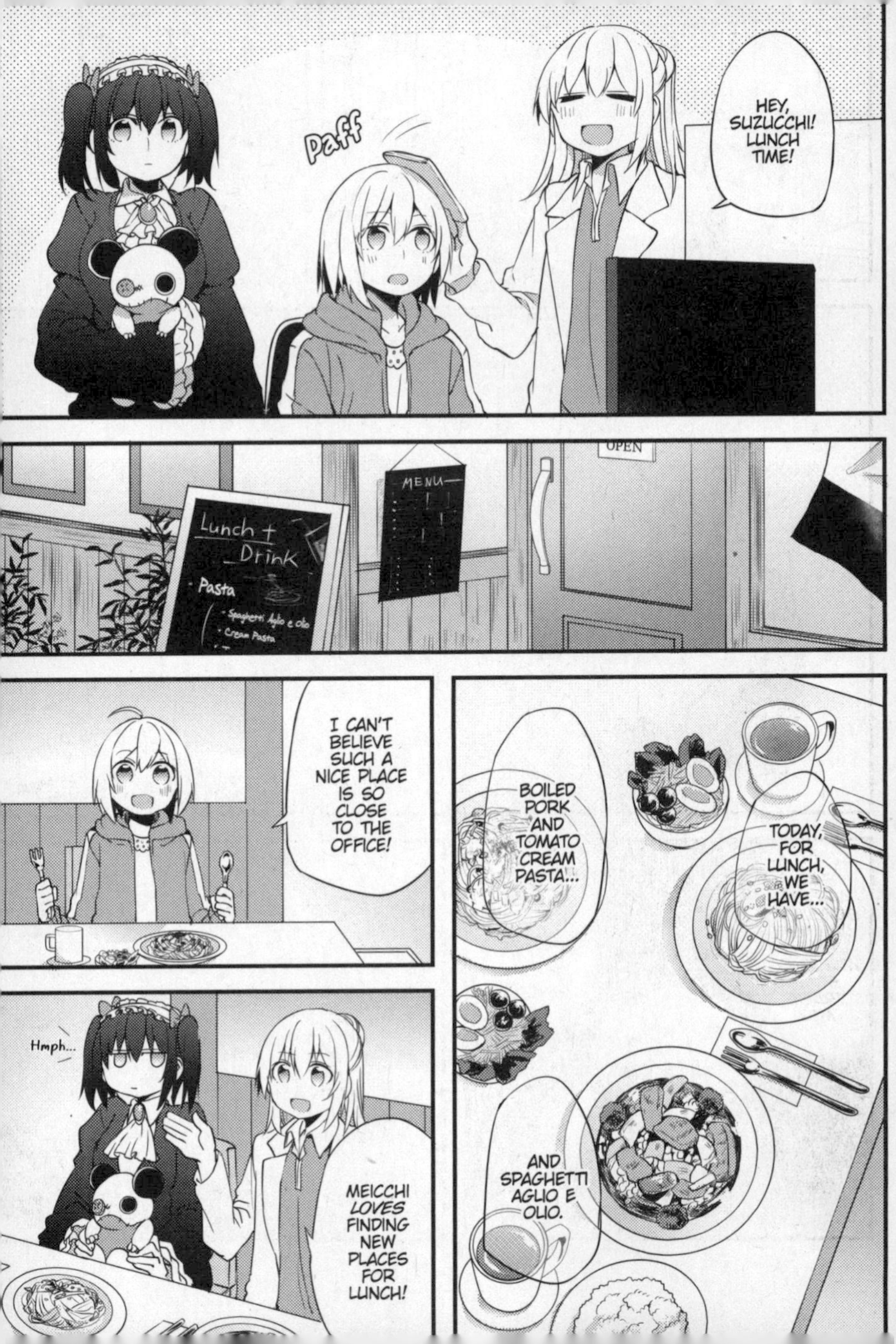
HEY, SUZUCCHI! LUNCH TIME!
Paff
OPEN
MENU
Lunch + Drink
Pasta
Spaghetti Aglio e olio
Cream Pasta
TODAY, FOR LUNCH, WE HAVE...
BOILED PORK AND TOMATO CREAM PASTA...
AND SPAGHETTI AGLIO E OLIO.
I CAN'T BELIEVE SUCH A NICE PLACE IS SO CLOSE TO THE OFFICE!
MEICCHI LOVES FINDING NEW PLACES FOR LUNCH!
Hmph...

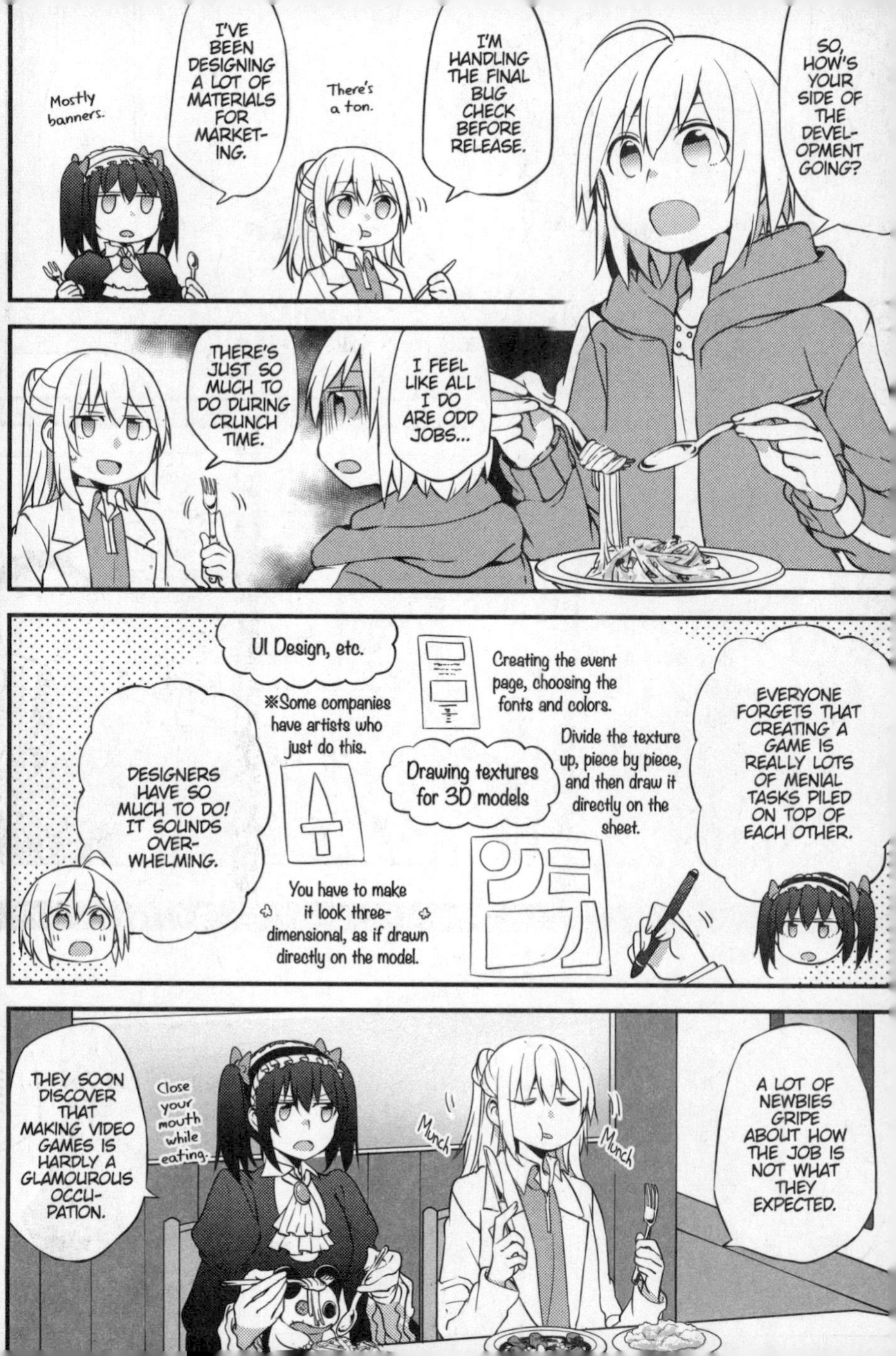
SO, HOW'S YOUR SIDE OF THE DEVEL-OPMENT GOING?
I'M HANDLING THE FINAL BUG CHECK BEFORE RELEASE.
There's a ton.
I'VE BEEN DESIGNING A LOT OF MATERIALS FOR MARKET-ING.
Mostly banners.
I FEEL LIKE ALL I DO ARE ODD JOBS...
THERE'S JUST SO MUCH TO DO DURING CRUNCH TIME.
EVERYONE FORGETS THAT CREATING A GAME IS REALLY LOTS OF MENIAL TASKS PILED ON TOP OF EACH OTHER.
Creating the event page, choosing the fonts and colors.
UI Design, etc.
※Some companies have artists who just do this.
Divide the texture up, piece by piece, and then draw it directly on the sheet.
Drawing textures for 3D models
You have to make it look three-dimensional, as if drawn directly on the model.
DESIGNERS HAVE SO MUCH TO DO! IT SOUNDS OVER-WHELMING.
A LOT OF NEWBIES GRIPE ABOUT HOW THE JOB IS NOT WHAT THEY EXPECTED.
Munch
Munch
Close your mouth while eating.
THEY SOON DISCOVER THAT MAKING VIDEO GAMES IS HARDLY A GLAMOUROUS OCCU-PATION.

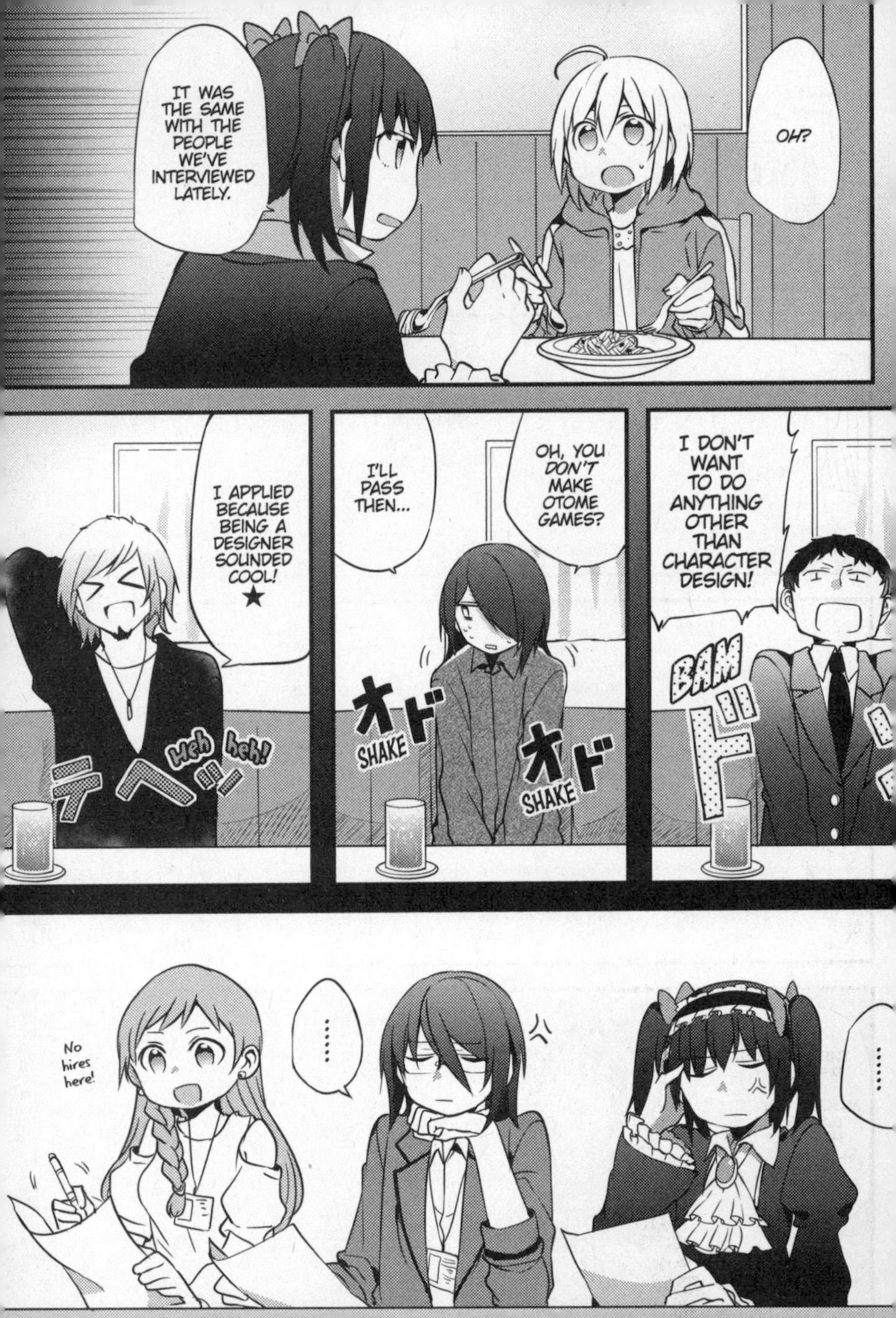
OH?
IT WAS THE SAME WITH THE PEOPLE WE'VE INTERVIEWED LATELY.
I DON'T WANT TO DO ANYTHING OTHER THAN CHARACTER DESIGN!
BAM
OH, YOU DON'T MAKE OTOME GAMES?
I'LL PASS THEN...
SHAKE
SHAKE
I APPLIED BECAUSE BEING A DESIGNER SOUNDED COOL! ★
Heh heh!
...
......
No hires here!

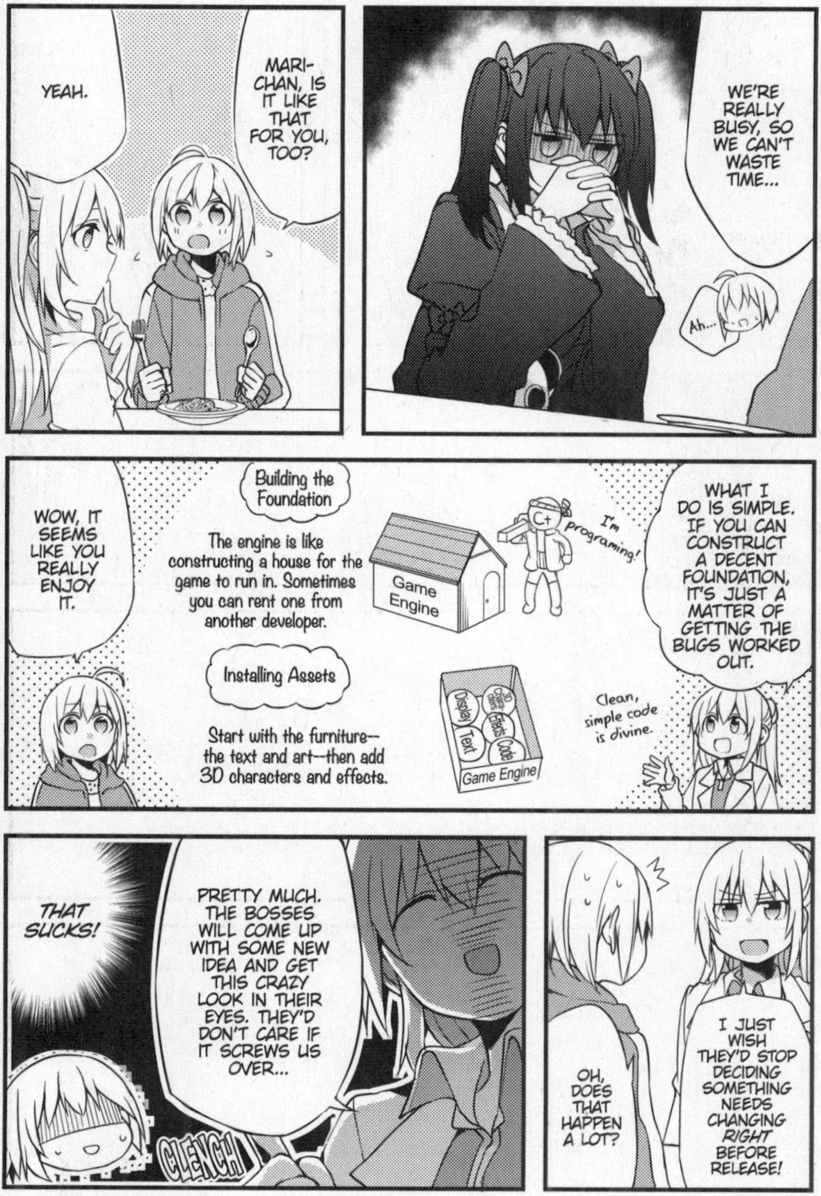
WE'RE REALLY BUSY, SO WE CAN'T WASTE TIME...
Ah...
MARI-CHAN, IS IT LIKE THAT FOR YOU, TOO?
YEAH.
WHAT I DO IS SIMPLE. IF YOU CAN CONSTRUCT A DECENT FOUNDATION, IT'S JUST A MATTER OF GETTING THE BUGS WORKED OUT.
Clean, simple code is divine.
I'm programing!
C+
Game Engine
Building the Foundation
The engine is like constructing a house for the game to run in. Sometimes you can rent one from another developer.
3D Characters
Effects
Code
Display
Text
Game Engine
Installing Assets
Start with the furniture--the text and art--then add 3D characters and effects.
WOW, IT SEEMS LIKE YOU REALLY ENJOY IT.
I JUST WISH THEY'D STOP DECIDING SOMETHING NEEDS CHANGING *RIGHT* BEFORE RELEASE!
OH, DOES THAT HAPPEN A LOT?
PRETTY MUCH. THE BOSSES WILL COME UP WITH SOME NEW IDEA AND GET THIS CRAZY LOOK IN THEIR EYES. THEY'D DON'T CARE IF IT SCREWS US OVER...
THAT SUCKS!
CLENCH

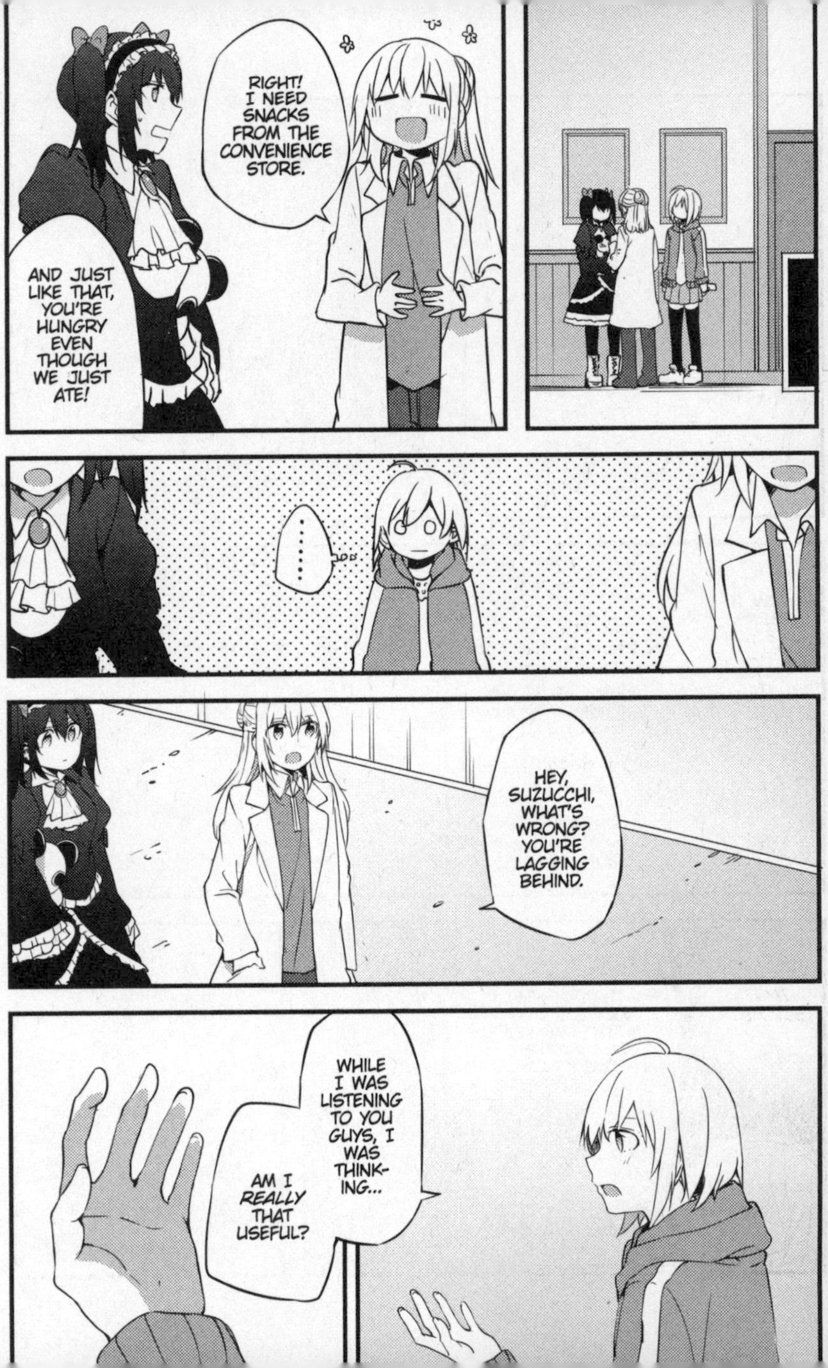
RIGHT! I NEED SNACKS FROM THE CONVENIENCE STORE.
AND JUST LIKE THAT, YOU'RE HUNGRY EVEN THOUGH WE JUST ATE!
......
HEY, SUZUCCHI, WHAT'S WRONG? YOU'RE LAGGING BEHIND.
WHILE I WAS LISTENING TO YOU GUYS, I WAS THINKING...
AM I *REALLY* THAT USEFUL?

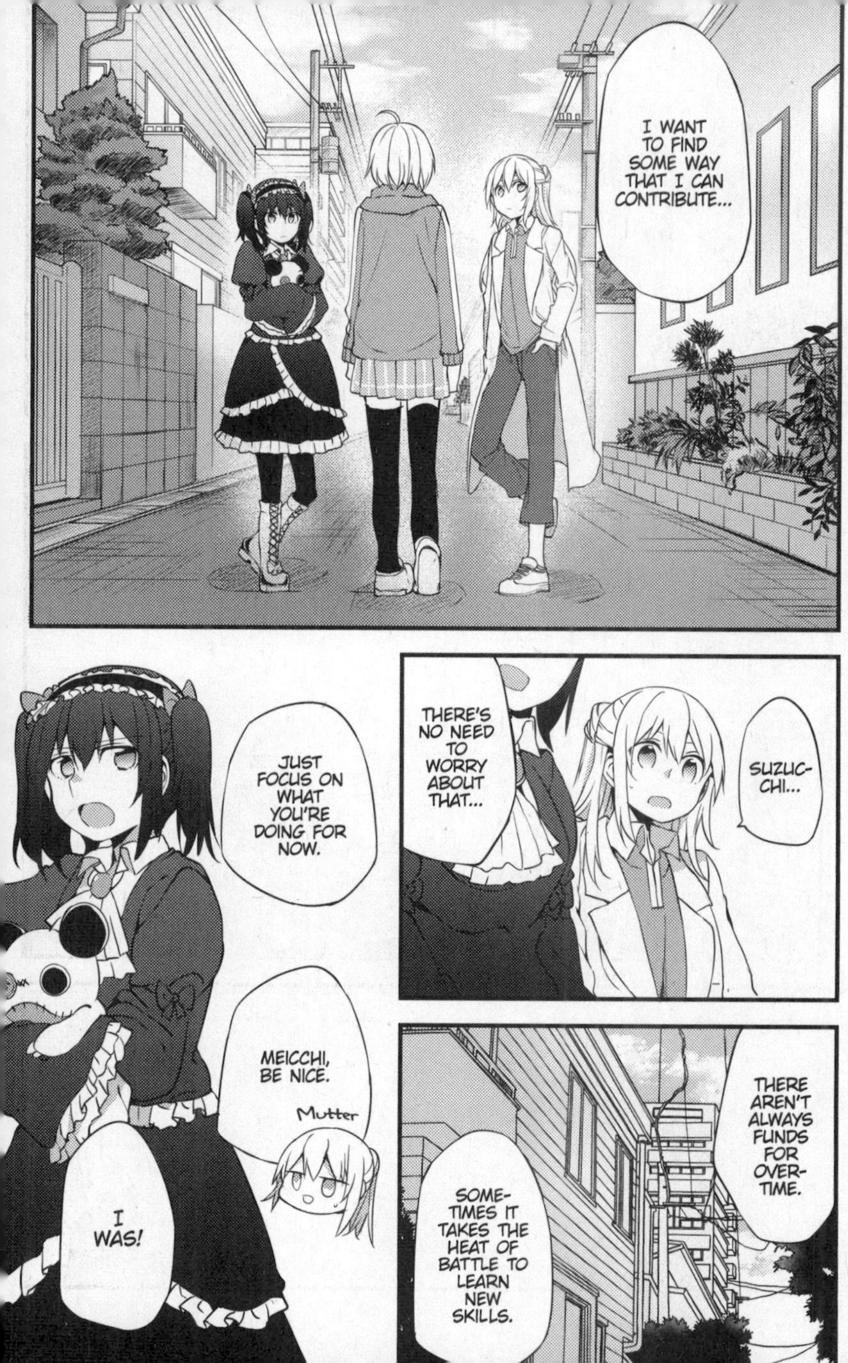
I WANT TO FIND SOME WAY THAT I CAN CONTRIBUTE...
SUZUC-CHI...
THERE'S NO NEED TO WORRY ABOUT THAT...
THERE AREN'T ALWAYS FUNDS FOR OVER-TIME.
SOME-TIMES IT TAKES THE HEAT OF BATTLE TO LEARN NEW SKILLS.
JUST FOCUS ON WHAT YOU'RE DOING FOR NOW.
MEICCHI, BE NICE.
Mutter
I WAS!

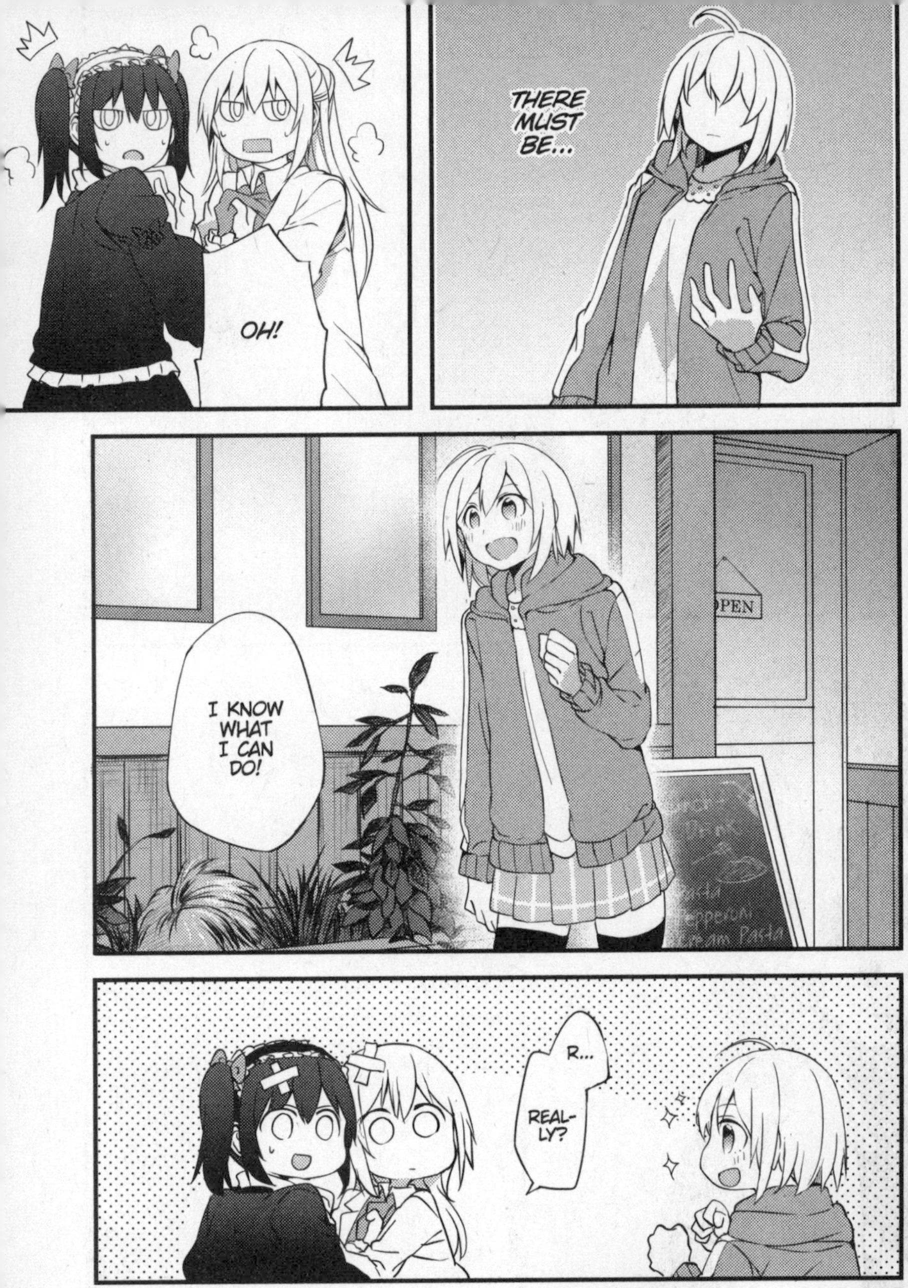
THERE MUST BE...
OH!
OPEN
I KNOW WHAT I CAN DO!
R... REAL-LY?

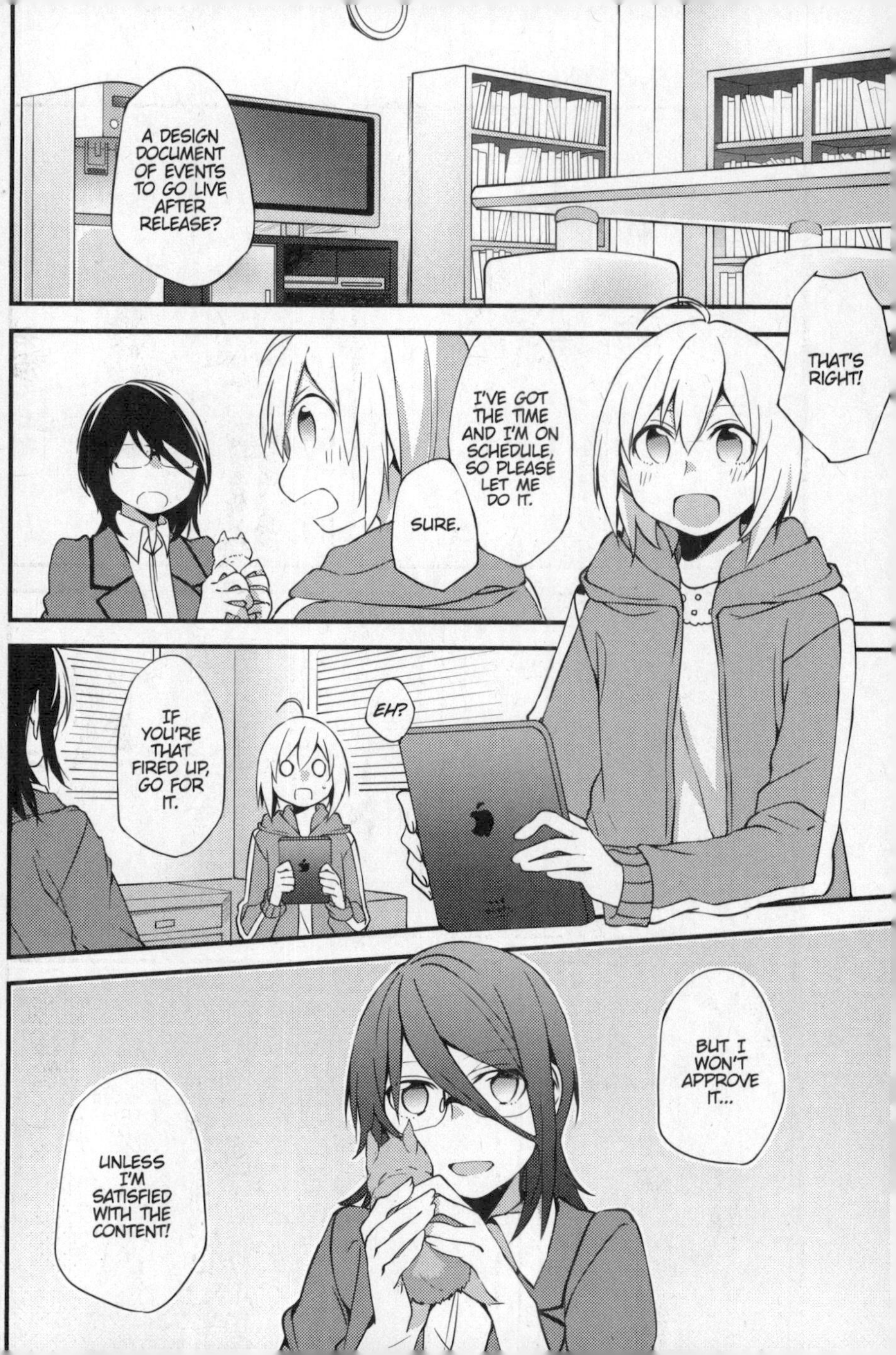
A DESIGN DOCUMENT OF EVENTS TO GO LIVE AFTER RELEASE?
THAT'S RIGHT!
I'VE GOT THE TIME AND I'M ON SCHEDULE, SO PLEASE LET ME DO IT.
SURE.
EH?
IF YOU'RE THAT FIRED UP, GO FOR IT.
BUT I WON'T APPROVE IT...
UNLESS I'M SATISFIED WITH THE CONTENT!

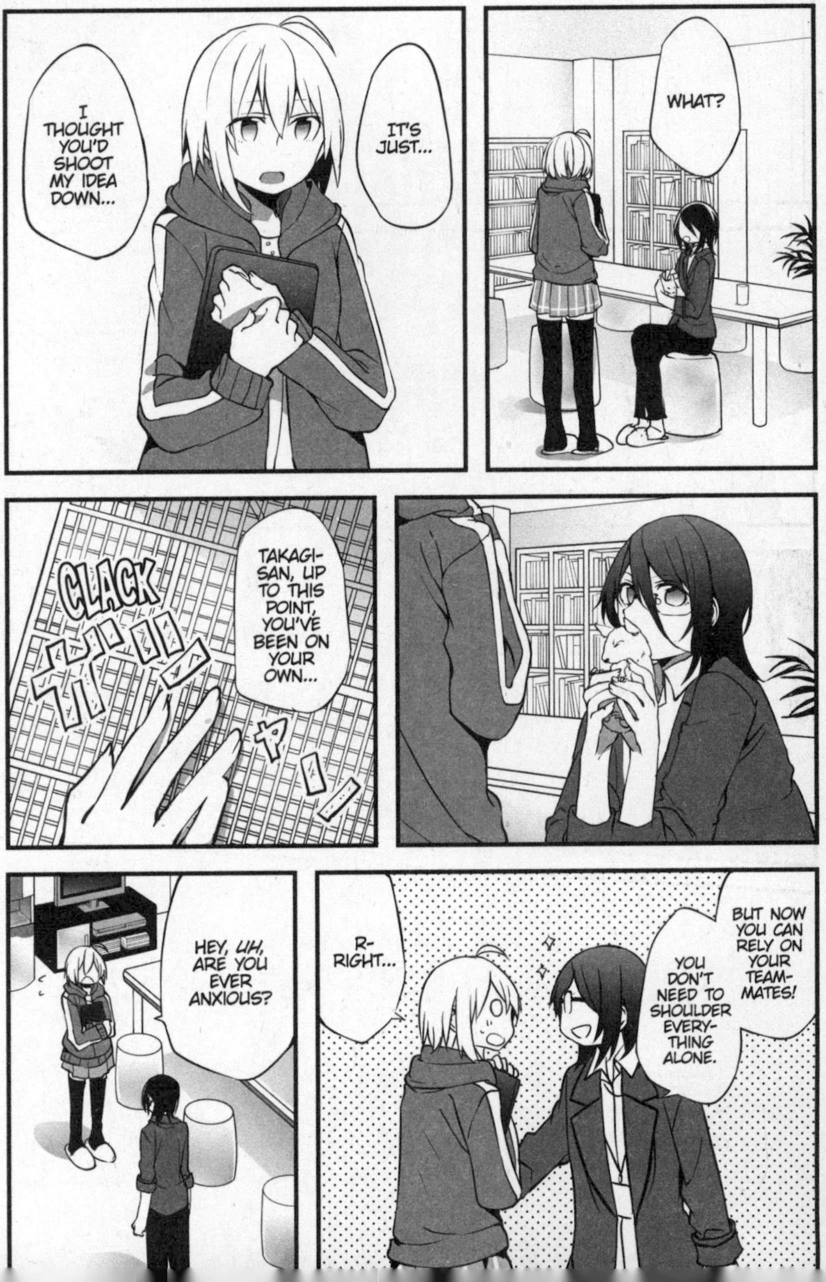
WHAT?
IT'S JUST...
I THOUGHT YOU'D SHOOT MY IDEA DOWN...
TAKAGI-SAN, UP TO THIS POINT, YOU'VE BEEN ON YOUR OWN...
CLACK
BUT NOW YOU CAN RELY ON YOUR TEAM-MATES!
YOU DON'T NEED TO SHOULDER EVERY-THING ALONE.
R-RIGHT...
HEY, UH, ARE YOU EVER ANXIOUS?

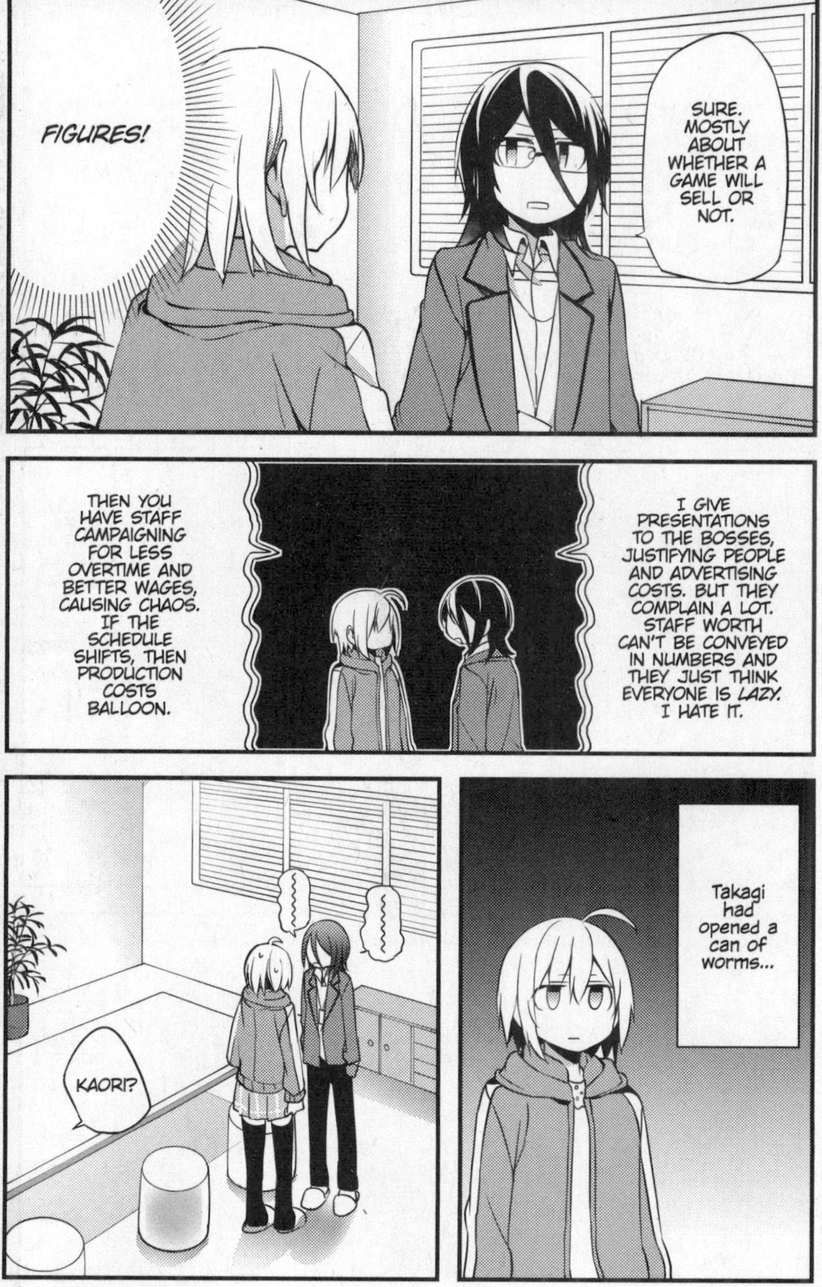
SURE. MOSTLY ABOUT WHETHER A GAME WILL SELL OR NOT.
FIGURES!
I GIVE PRESENTATIONS TO THE BOSSES, JUSTIFYING PEOPLE AND ADVERTISING COSTS. BUT THEY COMPLAIN A LOT. STAFF WORTH CAN'T BE CONVEYED IN NUMBERS AND THEY JUST THINK EVERYONE IS *LAZY.* I HATE IT.
THEN YOU HAVE STAFF CAMPAIGNING FOR LESS OVERTIME AND BETTER WAGES, CAUSING CHAOS. IF THE SCHEDULE SHIFTS, THEN PRODUCTION COSTS BALLOON.
Takagi had opened a can of worms...
KAORI?

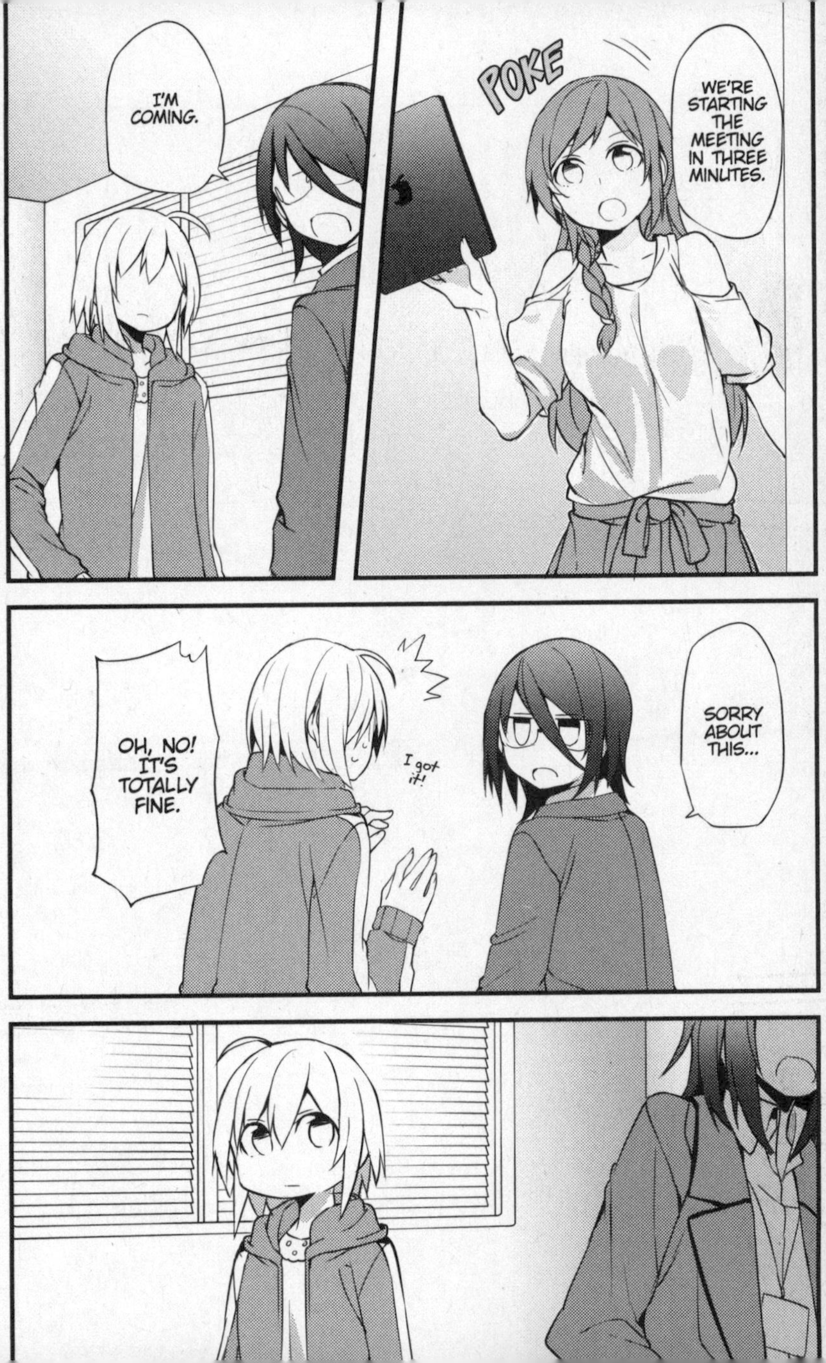
WE'RE STARTING THE MEETING IN THREE MINUTES.
POKE
I'M COMING.
SORRY ABOUT THIS...
I got it!
OH, NO! IT'S TOTALLY FINE.

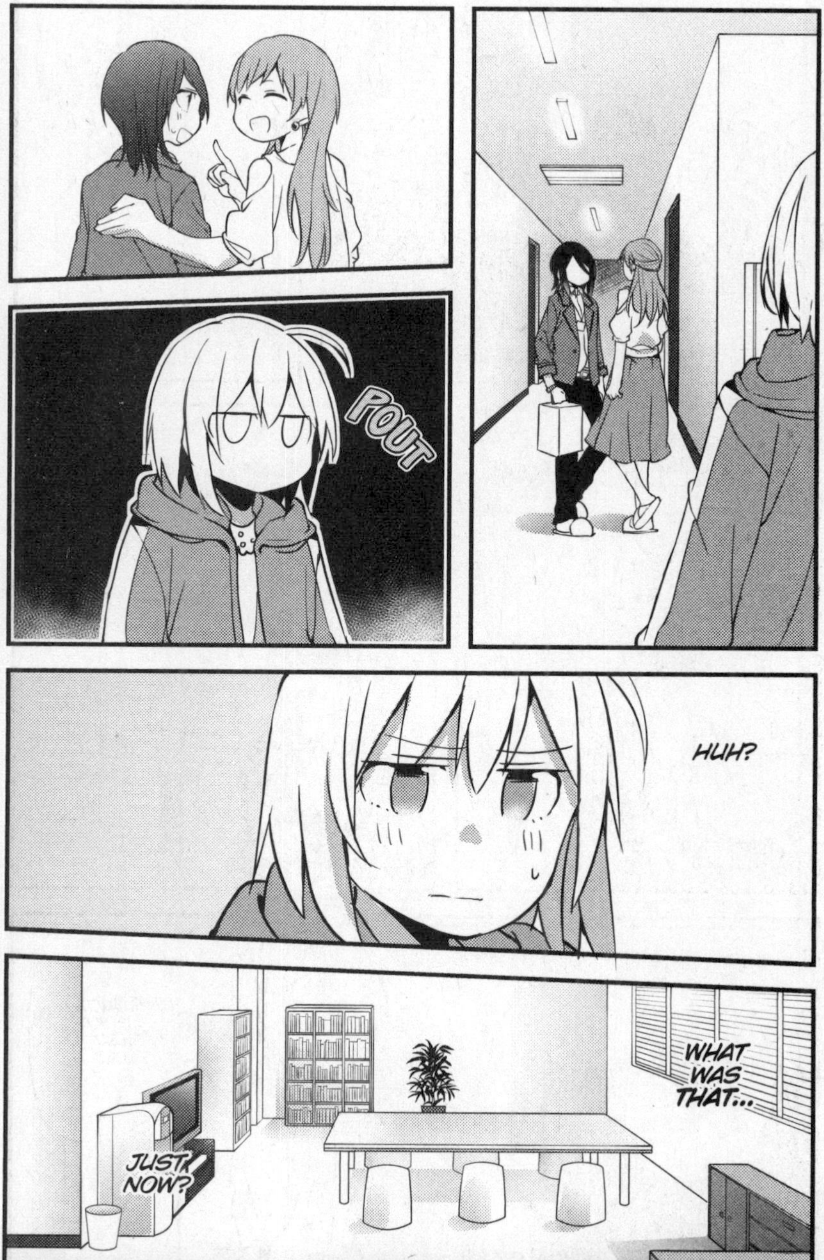
POUT
HUH?
WHAT WAS THAT...
JUST NOW?

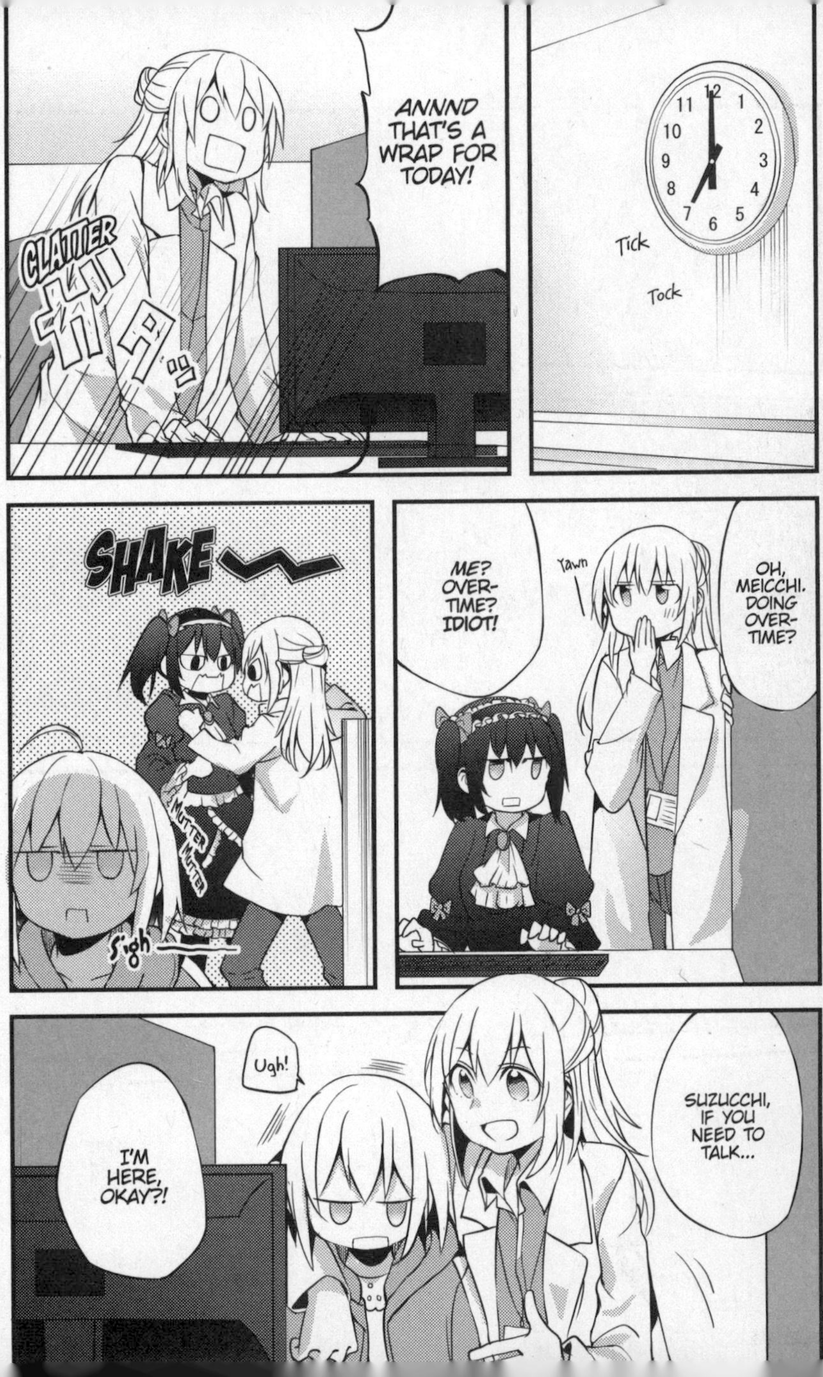
Tick
Tock
ANNND THAT'S A WRAP FOR TODAY!
CLATTER
ガタッ
OH, MEICCHI. DOING OVER-TIME?
Yawn
ME? OVER-TIME? IDIOT!
SHAKE
MUTTER MUTTER
Sigh
SUZUCCHI, IF YOU NEED TO TALK...
Ugh!
I'M HERE, OKAY?!

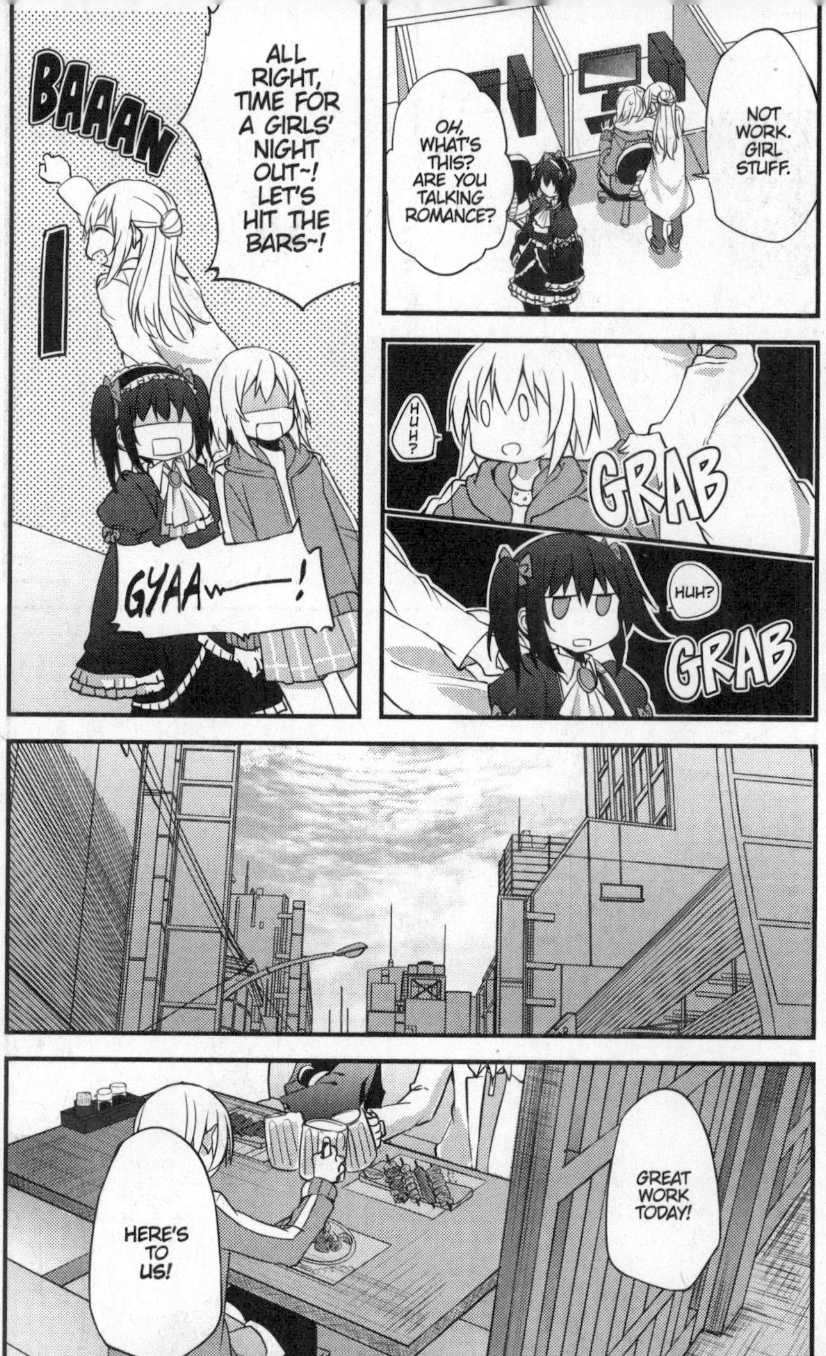
NOT WORK. GIRL STUFF.
OH, WHAT'S THIS? ARE YOU TALKING ROMANCE?
HUH?
GRAB
HUH?
GRAB
ALL RIGHT, TIME FOR A GIRLS' NIGHT OUT~! LET'S HIT THE BARS~!
BAAAN
GYAA—!
GREAT WORK TODAY!
HERE'S TO US!

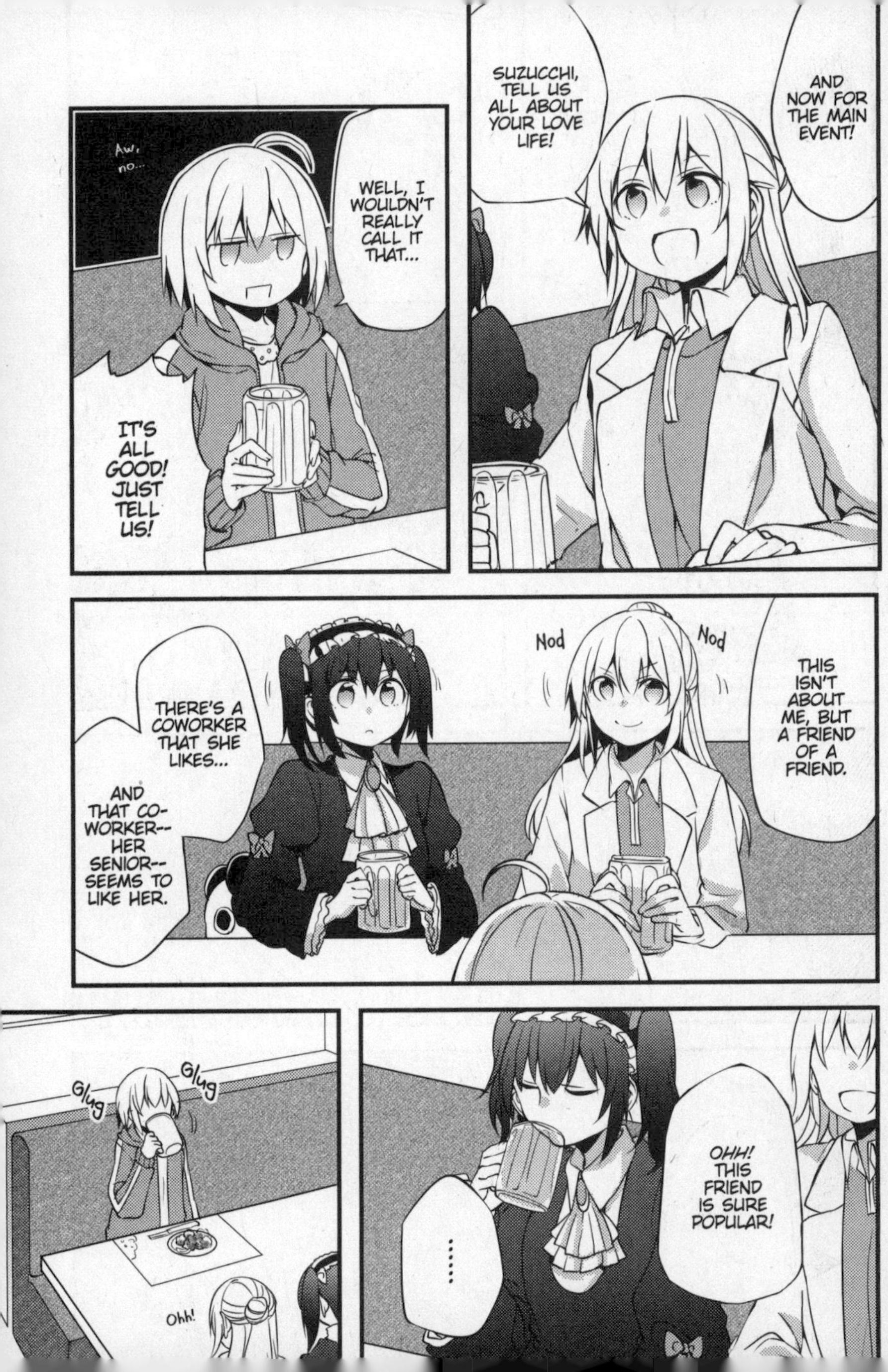

AND NOW FOR THE MAIN EVENT!
SUZUCCHI, TELL US ALL ABOUT YOUR LOVE LIFE!
WELL, I WOULDN'T REALLY CALL IT THAT...
Aw, no...
IT'S ALL GOOD! JUST TELL US!
Nod
Nod
THIS ISN'T ABOUT ME, BUT A FRIEND OF A FRIEND.
THERE'S A COWORKER THAT SHE LIKES...
AND THAT CO-WORKER--HER SENIOR--SEEMS TO LIKE HER.
OHH! THIS FRIEND IS SURE POPULAR!
......
Glug
Glug
Ohh!

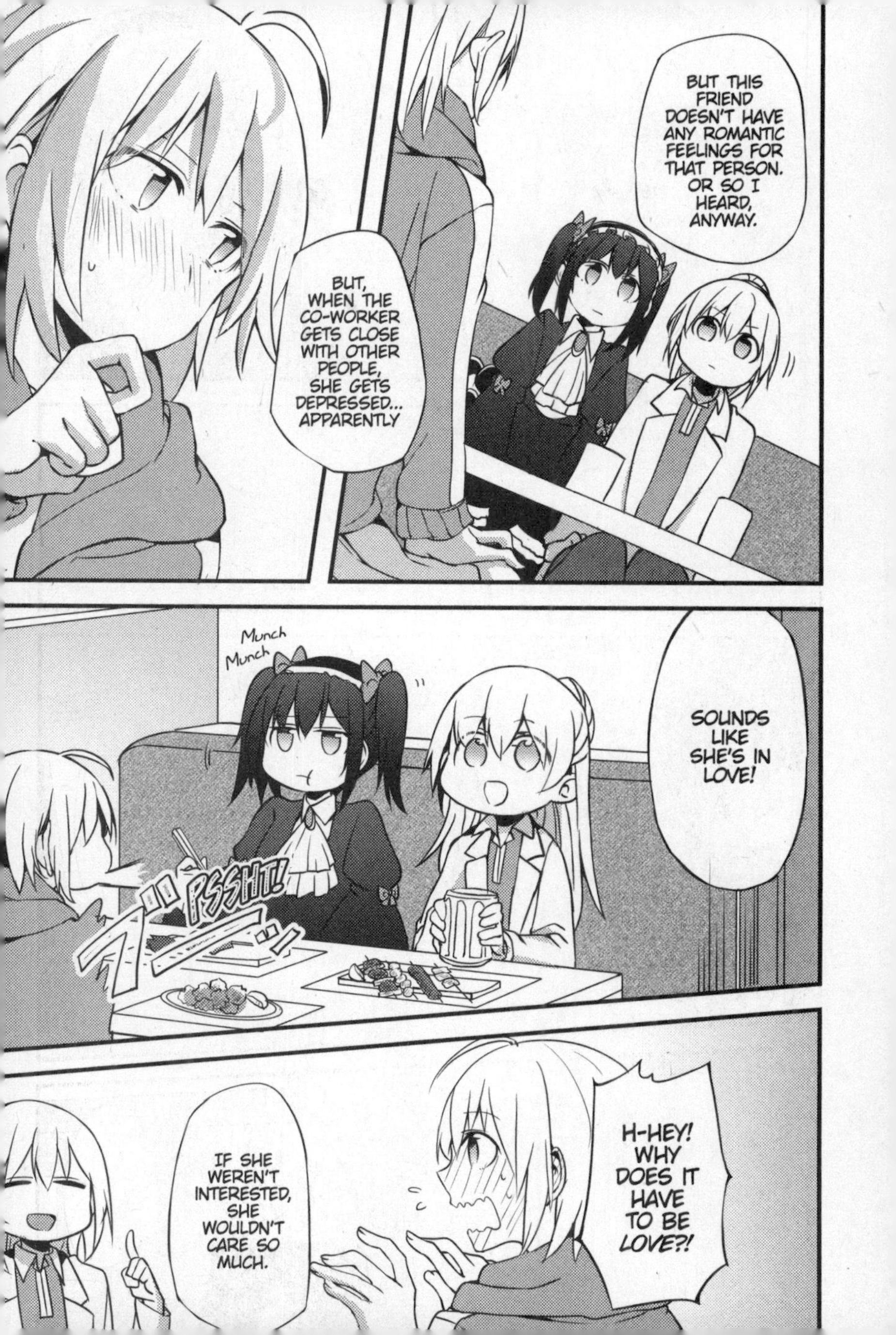
BUT THIS FRIEND DOESN'T HAVE ANY ROMANTIC FEELINGS FOR THAT PERSON. OR SO I HEARD, ANYWAY.
BUT, WHEN THE CO-WORKER GETS CLOSE WITH OTHER PEOPLE, SHE GETS DEPRESSED... APPARENTLY
SOUNDS LIKE SHE'S IN LOVE!
Munch Munch
PSSHT!
H-HEY! WHY DOES IT HAVE TO BE LOVE?!
IF SHE WEREN'T INTERESTED, SHE WOULDN'T CARE SO MUCH.

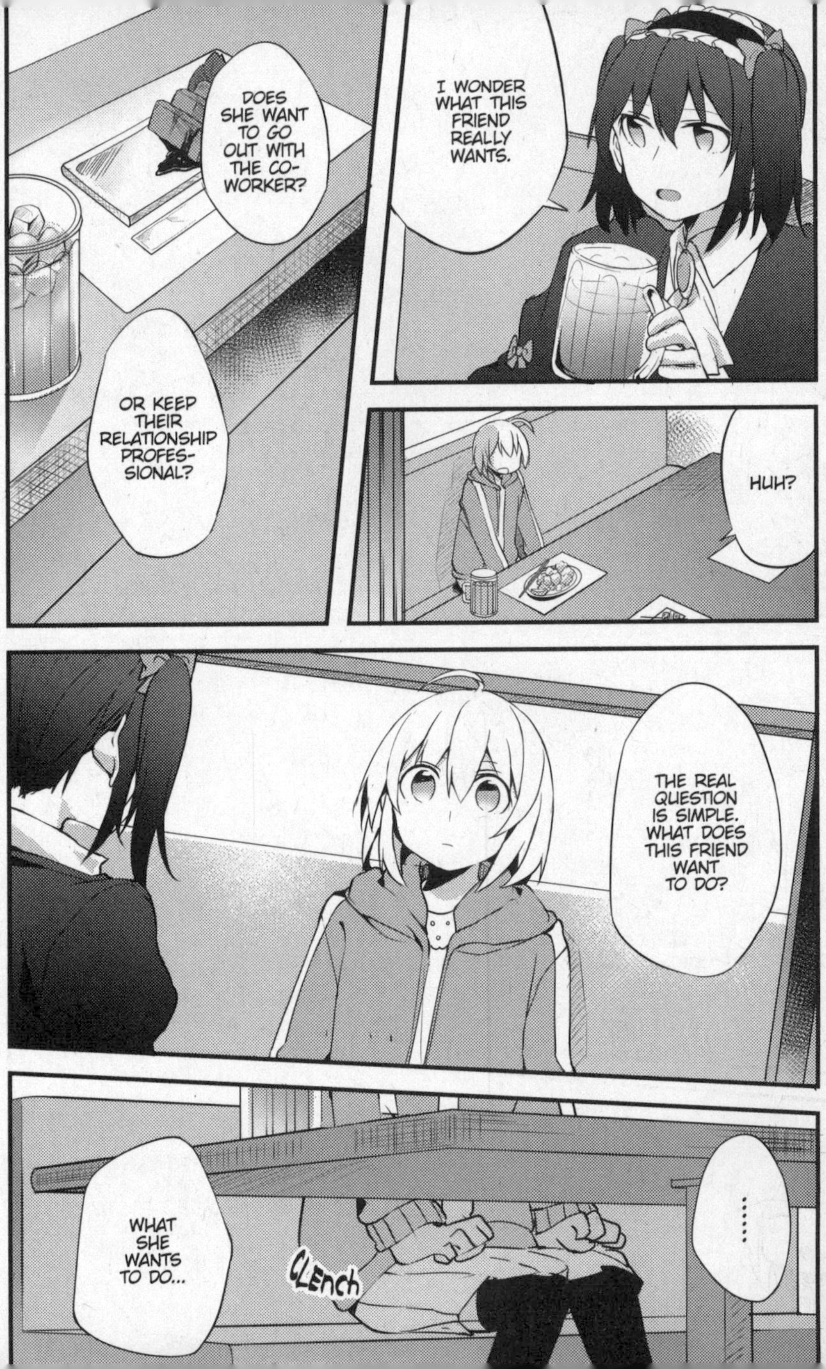
I WONDER WHAT THIS FRIEND REALLY WANTS.
HUH?
DOES SHE WANT TO GO OUT WITH THE CO-WORKER?
OR KEEP THEIR RELATIONSHIP PROFES-SIONAL?
THE REAL QUESTION IS SIMPLE. WHAT DOES THIS FRIEND WANT TO DO?
......
WHAT SHE WANTS TO DO...
CLENCH

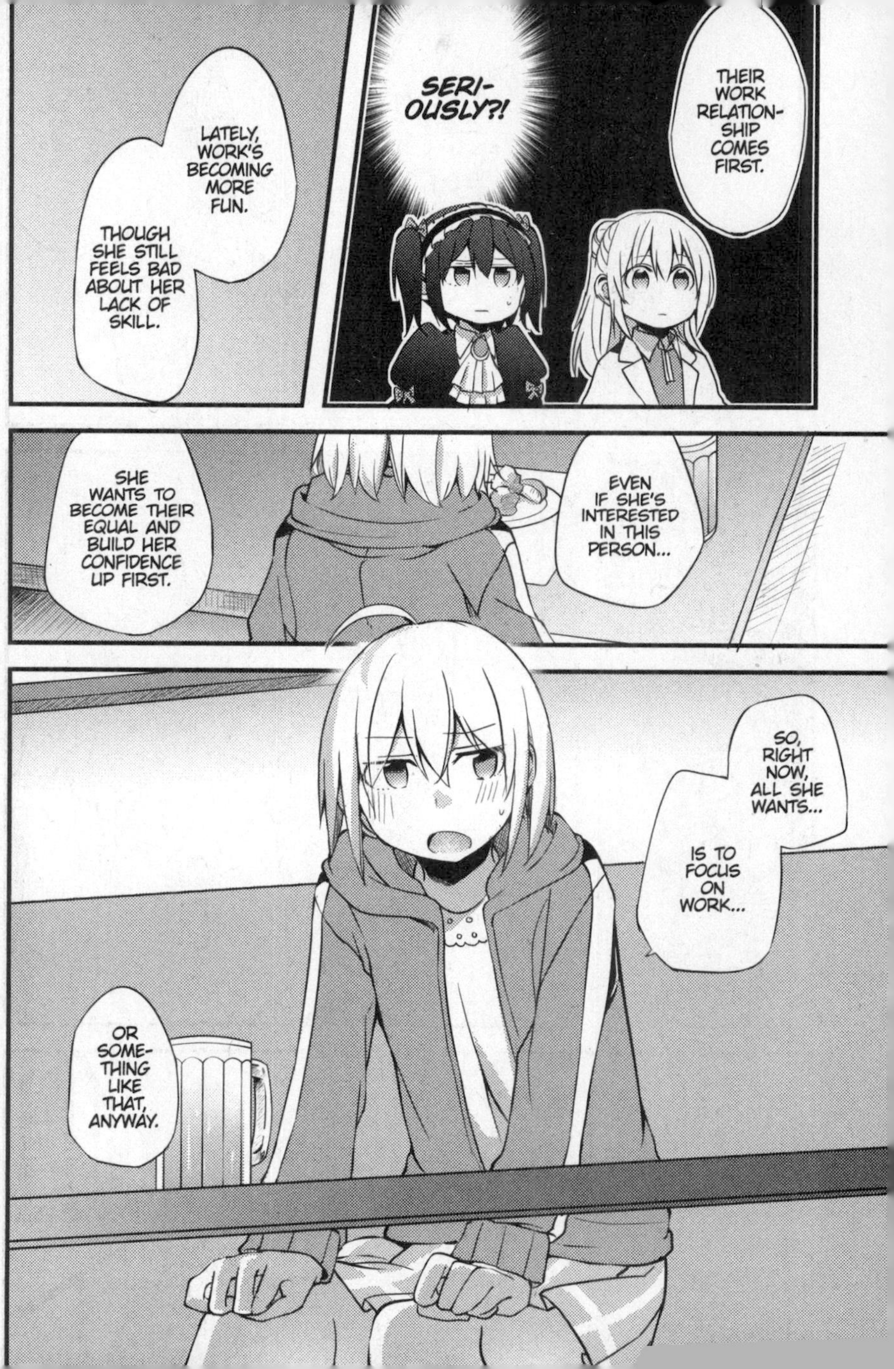
THEIR WORK RELATIONSHIP COMES FIRST.
SERIOUSLY?!
LATELY, WORK'S BECOMING MORE FUN.
THOUGH SHE STILL FEELS BAD ABOUT HER LACK OF SKILL.
EVEN IF SHE'S INTERESTED IN THIS PERSON...
SHE WANTS TO BECOME THEIR EQUAL AND BUILD HER CONFIDENCE UP FIRST.
SO, RIGHT NOW, ALL SHE WANTS...
IS TO FOCUS ON WORK...
OR SOMETHING LIKE THAT, ANYWAY.

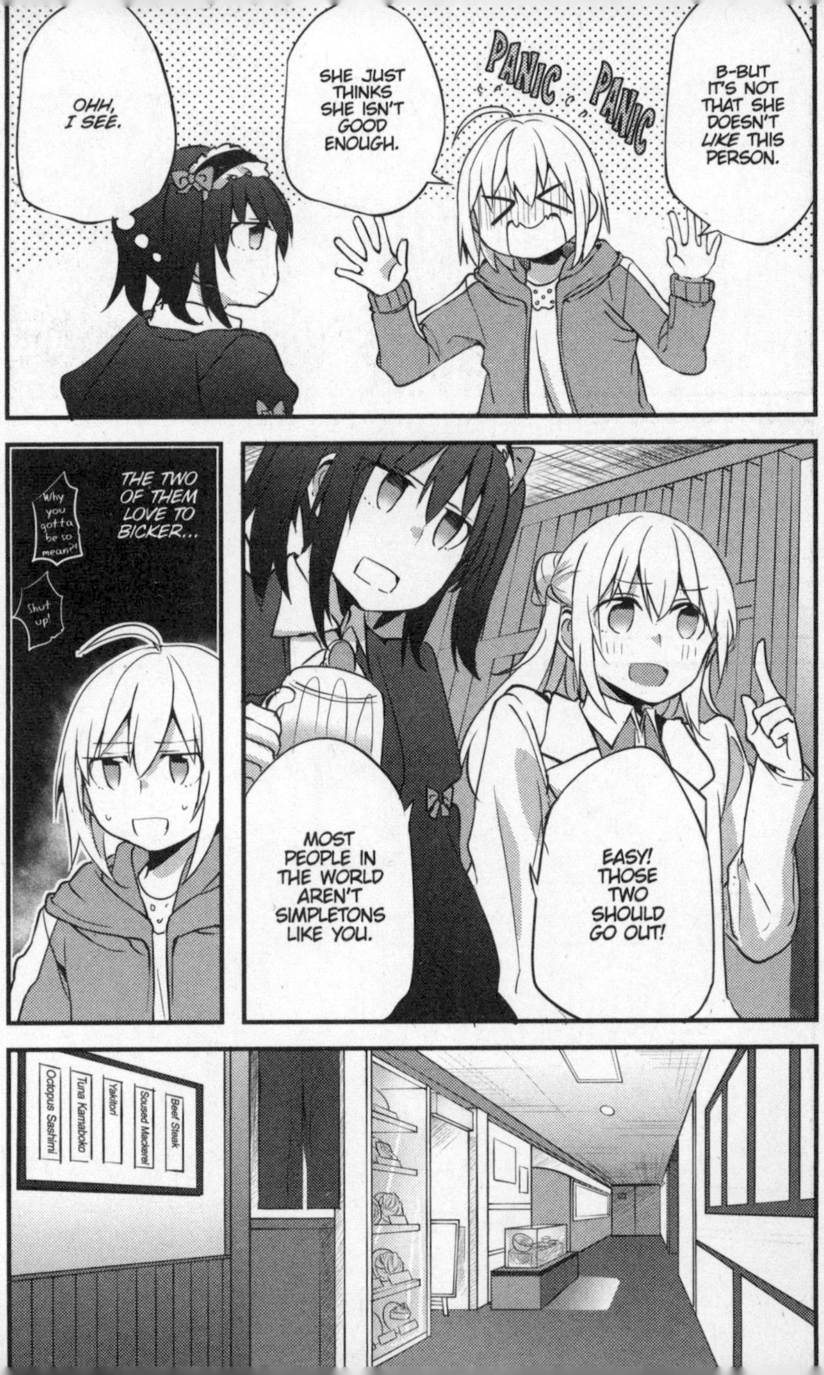
B-BUT IT'S NOT THAT SHE DOESN'T LIKE THIS PERSON.
PANIC PANIC
SHE JUST THINKS SHE ISN'T GOOD ENOUGH.
OHH, I SEE.
EASY! THOSE TWO SHOULD GO OUT!
MOST PEOPLE IN THE WORLD AREN'T SIMPLETONS LIKE YOU.
THE TWO OF THEM LOVE TO BICKER...
Why you gotta be so mean?!
Shut up!
Beef Steak
Soused Mackerel
Yakitori
Tuna Kamaboko
Octopus Sashimi

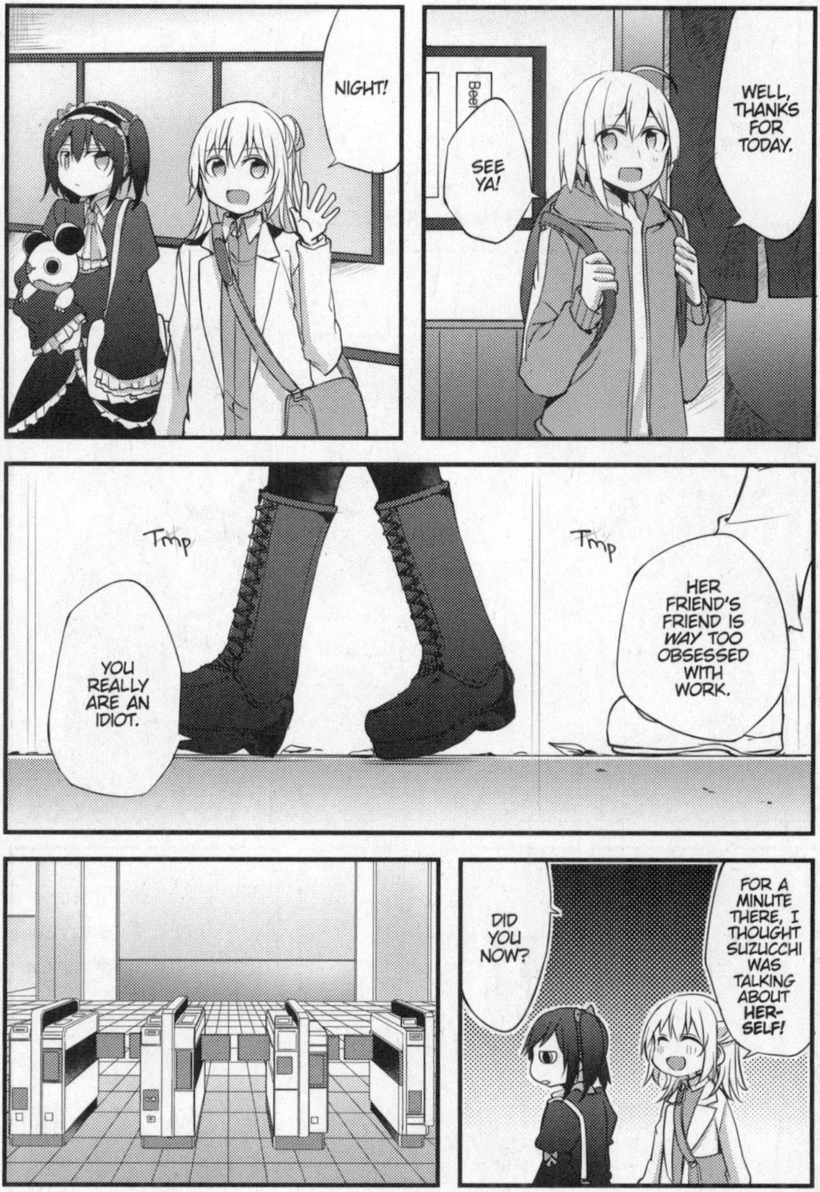

WELL, THANKS FOR TODAY.
SEE YA!
NIGHT!
Tmp
HER FRIEND'S FRIEND IS *WAY* TOO OBSESSED WITH WORK.
Tmp
YOU REALLY ARE AN IDIOT.
FOR A MINUTE THERE, I THOUGHT SUZUCCHI WAS TALKING ABOUT HER-SELF!
DID YOU NOW?

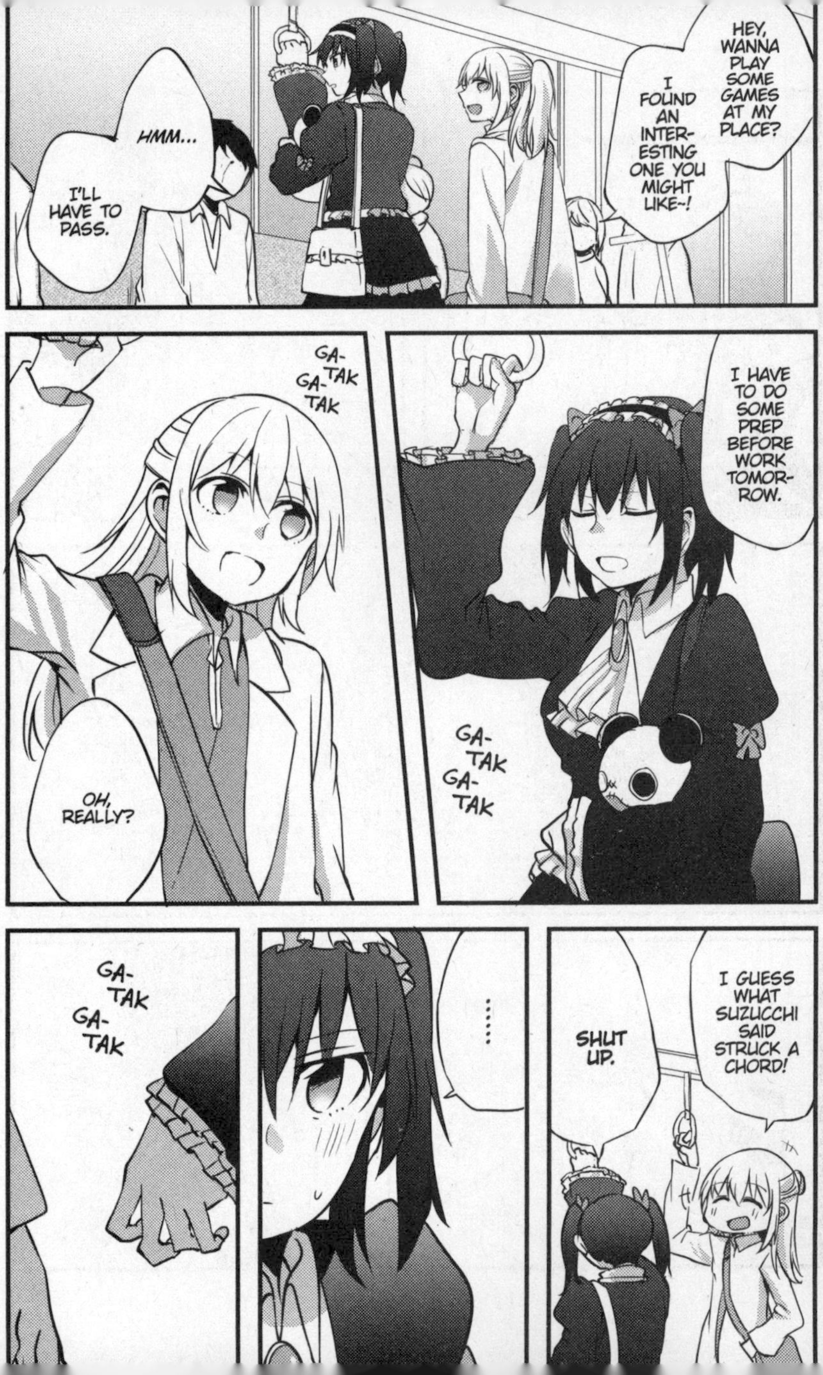
HEY, WANNA PLAY SOME GAMES AT MY PLACE?
I FOUND AN INTER-ESTING ONE YOU MIGHT LIKE~!
HMM...
I'LL HAVE TO PASS.
I HAVE TO DO SOME PREP BEFORE WORK TOMOR-ROW.
GA-TAK GA-TAK
GA-TAK GA-TAK
OH, REALLY?
I GUESS WHAT SUZUCCHI SAID STRUCK A CHORD!
SHUT UP.
......
GA-TAK GA-TAK

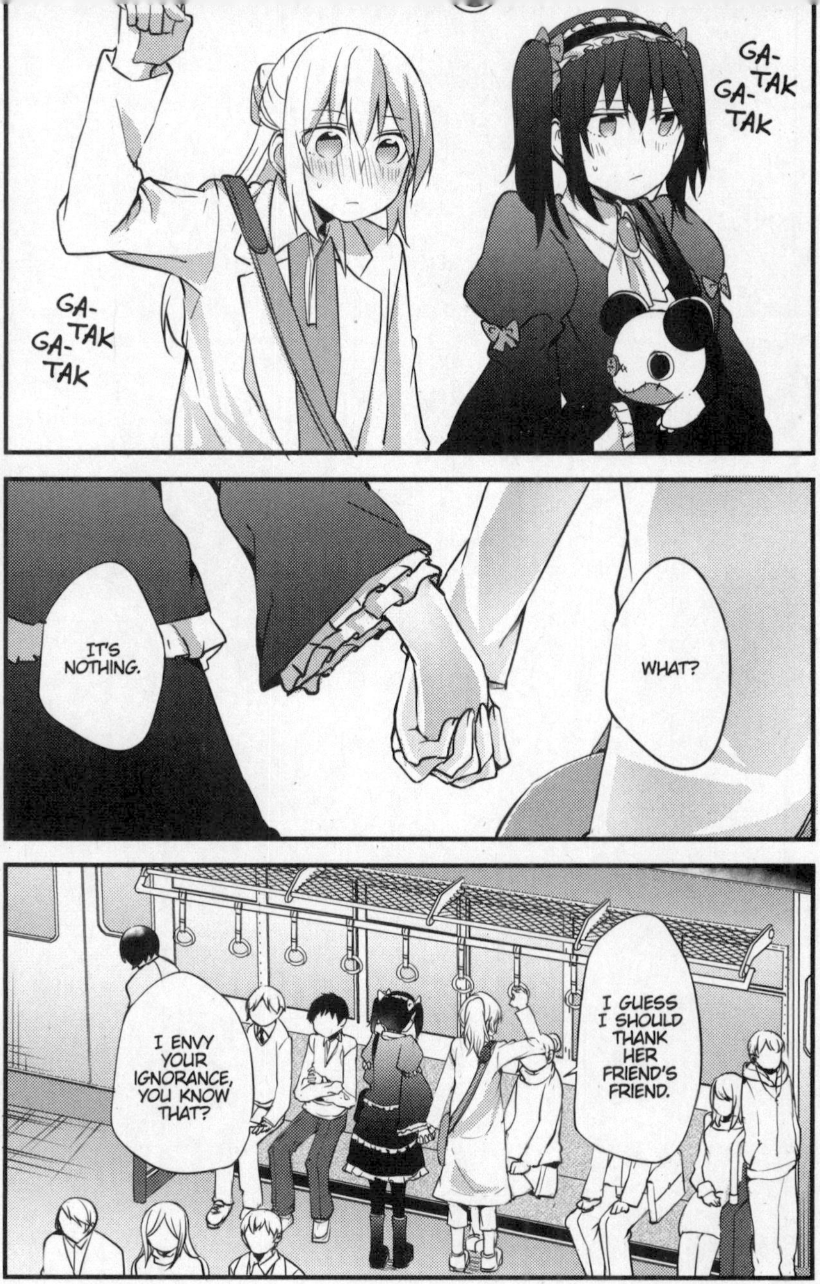
GA-TAK GA-TAK
GA-TAK GA-TAK
WHAT?
IT'S NOTHING.
I GUESS I SHOULD THANK HER FRIEND'S FRIEND.
I ENVY YOUR IGNORANCE, YOU KNOW THAT?

Now Loading...!

Now Loading...!

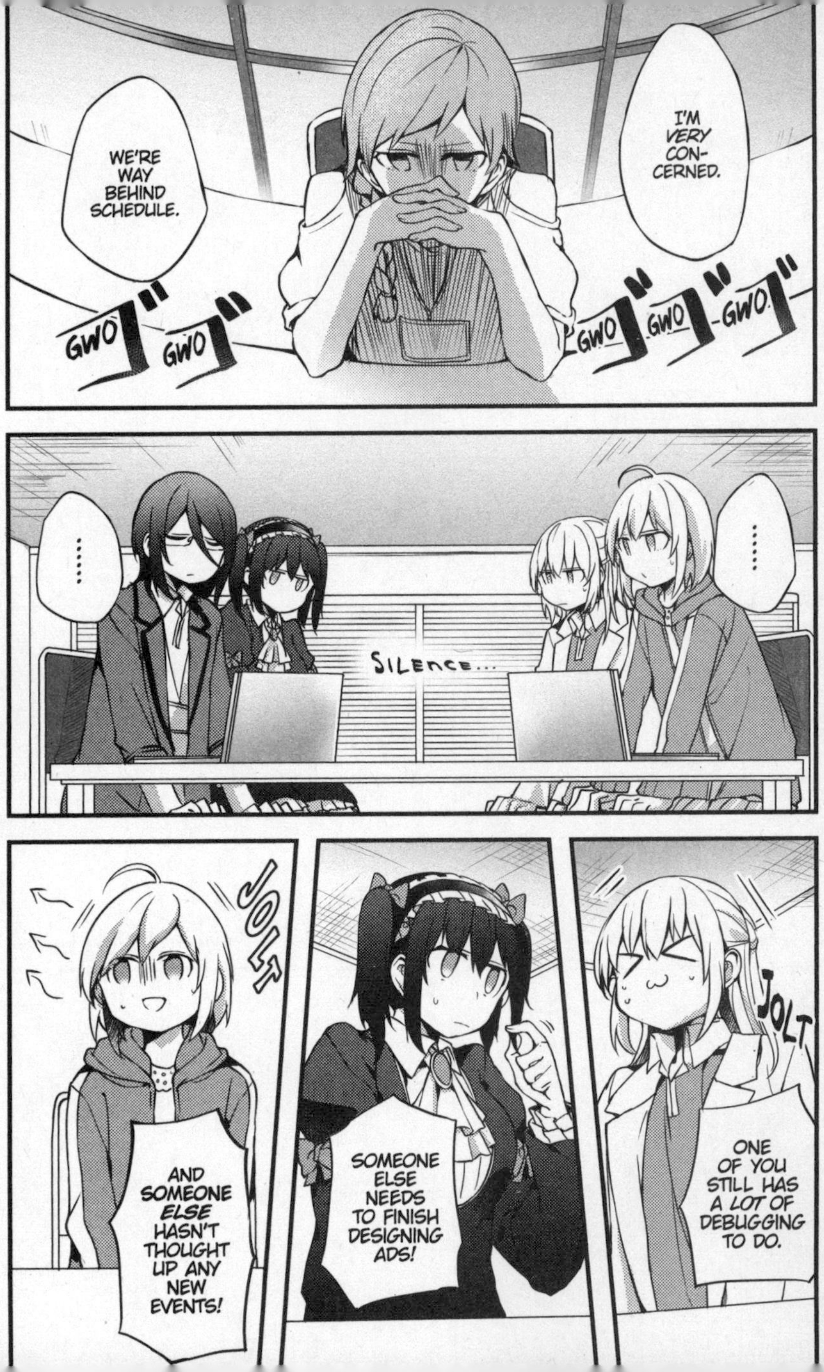
I'M VERY CON-CERNED.
WE'RE WAY BEHIND SCHEDULE.
GWO GWO-GWO
GWO GWO
......
......
SILENCE...
ONE OF YOU STILL HAS A *LOT* OF DEBUGGING TO DO.
JOLT
SOMEONE ELSE NEEDS TO FINISH DESIGNING ADS!
AND SOMEONE *ELSE* HASN'T THOUGHT UP ANY NEW EVENTS!
JOLT

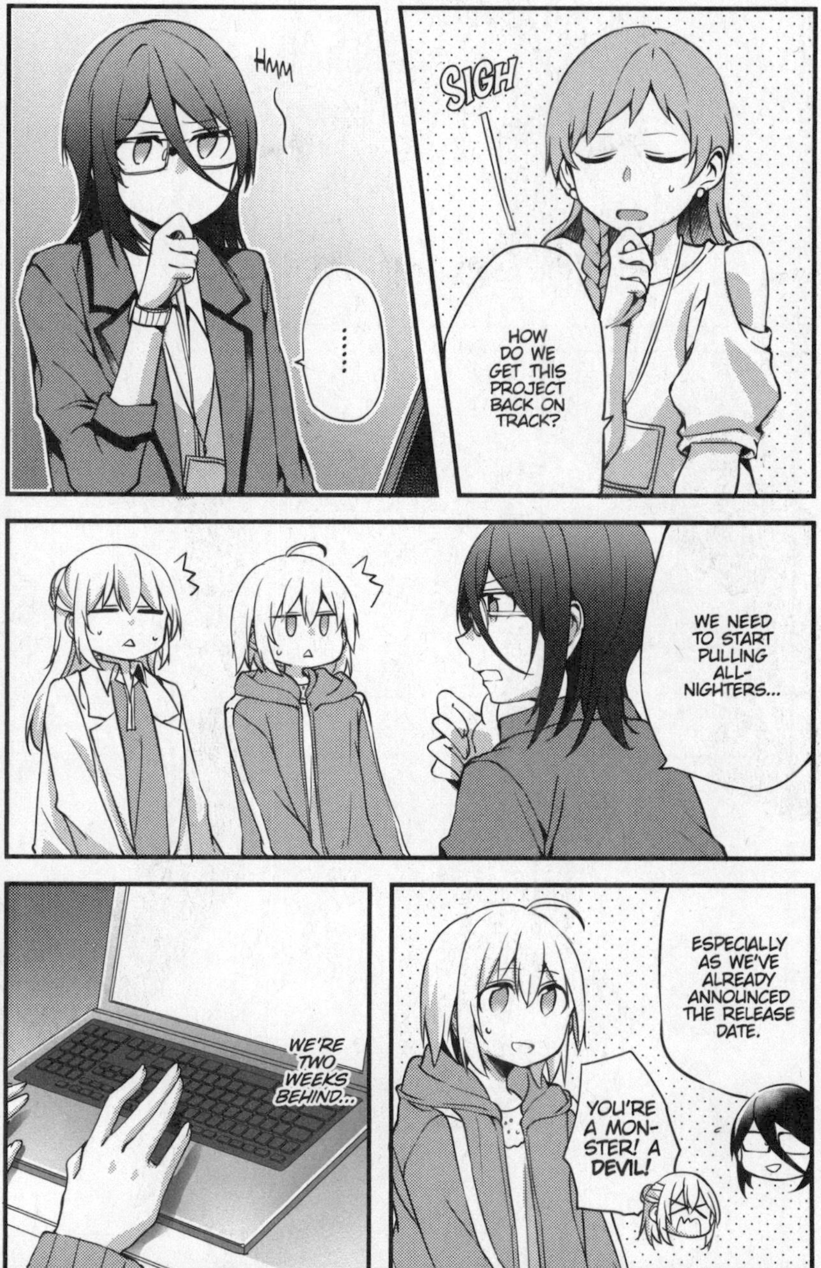
HMM
......
SIGH
HOW DO WE GET THIS PROJECT BACK ON TRACK?
WE NEED TO START PULLING ALL-NIGHTERS...
WE'RE TWO WEEKS BEHIND...
ESPECIALLY AS WE'VE ALREADY ANNOUNCED THE RELEASE DATE.
YOU'RE A MON-STER! A DEVIL!

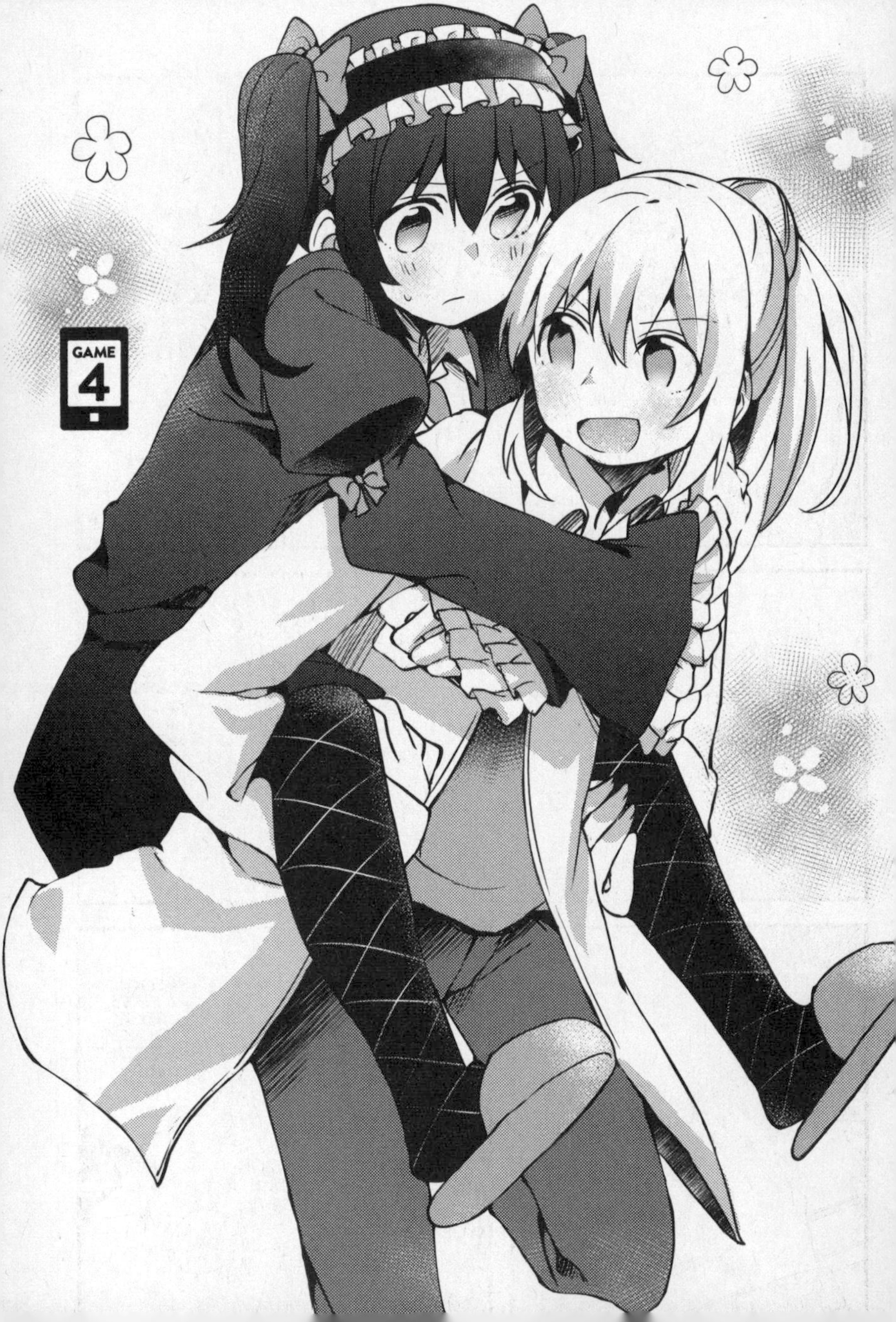
GAME
4

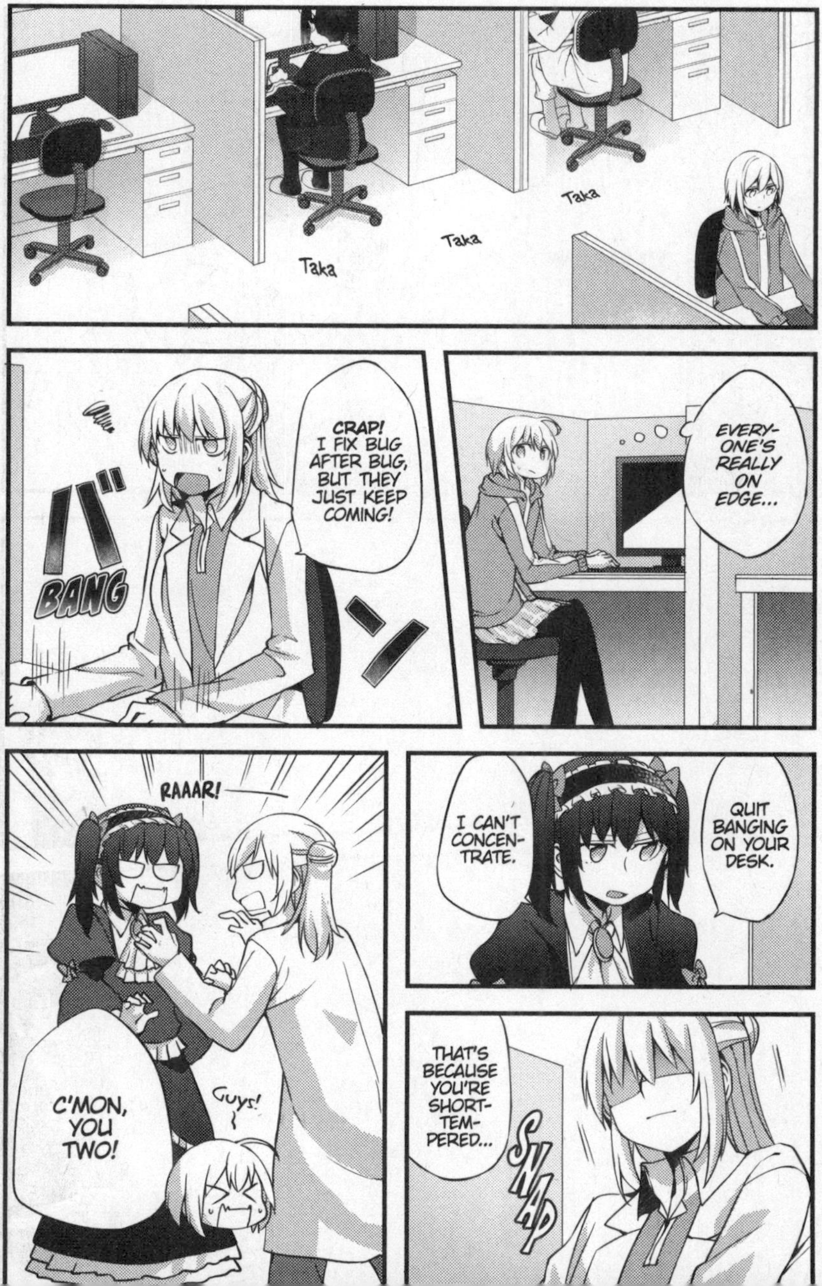

Taka
Taka
Taka
EVERY-ONE'S REALLY ON EDGE...
CRAP! I FIX BUG AFTER BUG, BUT THEY JUST KEEP COMING!
BANG
QUIT BANGING ON YOUR DESK.
I CAN'T CONCEN-TRATE.
THAT'S BECAUSE YOU'RE SHORT-TEM-PERED...
SNAP
RAAAR!
Guys!
C'MON, YOU TWO!

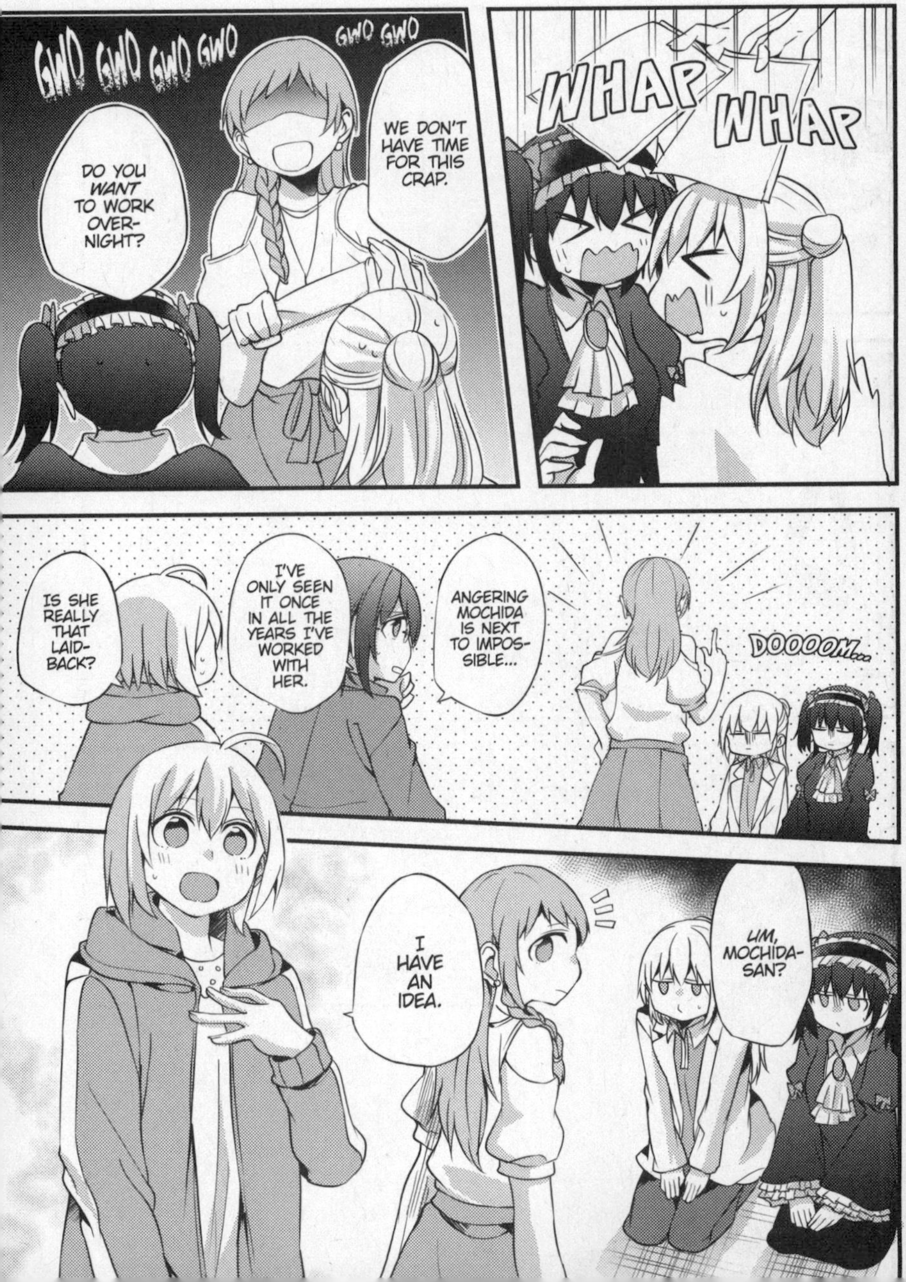
WHAP
WHAP
GWO GWO
WE DON'T HAVE TIME FOR THIS CRAP.
GWO GWO GWO GWO
DO YOU WANT TO WORK OVER-NIGHT?
DOOOOM...
ANGERING MOCHIDA IS NEXT TO IMPOS-SIBLE...
I'VE ONLY SEEN IT ONCE IN ALL THE YEARS I'VE WORKED WITH HER.
IS SHE REALLY THAT LAID-BACK?
UM, MOCHIDA-SAN?
I HAVE AN IDEA.

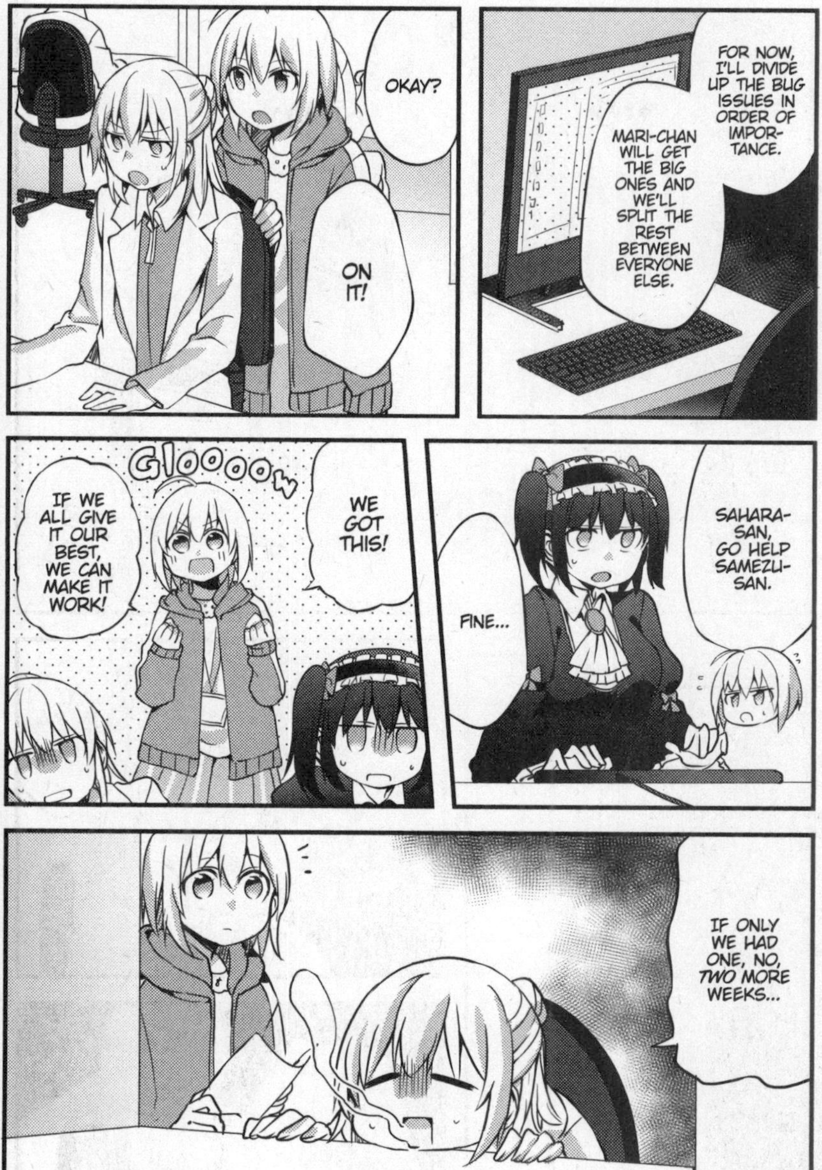
FOR NOW, I'LL DIVIDE UP THE BUG ISSUES IN ORDER OF IMPOR-TANCE.
MARI-CHAN WILL GET THE BIG ONES AND WE'LL SPLIT THE REST BETWEEN EVERYONE ELSE.
OKAY?
ON IT!
SAHARA-SAN, GO HELP SAMEZU-SAN.
FINE...
WE GOT THIS!
Glooooow
IF WE ALL GIVE IT OUR BEST, WE CAN MAKE IT WORK!
IF ONLY WE HAD ONE, NO, *TWO* MORE WEEKS...

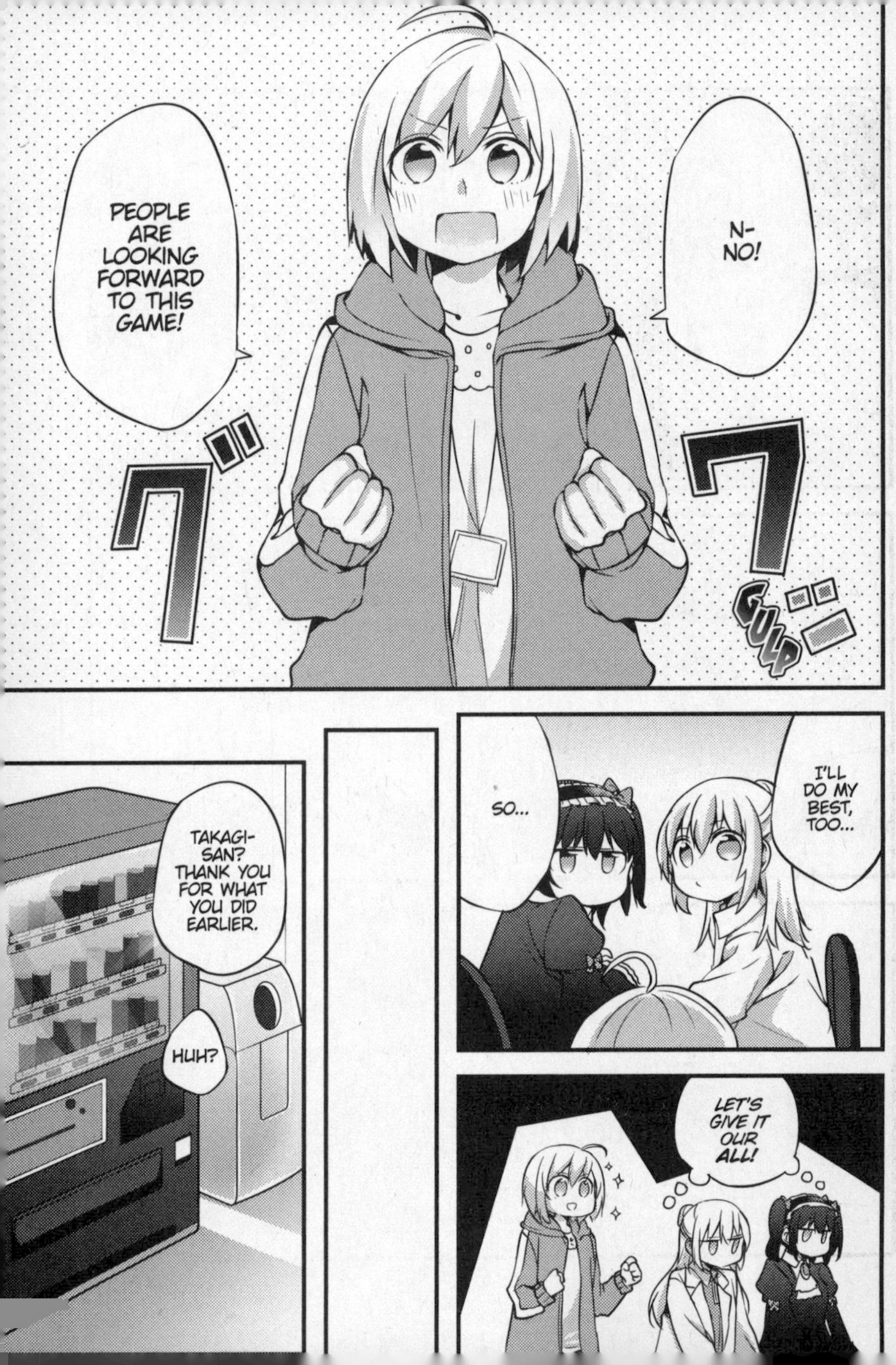
N- NO!
PEOPLE ARE LOOKING FORWARD TO THIS GAME!
GULP
I'LL DO MY BEST, TOO...
SO...
LET'S GIVE IT OUR ALL!
TAKAGI-SAN? THANK YOU FOR WHAT YOU DID EARLIER.
HUH?

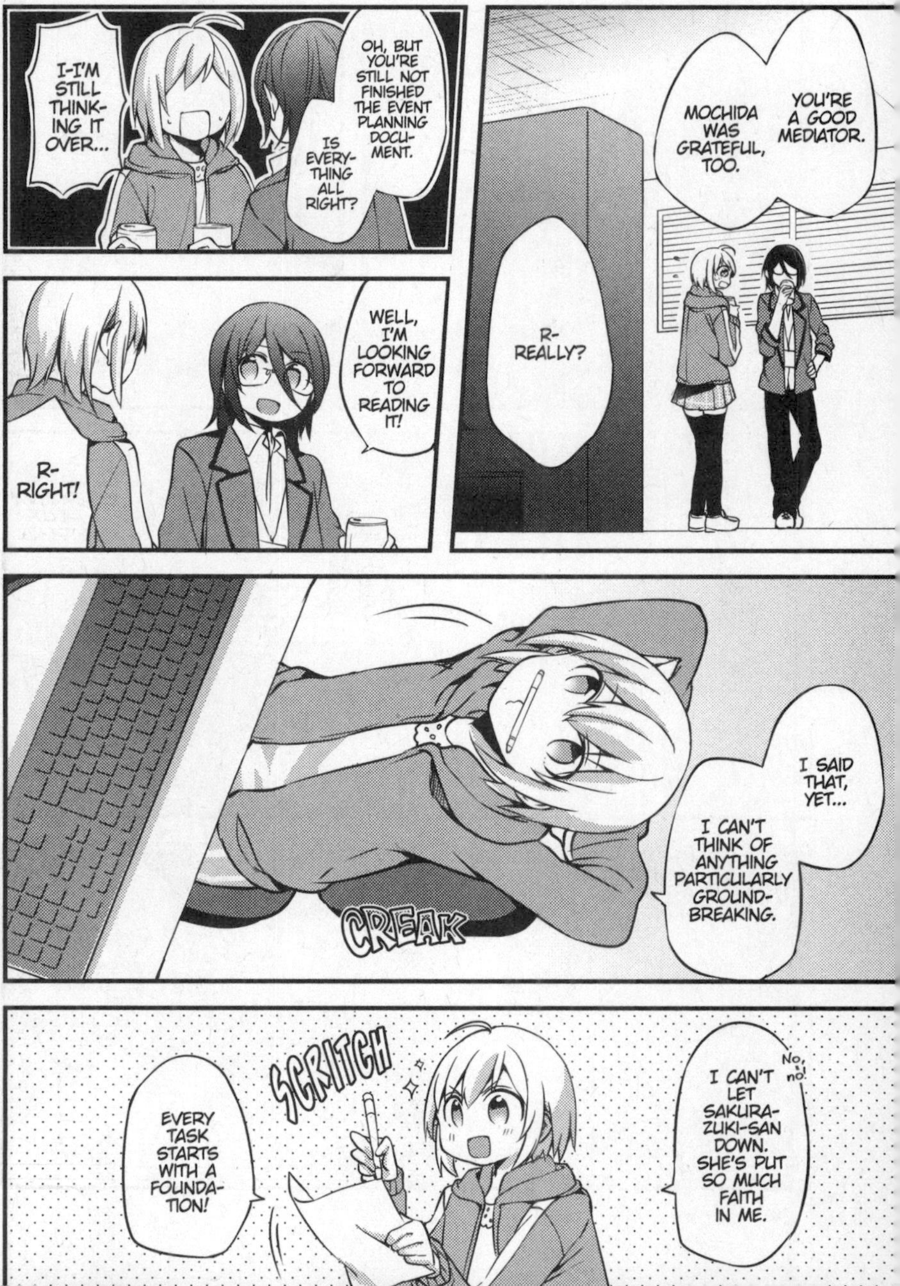
YOU'RE A GOOD MEDIATOR.
MOCHIDA WAS GRATEFUL, TOO.
R-REALLY?
OH, BUT YOU'RE STILL NOT FINISHED THE EVENT PLANNING DOCU-MENT.
IS EVERY-THING ALL RIGHT?
I-I'M STILL THINK-ING IT OVER...
WELL, I'M LOOKING FORWARD TO READING IT!
R-RIGHT!
I SAID THAT, YET...
I CAN'T THINK OF ANYTHING PARTICULARLY GROUND-BREAKING.
CREAK
No, no!
I CAN'T LET SAKURA-ZUKI-SAN DOWN. SHE'S PUT SO MUCH FAITH IN ME.
SCRITCH
EVERY TASK STARTS WITH A FOUNDA-TION!

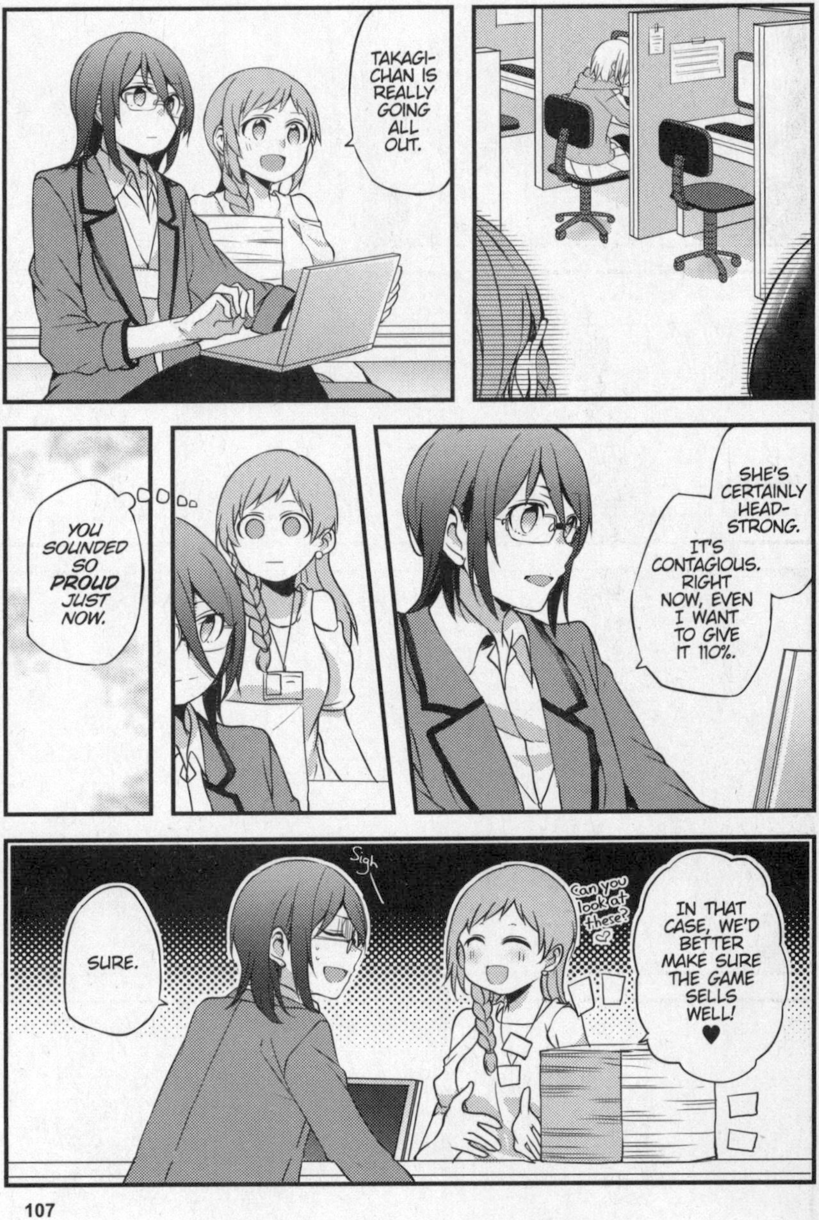
TAKAGI-CHAN IS REALLY GOING ALL OUT.
SHE'S CERTAINLY HEAD-STRONG.
IT'S CONTAGIOUS. RIGHT NOW, EVEN I WANT TO GIVE IT 110%.
YOU SOUNDED SO PROUD JUST NOW.
IN THAT CASE, WE'D BETTER MAKE SURE THE GAME SELLS WELL! ♥
Can you look at these? ♡
Sigh
SURE.

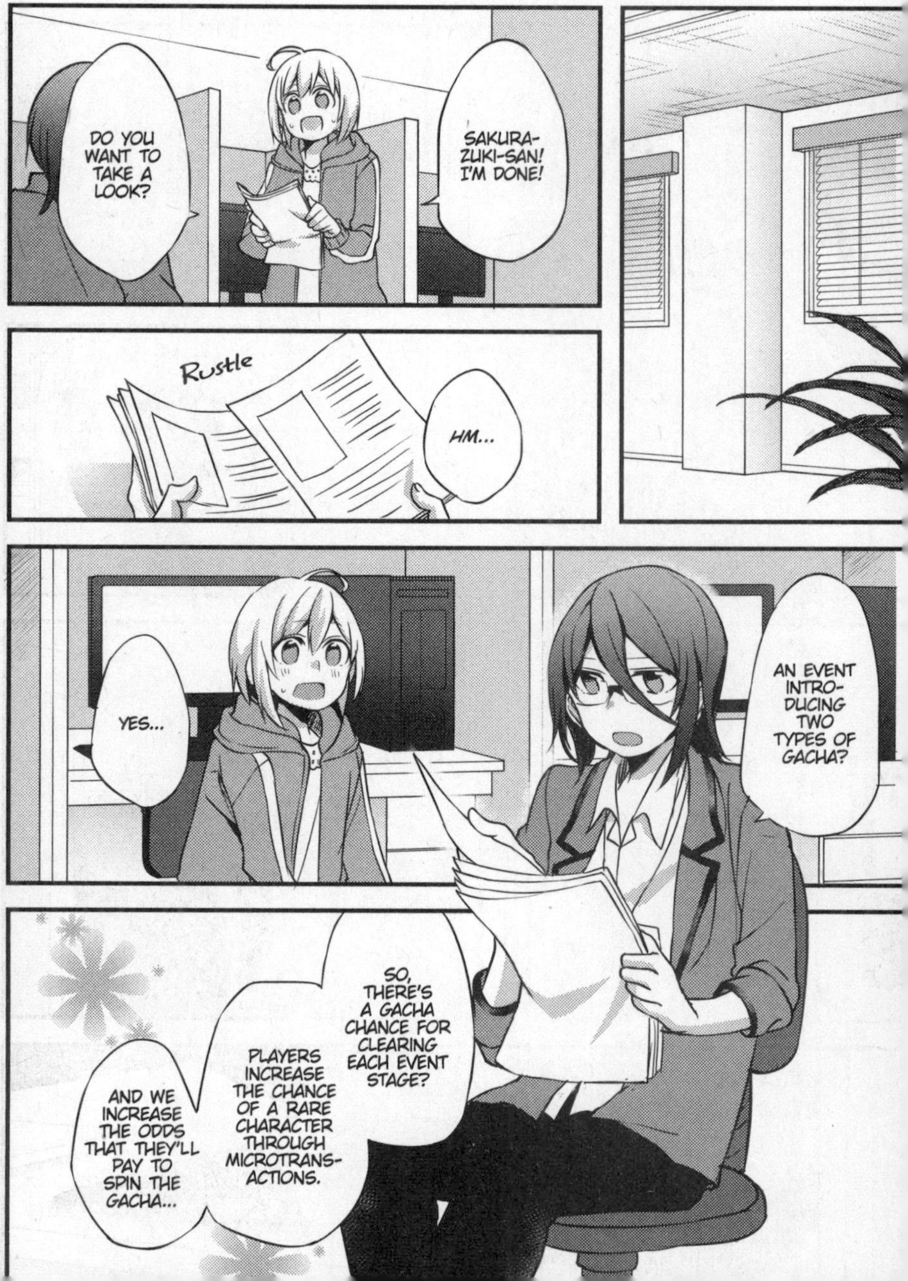
SAKURAZUKI-SAN! I'M DONE!
DO YOU WANT TO TAKE A LOOK?
Rustle
HM...
AN EVENT INTRODUCING TWO TYPES OF GACHA?
YES...
SO, THERE'S A GACHA CHANCE FOR CLEARING EACH EVENT STAGE?
PLAYERS INCREASE THE CHANCE OF A RARE CHARACTER THROUGH MICROTRANSACTIONS.
AND WE INCREASE THE ODDS THAT THEY'LL PAY TO SPIN THE GACHA...

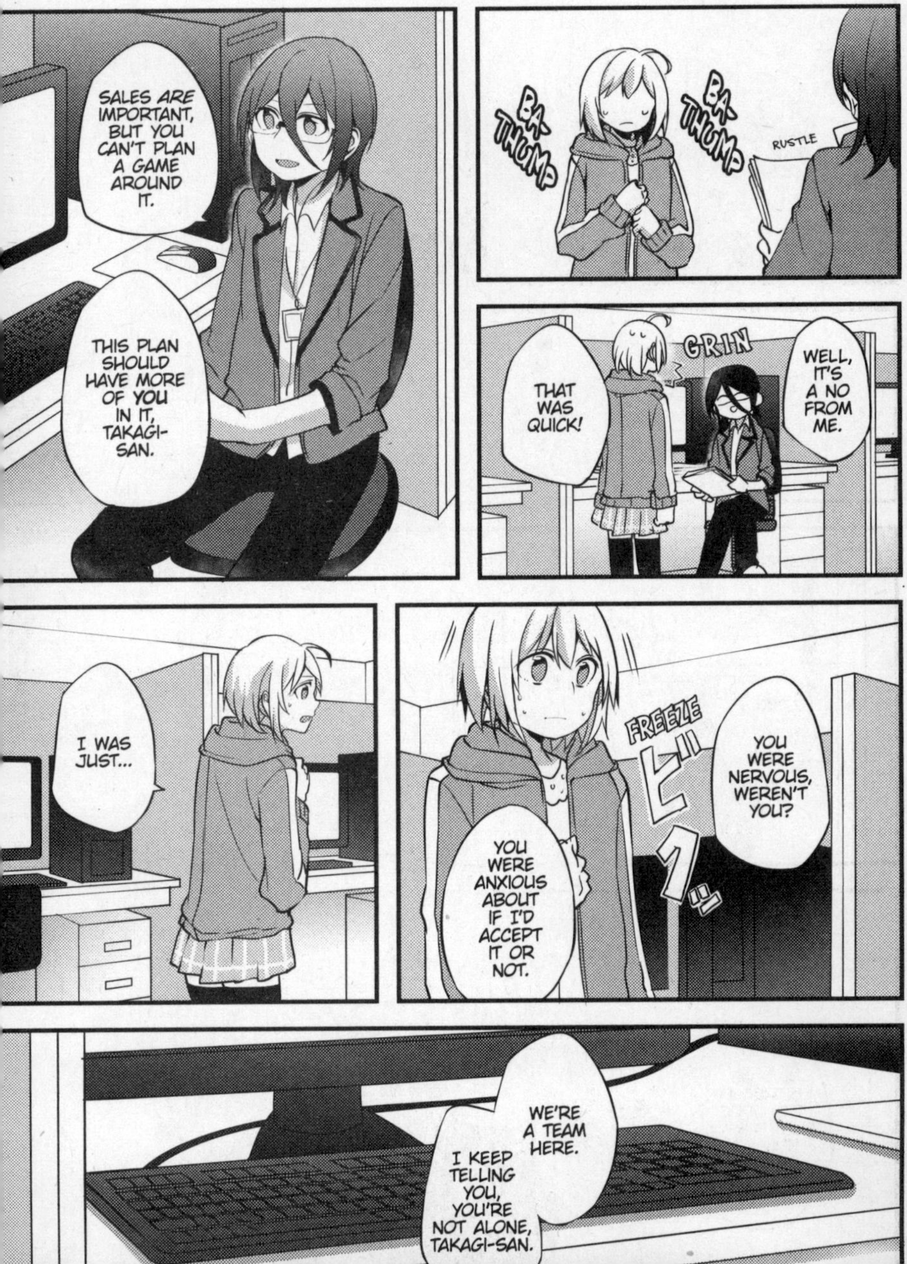
BA THUMP
BA THUMP
RUSTLE
WELL, IT'S A NO FROM ME.
GRIN
THAT WAS QUICK!
SALES ARE IMPORTANT, BUT YOU CAN'T PLAN A GAME AROUND IT.
THIS PLAN SHOULD HAVE MORE OF YOU IN IT, TAKAGI-SAN.
YOU WERE NERVOUS, WEREN'T YOU?
FREEZE
YOU WERE ANXIOUS ABOUT IF I'D ACCEPT IT OR NOT.
I WAS JUST...
WE'RE A TEAM HERE.
I KEEP TELLING YOU, YOU'RE NOT ALONE, TAKAGI-SAN.

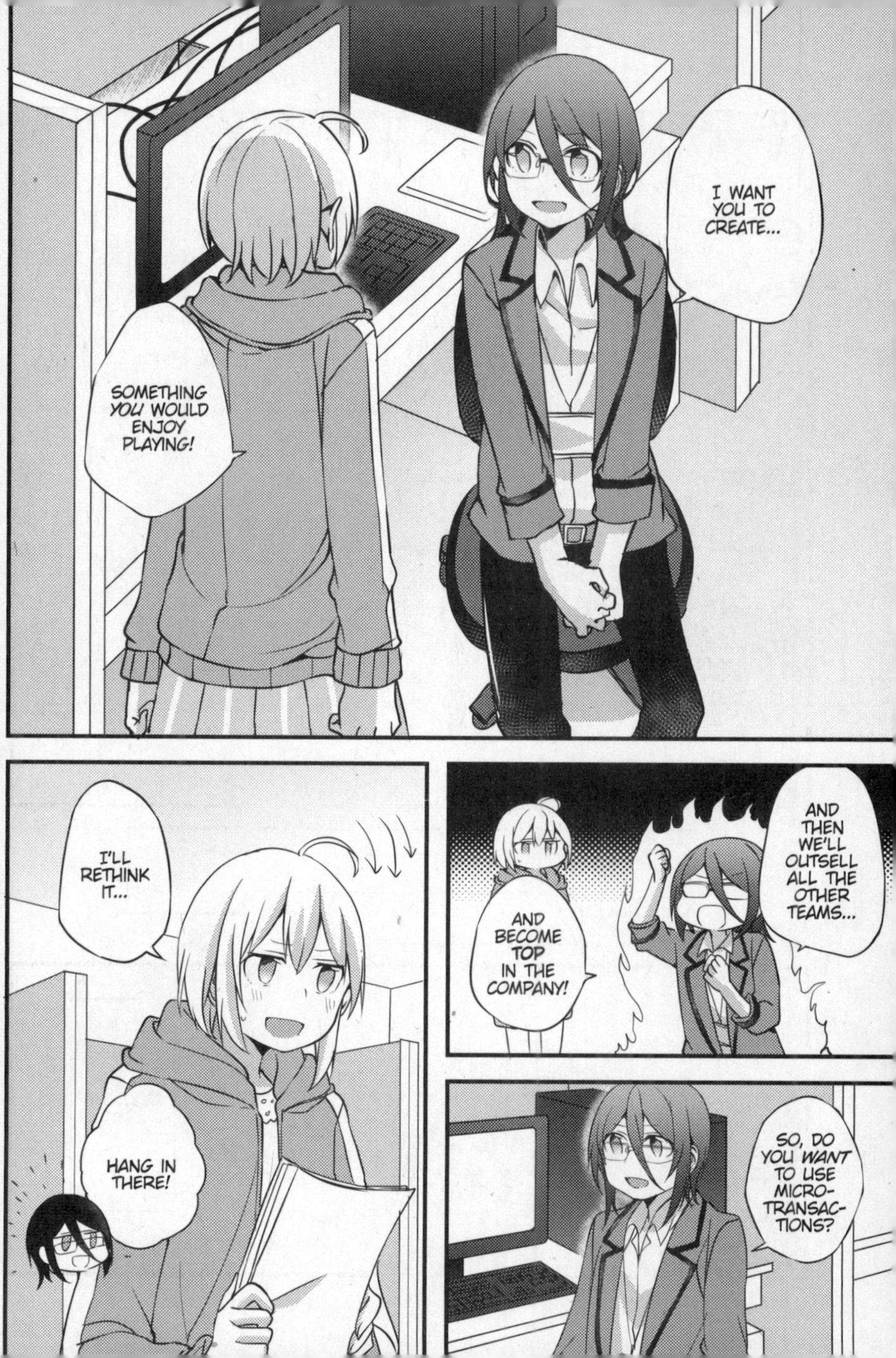
I WANT YOU TO CREATE...
SOMETHING YOU WOULD ENJOY PLAYING!
AND THEN WE'LL OUTSELL ALL THE OTHER TEAMS...
AND BECOME TOP IN THE COMPANY!
SO, DO YOU WANT TO USE MICRO-TRANSACTIONS?
I'LL RETHINK IT...
HANG IN THERE!

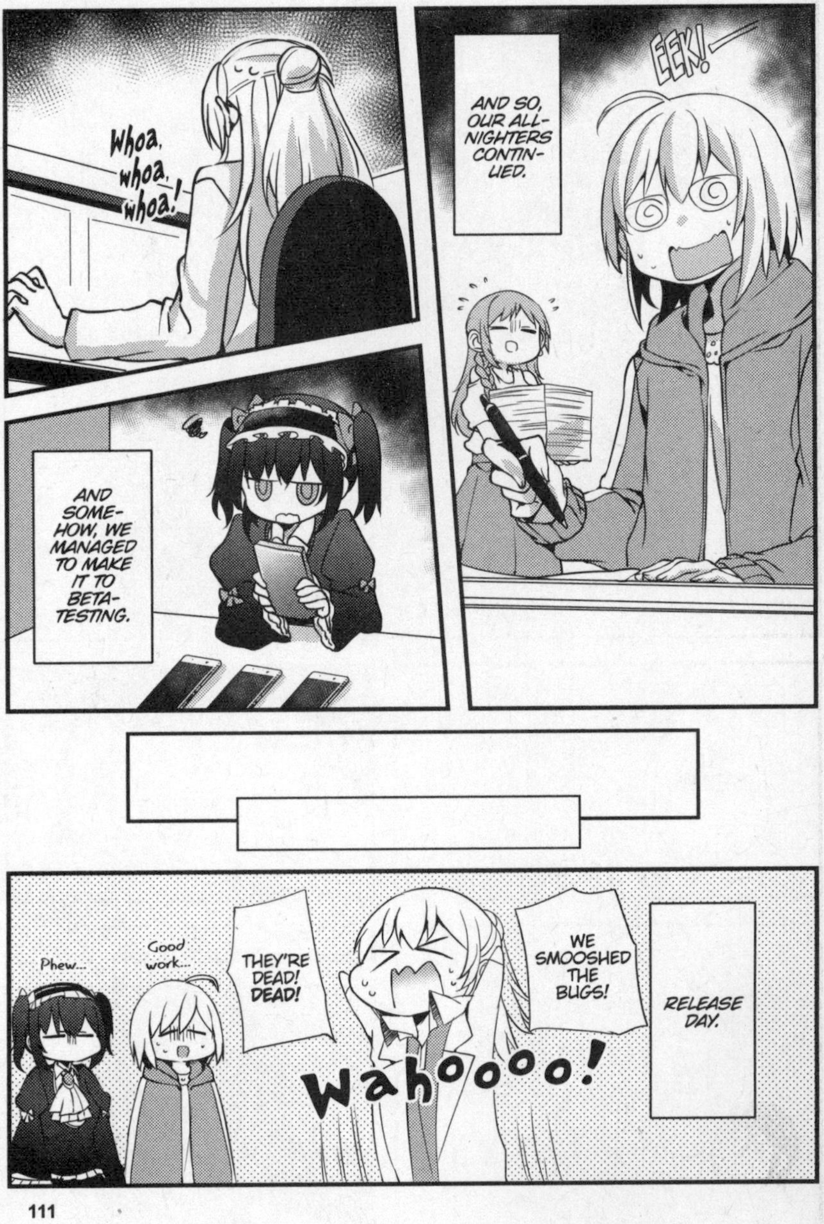
AND SO, OUR ALL-NIGHTERS CONTINUED.
EEK!
Whoa, whoa, whoa!
AND SOMEHOW, WE MANAGED TO MAKE IT TO BETA-TESTING.
RELEASE DAY.
WE SMOOSHED THE BUGS!
THEY'RE DEAD! DEAD!
Wahooooo!
Good work...
Phew...

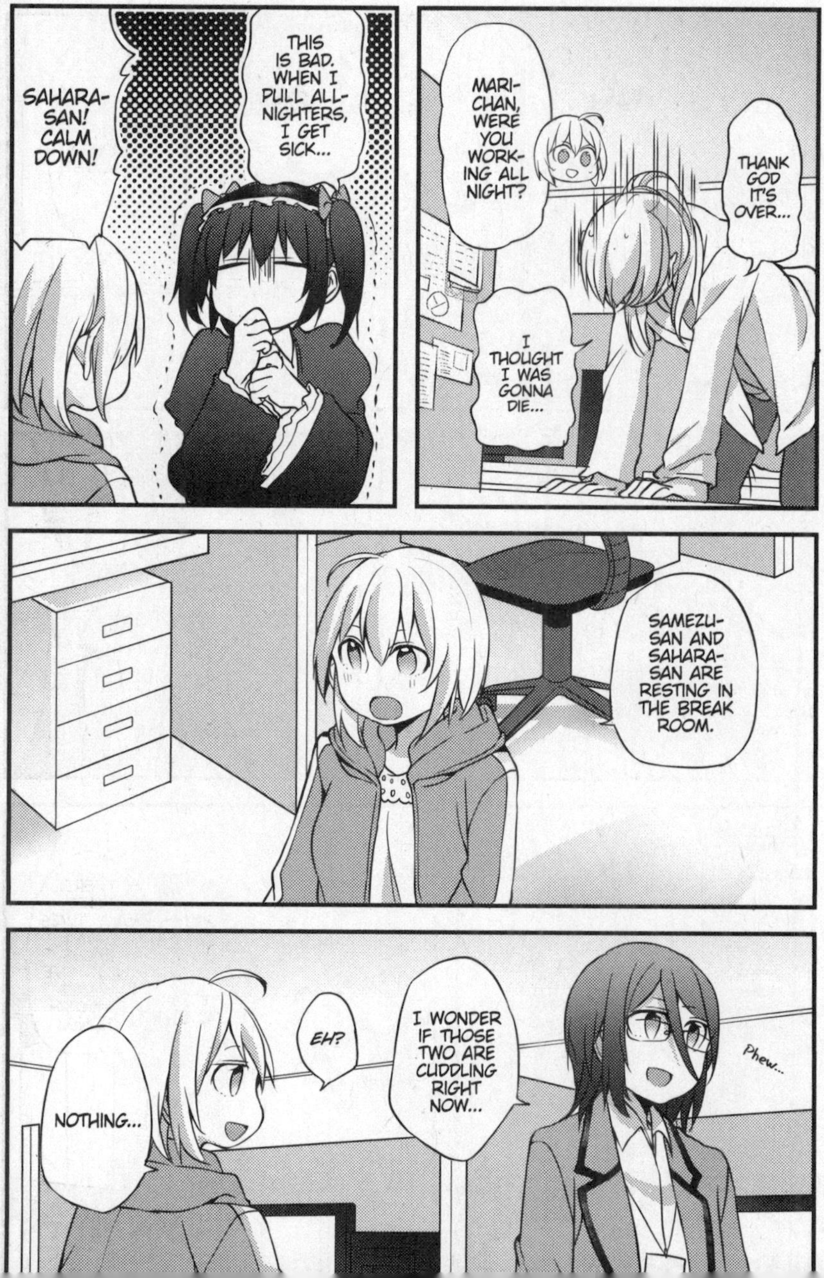
THANK GOD IT'S OVER...
MARI-CHAN, WERE YOU WORKING ALL NIGHT?
I THOUGHT I WAS GONNA DIE...
THIS IS BAD. WHEN I PULL ALL-NIGHTERS, I GET SICK...
SAHARA-SAN! CALM DOWN!
SAMEZU-SAN AND SAHARA-SAN ARE RESTING IN THE BREAK ROOM.
Phew...
I WONDER IF THOSE TWO ARE CUDDLING RIGHT NOW...
EH?
NOTHING...

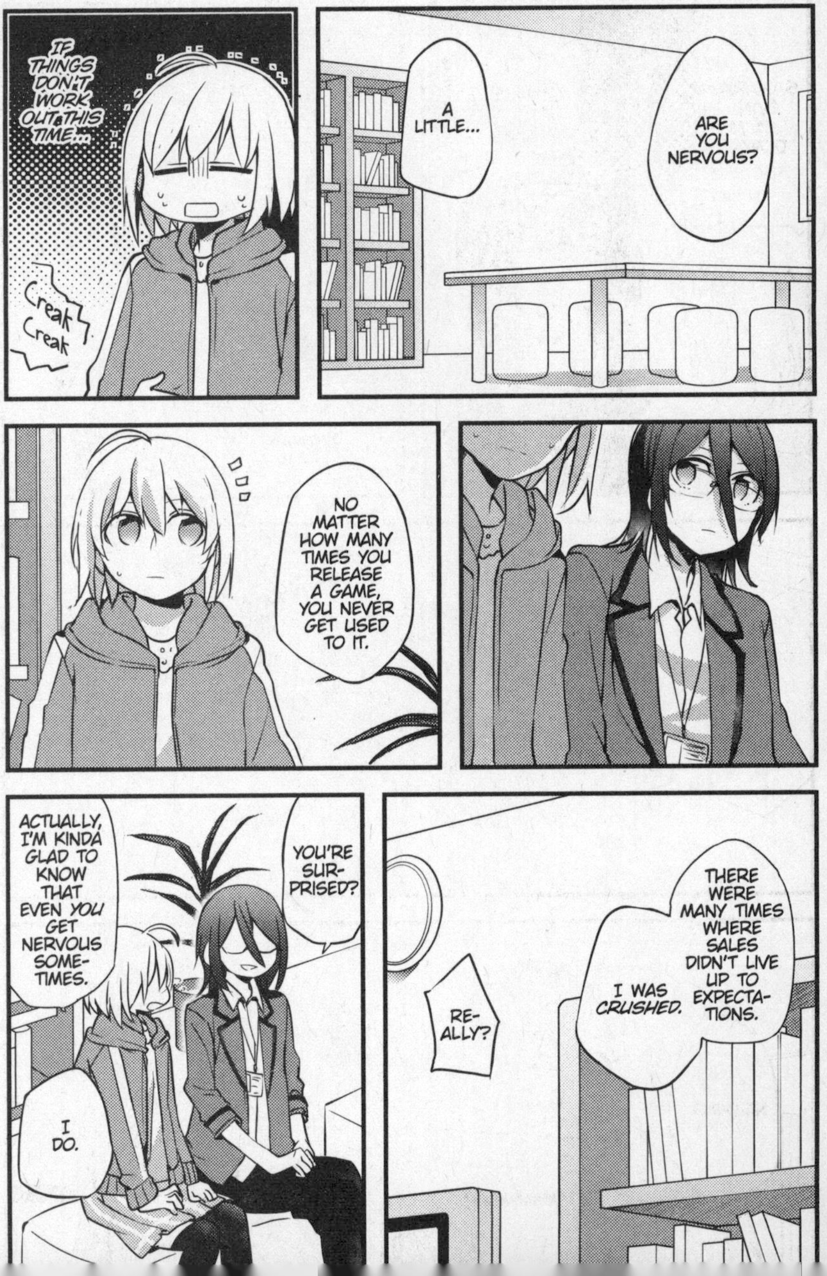
ARE YOU NERVOUS?
A LITTLE...
IF THINGS DON'T WORK OUT THIS TIME...
Creak Creak
NO MATTER HOW MANY TIMES YOU RELEASE A GAME, YOU NEVER GET USED TO IT.
THERE WERE MANY TIMES WHERE SALES DIDN'T LIVE UP TO EXPECTATIONS.
I WAS CRUSHED.
REALLY?
YOU'RE SURPRISED?
ACTUALLY, I'M KINDA GLAD TO KNOW THAT EVEN YOU GET NERVOUS SOMETIMES.
I DO.

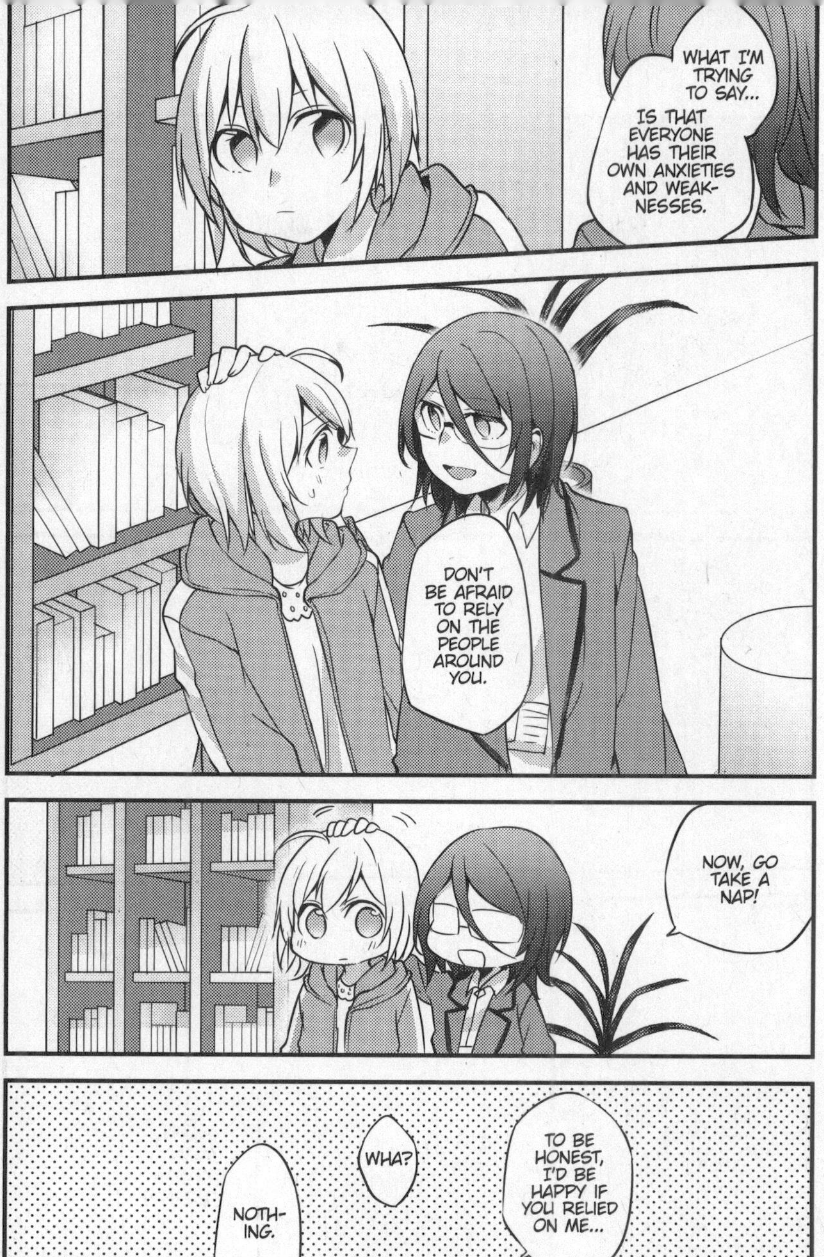
WHAT I'M TRYING TO SAY...
IS THAT EVERYONE HAS THEIR OWN ANXIETIES AND WEAK-NESSES.
DON'T BE AFRAID TO RELY ON THE PEOPLE AROUND YOU.
NOW, GO TAKE A NAP!
TO BE HONEST, I'D BE HAPPY IF YOU RELIED ON ME...
WHA?
NOTH-ING.

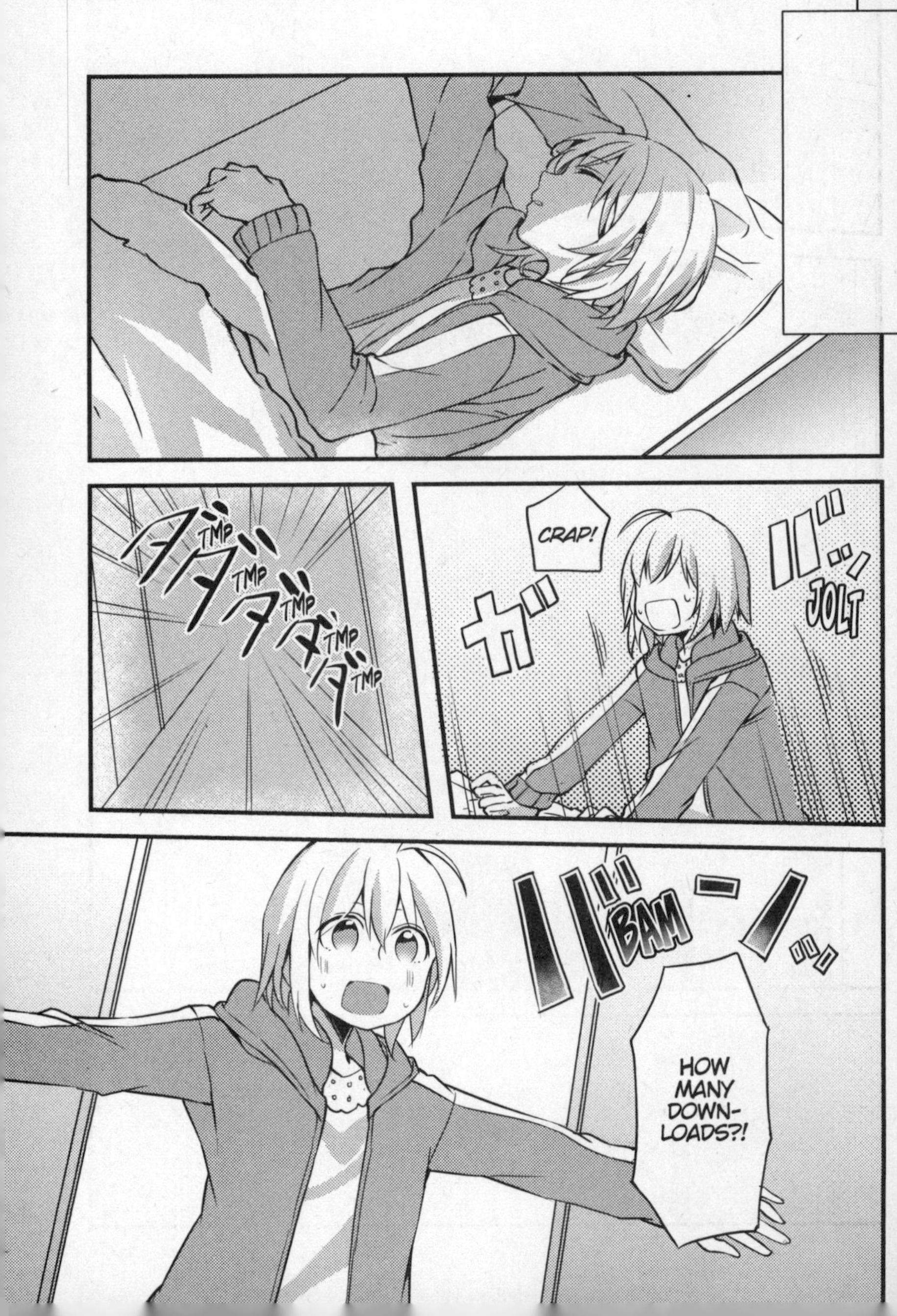
CRAP!
JOLT
TMP TMP TMP TMP TMP
BAM
HOW MANY DOWN-LOADS?!

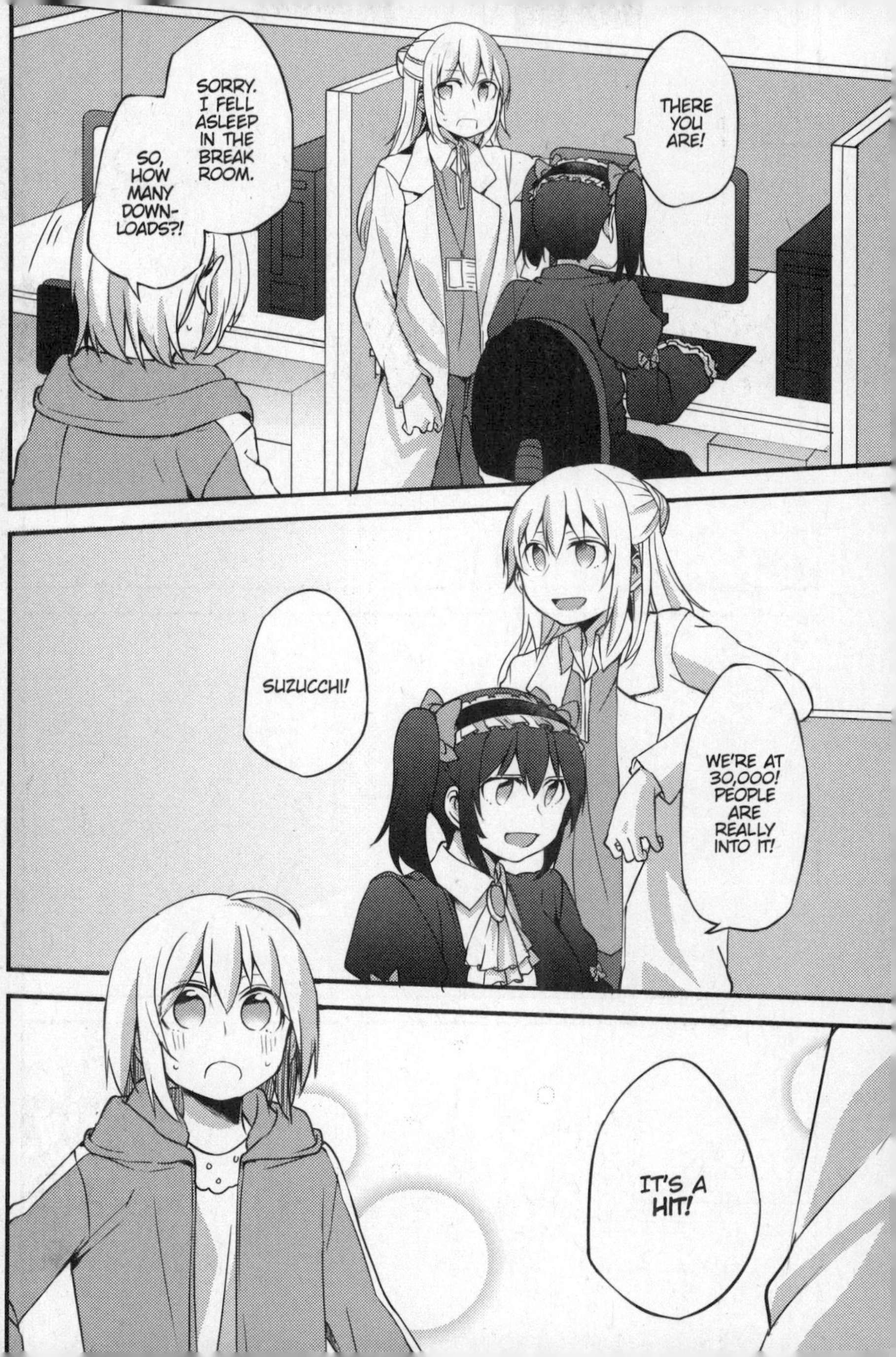
THERE YOU ARE!
SORRY. I FELL ASLEEP IN THE BREAK ROOM.
SO, HOW MANY DOWN-LOADS?!
WE'RE AT 30,000! PEOPLE ARE REALLY INTO IT!
SUZUCCHI!
IT'S A HIT!

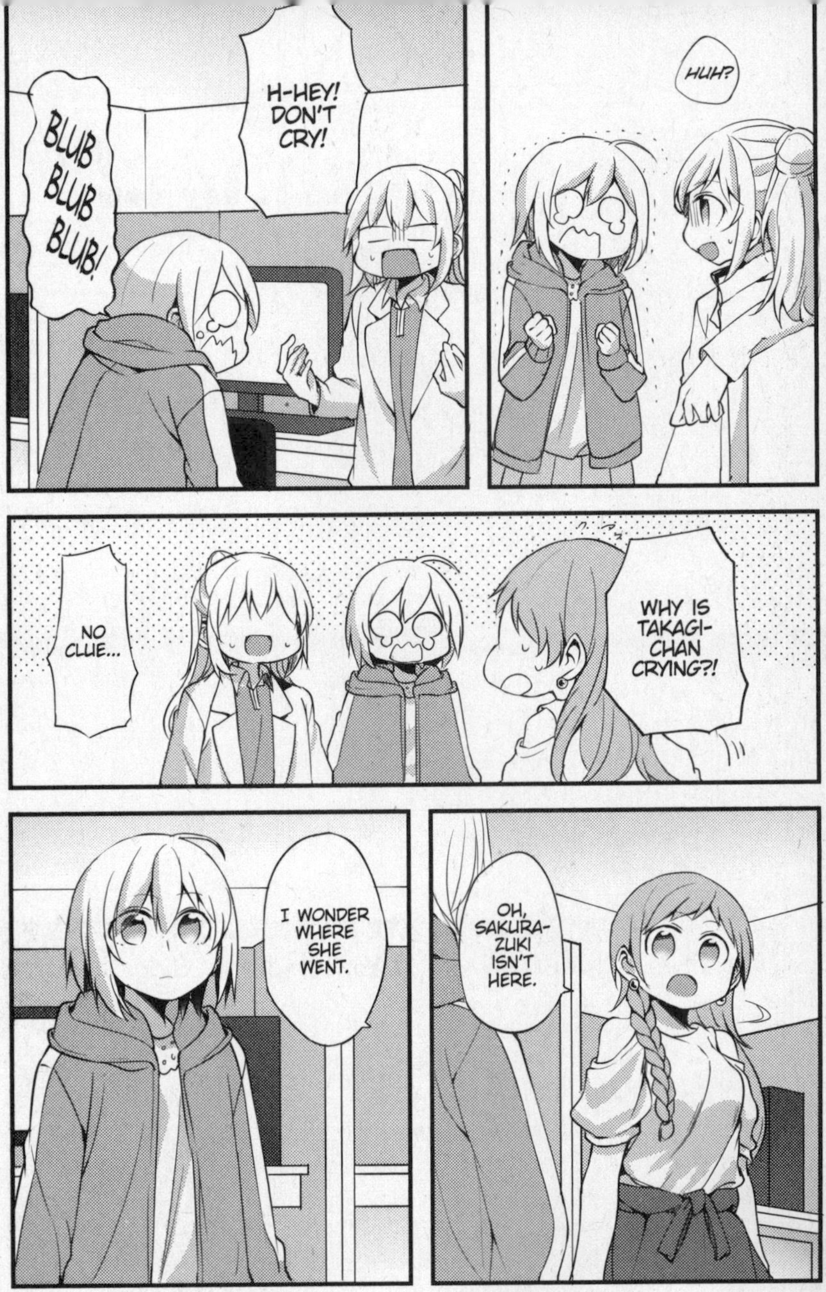
HUH?
H-HEY! DON'T CRY!
BLUB BLUB BLUB!
WHY IS TAKAGI-CHAN CRYING?!
NO CLUE...
OH, SAKURA-ZUKI ISN'T HERE.
I WONDER WHERE SHE WENT.

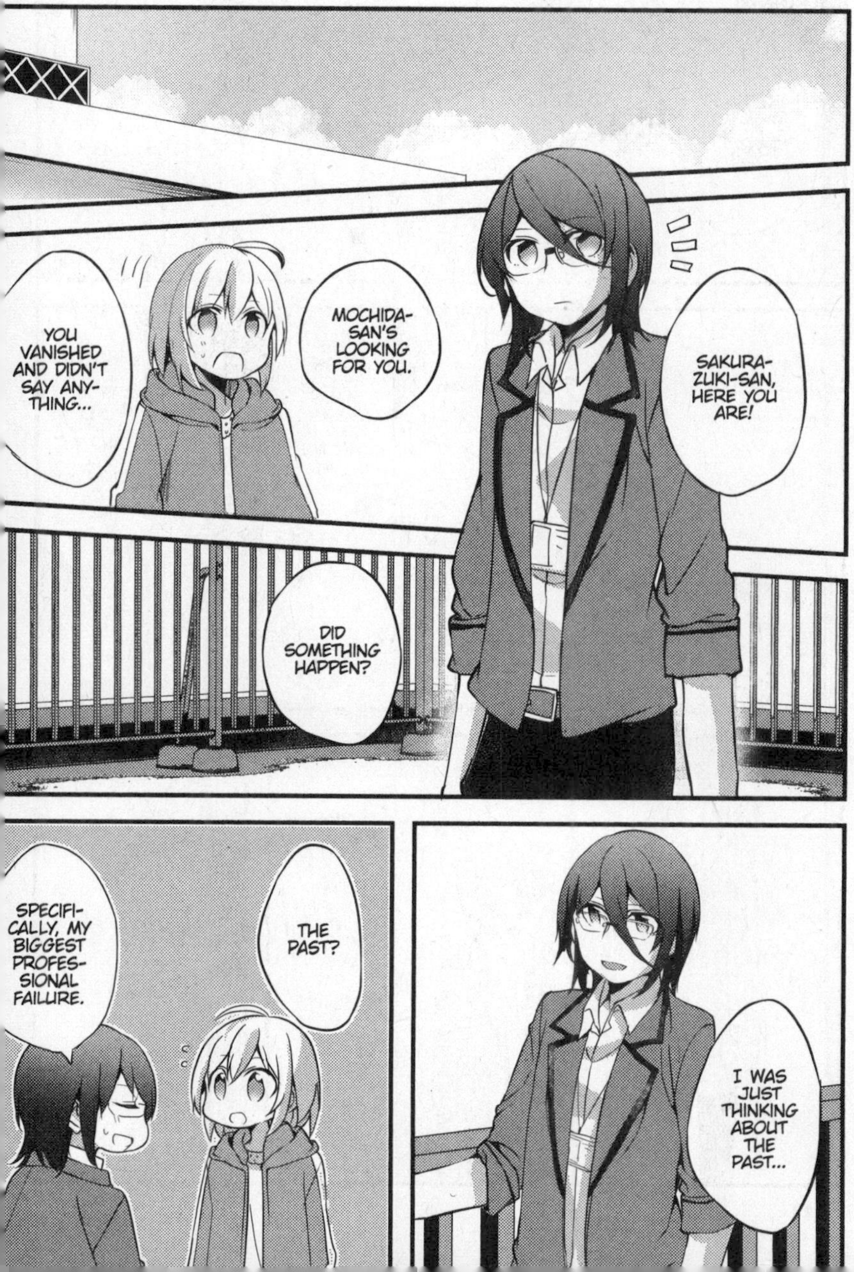
SAKURA-ZUKI-SAN, HERE YOU ARE!
MOCHIDA-SAN'S LOOKING FOR YOU.
YOU VANISHED AND DIDN'T SAY ANY-THING...
DID SOMETHING HAPPEN?
I WAS JUST THINKING ABOUT THE PAST...
THE PAST?
SPECIFI-CALLY, MY BIGGEST PROFES-SIONAL FAILURE.

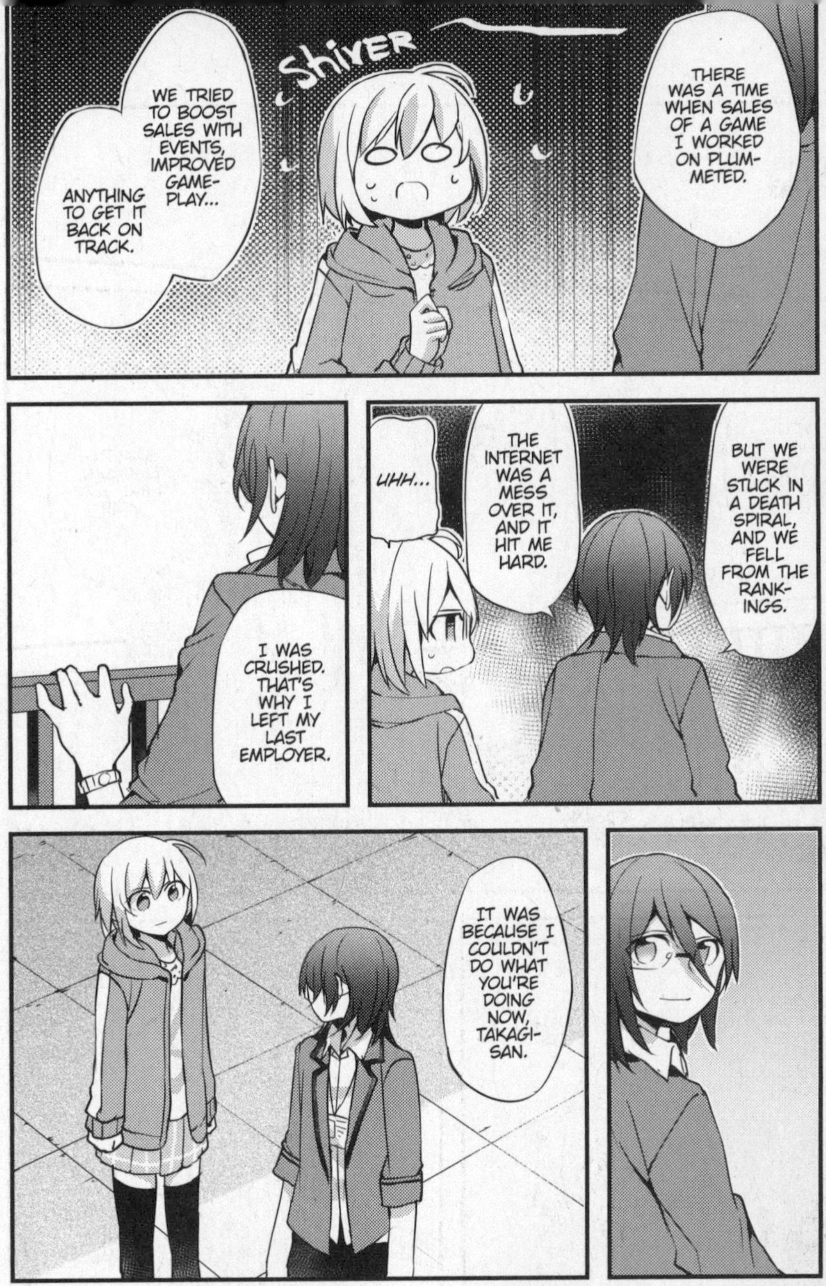
THERE WAS A TIME WHEN SALES OF A GAME I WORKED ON PLUM- METED.
WE TRIED TO BOOST SALES WITH EVENTS, IMPROVED GAME- PLAY...
ANYTHING TO GET IT BACK ON TRACK.
SHIVER
BUT WE WERE STUCK IN A DEATH SPIRAL, AND WE FELL FROM THE RANK- INGS.
THE INTERNET WAS A MESS OVER IT, AND IT HIT ME HARD.
UHH...
I WAS CRUSHED. THAT'S WHY I LEFT MY LAST EMPLOYER.
IT WAS BECAUSE I COULDN'T DO WHAT YOU'RE DOING NOW, TAKAGI- SAN.

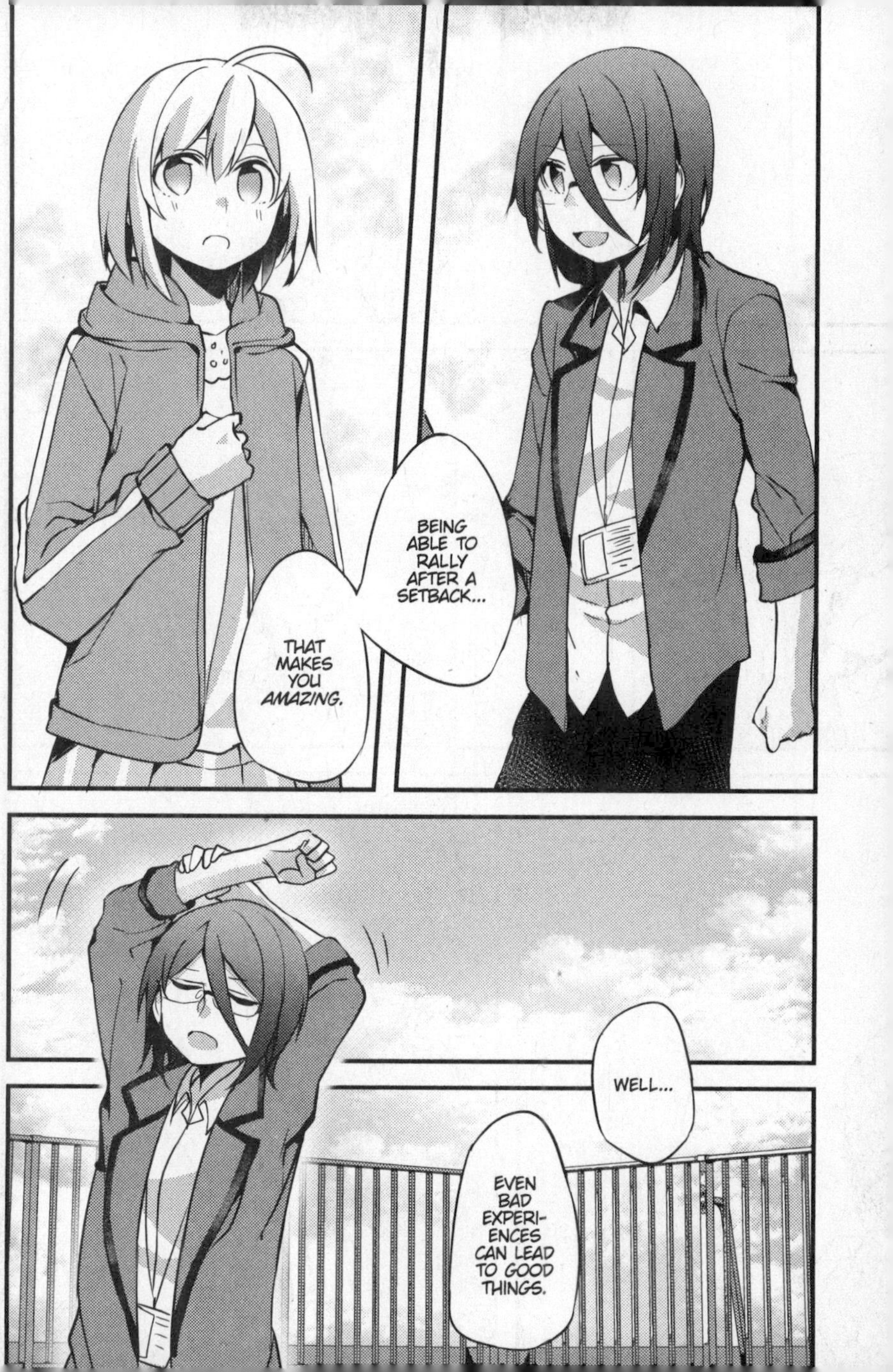
BEING ABLE TO RALLY AFTER A SETBACK...
THAT MAKES YOU AMAZING.
WELL...
EVEN BAD EXPERI- ENCES CAN LEAD TO GOOD THINGS.

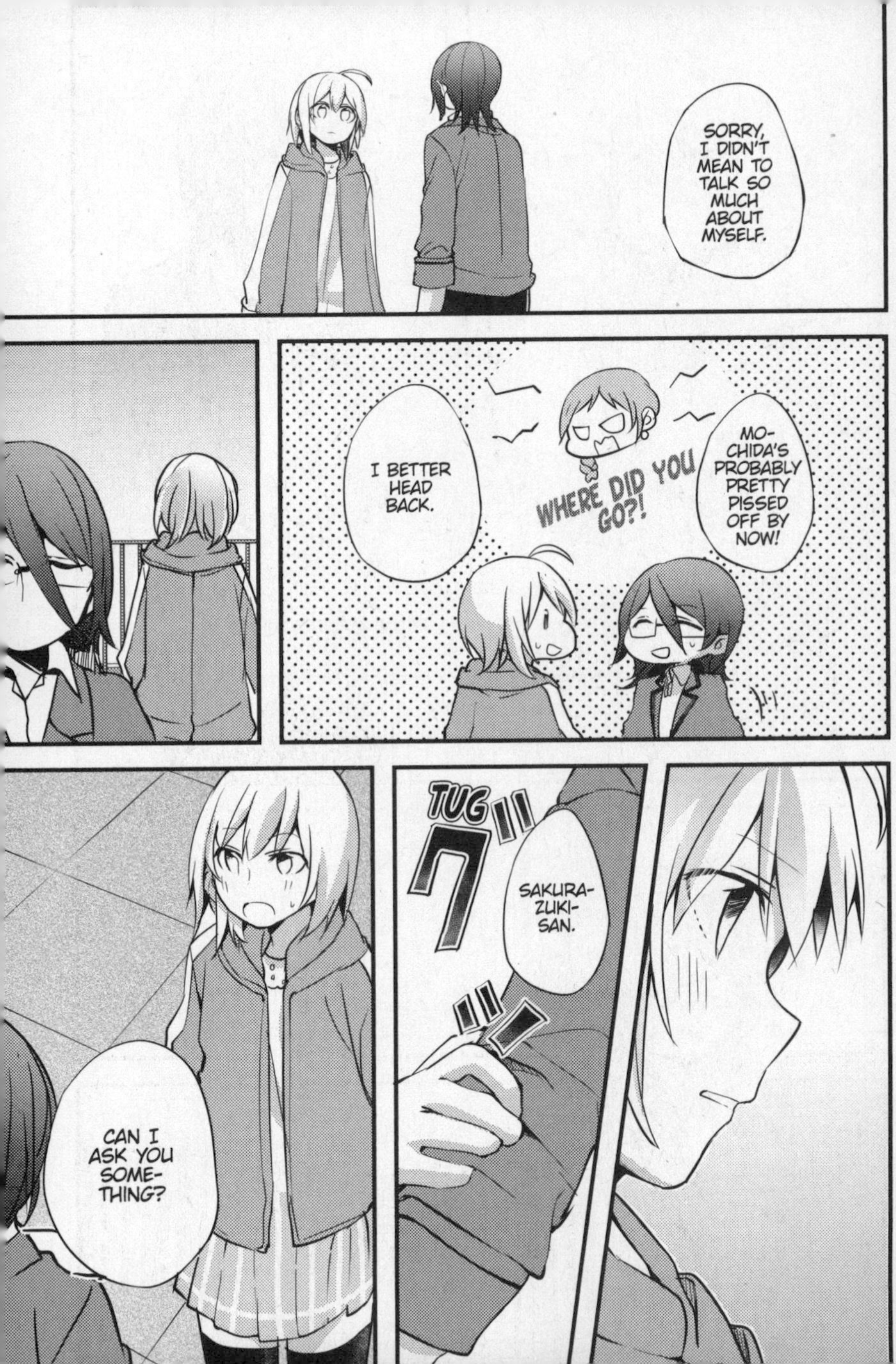
SORRY, I DIDN'T MEAN TO TALK SO MUCH ABOUT MYSELF.
MO-CHIDA'S PROBABLY PRETTY PISSED OFF BY NOW!
WHERE DID YOU GO?!
I BETTER HEAD BACK.
TUG
SAKURA-ZUKI-SAN.
CAN I ASK YOU SOME-THING?

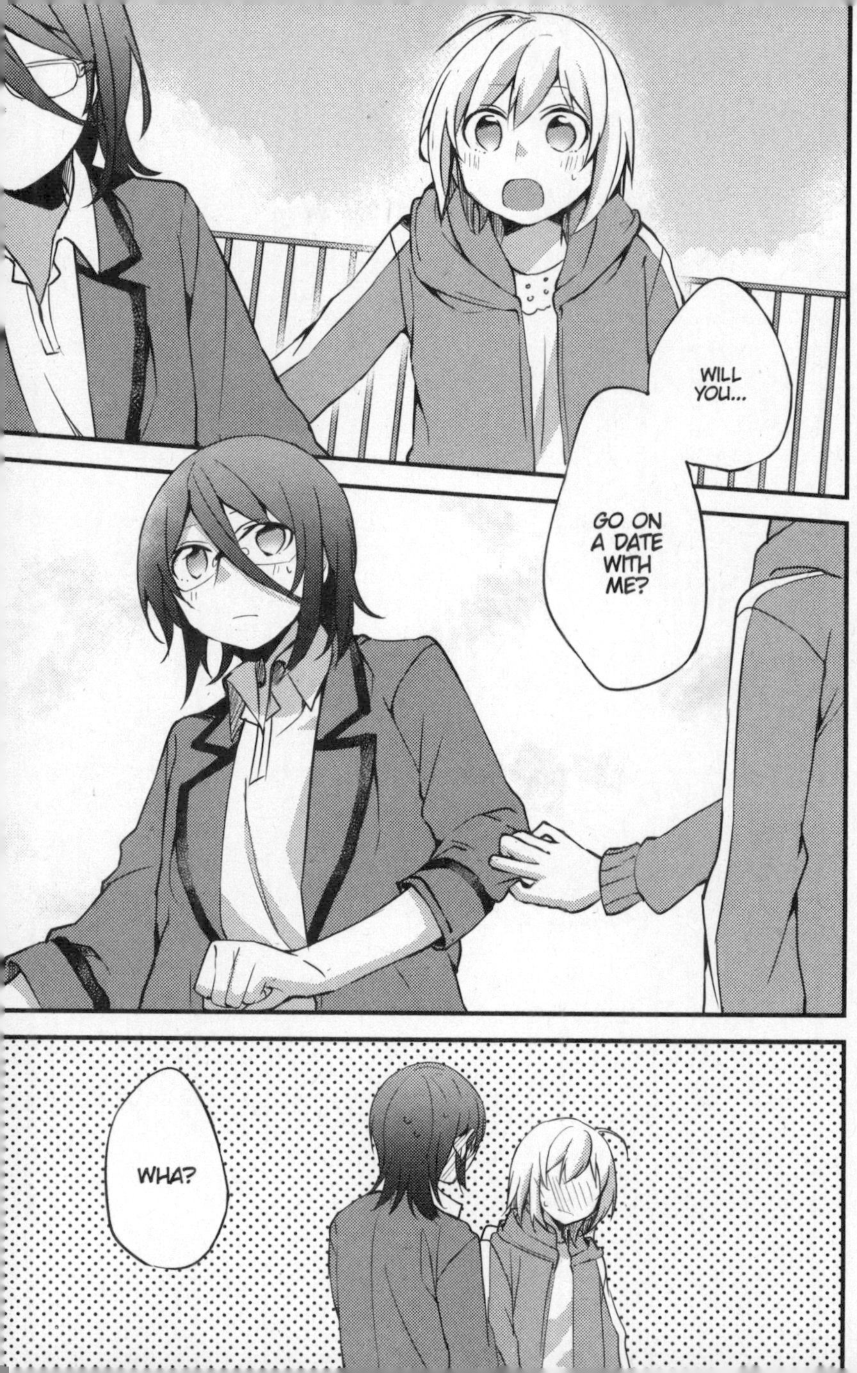
WILL YOU...
GO ON A DATE WITH ME?
WHA?

Now Loading...!

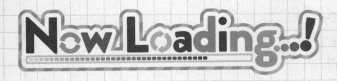

Now Loading...!

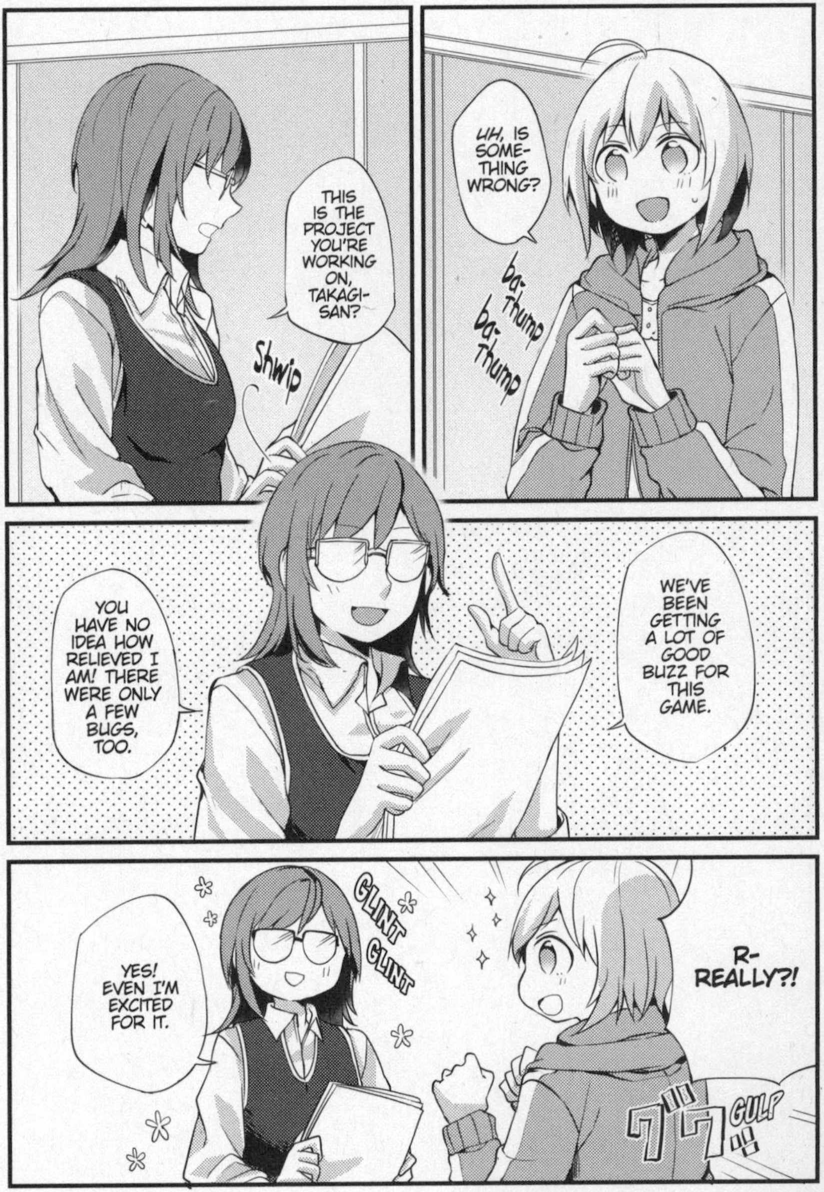
UH, IS SOMETHING WRONG?
ba-thump ba-thump
THIS IS THE PROJECT YOU'RE WORKING ON, TAKAGI-SAN?
Shwip
WE'VE BEEN GETTING A LOT OF GOOD BUZZ FOR THIS GAME.
YOU HAVE NO IDEA HOW RELIEVED I AM! THERE WERE ONLY A FEW BUGS, TOO.
R-REALLY?!
GLINT GLINT
YES! EVEN I'M EXCITED FOR IT.
GULP

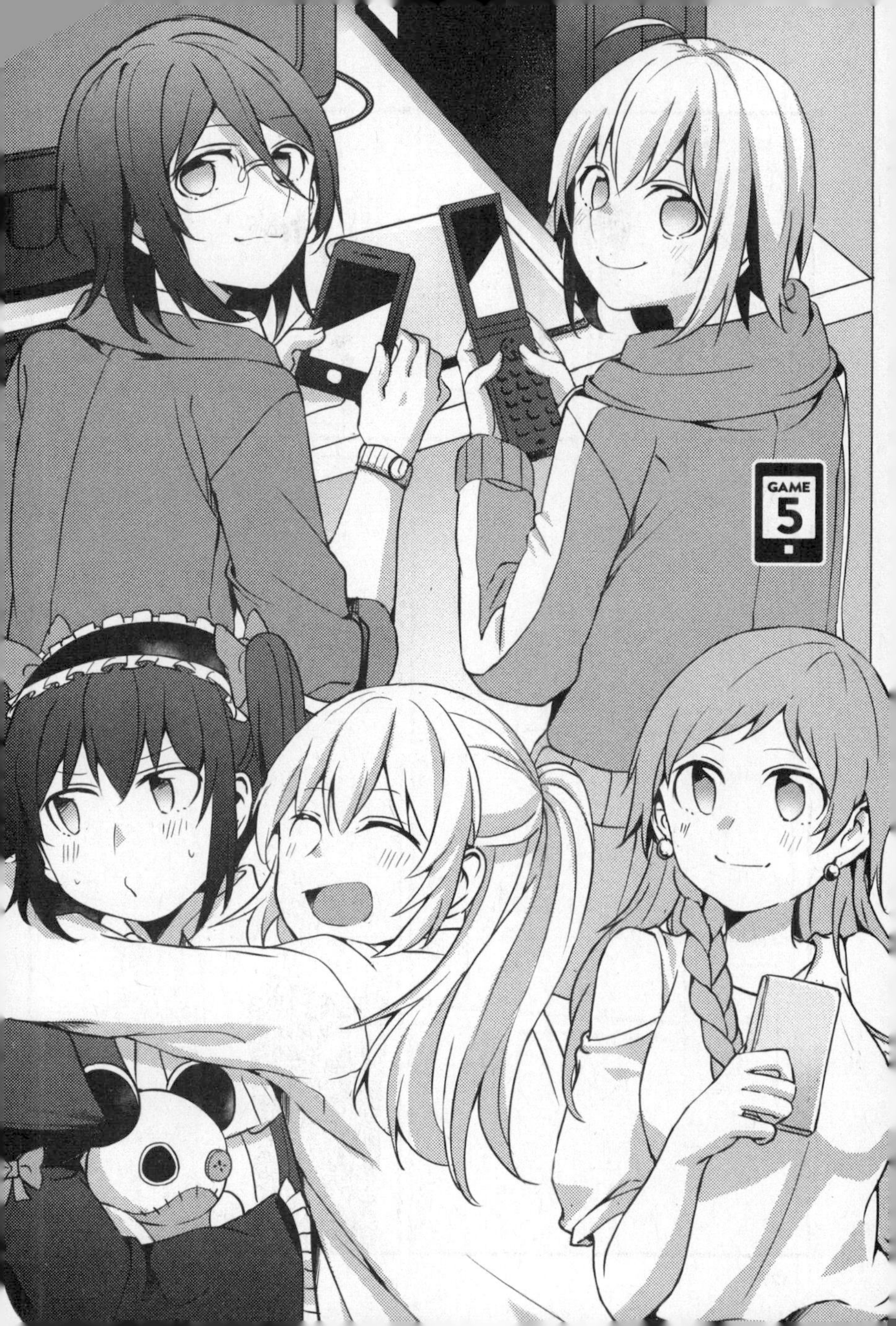
GAME
5

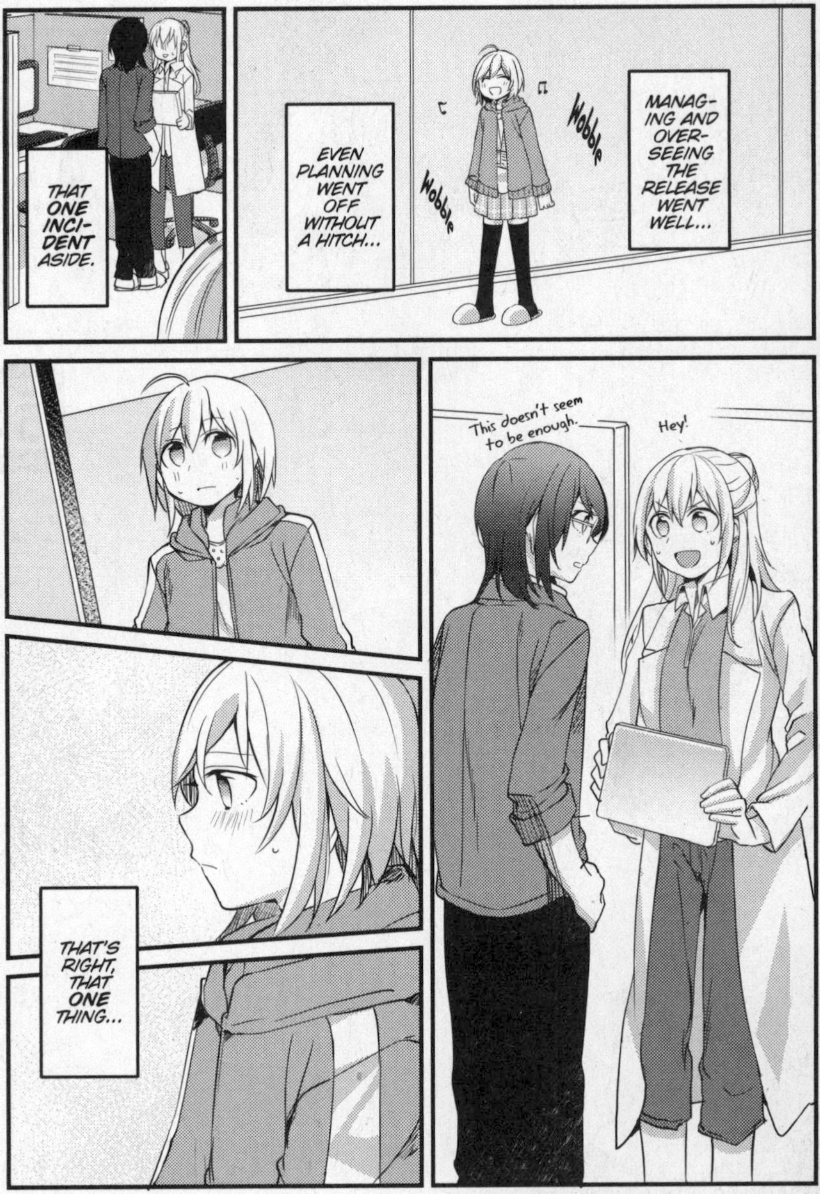
MANAG-ING AND OVER-SEEING THE RELEASE WENT WELL...
Wobble
Wobble
EVEN PLANNING WENT OFF WITHOUT A HITCH...
THAT ONE INCI-DENT ASIDE.
Hey!
This doesn't seem to be enough.
THAT'S RIGHT, THAT ONE THING...

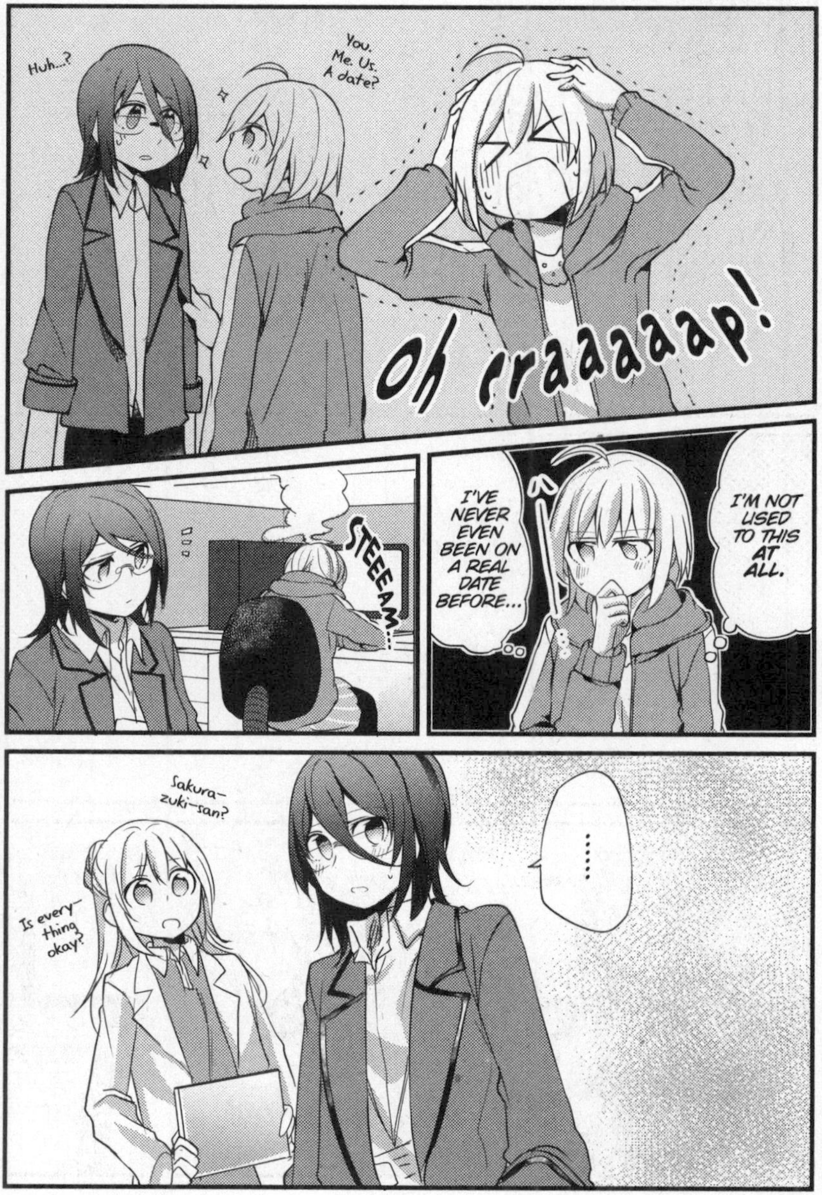
You. Me. Us. A date?
Oh craaaaaap!
Huh...?
I'M NOT USED TO THIS AT ALL.
I'VE NEVER EVEN BEEN ON A REAL DATE BEFORE...
STEEEAM...
......
Sakura-zuki-san?
Is every-thing okay?

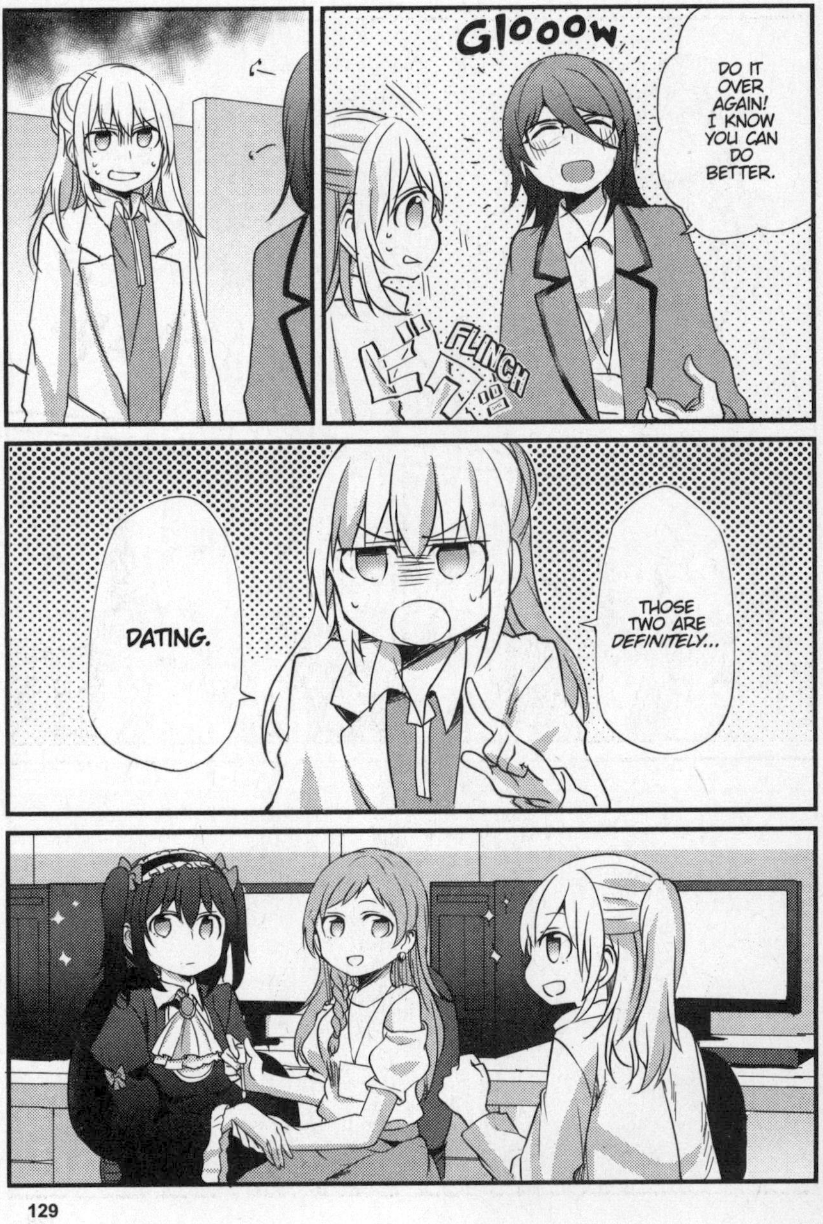
GlOOOW
DO IT OVER AGAIN! I KNOW YOU CAN DO BETTER.
FLINCH
THOSE TWO ARE DEFINITELY...
DATING.

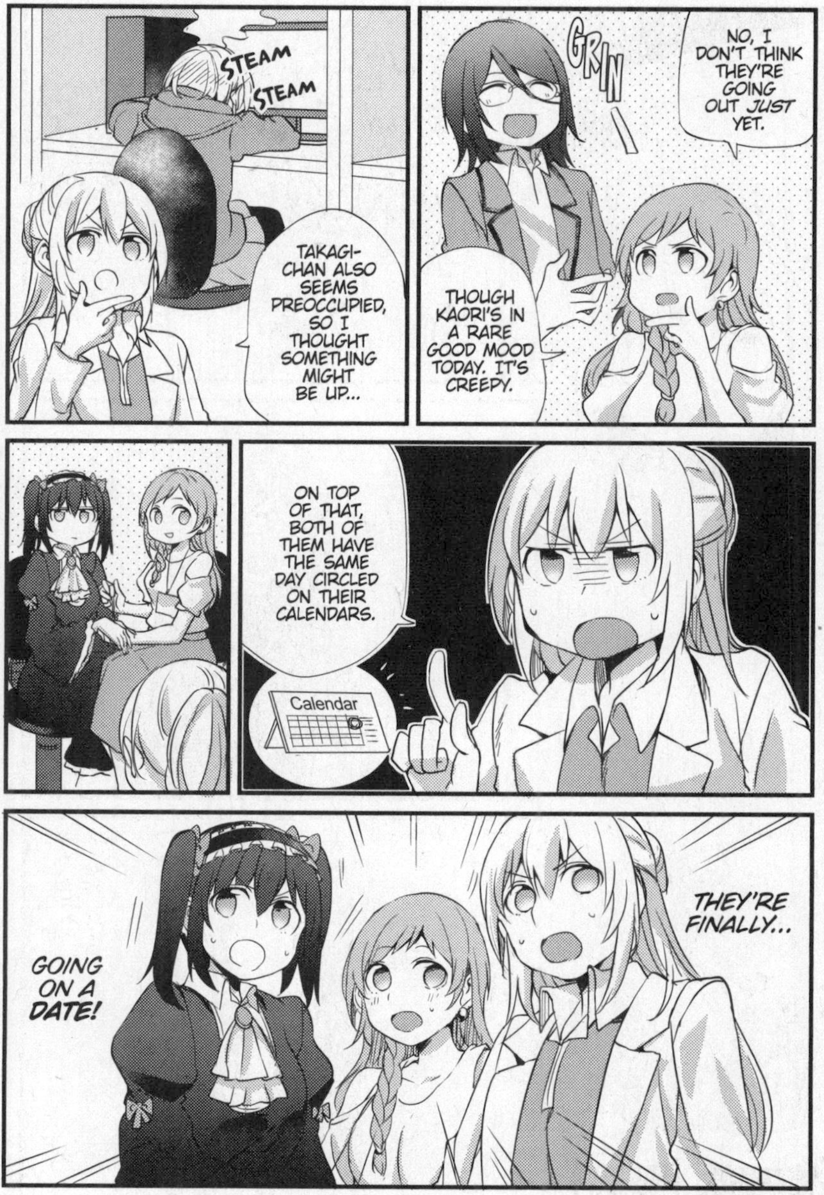
NO, I DON'T THINK THEY'RE GOING OUT *JUST* YET.
GRIN
THOUGH KAORI'S IN A RARE GOOD MOOD TODAY. IT'S CREEPY.
STEAM
STEAM
TAKAGI-CHAN ALSO SEEMS PREOCCUPIED, SO I THOUGHT SOMETHING MIGHT BE UP...
ON TOP OF THAT, BOTH OF THEM HAVE THE SAME DAY CIRCLED ON THEIR CALENDARS.
Calendar
THEY'RE FINALLY...
GOING ON A DATE!

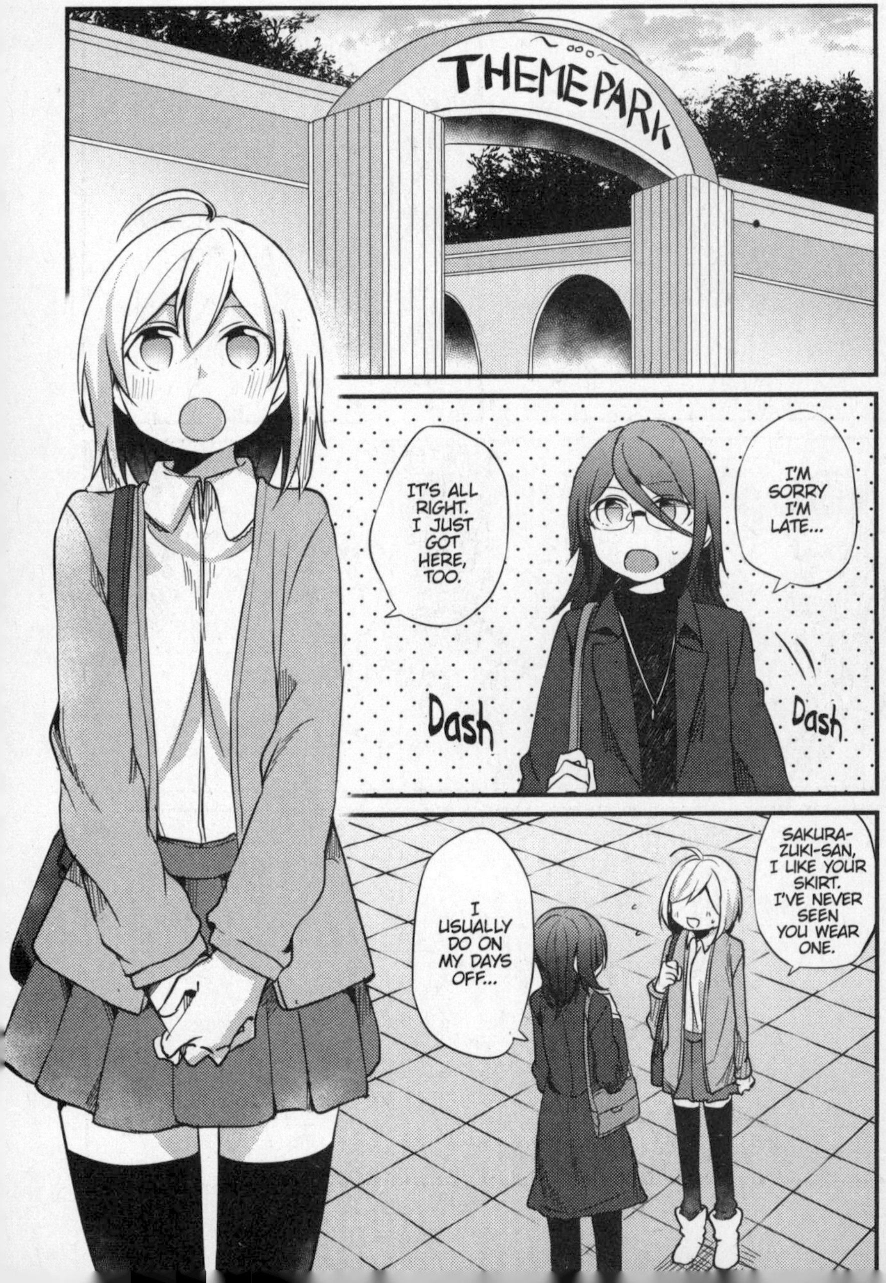
THEME PARK
I'M SORRY I'M LATE...
IT'S ALL RIGHT. I JUST GOT HERE, TOO.
Dash
Dash
SAKURAZUKI-SAN, I LIKE YOUR SKIRT. I'VE NEVER SEEN YOU WEAR ONE.
I USUALLY DO ON MY DAYS OFF...

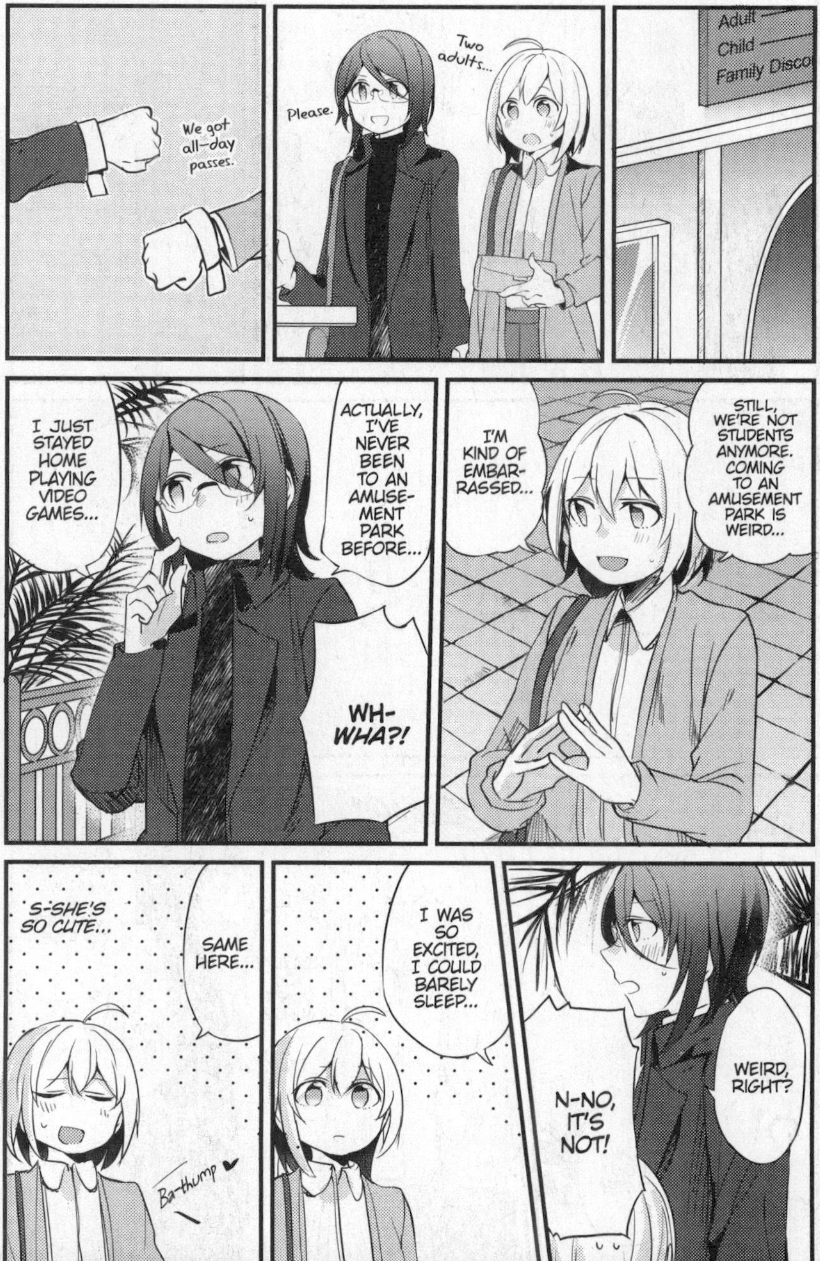

Adult
Child
Family Disco
Two adults...
Please.
We got all-day passes.
STILL, WE'RE NOT STUDENTS ANYMORE. COMING TO AN AMUSEMENT PARK IS WEIRD...
I'M KIND OF EMBARRASSED...
ACTUALLY, I'VE NEVER BEEN TO AN AMUSEMENT PARK BEFORE...
I JUST STAYED HOME PLAYING VIDEO GAMES...
WH-WHA?!
WEIRD, RIGHT?
N-NO, IT'S NOT!
I WAS SO EXCITED, I COULD BARELY SLEEP...
SAME HERE...
S-SHE'S SO CUTE...
Ba-thump

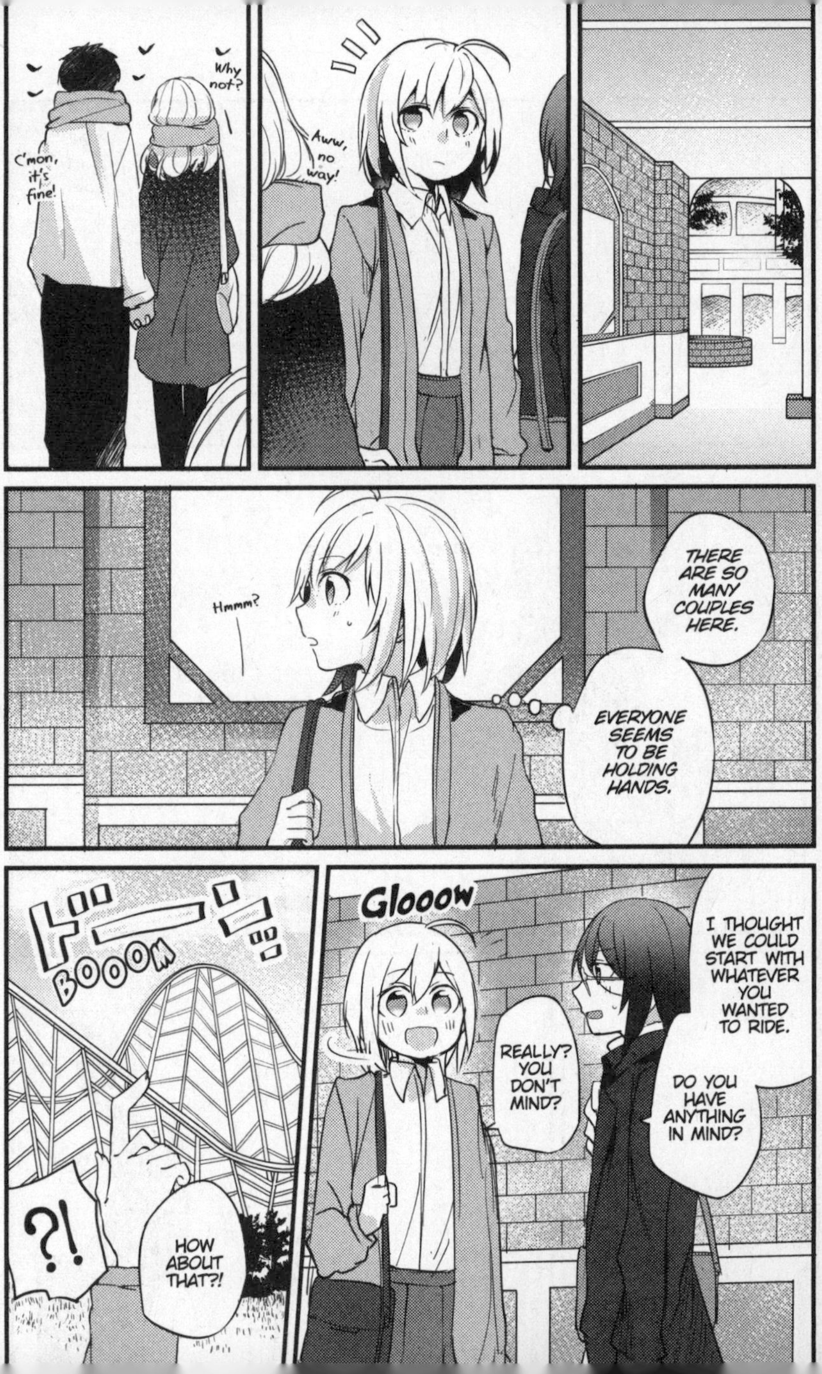
Aww, no way!
Why not?
C'mon, it's fine!
THERE ARE SO MANY COUPLES HERE.
EVERYONE SEEMS TO BE HOLDING HANDS.
Hmmm?
Glooow
I THOUGHT WE COULD START WITH WHATEVER YOU WANTED TO RIDE.
DO YOU HAVE ANYTHING IN MIND?
REALLY? YOU DON'T MIND?
ドーーン
BOOOM
HOW ABOUT THAT?!
?!

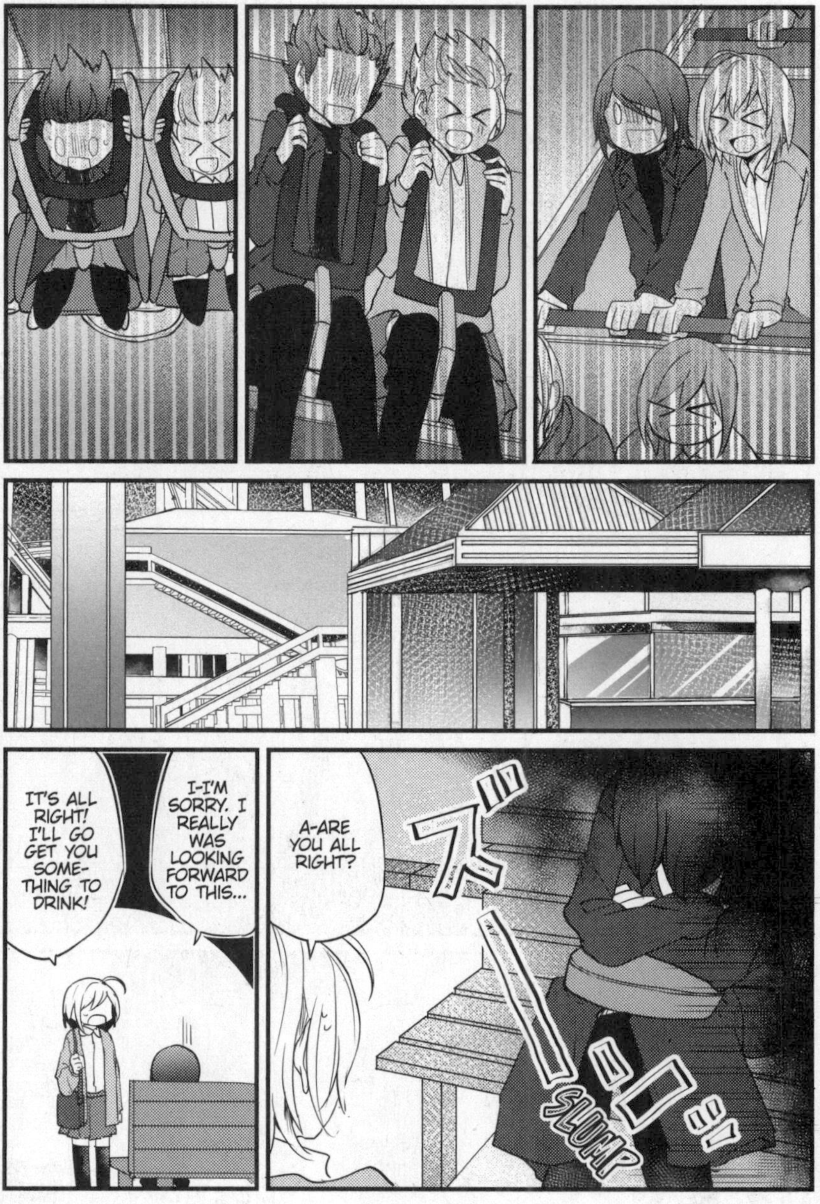
A-ARE YOU ALL RIGHT?
SLUMP
I-I'M SORRY. I REALLY WAS LOOKING FORWARD TO THIS...
IT'S ALL RIGHT! I'LL GO GET YOU SOME-THING TO DRINK!

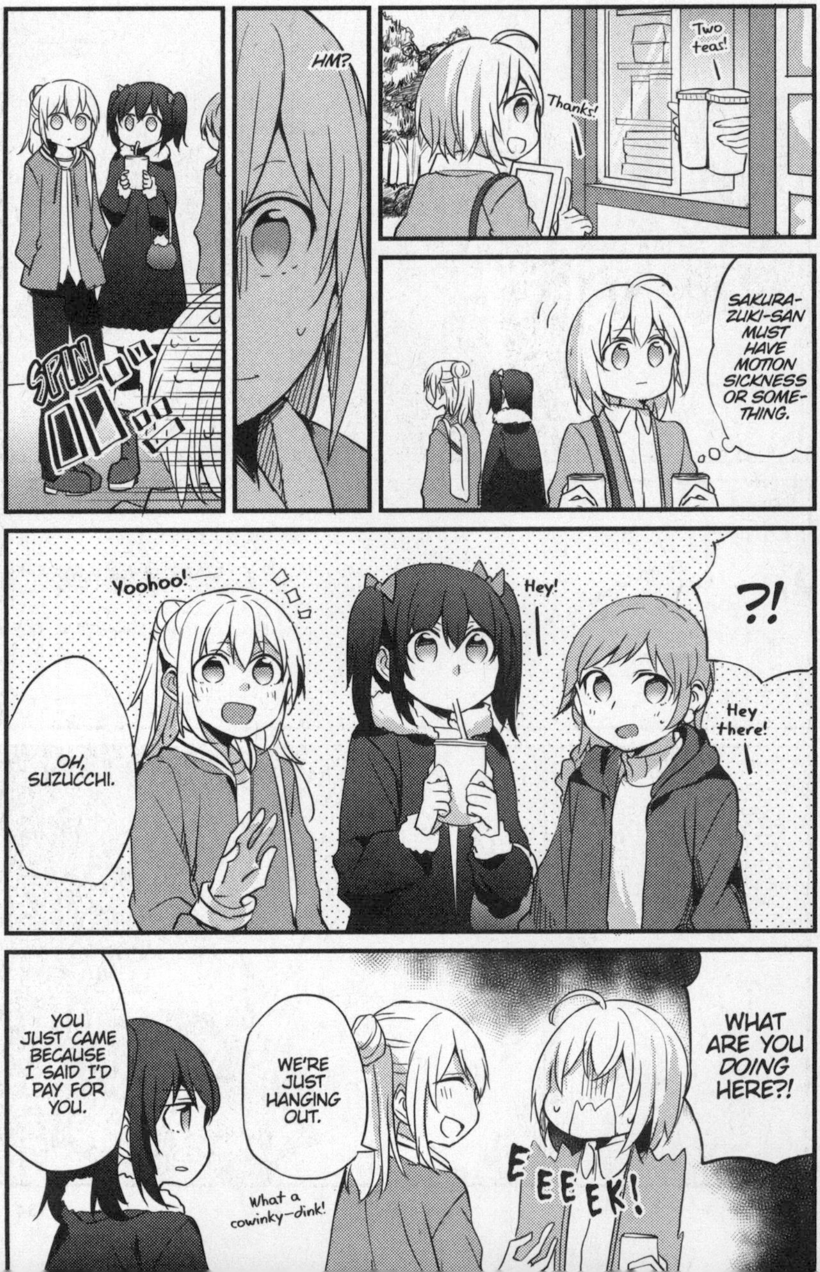
Two teas!
Thanks!
SAKURAZUKI-SAN MUST HAVE MOTION SICKNESS OR SOMETHING.
HM?
SPIN
?!
Hey there!
Hey!
Yoohoo!
OH, SUZUCCHI.
WHAT ARE YOU DOING HERE?!
EEEEK!
WE'RE JUST HANGING OUT.
What a cowinky-dink!
YOU JUST CAME BECAUSE I SAID I'D PAY FOR YOU.

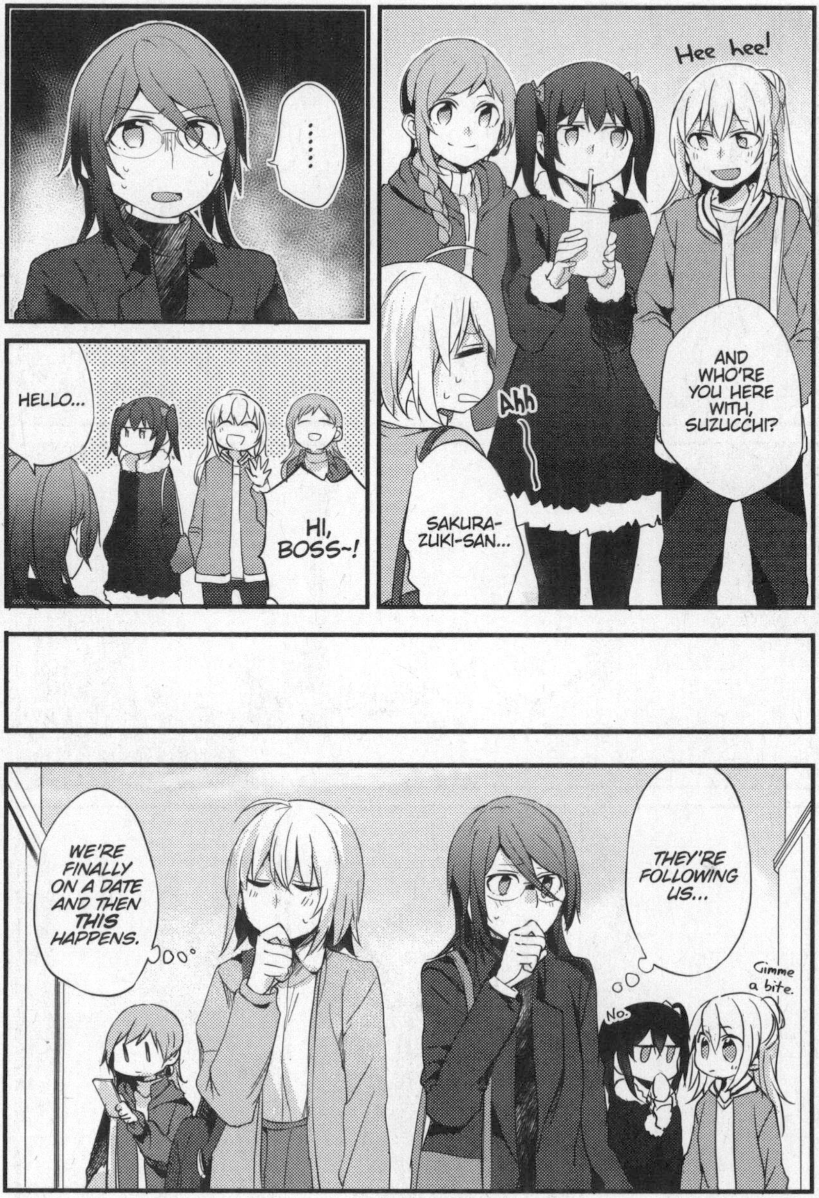
Hee hee!
AND WHO'RE YOU HERE WITH, SUZUCCHI?
Ahh
SAKURA-ZUKI-SAN...
......
HELLO...
HI, BOSS~!
THEY'RE FOLLOWING US...
Gimme a bite.
No.
WE'RE FINALLY ON A DATE AND THEN THIS HAPPENS.

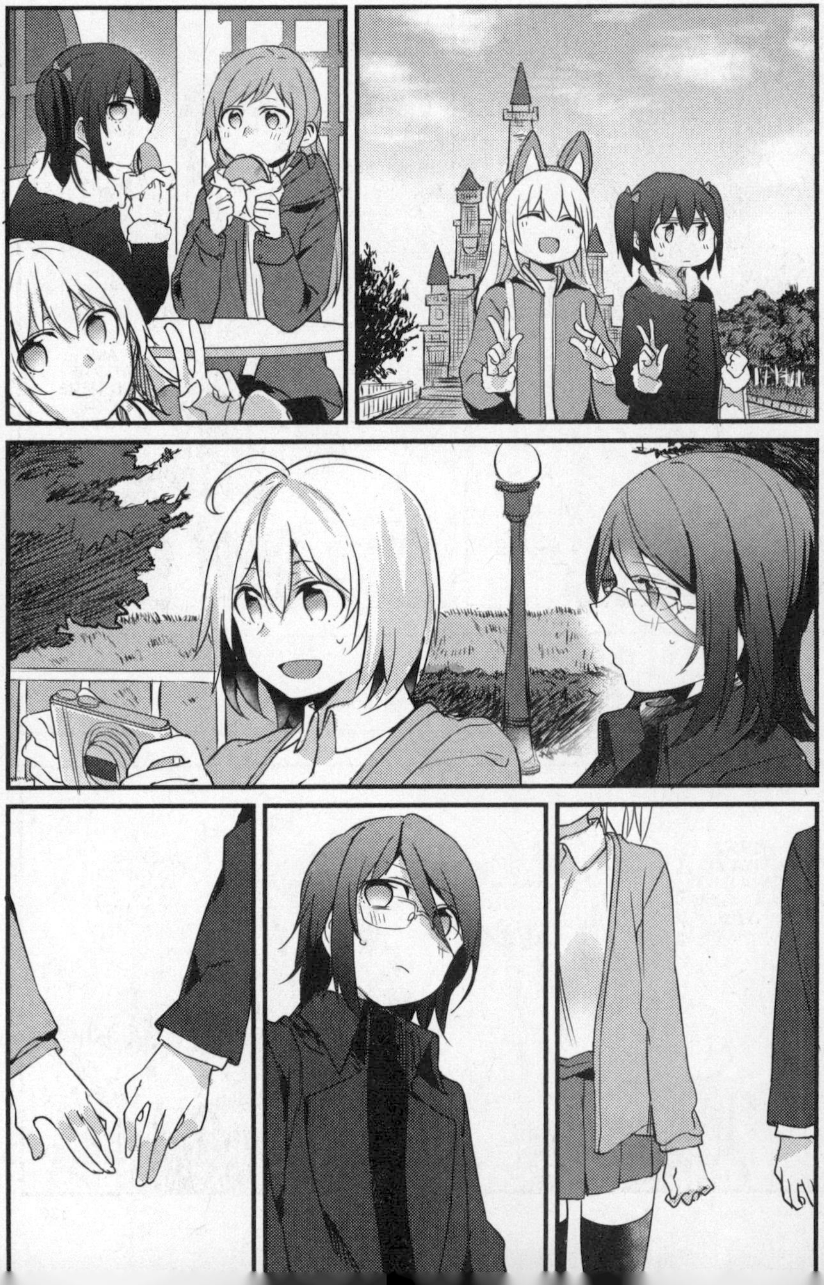

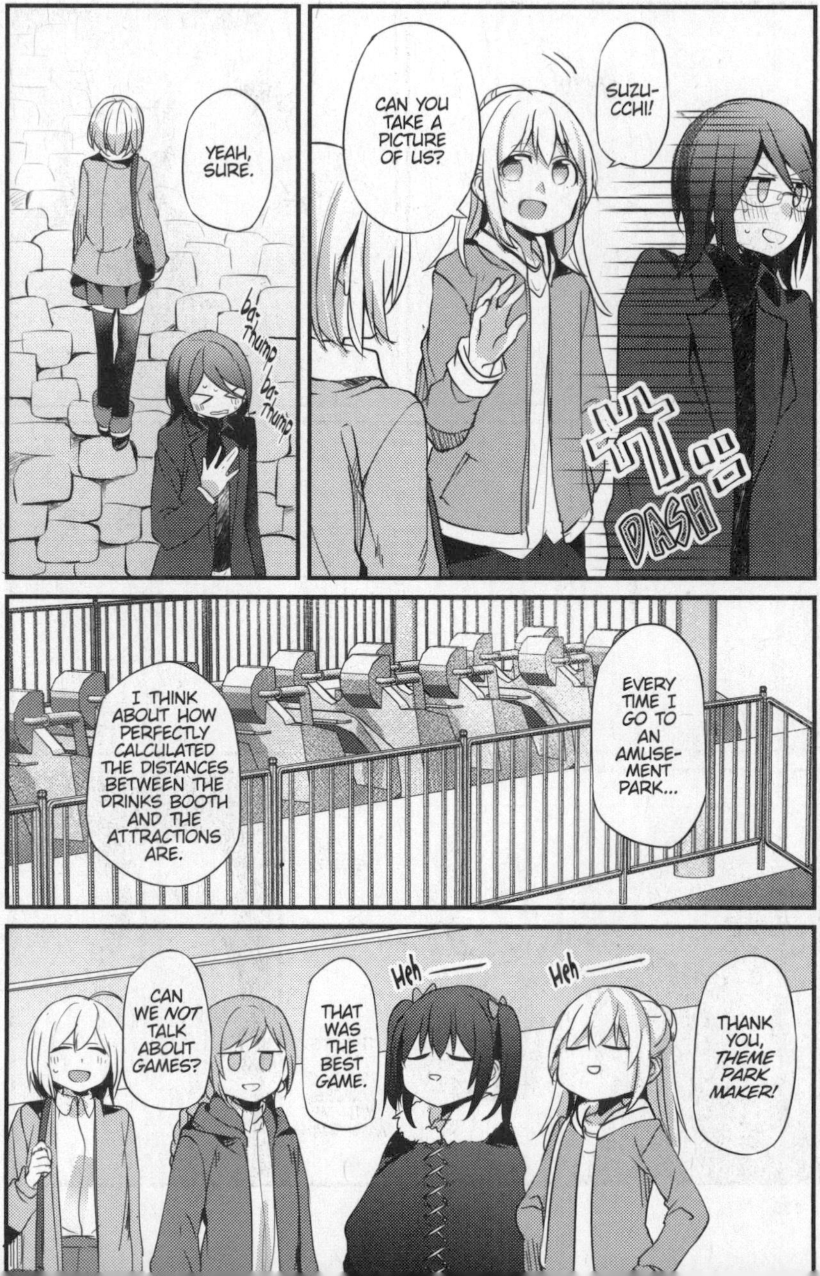
SUZU-CCHI!
CAN YOU TAKE A PICTURE OF US?
DASH
YEAH, SURE.
ba-thump ba-thump
EVERY TIME I GO TO AN AMUSEMENT PARK...
I THINK ABOUT HOW PERFECTLY CALCULATED THE DISTANCES BETWEEN THE DRINKS BOOTH AND THE ATTRACTIONS ARE.
Heh——
THANK YOU, *THEME PARK MAKER!*
Heh——
THAT WAS THE BEST GAME.
CAN WE *NOT* TALK ABOUT GAMES?

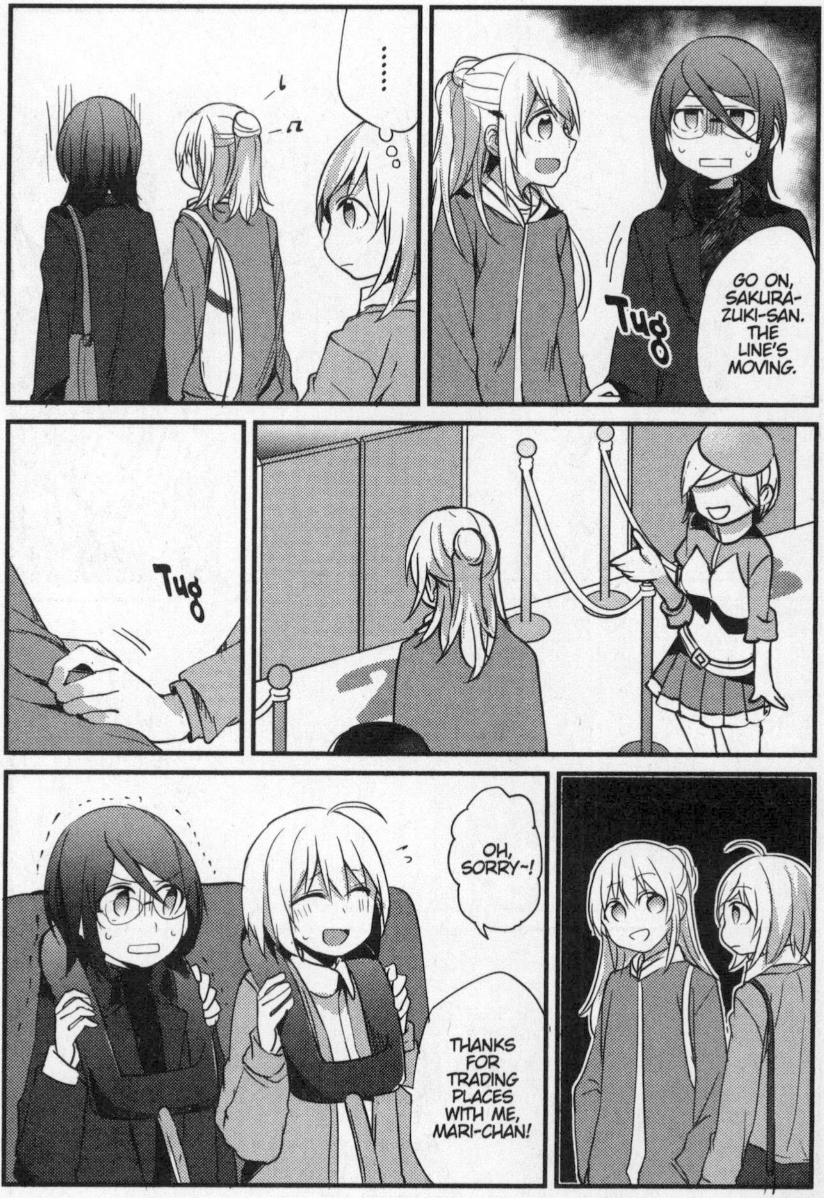
Tug
GO ON, SAKURA-ZUKI-SAN. THE LINE'S MOVING.
......
Tug
OH, SORRY~!
THANKS FOR TRADING PLACES WITH ME, MARI-CHAN!

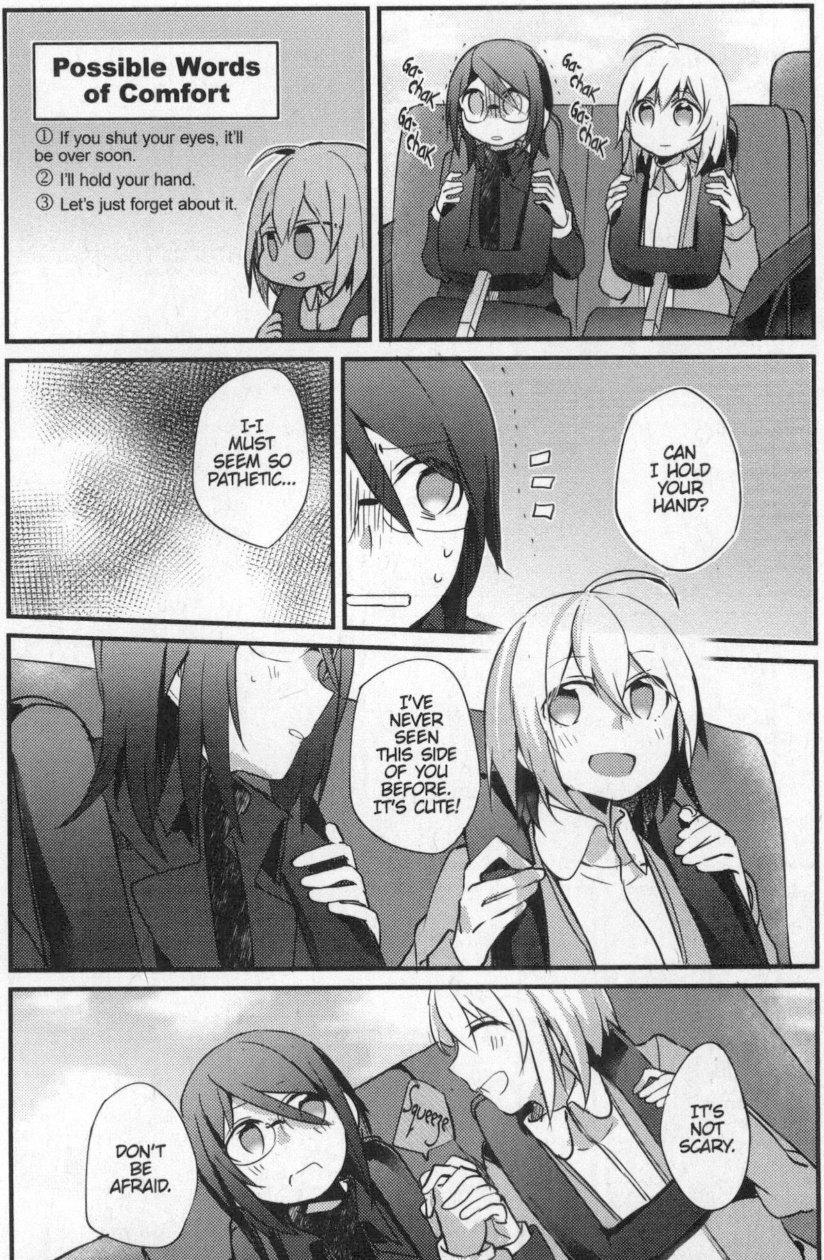
Ga-chak Ga-chak
Ga-chak Ga-chak
Possible Words of Comfort
① If you shut your eyes, it'll be over soon.
② I'll hold your hand.
③ Let's just forget about it.
CAN I HOLD YOUR HAND?
I-I MUST SEEM SO PATHETIC...
I'VE NEVER SEEN THIS SIDE OF YOU BEFORE. IT'S CUTE!
IT'S NOT SCARY.
Squeeze
DON'T BE AFRAID.

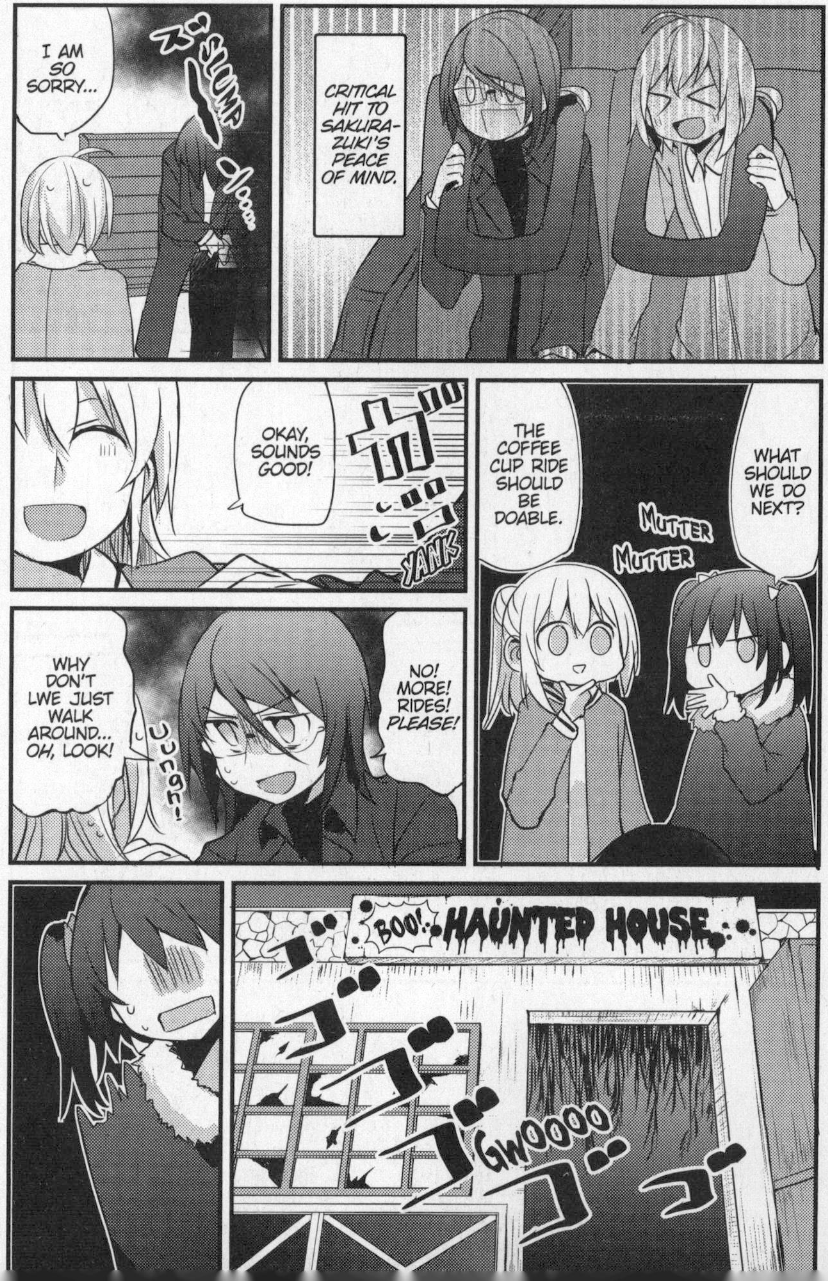
CRITICAL HIT TO SAKURAZUKI'S PEACE OF MIND.
I AM SO SORRY...
SLUMP
WHAT SHOULD WE DO NEXT?
MUTTER
MUTTER
THE COFFEE CUP RIDE SHOULD BE DOABLE.
OKAY, SOUNDS GOOD!
YANK
NO! MORE! RIDES! PLEASE!
Uungh!
WHY DON'T LWE JUST WALK AROUND... OH, LOOK!
BOO!
HAUNTED HOUSE
GWOOOO

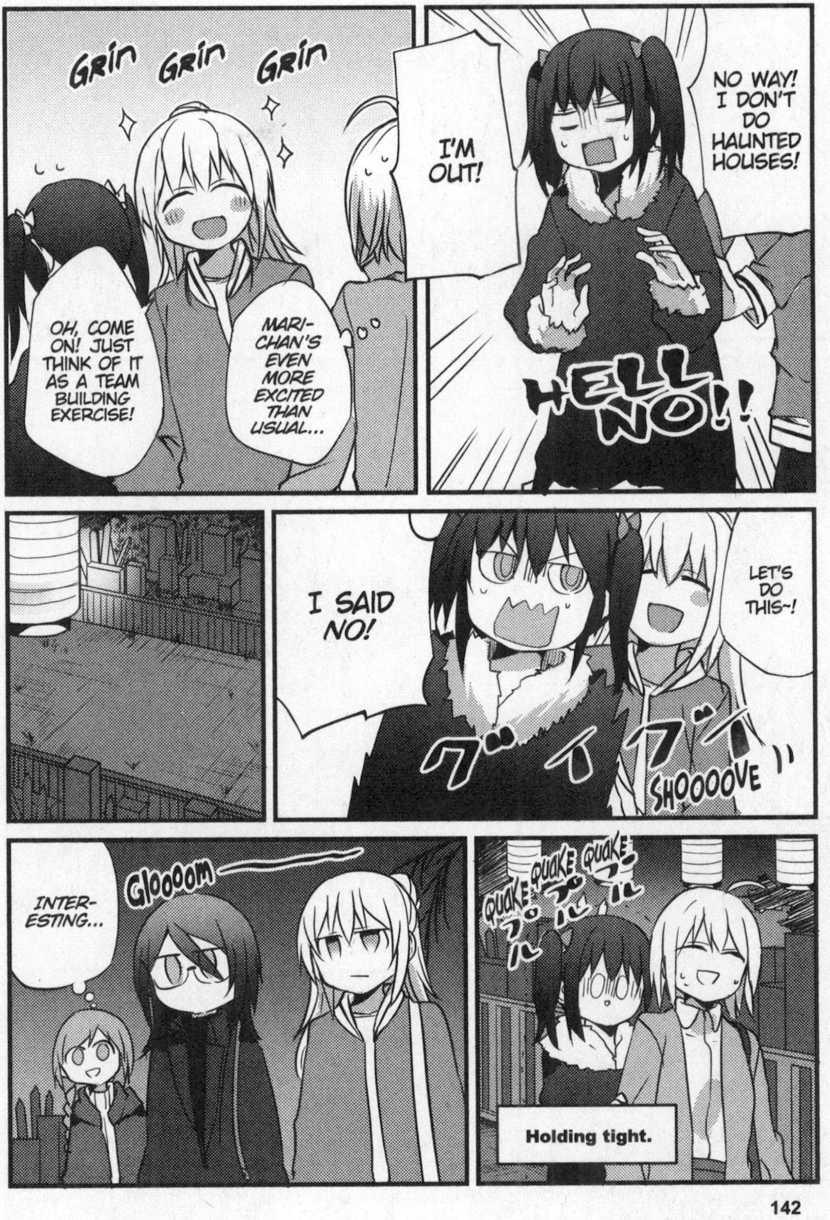

NO WAY! I DON'T DO HAUNTED HOUSES!
I'M OUT!
HELL NO!!
Grin Grin Grin
MARI-CHAN'S EVEN MORE EXCITED THAN USUAL...
OH, COME ON! JUST THINK OF IT AS A TEAM BUILDING EXERCISE!
LET'S DO THIS~!
I SAID NO!
SHOOOOVE
QUAKE QUAKE QUAKE
Holding tight.
Gloooom
INTER-ESTING...

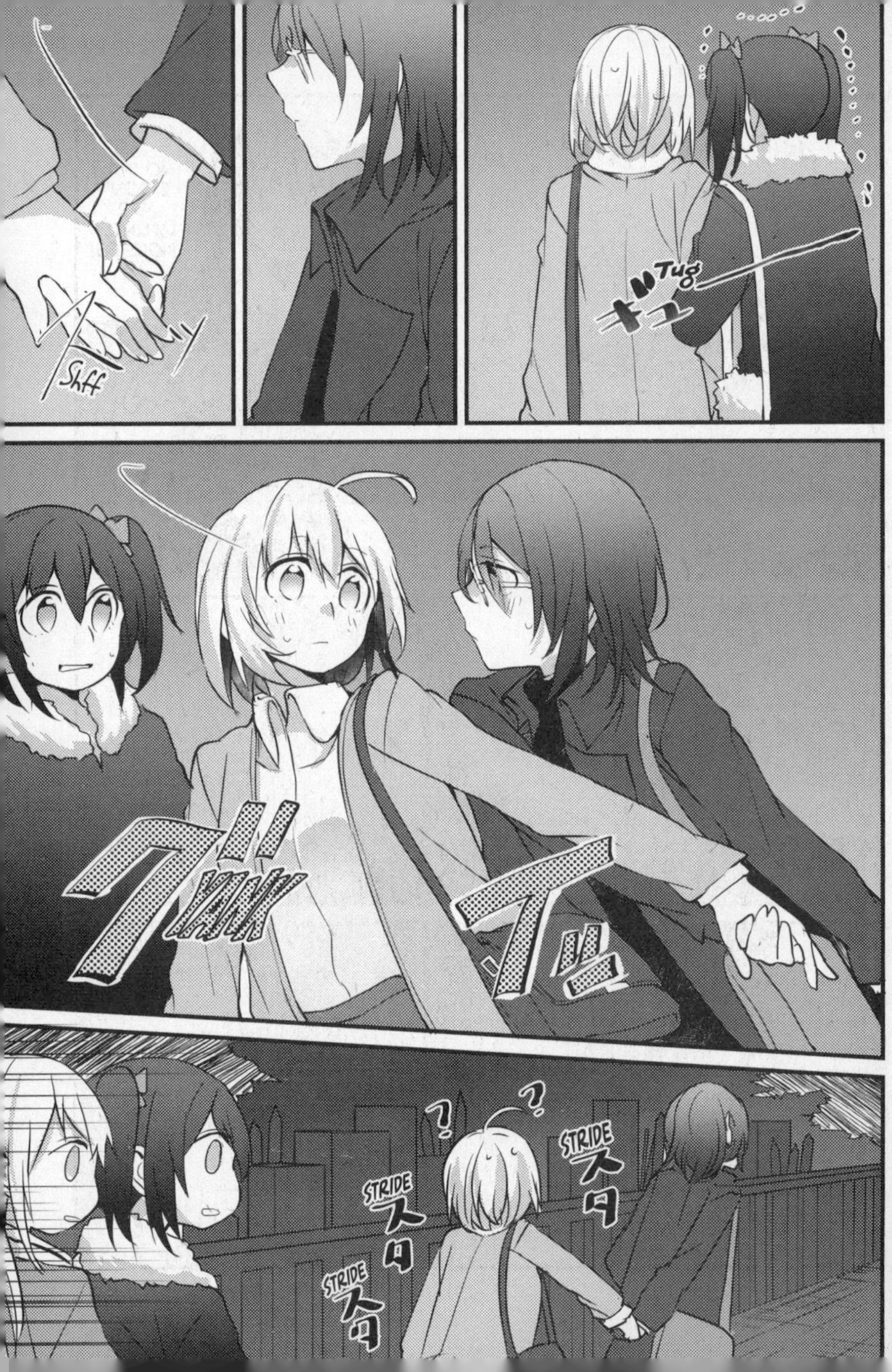
Tug
Shff
STRIDE
STRIDE
STRIDE

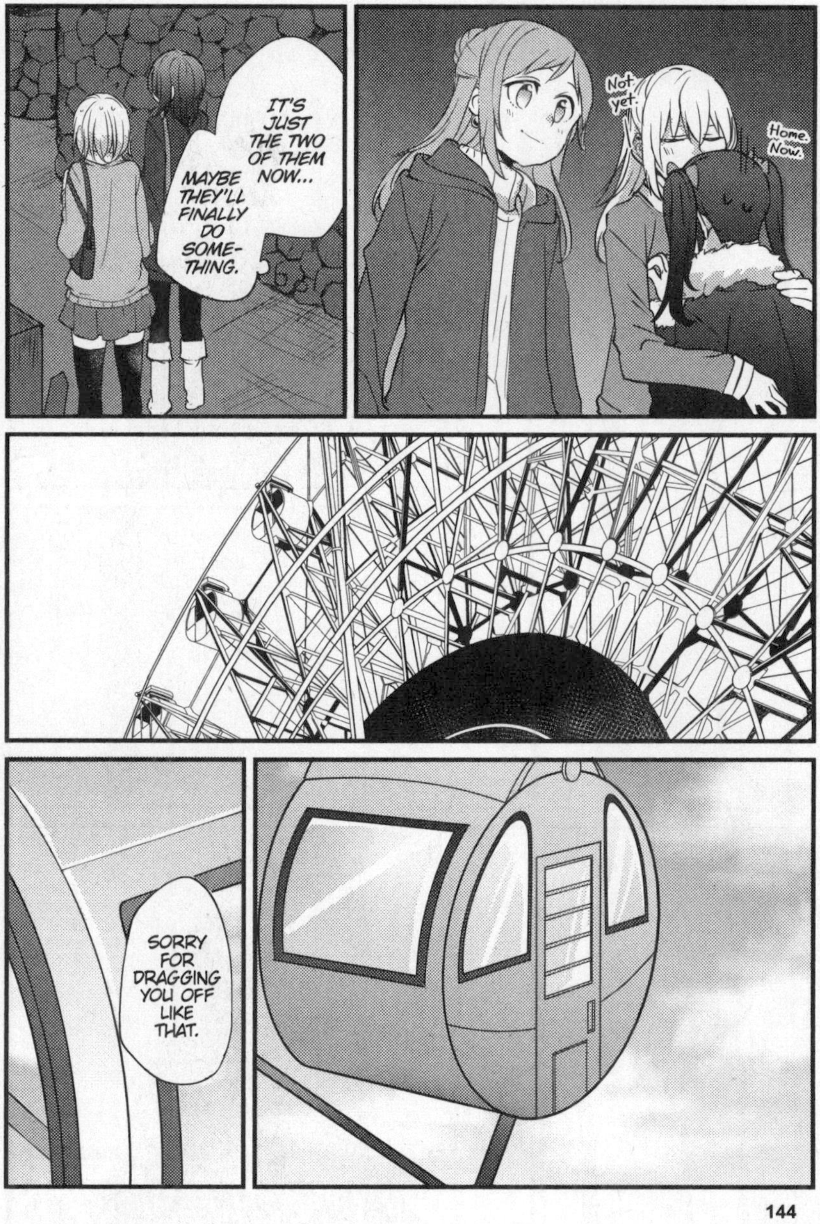
Home. Now.
Not yet.
IT'S JUST THE TWO OF THEM NOW...
MAYBE THEY'LL FINALLY DO SOMETHING.
SORRY FOR DRAGGING YOU OFF LIKE THAT.

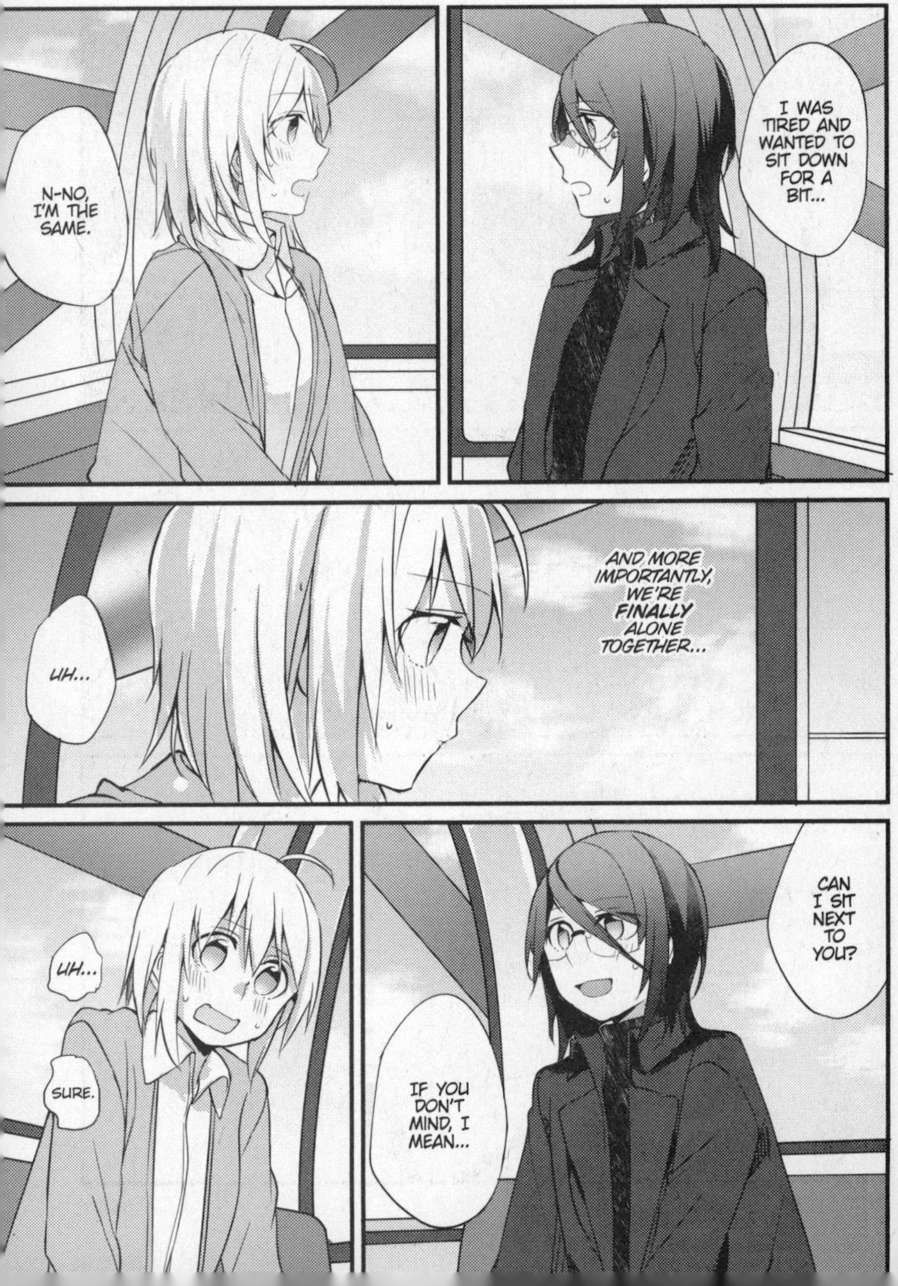
I WAS TIRED AND WANTED TO SIT DOWN FOR A BIT...
N-NO, I'M THE SAME.
AND MORE IMPORTANTLY, WE'RE FINALLY ALONE TOGETHER...
UH...
CAN I SIT NEXT TO YOU?
IF YOU DON'T MIND, I MEAN...
UH...
SURE.

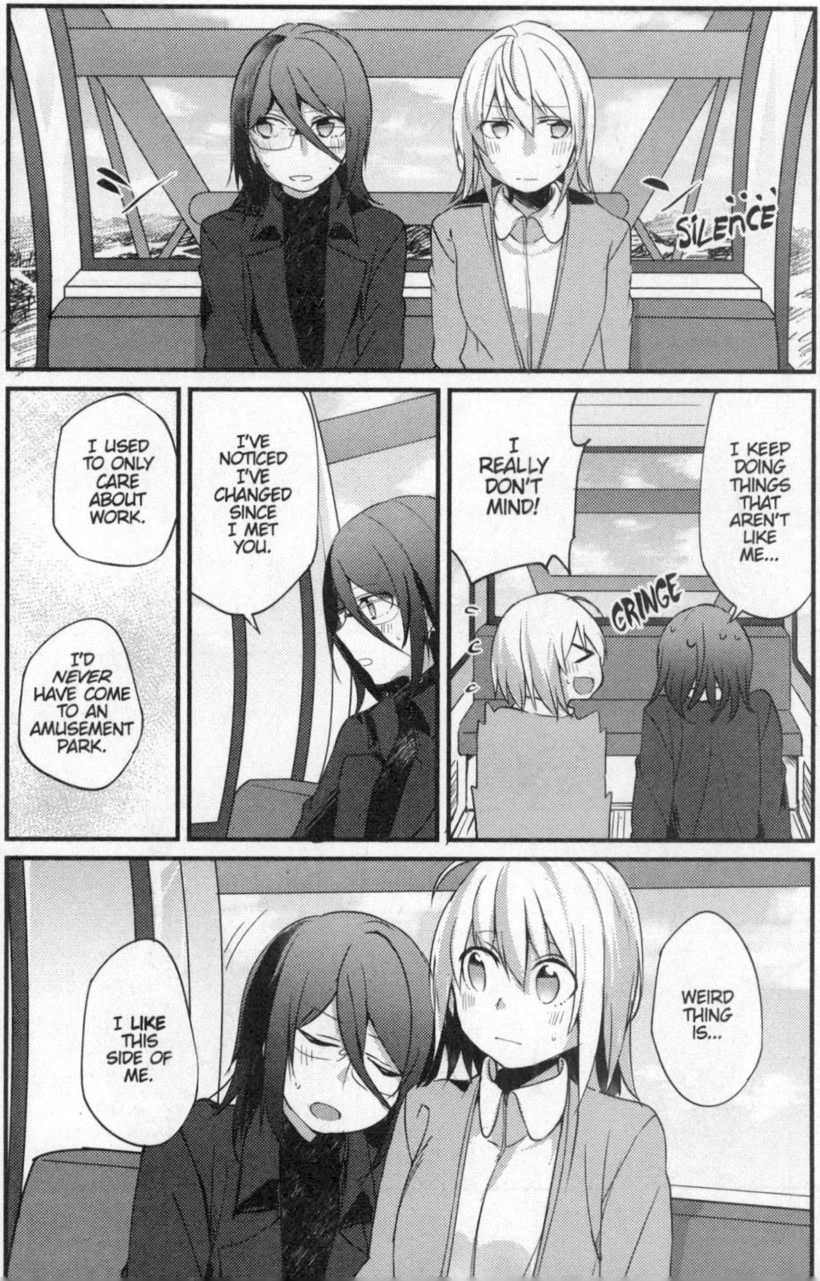
...
SILENCE
I KEEP DOING THINGS THAT AREN'T LIKE ME...
I REALLY DON'T MIND!
CRINGE
I'VE NOTICED I'VE CHANGED SINCE I MET YOU.
I USED TO ONLY CARE ABOUT WORK.
I'D *NEVER* HAVE COME TO AN AMUSEMENT PARK.
WEIRD THING IS...
I LIKE THIS SIDE OF ME.

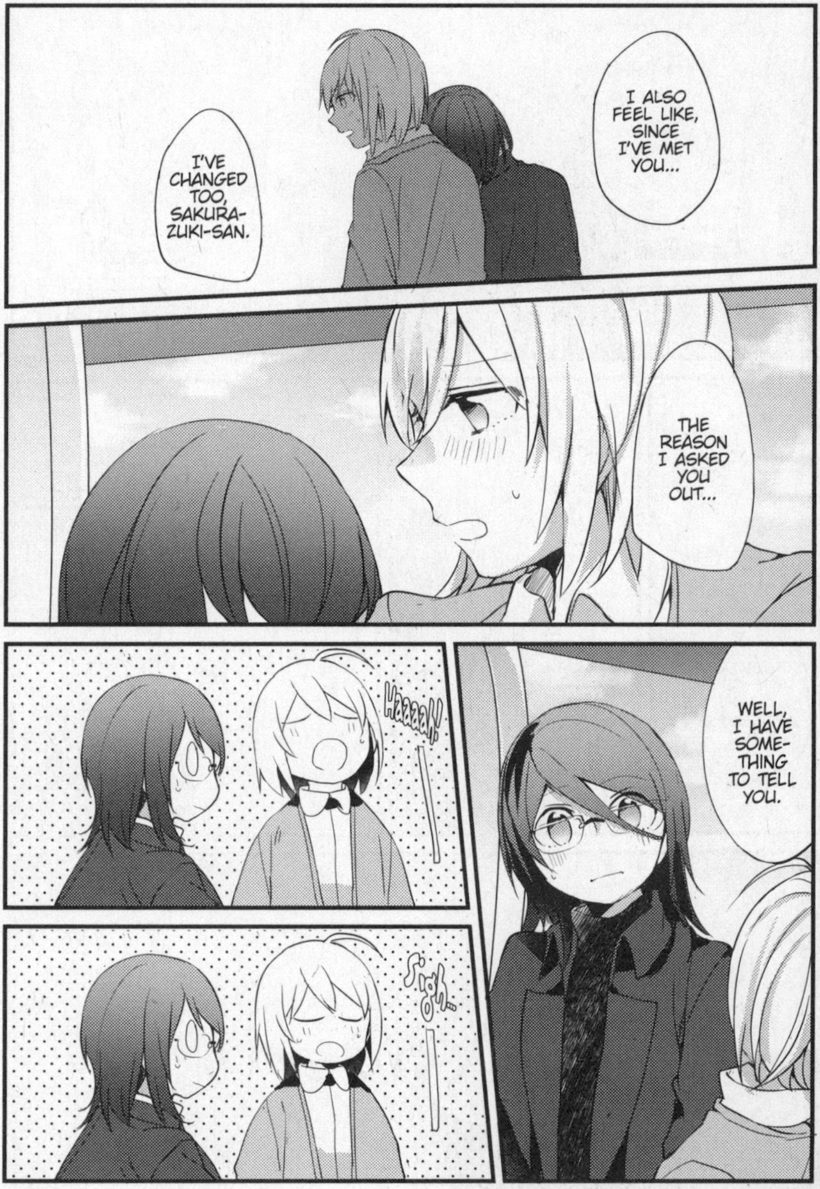
I ALSO FEEL LIKE, SINCE I'VE MET YOU...
I'VE CHANGED TOO, SAKURA-ZUKI-SAN.
THE REASON I ASKED YOU OUT...
WELL, I HAVE SOME-THING TO TELL YOU.
Haaaah!
Sigh...

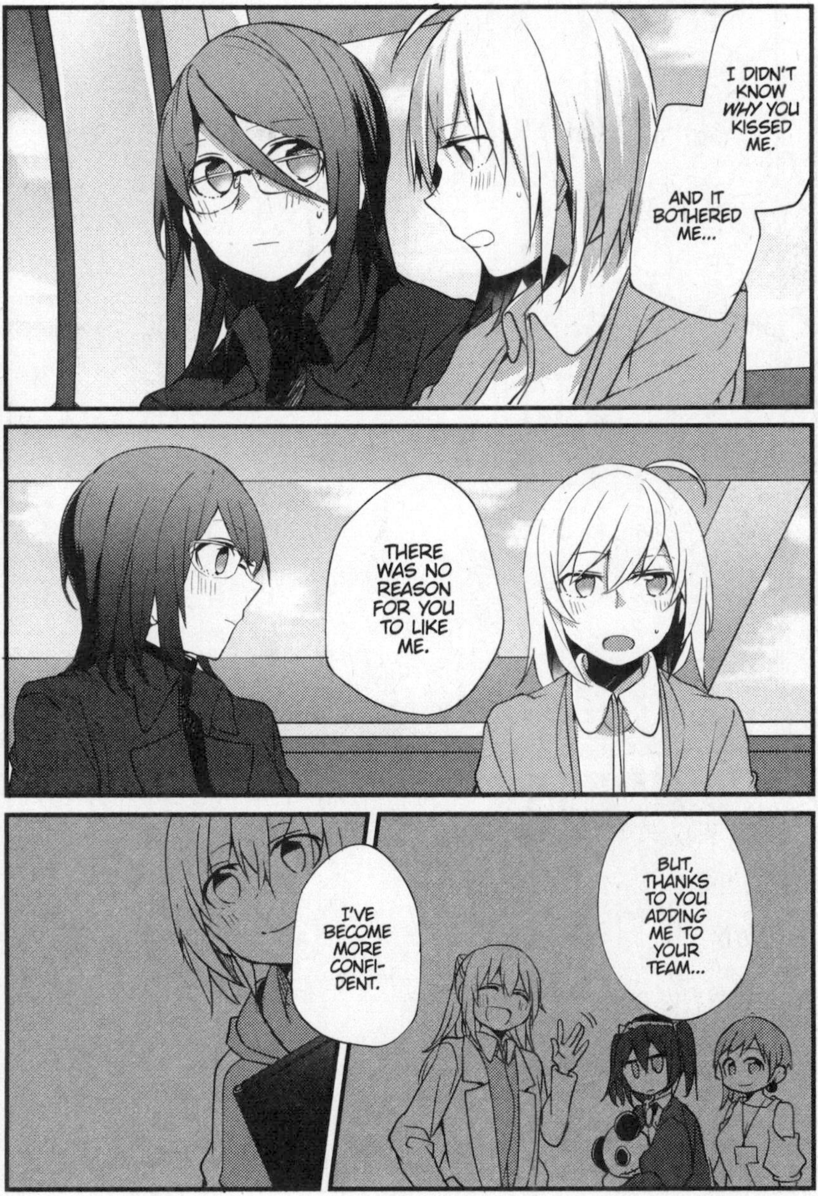
I DIDN'T KNOW *WHY* YOU KISSED ME.
AND IT BOTHERED ME...
THERE WAS NO REASON FOR YOU TO LIKE ME.
BUT, THANKS TO YOU ADDING ME TO YOUR TEAM...
I'VE BECOME MORE CONFI-DENT.

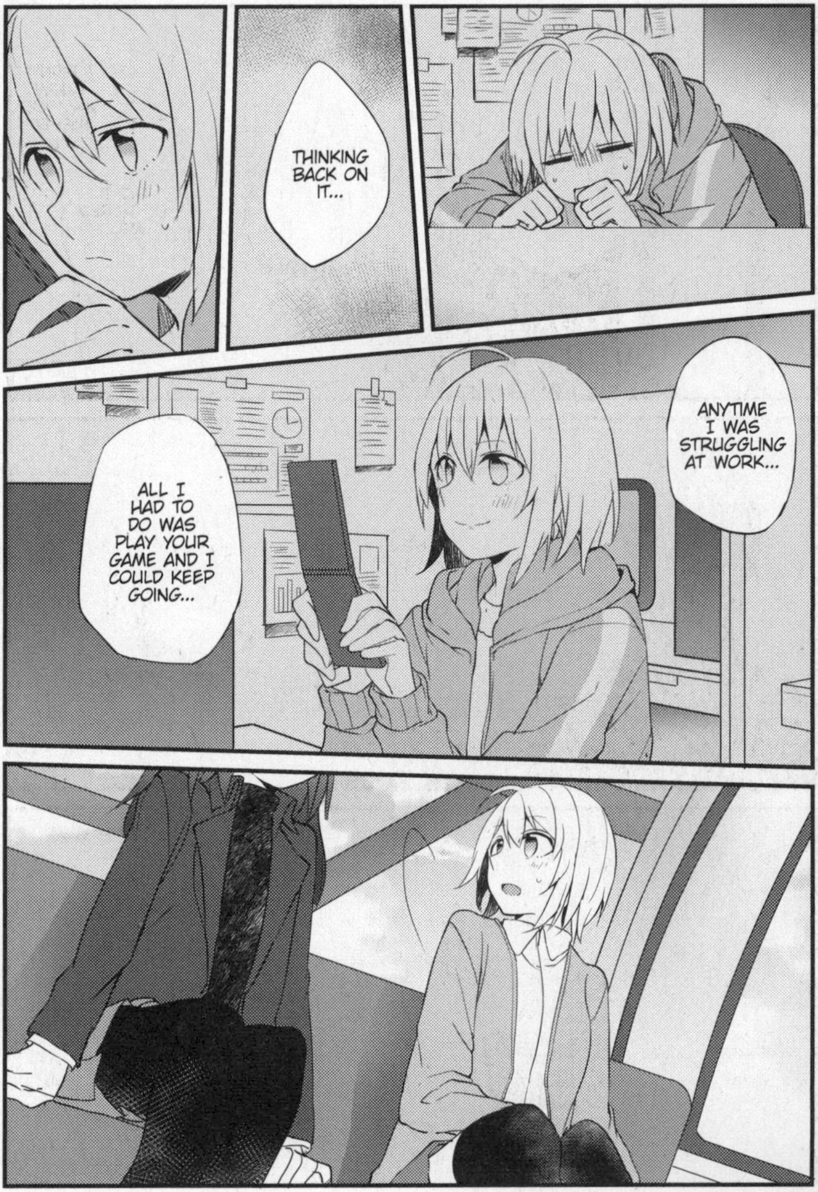
THINKING BACK ON IT...
ANYTIME I WAS STRUGGLING AT WORK...
ALL I HAD TO DO WAS PLAY YOUR GAME AND I COULD KEEP GOING...

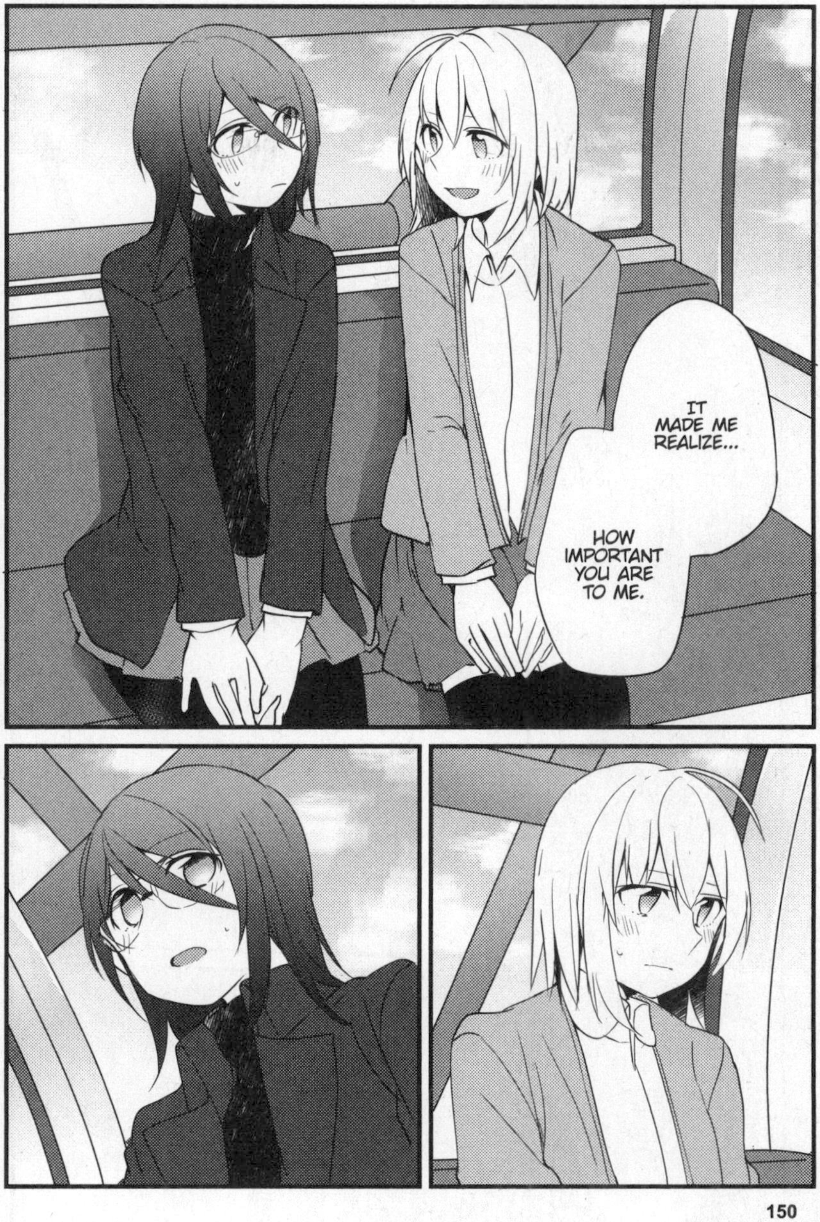
IT MADE ME REALIZE...
HOW IMPORTANT YOU ARE TO ME.

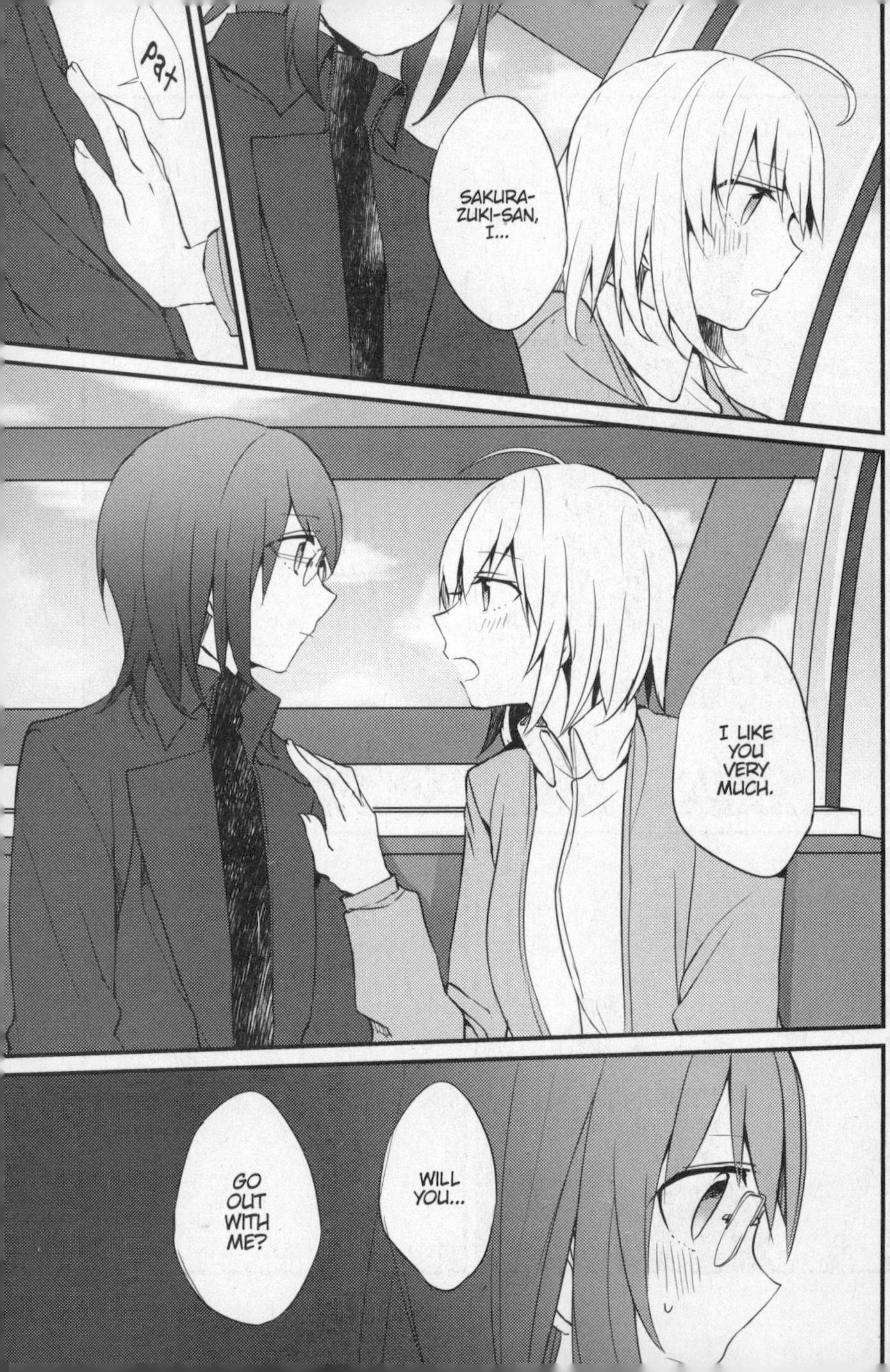
SAKURA-ZUKI-SAN, I...
pat
I LIKE YOU VERY MUCH.
WILL YOU...
GO OUT WITH ME?

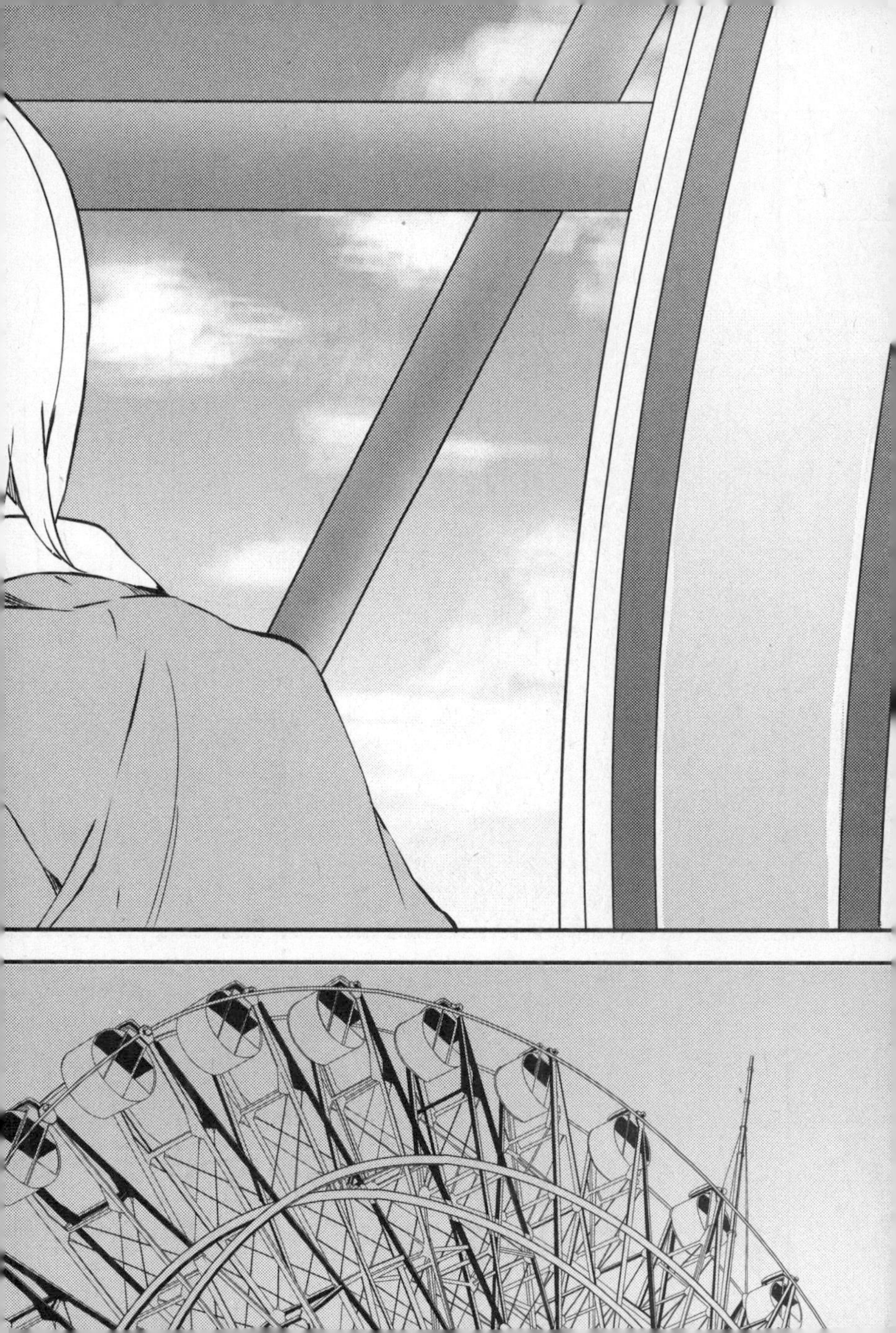

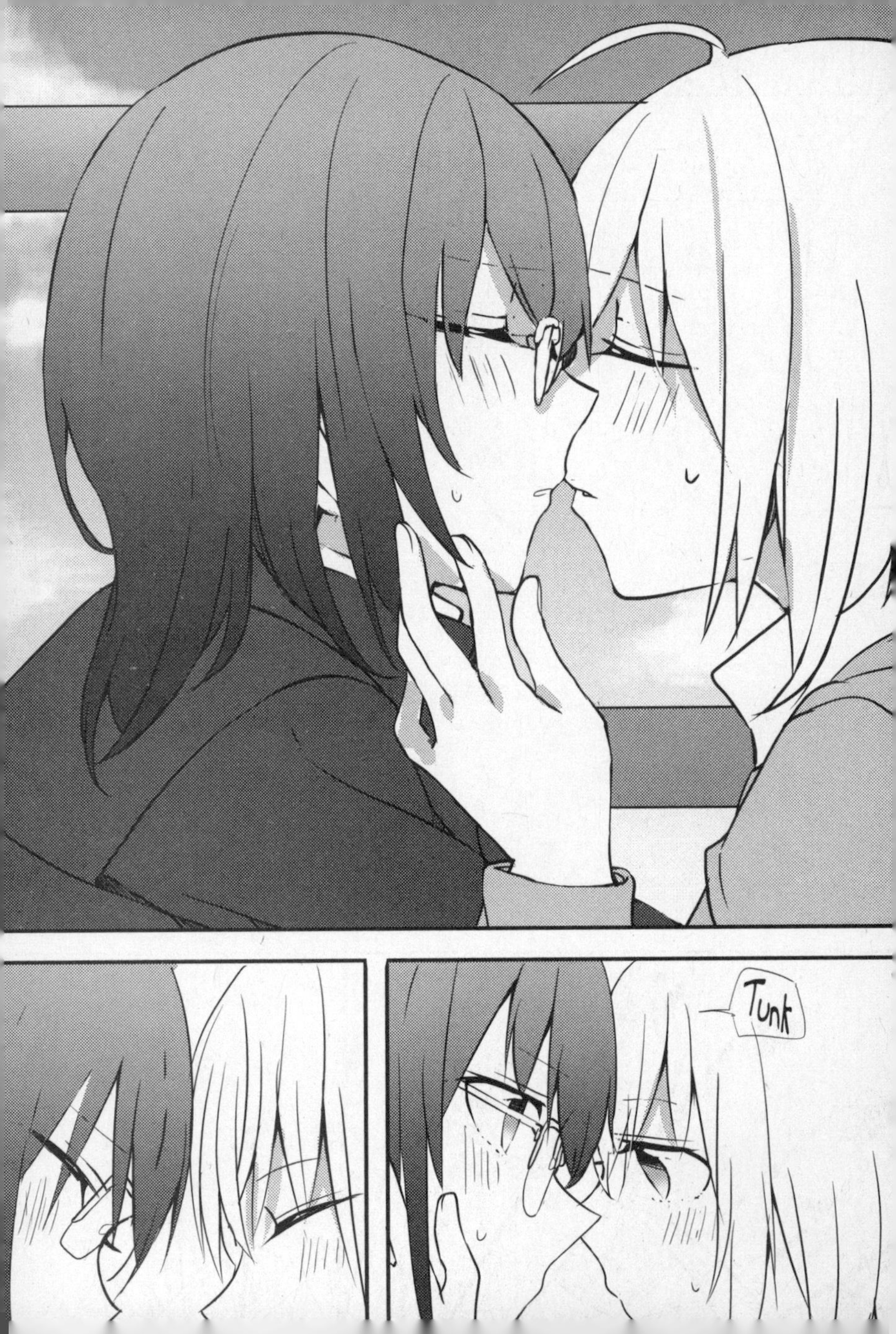
Tunk

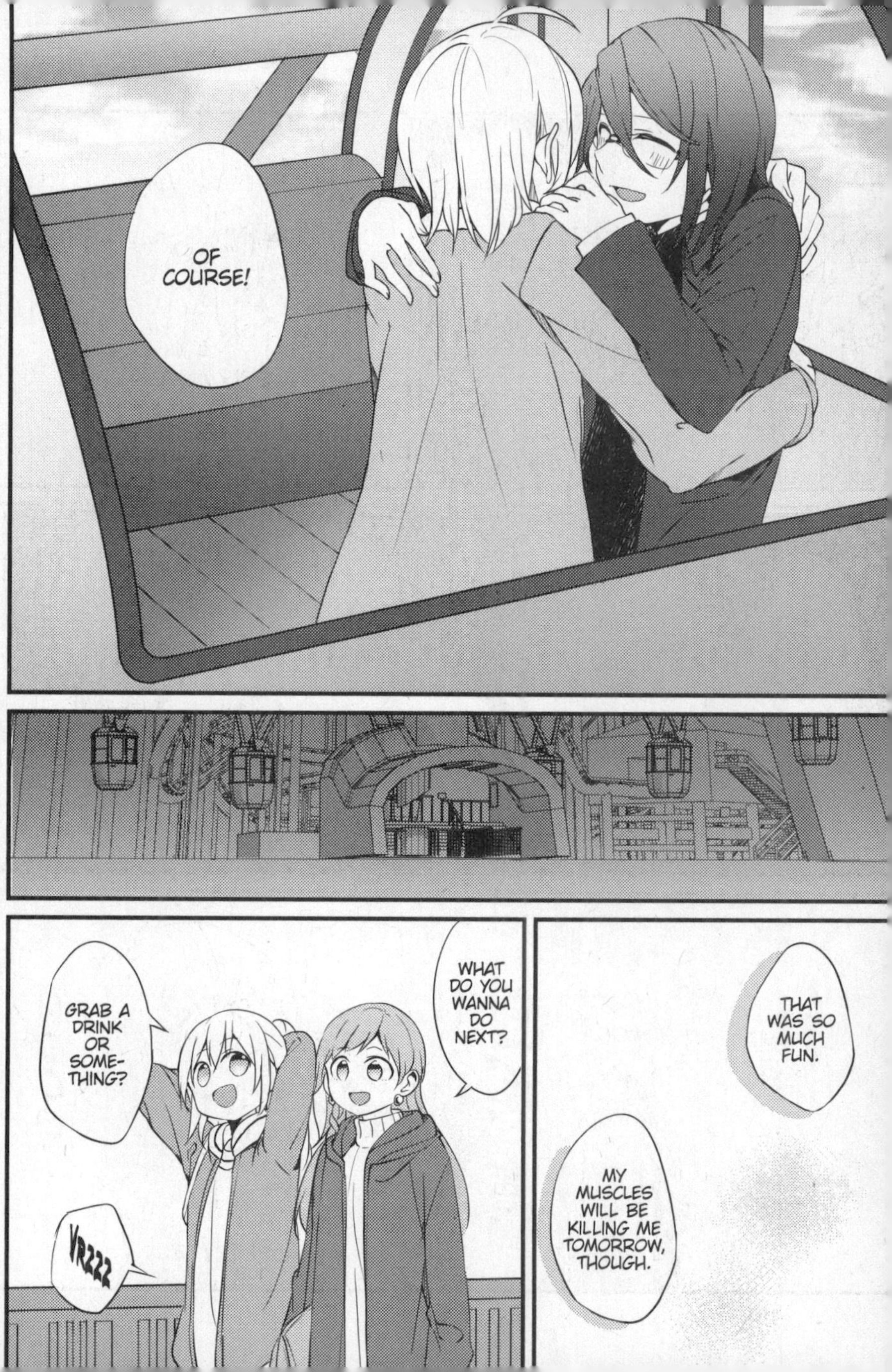
OF COURSE!
THAT WAS SO MUCH FUN.
MY MUSCLES WILL BE KILLING ME TOMORROW, THOUGH.
WHAT DO YOU WANNA DO NEXT?
GRAB A DRINK OR SOME-THING?
VRZZZ

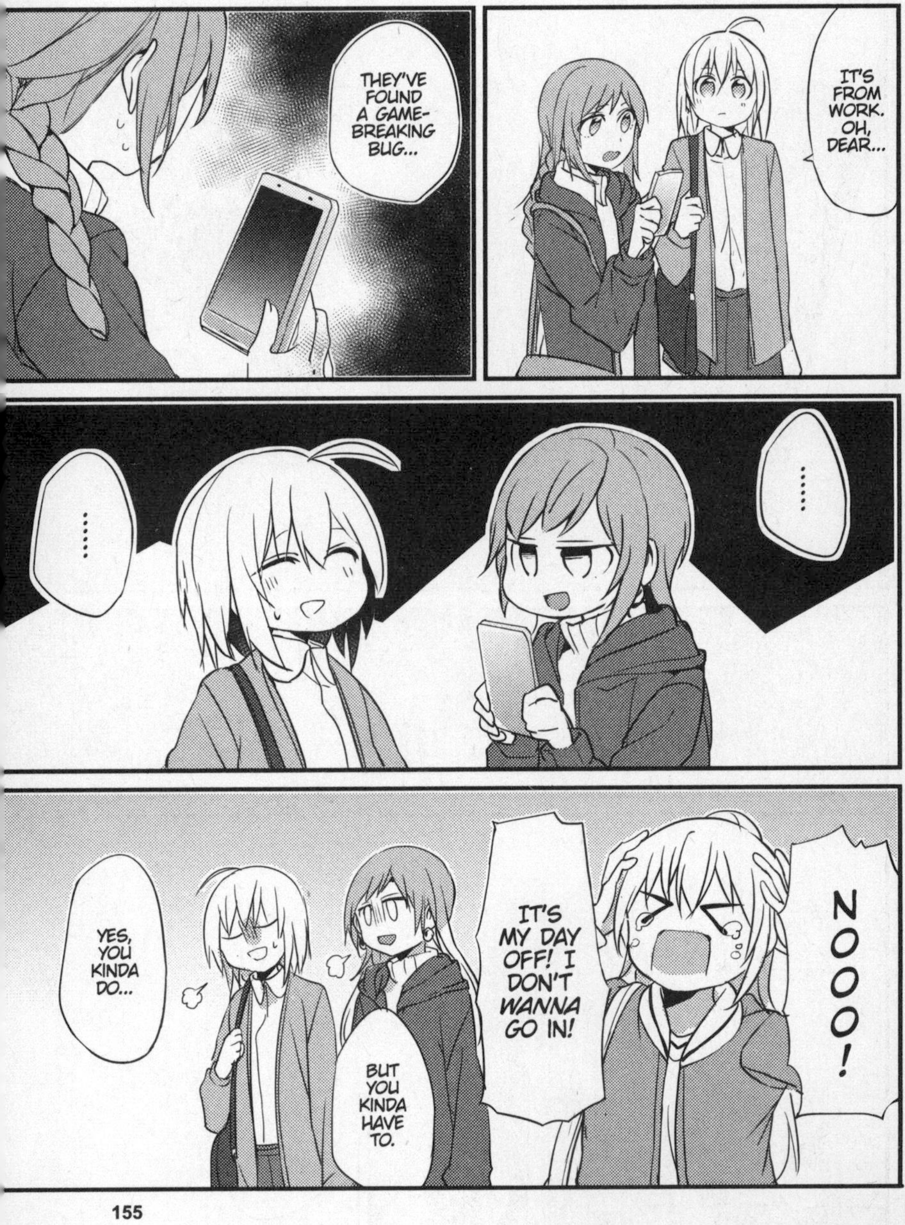
IT'S FROM WORK. OH, DEAR...
THEY'VE FOUND A GAME-BREAKING BUG...
......
......
NOOOO!
IT'S MY DAY OFF! I DON'T WANNA GO IN!
BUT YOU KINDA HAVE TO.
YES, YOU KINDA DO...

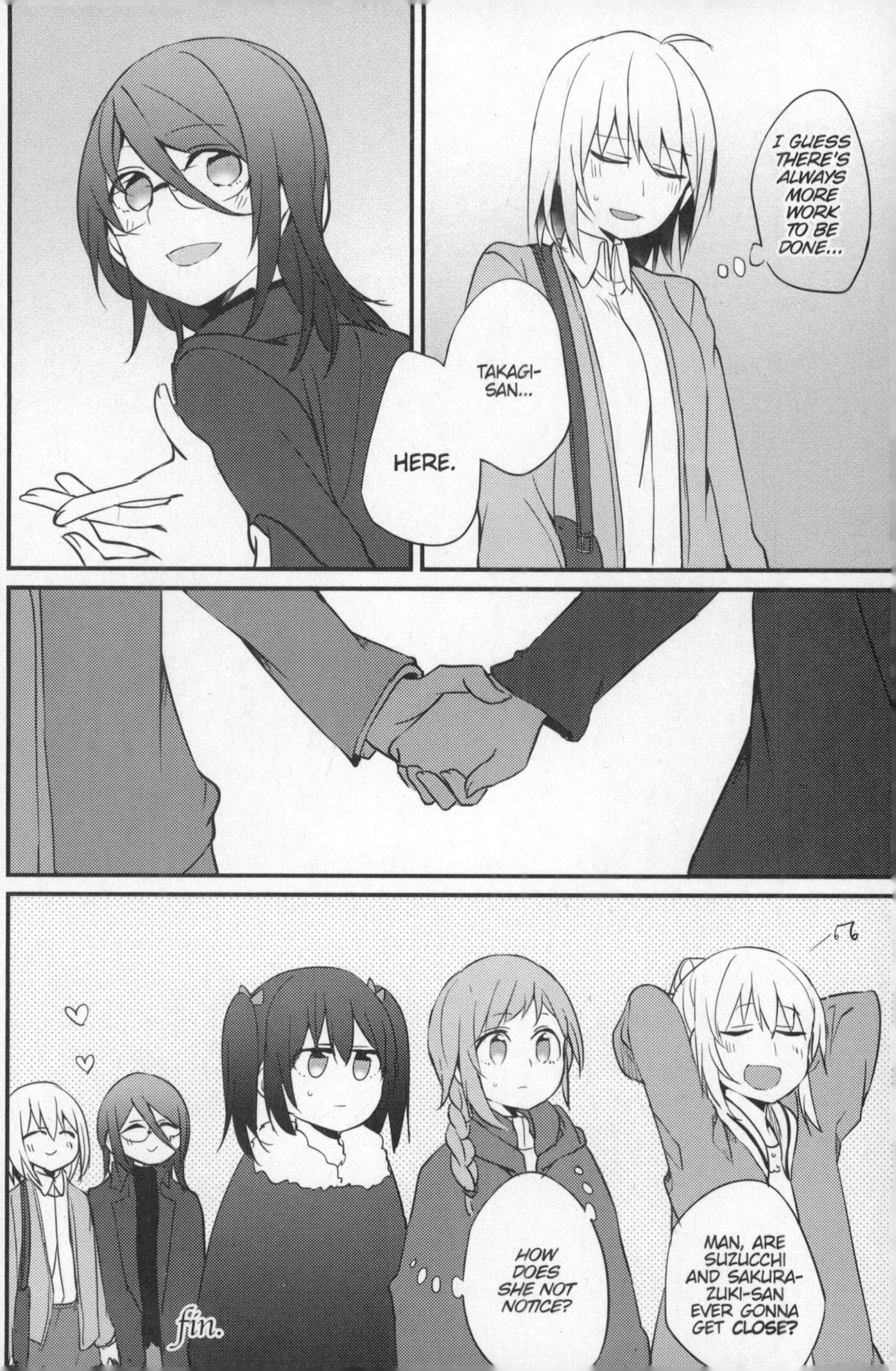
I GUESS THERE'S ALWAYS MORE WORK TO BE DONE...
TAKAGI-SAN... HERE.
MAN, ARE SUZUCCHI AND SAKURAZUKI-SAN EVER GONNA GET CLOSE?
HOW DOES SHE NOT NOTICE?
fin.

Now Loading...!

Customer Support 1

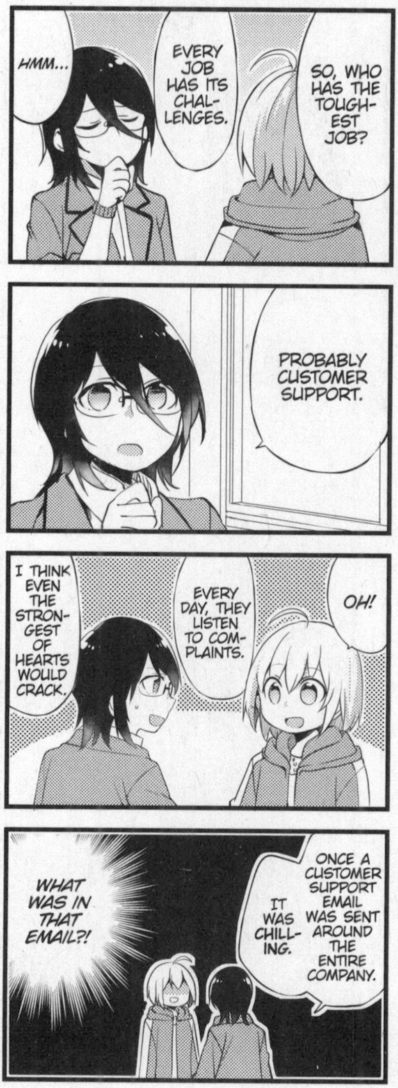
SO, WHO HAS THE TOUGH-EST JOB?
EVERY JOB HAS ITS CHAL-LENGES.
HMM...
PROBABLY CUSTOMER SUPPORT.
OH!
EVERY DAY, THEY LISTEN TO COM-PLAINTS.
I THINK EVEN THE STRON-GEST OF HEARTS WOULD CRACK.
ONCE A CUSTOMER SUPPORT EMAIL WAS SENT AROUND THE ENTIRE COMPANY.
IT WAS CHILL-ING.
WHAT WAS IN THAT EMAIL?!

Customer Support 2

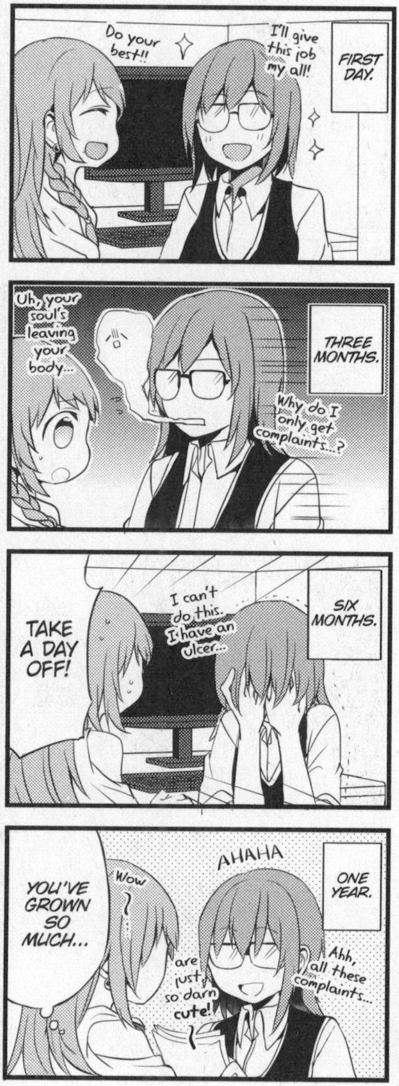
FIRST DAY.
I'll give this job my all!
Do your best!!
THREE MONTHS.
Uh, your soul's leaving your body...
Why do I only get complaints...?
SIX MONTHS.
I can't do this. I have an ulcer...
TAKE A DAY OFF!
ONE YEAR.
AHAHA
Wow
YOU'VE GROWN SO MUCH...
Ahh, all these complaints...
are just so darn cute!

That's That

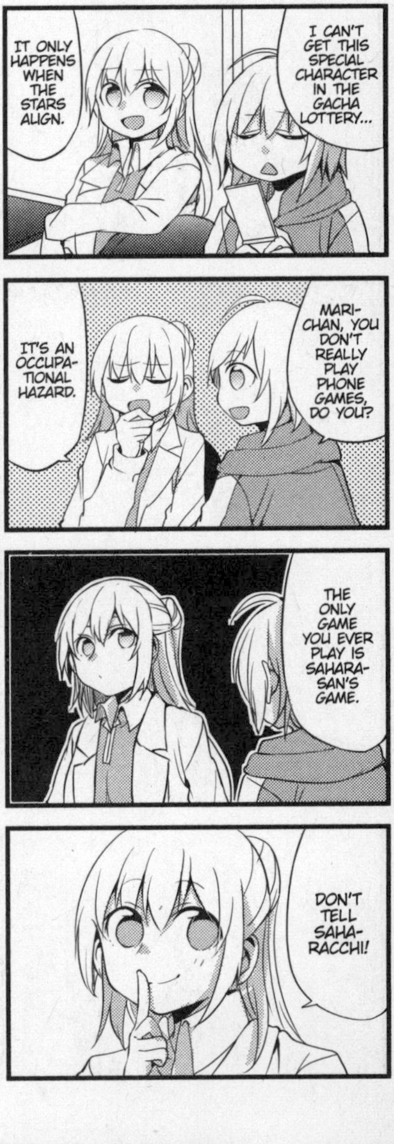
I CAN'T GET THIS SPECIAL CHARACTER IN THE GACHA LOTTERY...
IT ONLY HAPPENS WHEN THE STARS ALIGN.
MARI-CHAN, YOU DON'T REALLY PLAY PHONE GAMES, DO YOU?
IT'S AN OCCUPATIONAL HAZARD.
THE ONLY GAME YOU EVER PLAY IS SAHARA-SAN'S GAME.
DON'T TELL SAHARACCHI!

It's So Hard

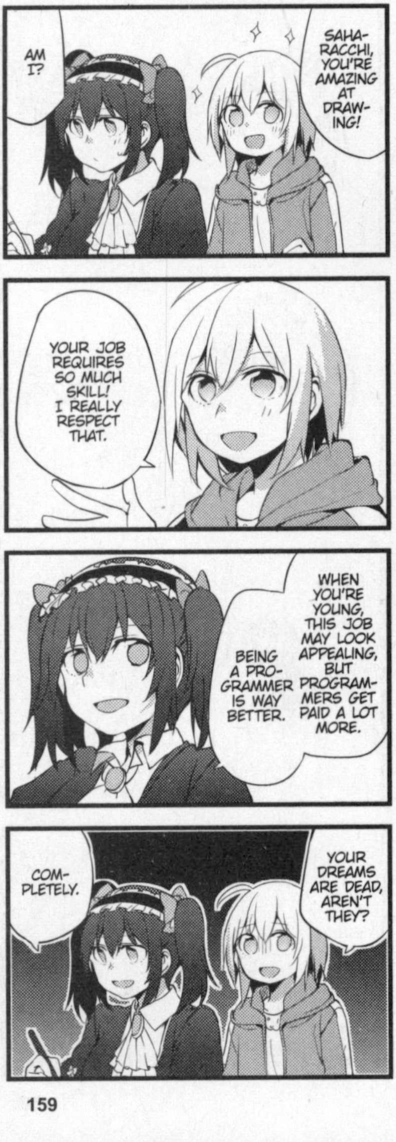
SAHARACCHI, YOU'RE AMAZING AT DRAWING!
AM I?
YOUR JOB REQUIRES SO MUCH SKILL! I REALLY RESPECT THAT.
WHEN YOU'RE YOUNG, THIS JOB MAY LOOK APPEALING, BUT PROGRAMMERS GET PAID A LOT MORE.
BEING A PROGRAMMER IS WAY BETTER.
YOUR DREAMS ARE DEAD, AREN'T THEY?
COMPLETELY.

Hobbies

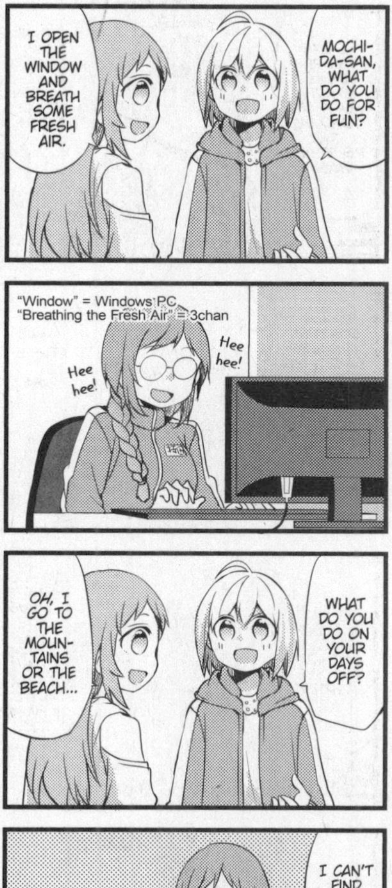
MOCHIDA-SAN, WHAT DO YOU DO FOR FUN?
I OPEN THE WINDOW AND BREATH SOME FRESH AIR.
“Window” = Windows PC
“Breathing the Fresh Air” = 3chan
Hee hee!
Hee hee!
WHAT DO YOU DO ON YOUR DAYS OFF?
OH, I GO TO THE MOUNTAINS OR THE BEACH...
I CAN'T FIND ANY OF THE STUFF I NEED.
Same here.

Shelter from the Storm

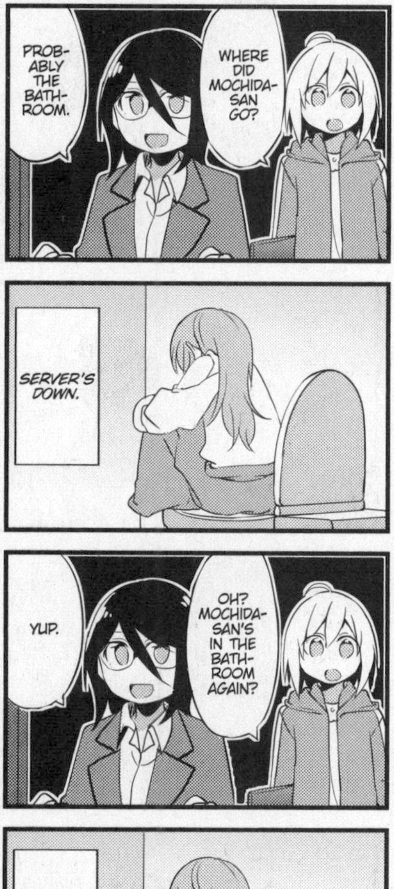
WHERE DID MOCHIDA-SAN GO?
PROBABLY THE BATHROOM.
SERVER'S DOWN.
OH? MOCHIDA-SAN'S IN THE BATHROOM AGAIN?
YUP.
SKIPPING SALES REPORT MEETING.

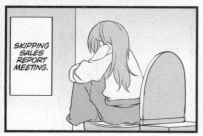

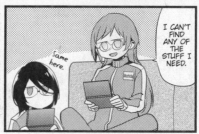

Youth

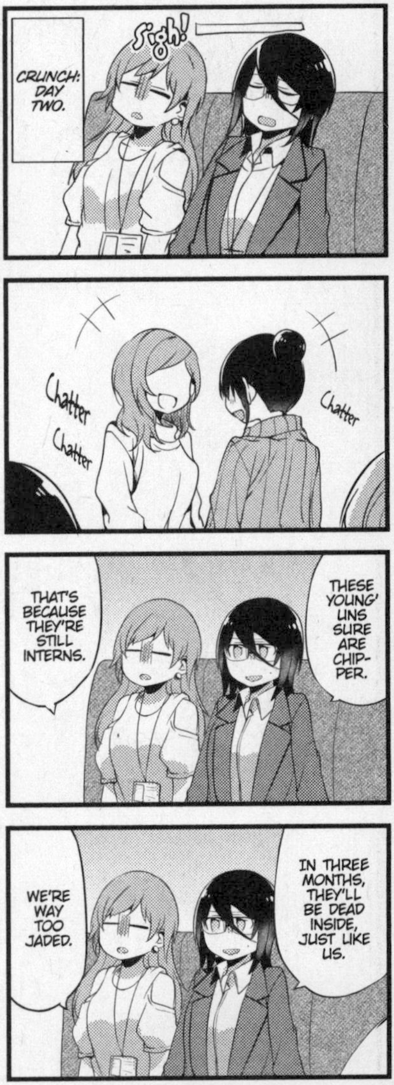

sigh!
CRUNCH: DAY TWO.
Chatter
Chatter
Chatter
THESE YOUNG' UNS SURE ARE CHIPPER.
THAT'S BECAUSE THEY'RE STILL INTERNS.
IN THREE MONTHS, THEY'LL BE DEAD INSIDE, JUST LIKE US.
WE'RE WAY TOO JADED.

Things You Hate, Things You Like

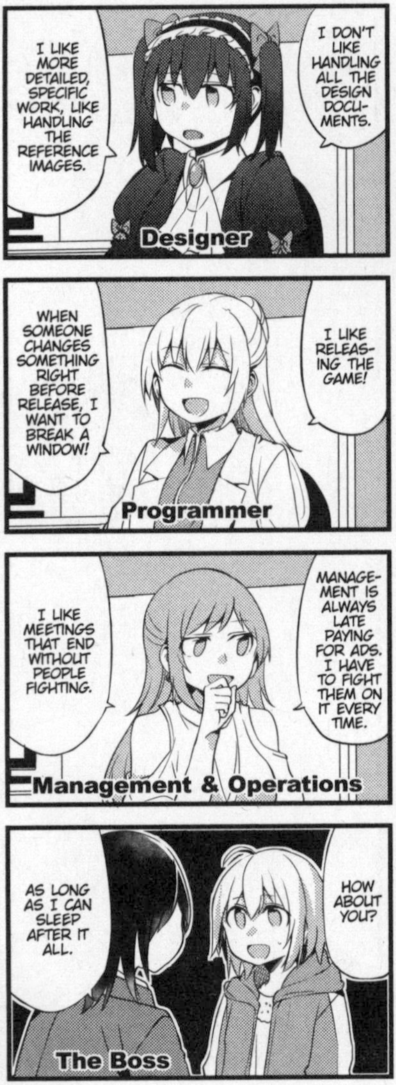

I DON'T LIKE HANDLING ALL THE DESIGN DOCUMENTS.
I LIKE MORE DETAILED, SPECIFIC WORK, LIKE HANDLING THE REFERENCE IMAGES.
Designer
I LIKE RELEASING THE GAME!
WHEN SOMEONE CHANGES SOMETHING RIGHT BEFORE RELEASE, I WANT TO BREAK A WINDOW!
Programmer
MANAGEMENT IS ALWAYS LATE PAYING FOR ADS. I HAVE TO FIGHT THEM ON IT EVERY TIME.
I LIKE MEETINGS THAT END WITHOUT PEOPLE FIGHTING.
Management & Operations
HOW ABOUT YOU?
AS LONG AS I CAN SLEEP AFTER IT ALL.
The Boss

A Terrible Experience

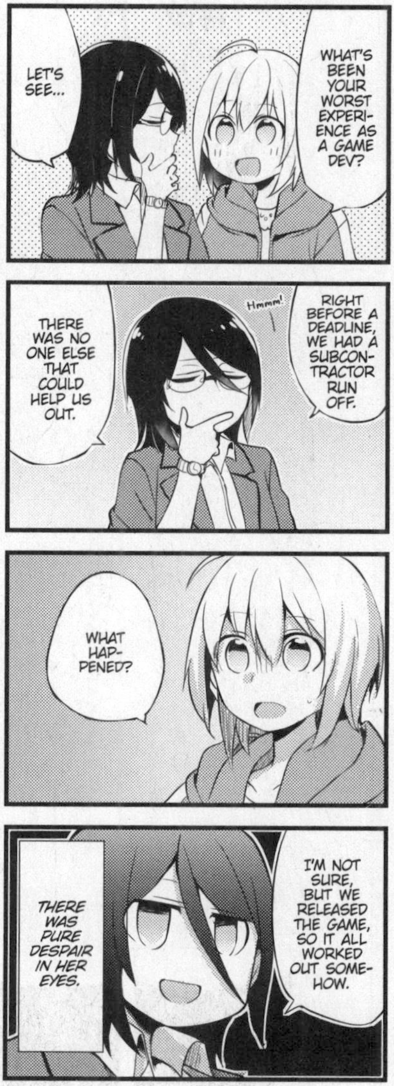
WHAT'S BEEN YOUR WORST EXPERIENCE AS A GAME DEV?
LET'S SEE...
Hmmm!
RIGHT BEFORE A DEADLINE, WE HAD A SUBCONTRACTOR RUN OFF.
THERE WAS NO ONE ELSE THAT COULD HELP US OUT.
WHAT HAPPENED?
I'M NOT SURE, BUT WE RELEASED THE GAME, SO IT ALL WORKED OUT SOME-HOW.
THERE WAS PURE DESPAIR IN HER EYES.

A Singles' Mixer with Co-workers

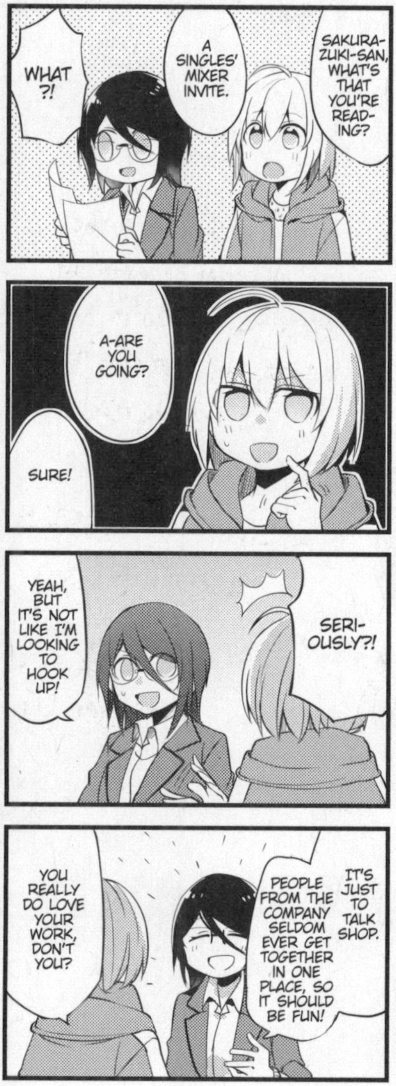
SAKURA-ZUKI-SAN, WHAT'S THAT YOU'RE READ-ING?
A SINGLES' MIXER INVITE.
WHAT ?!
A-ARE YOU GOING?
SURE!
SERI-OUSLY?!
YEAH, BUT IT'S NOT LIKE I'M LOOKING TO HOOK UP!
IT'S JUST TO TALK SHOP.
PEOPLE FROM THE COMPANY SELDOM EVER GET TOGETHER IN ONE PLACE, SO IT SHOULD BE FUN!
YOU REALLY DO LOVE YOUR WORK, DON'T YOU?

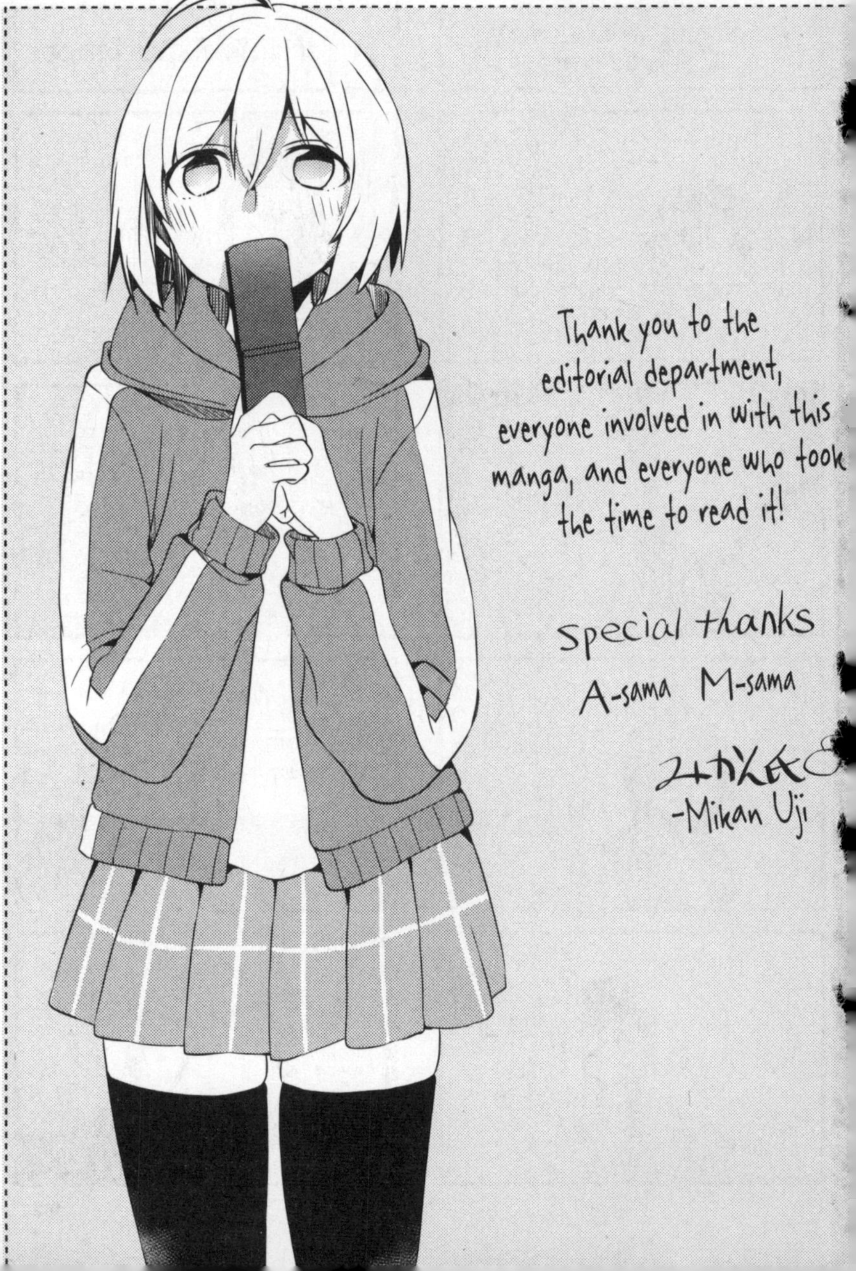

Thank you to the editorial department, everyone involved in with this manga, and everyone who took the time to read it!
Special thanks
A-sama M-sama
-Mikan Uji

SEVEN SEAS ENTERTAINMENT PRESENTS

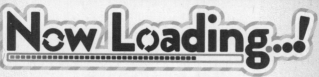

Now Loading...!

story and art by **MIKANUJI**

TRANSLATION
Amber Tamosaitis

ADAPTATION
Asha Bardon

LETTERING AND RETOUCH
CK Russell

COVER DESIGN
KC Fabellon

PROOFREADER
B. Lana Guggenheim

EDITOR
Shannon Fay

PRODUCTION MANAGER
Lissa Pattillo

EDITOR-IN-CHIEF
Adam Arnold

PUBLISHER
Jason DeAngelis

First published in Japan in 2017 by ICHIJINSHA Inc., Tokyo.
English translation rights arranged with ICHIJINSHA Inc., Tokyo.

ISBN: 978-1-626929-84-

Printed in Canada

First Printing: January 2

10 9 8 7 6 5 4 3 2

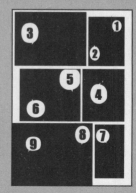

FOLLOW US ONLINE: ***www.sevenseasentertainment.com***

READING DIRECTIONS

This book reads from ***right to left***, Japanese style. If this is your first time reading manga, you start reading from the top right panel on each page and take it from there. If you get lost, just follow the numbered diagram here. It may seem backwards at first, but you'll get the hang of it! Have fun!!

1
2
3
4
5
6
7
8
9